and tribune Detroit post

Zachariah Chandler

An outline sketch of his life and public services

and tribune Detroit post

Zachariah Chandler
An outline sketch of his life and public services

ISBN/EAN: 9783337312749

Printed in Europe, USA, Canada, Australia, Japan

Cover: Foto ©Raphael Reischuk / pixelio.de

More available books at **www.hansebooks.com**

ZACHARIAH CHANDLER:

AN OUTLINE SKETCH

OF

His Life and Public Services.

BY

THE DETROIT POST AND TRIBUNE.

WITH AN INTRODUCTORY LETTER

FROM

JAMES G. BLAINE, OF MAINE.

O iron nerve to true occasion true,
O fall'n at length that tower of strength
Which stood four - square to all the winds that blew !
—*Tennyson.*

DETROIT:
THE POST AND TRIBUNE COMPANY, PUBLISHERS.
R. D. S. TYLER & CO., DETROIT.   TYLER & CO., CHICAGO.
CHARLES DREW, NEW YORK.   WM. H. THOMPSON & CO., BOSTON.
J. M. OLCOTT, INDIANAPOLIS.
1880.

Electrotyped by
A. W. HABBIN, Detroit.

PRESS OF
WRIGHTSON & CO.,
CINCINNATI, O.

IT is stated elsewhere that this work is written "By The Detroit Post and Tribune." Unusual as this form of announcement is on the title-pages of books, there certainly may be an authorial as well as an editorial impersonality; in this case the phrase succinctly expresses the fact, namely, that the volume represents the joint labors of the staff of The Post and Tribune, alike in the collection and the treatment of its material.

While its preparation has been almost wholly a matter of original research, such use as was necessary has been made of historical data contained in "The Centennial History of Bedford, N. H.," published in 1851, in Horace Greeley's "American Conflict," and in Henry Wilson's "History of the Rise and Fall of the Slave Power."

Needed information has been furnished by those intimately connected with Mr. Chandler, but the work has not been submitted to their revision, and they are not responsible for the form of the narrative, nor for the personal estimate it embodies.

This book presents a sketch of the life and the public services of a remarkable man. It has been written from the standpoint of political sympathy, and with the hope of deepening the wholesome influences so powerfully exerted upon public sentiment in his lifetime by Zachariah Chandler. The aim has been to make it accurate in statement, and to see that its chapters should fairly draw, in outline at least, the picture of the career of a genuine leader of men.

INTRODUCTORY LETTER.

To the Editors of The Post and Tribune :

I am unable to give any personal or special incidents in the life of Mr. Chandler not open to his biographers from other sources. I was not so intimate in my relations with him as were some others, nor did I know him better than many others who like myself were associated with him in public life for a long period. I knew him well, however, both on the side of his private life and his public life, and in every phase he was a man of strong character.

The time in which a man lives, and the circumstances by which he is surrounded, control his fate even more largely than his personal and inherent qualities. Mr. Chandler was fortunate in the time of his removal to the West, fortunate in the era which brought him into public life. When he became a citizen of Michigan the days of hard pioneer life were ending, extensive cultivation of the soil had begun, products for shipment were large and rapidly increasing. Facilities for transportation were already great. The Erie Canal had been open for several years, and steamers had multiplied on the Great Lakes. Everything was in readiness for a strong - minded, energetic, competent man of business, and Mr. Chandler had the good fortune to settle in Detroit at the precise point of time when the elements of success were within his grasp. For a quarter of a century thereafter his career was that of a business man intensely devoted to his private interests, and participating in public affairs only as an incident and with no effort to secure advancement. The result of this steady devotion to business was that Mr. Chandler found himself at forty-four years of age possessed of a large property, constantly and rapidly increasing in value.

Coincident with this condition in his financial fortunes came a crisis in the political affairs of the country, involving the class of questions which took deep hold on the mind and the heart of Mr. Chandler. The curbing of the slave power, the assertion and maintenance of freedom on free soil, undying devotion to the Union of the States, and the bold defense of the rights of the citizen — these were the issues which in various phases absorbed the public mind from the repeal of the Missouri compromise in 1854 down to the close of Mr. Chandler's life. And on all the issues presented for consideration for twenty-five years Mr. Chandler never halted, never wearied, never grew timid, never was willing to compromise. On these great questions he became the leader of Michigan, and Michigan kept Mr. Chandler at the front during the prolonged struggle which has wrought such mighty changes in the history of the American people.

It is a noteworthy fact, not infrequently adverted to, that the political opinions of Michigan both as Territory and State, for a period of sixty years, were represented, and indeed in no small degree formed, by two men of New Hampshire birth. From 1819 to 1854 General Cass was the accepted political leader of

Michigan, and only once in all that long period of thirty-five years did her people fail to follow him. That was in 1840, when the old pioneers and the soldiers of 1812 — generally the friends of Cass — refused his leadership, and voted for the older pioneer and the more illustrious chieftain, William Henry Harrison. From 1854 till Mr. Chandler's death the dominant opinion of Michigan was with him; and her people followed him, trusted him, believed in him. During that quarter of a century the population of the State more than trebled in number, but the strength of Chandler with the newcomers seemed as great as with the older population with whom he had begun the struggle of life in the Territory of Michigan. The old men stood firmly by him in the faith and confidence of an ancient friendship, and the young men followed with an enthusiasm which grew into affection, and with an affection which ripened into reverence.

Mr. Chandler's life in Washington, apart from his public service, was a notable event in the history of the capital. His wealth enabled him to be generous and hospitable, and his elegant mansion was a center of attraction for many years. Nor were the guests confined to one party. Mr. Chandler was personally popular with his political opponents, and the leading men of the Democratic party often sat at his table and forgot in the genial host, and the frank, sincere man, all the bitterness that might have come from conflict in the partisan arena.

It is fitting that Mr. Chandler's life be written. It is due, first of all, to his memory. It is due to those who come after

him. It is due to the great State whose Senator he was, whose
interests he served, whose honor he upheld. I am glad the work
is committed to competent friends, who can discriminate between
honest approval and inconsiderate praise, and who with strict
adherence to truth can find in his career so much that is honorable, so much that is admirable, so little that is censurable, and
nothing that is mean.

Very sincerely yours,

JAMES G. BLAINE.

WASHINGTON, February 15, 1880.

TABLE OF CONTENTS.

CHAPTER IV.

The Panorama of Northwestern Development.

CHAPTER V.

The Commencement of Political Activity—Record as an Anti-Slavery Whig.

CHAPTER VI.

The Formation of the Republican Party.

CHAPTER VII.

The First Election to the Senate.

CHAPTER VIII.

THE DEVELOPMENT OF THE SOUTHERN CONSPIRACY — THE ELECTION OF ABRAHAM LINCOLN.

CHAPTER IX.

SERVICES TO THE CAUSE OF THE PROTECTION OF HOME INDUSTRY.

CHAPTER X.

SERVICES TO NORTHWESTERN COMMERCIAL INTERESTS AND THE CAUSE OF INTERNAL IMPROVEMENTS.

CHAPTER XI.

THE OUTBREAK OF THE REBELLION — NO COMPROMISE OF CONSTITUTIONAL RIGHTS.

CHAPTER XII.

THE COMMENCEMENT OF THE CIVIL WAR.

CHAPTER XIII.

THE COMMITTEE ON THE CONDUCT OF THE WAR.

CHAPTER XIV.

THE VIGOROUS PROSECUTION OF THE WAR.

CHAPTER XV.

THE PRESIDENTIAL CAMPAIGN OF 1864.

CHAPTER XVI.

CHAPTER XVII.

CHAPTER XVIII.

CHAPTER XIX.

SECRETARY OF THE INTERIOR IN THE CABINET OF PRESIDENT GRANT.

CHAPTER XX.

THE PRESIDENTIAL ELECTION OF 1876 — AT HOME — THE MARSH FARM NEAR LANSING.

APPENDIX.

2

LIST OF ILLUSTRATIONS.

ZACHARIAH CHANDLER.

CHAPTER I.

IN the valley of the Merrimack, fifty miles northwest from Boston, is the New Hampshire town of Bedford. It is a community of thrifty farms, with striking characteristics, and almost a century and a half of entertaining history. Simplicity of manners and sturdiness of character prevail among its people to-day, and the vigor of the stock of its original settlers, the loftiness of their traditions, and the puritanism of its civilization have made it a nursery of strong men.

King Philip's War ended in a Pyrrhic victory for the New England provinces. The subjugation of the savages was only accomplished when one in twenty of the men among the colonists had fallen and a like proportion of their families was houseless, and it left behind it what was in those days a heavy debt. More than half a century elapsed before there was any substantial recognition of the claims of the survivors of that war and their descendants. It was not until 1732, after numerous petitions and prolonged discussion, that "the Great and General Court of Massachusetts" granted land enough for two townships "to the soldiers who had served in King Philip's or the Narragansett War and to their surviving heirs-at-law." This grant was subsequently enlarged to seven townships, as appears from the following record of proceedings in "the Great and General Court or Assembly for His Majestie's Province of the Massachusetts Bay," under date of April 26, 1733 :

A Petition of a Committee for the Narragansett Soldiers, showing that there are the number of Eight Hundred and Forty Persons entered as officers and soldiers in the late Narragansett War, Praying that there may be such an addition of Land granted to them, as may allow a Tract of six miles Square to each one hundred and twenty men so admitted.

In the House of Representatives, Read, and Ordered that the Prayer of the Petition be granted, and that Major Chandler, Mr. Edward Shove, Col. Thomas Tileston, Mr. John Hobson and Mr. Samuel Chandler (or any three of them,) be a Committee fully authorized and empowered to survey and lay out five more Tracts of Land for Townships, of the Contents of Six miles Square each, in some of the unappropriated lands of this Province ; and that the said land, together with the two towns before granted, be granted and disposed of to the officers and soldiers or their lawful Representatives, as they are or have been allowed by this Court, being eight hundred and forty in number, in the whole, and in full satisfaction of the Grant formerly made them by the General Court, as a reward for their public service. And the Grantees shall be obliged to assemble within as short time as they can conveniently, not exceeding the space of two months, and proceed to the choice of Committees, respectively, to regulate each Propriety or Township which is to be held and enjoyed by one hundred and twenty of the Grantees, each in equal Proportion, who shall pass such orders and rules as will effectually oblige them to settle Sixty families, at least, within each Township, with a learned, orthodox ministry, within the space of seven years of the date of this Grant. Provided, always, that if the said Grantees shall not effectually settle the said number of families in each Township, and also lay out a lot for the first settled minister, one for the ministry, and one for the school, in each of the said townships, they shall have no advantage of, but forfeit their respective grants, anything to the contrary contained notwithstanding. The Charge of the Survey to be paid by the Province.

In Council read and concur'd.   J. BELCHER.

In June of 1733 these grantees met on Boston Common for the purpose of making a division of the lands thus appropriated, but twenty veterans of the Narragansett War being then living. They organized into seven societies, each representing one hundred and twenty persons, and each represented by an executive committee of three. These committees convened in Boston on the 17th of October, 1733, and, by drawing numbers from a hat, apportioned to their societies the following seven townships set apart from the public domain under the grant: No. 1, in Maine, now called Buxton; No. 2, Westminster, Mass.; No. 3, Souhegan-West, now Amherst, N. H.; No. 4, originally at the Falls of the Amoskeag, where Goffstown now is (subsequently exchanged for lands in Hampden county, Mass.); No. 5, Souhegan-East, N. H.; No. 6, Templeton, Mass.; No. 7, Gorham, Me. Thomas Tileston, of Dorchester, drew "Number 5, Souhegan-East;" of the one hundred and twenty grantees whom he represented, fifty-seven belonged to Boston, fifteen to Roxbury, seven to Dorchester, two to Milton, five to Braintree, four to Weymouth, thirteen to Hingham, four to Dedham, two to Hull, one to Medfield, five to Scituate, and one to Newport, R. I. In the fifteen Roxbury grantees was Zechariah Chandler, who was one of the few who personally took up land under the grant and settled upon it one of his own family. As a rule the grantees sold their claims to others. On the town records Zechariah Chandler's name is signed in the right of his wife's father, Thomas Bishop, who served against King Philip. His son, Thomas Chandler, took possession of the land and was among the pioneers of the town. To-day the Chandler family is believed to be the only representative in Bedford of the original grantees. It was in 1737, 1738, and 1739 that systematic settlement practically began in this part of the Merrimack valley.

In 1741 New Hampshire became a separate province, and in 1748 the farmers of Souhegan-East, finding themselves without any township organization and without the power to legally transact corporate business, called upon the government for relief. As a result, it is recorded that on the 11th of April in that year Gov. Benning Wentworth informed the Council of New

Hampshire "of the situation of a number of persons inhabiting "a place called Souhegan-East, within this Province, that were "without any township or District, and had not the privilege of "a town in choosing officers for regulating their affairs, such as "raising money for the ministry," etc. Thereupon a provisional township organization was authorized, under which the municipality was managed until 1750, when, on the 10th of May, the following petition was sent to the Governor, signed by thirty-eight citizens, among them Thomas Chandler:

To his Excellency, Benning Wentworth, Esq., Governor and Commander-in-Chief of his Majesty's Province of New Hampshire, and to the Honorable, his Majesty's Council, assembled at Portsmouth, May 10, 1750.

The humble Petition of the subscribers, inhabitants of Souhegan-East, so-called, sheweth, That your Petitioners are major part of said Souhegan ; that your petitioners, as to our particular persuasion in Christianity, are generally of the Presbyterian denomination ; that your petitioners, through a variety of causes, having long been destitute of the gospel, are now desirous of taking proper steps in order to have it settled among us in that way of discipline which we judge to tend most to our edification ; that your petitioners, not being incorporated by civil authority, are in no capacity to raise those sums of money, which may be needful in order to our proceeding in the above important affair. May it therefore please your Excellency, and Honors, to take the case of your petitioners under consideration, and to incorporate us into a town or district, or in case any part of our inhabitants should be taken off by any neighboring district, to grant that those of our persuasion, who are desirous of adhering to us, may be excused from supporting any other parish charge, than where they conscientiously adhere, we desiring the same liberty to those within our bounds, if any there be, and your petitioners shall ever pray, &c.

This petition was presented on May 18, 1750, to the Council, which unanimously advised the granting of a charter, and this the Governor did upon the following day. The name of the town was changed by Governor Wentworth from Souhegan-East to Bedford, it is said in honor of the fourth Duke of Bedford, then Secretary of State in the ministry of George II. This was the formal organization of the present town, which has a territorial extent of about twenty thousand acres of land.

Of the early population of this and neighboring towns "The Centennial History of Bedford" (published in 1851) says:

With few exceptions the early inhabitants of the town were from the North of Ireland or from the then infant settlement of Londonderry, N. H., to which they had recently emigrated from Ireland. Their ancestors were of Scotch origin. About the middle of the seventeenth century they went in considerable numbers from Argylshire, in the West of Scotland, to the counties of Londonderry and Antrim, in the North of Ireland, from which in 1718 a great emigration took place to this country. Some arrived at Boston, and some at Casco Bay near Portland, which last were the settlers of Londonderry. Many towns in this vicinity were settled from this colony. Windham, Chester, Litchfield, Manchester, Bedford, Goffstown, New Boston, Antrim, Peterborough and Acworth derived from Londonderry a considerable proportion of their first inhabitants.

Many of their descendants have risen to high respectability, among whom are numbered four Governors of New Hampshire, one of the signers of the Declaration of Independence, several distinguished officers in the Revolutionary War and in the last war with Great Britain, including Stark, Reid, Miller, and McNeil, a President of Bowdoin College, some Members of Congress, and several distinguished ministers of the gospel.

It was a Scottish stock, with an Irish preceding the American transplanting, that peopled Bedford. There were among its original settlers a few families of English and fewer still of pure Milesian extraction, but the Scotch descent was overwhelmingly predominant, and the austere theology and noble traditions of the Kirk of Scotland formed the leaven of the community. Their religious history dated back to John Knox. Their immediate ancestors were the sturdy Presbyterians with whom James I. colonized depopulated Ulster after he had crushed the Catholic uprisings. Those involuntary colonists made that the most prosperous of the Irish provinces, and at a critical moment for the cause of Protestantism added to the annals of heroic endurance the defense of Londonderry against the army of James II. But to their simple and tenacious faith the tithes and rents of the Anglican Church were scarcely less abhorrent than Catholic persecution, and the example of Puritan emigration ultimately led them by thousands to American shores. Much of this tide of settlement was diverted by the Puritan pre-occupation of New England soil to the Middle and Southern States, but a strong current set up into northern New England and occupied (with much other territory) the valley of the Merrimack. It was to these Scotch-Irish Presbyterians that the greater number of the grantees of Bedford — as a rule the descendants of Massachusetts Puritans — sold their claims, and the community became what their labors and influence made it. The Chandler (representing an original grantee) was one of the few Bedford families which sprang from English stock and possessed Puritan antecedents.

The settlement of Bedford was thus the outgrowth of an unquenchable thirst for civil and religious liberty. A profound conscientiousness added these simple, devout, frugal, and industrious people to the pioneer assailants of the North American wilderness. The ancient records and the published annals of the town afford a quaintly interesting picture of early New England civilization. Its background is the rock of religious faith, and to repeat the chronicles of the Bedford church for the eighteenth century is to write the history of the township for that period. The original grant required the maintenance of "a learned, orthodox ministry." The petition for the charter of Bedford set forth that "your petitioners, as to our particular persuasion in Christianity, are generally of the Presbyterian denomination," and assigned as the chief reason for asking incorporation that they "having been long destitute of the gospel, are now desir-"ous of taking the proper steps in order to have it settled "among us," but "not being incorporated by civil authority are "in no capacity to raise those sums of money which may be need-ful." The official records of formal township proceedings abound in such entries as these:

Feb. 15, 1748. *Voted* — That one third of the time, Preaching shall be to accommodate the inhabitants at the upper end of the town ; one other third part, at the lower end of the town; the last third, about Strawberrie hill

July 26, 1750. *Voted*, There be a call given to the Rev. Mr. Alexander Boyd, to the work of the ministry in this town.

March 28, 1753. *Voted*, Unanimously, to present a call for Mr. Alexander McDowell, to the Rev'd Presbytery for the work of the ministry in this town.

March 13, 1757. *Voted*,—That Capt. Moses Barron, Robert Walker, and Samuel Patten, be a committee for boarding and shingling the meeting-house.

March, 1767. *Voted*,—That the same committee who built the pulpit, paint it, and paint it the same color the Rev. Mr. McGregor's pulpit is, in Londonderry.

June, 1768. The meeting-house glass lent out*; Matthew Little's account of the same. David Moore had from Matthew Little, six squares of the meeting-house glass ; Daniel Moor had 4 squares of the same, Dea. Gilmore had of the same, 24 squares. *November* 20, 1768, The Rev. Mr. John Houston, had 24 squares of the same ; Hugh Campbell had 12 squares of the same ; Dea. Smith is to pay Whitfield Gilmore 6 squares of the same ; James Wallace had 15 squares of the same ; John Bell had 9 squares of the same ; Joseph Scobey, one quart of oil.

A true record.   Attest, WILLIAM WHITE, *Town Clerk.*

[Extract from the "town meeting warrant" (call) for 1779] : As for some time past, the Sabbath has been greatly profaned, by persons traveling with burthens upon the same, when there is no necessity for it,—to see whether the town will not try to provide some remedy for the same, for the future.

The Bedford church has been ever the center of all public activity. Its officers have been the officers of the town. From its pulpit have been made all formal announcements. Within its walls have been inspired every important home measure, and its influence has stimulated each wise public action. In the early records the school-house also shares prominence with the meeting-house, and the later generations of Bedford's inhabitants were men and women of solid primary education and thorough religious training. Thrift and industry made them prosperous, and they raised large families of powerful men and vigorous women. The mothers and daughters shared in the field work, and even

---

*The glass for the meeting-house was procured before the building was ready for it, and it was loaned to different members ; the careful record kept shows how scarce and costly an article it then was.

carried on foot to Boston the linen thread from their busy spinning wheels. Physical and moral strength characterized the race,
and they built up a community of comfortable homes, severe
virtues, strong religious instincts, a stern morality, and long lives.
Neither poverty nor riches were to be found among them, and
the simplest habits prevailed. Silks were unknown, and home-
made linen was the choicest fabric. Brown bread was the staple
of life, and wheat flour a luxury. Tea and coffee were rarely
seen, but barley broth was on all tables. Shoes were only worn
in winter, except to church on Sundays when they were carried
in the hand to the neighborhood of the meeting-house. The
saddle and pillion were used in journeys. Splinters and knots of
pitch pine furnished lights. The hymns were " deaconed out "
by the line at the meeting-house, and at the appearance of the
first bass-viol in the gallery (about 1790) there was a fierce
rebellion among the more austere of the worshipers. There was
community of effort in all important enterprises, and no man
needed aught if his neighbor could supply it.

But this frontier picture is not wholly stern in its lines.
Along with this simplicity of life and severity of religious doctrine there was no lack of frolic and rough joking, and the other
rugged characteristics were relieved by shrewd wit and native
humor. The annals of Bedford are entertaining and abound in
such anecdotes as these: Deacon John Orr (the grandfather of
the mother of Zachariah Chandler) was a sturdy Irish-Scotchman,
whose temper under extreme provocation once got the better of
his devoutness and led him into a vigorous profanity of speech.
This glaring dereliction in a church officer called for reprimand,
and he was waited upon by the minister and a delegation of his
brethren who asked, "How could you suffer yourself to speak
so?" "Why, what was it?" His offending language was
repeated to him. "And what o' that!" said he, "D'ye expect
me to be a' spirit and nae flesh?" Late in life Deacon Orr

visited Boston with a load of produce and put up at a house of
entertainment where, after he had drank several cups of tea, and
refused a final invitation, the landlady said that it was customary
to turn the cup upside down to show that no more was wanted.
He apologized and promised to remember the injunction. The
next morning he partook of a huge bowl of bread and milk for
breakfast, and not wanting the whole laid down his spoon and
turned the dish upside down with its contents on the table. The
hostess was naturally angry, but was met with the statement that
he had merely followed her own direction. The answer of a
brother deacon to one of the congregation who complained, " I
could na mak yesterday's preaching come together," was a com-
pend of practical Christianity: " Trouble yourself na' about that,
" man — a' ye have to do, man, is to fear God and keep His
" commandments." It is also told that the objections of one of
the staunch Scotch Presbyterians of Bedford to the marriage of
his daughter with an urgent suitor of Catholic parentage were
overcome by the apt query, " If a man happened to be born in
a stable would that make him a horse ?" And to one of the
rural theologians of the town is credited this contribution to
ecclesiastical distinctions: " The difference between the Presby-
" terians and Congregationalists is this: The Congregationalist
" goes home and eats a regular dinner between services, but the
" Presbyterian postpones his until after meeting." After a most
vigorous quarrel between the minister and one of the flock over
a boundary line dispute, the wrathful member of the congregation was prompt at service on Sunday with the following
explanation: " I'd have ye to know, if I did quarrel with the
minister, I did not quarrel with the Gospel."

That this was a community of uncompromising patriotism
follows from its character. In the French and Indian war the
New England forces were at one time under command of Col.
John Goffe, of Bedford, and the number of privates enlisted from

that town was large. The New Hampshire regiment which joined
the expedition of General Amherst against Canada, commanded
by Colonel Goffe, was raised largely among the Scotch-Irish
emigrants of Hillsborough and Rockingham counties, and had in
its ranks many Bedford men. In the Revolutionary War a large
portion of its able-bodied citizens were in the first American
army that beleaguered Boston and fought at Bunker Hill; nearly
or quite half of all who could handle a musket were with Stark
at Bennington, and with Gates at Saratoga. General Stark lived
but a few rods from the town line on the north, and one of his
most trusted officers was Lieutenant, afterwards Colonel, John
Orr, of Bedford. The town records abound with votes taken to
carry out the measures proposed by the Continental Congress,
and also chronicle one case of semi-Toryism and its punishment.
In 1776 Congress advised the disarming of all who were dis-
affected towards the American cause, and the selectmen of the
New Hampshire towns circulated this pledge among their people:

In consequence of the above Resolution of the Continental Congress, and
to show our determination in joining our American brethren, in defending the
lives, liberties, and properties of the inhabitants of the United Colonies, We,
the Subscribers, do hereby solemnly engage and promise, that we will, to the
utmost of our power, at the risk of our lives and fortunes, with arms, oppose
the hostile proceedings of the British Fleets and Armies against the United
American Colonies.

Among its Bedford signers were John Orr, Zachariah Chandler, and Samuel Patten (all ancestors of Zachariah Chandler,)
and the report made from that town was this:

To the honorable, the Council and House of Representatives, for the Colony of
New Hampshire, to be convened in Exeter, in said Colony, on Wednesday,
5th inst.

Pursuant to the within precept, we have taken pains to know the minds
of the inhabitants of the town of Bedford, with respect to the within obligation, and find none unwilling to sign the same, except *the Rev. John Houston*,
who declines signing the said obligation, for the following reasons: Firstly,
Because he did not apprehend that the honorable Committee meant that Min-

isters should take up arms, as being inconsistent with their ministerial charge, Secondly, Because he was already confined to the County of Hillsborough, therefore, he thinks he ought to be set at liberty before he should sign the said obligation. Thirdly, Because there are three men belonging to his family already enlisted in the Continental Army.

Mr. Houston, who was thus officially reported as the only Bedford Tory, had occupied the town pulpit for over fifteen years, and was a man of scholarship and purity, but he had become a loyalist in sympathy at the outbreak of the Revolutionary troubles, and was as inflexible in conviction as his neighbors. Originally (in 1756) the town had voted that his salary should be at the rate of forty pounds sterling a year for such Sundays as they desired his services. When they felt unable to pay they voted him one or more Sundays for himself, and then deducted from his salary proportionately. In 1775, after prolonged controversy with him, his case was brought before town-meeting (on June 15th), and he was unanimously dismissed by the adoption of a vote setting off for his own use all the Sabbaths remaining in the calendar year. The town records contain this explanation of the action:

June 15, 1775. *Voted* — Whereas, we find that the Rev'd Mr. John Houston, after a great deal of tenderness and pains taken with him, both in public and private, and toward him, relating to his speeches, frequently made both in public and private, against the rights and privileges of America, and his vindicating of King and Parliament in their present proceedings against the Americans ; and having not been able hitherto to bring him to a sense of his error, and he has thereby rendered himself despised by people in general, and by us in particular, and that he has endeavored to intimidate us against maintaining the just rights of America : Therefore, we think it not our duty as men or Christians, to have him preach any longer with us as our minister.

The resolute and uncompromising spirit, which thus sternly resented and punished unpatriotic sympathies in one whom the people had been accustomed to hold in reverence, was manifested on all occasions. This is a document of later date, signed by a Bedford committee, which seems not to have been suggested by any outside action, but to have resulted from the impulses of the citizens themselves:

Bedford, May 31, 1788.

To Lieut. John Orr, Representative at the General Court of the State of New Hampshire : —

Sir : — Although we have full confidence in you: fidelity and public virtue, and conceive that you would at all times pursue such measures only as tend to the public good, yet upon the particular occasion of our instructing you, we conceive that it will be an advantage to have your sentiments fortified by those of your constituents.

The occasion is this ; the return of those persons to this country, who are known in Great Britain by the name of loyalist, but in America, by those of conspirators, absentees, and tories ;

We agree that you use your influence that these persons do not receive the least encouragement to return to dwell among us, they not deserving favor, as they left us in the righteous cause we were engaged in, fighting for our undoubted rights and liberties, and as many of them acted the part of the most inveterate enemies.

And further,— that they do not receive any favor of any kind, as we esteem them as persons not deserving it, but the contrary.

You are further directed to use your influence, that those who are already returned, be treated according to their deserts.

In the War of 1812 there were more than two hundred men in Bedford armed and in readiness to march whenever called upon, and in this two hundred was one company of about sixty men over forty years of age and therefore exempt from military duty.   In the War of the Rebellion Bedford invariably filled its quota without draft and without high bounties, and it paid its war debt promptly.

It was in this community of stalwart, clear-headed, freedom-loving, sturdily honest, and uncompromisingly sincere men and women, that Zachariah Chandler was born and that the foundations of his character were durably laid.

CHAPTER II.

THE Chandlers of New England are the descendants of William Chandler, who came from England in the days of the Puritan immigration — about 1637 — and settled in Roxbury, in the Massachusetts Bay Colony. The Chandlers of Bedford, N. II., are the posterity of one of his descendants, Zechariah Chandler of Roxbury, who was among the grantees of Souhegan-East in the right of his wife, the daughter of a soldier in King Philip's War. They were the conspicuous English family in that Scotch-Irish Presbyterian settlement, and their farm is the only one in that town which is still in possession of the lineal descendants of an original grantee. That Zechariah Chandler was a man of some means is shown by this document, which is still on record and reads curiously enough in the biography of a most inveterate and powerful opponent of slavery and the slave power :

BOSTON, November 11, 1740.

Received of Mr. Zechariah Chandler, one hundred and ten pounds, in full, for a Negro Boy, sold and delivered him for my master, John Jones.

£110   WM. MERCHANT, Jun'r.

This slave was taken to Bedford, but soon freed by his owner, when he assumed the name of Primas Chandler. Although past the usual military age, in 1775 he enlisted as a private in the service of the colonies, was captured by the British at "The Cedars" and was never afterwards heard from by his friends. He left a wife and two sons in Bedford, but his family has since become extinct.

The first settlers in Bedford located chiefly on the rocky and hilly territory which is now the central and most thickly inhabited portion of the town. East of this, in the smooth and fertile intervale of the Merrimack, judging by the names on the most ancient maps, the settlers were chiefly of English descent, and among them was Thomas Chandler, the son of Zechariah, and the first actual occupant of the land granted to his father. He married Hannah, a daughter of Col. John Goffe, by whom he had four children — three daughters and a son named also Zachariah, who married Sarah Patten, the second daughter of Capt. Samuel Patten. This Zachariah, the grandfather of his namesake, the Senator, died on April 20, 1830, at the age of 79, and his widow died in 1842, aged nearly 94. From them were descended the two families of Chandlers, who in the present generation have been prominent in Bedford.

The oldest son of Zachariah was named Thomas, and was born August 10, 1772. He had four children — Asenath, who married Stephen Kendrick, of Nashville; Sarah, who married Caleb Kendrick; Hannah, who married Rufus Kendrick, a well-known citizen of Boston; and Adam, who now lives in Manchester, where also reside his three sons, Henry and Byron, who are connected with the Amoskeag National Bank, and John, who is a prominent merchant of that city. The only daughter of Zachariah, Sarah, remained single, and lived at the old homestead, which had become her property, until her death in 1852. Throughout that whole region she was known for years as "'Aunt Sarah."

Samuel, the second son of Zachariah, was born May 28, 1774, and married Margaret Orr, the oldest daughter of General Stark's most trusted officer, Col. John Orr. They had seven children, one of whom died in infancy. Those who reached maturity were Mary Jane, who was successively married to the Rev. Cyrus Downs, the Rev. David P. Smith, and the Rev. Samuel Lee, and

THE CHANDLER HOMESTEAD, AT BEDFORD, N. H.

3

who is still living, the last surviving member of the seven, at
the present homestead; Annis, who married Franklin Moore and
became a resident of Detroit; Samuel, Jr., who, after four years
at Dartmouth and Union colleges, lost his health and died in
Detroit in 1835; Zachariah, the subject of this memorial volume;
and John Orr, who, after graduating at Dartmouth, spent one
year in Andover Theological Seminary, came in feeble health to
Detroit where he was tenderly cared for by his brother, and finally
went by way of New Orleans to Cuba, where he died in January, 1839, his remains being subsequently removed to the Bedford
burying-ground.   The father, Samuel, died in Bedford on January 11, 1870, at the age of 95, and the mother in 1855, at the
age of 81.

The Chandlers during the three generations from Thomas
to Samuel were thus allied by marriage to three of the most
noted families, not only in Bedford but in New Hampshire,
the Goffes, Pattens and Orrs.   They were generally long-lived,
although consumption developed in different generations, and
were always prominent in town and church matters.   The
Thomas Chandler who first settled in Bedford was one of the
signers of the petition for incorporation in 1750, and was conspicuously connected with all local movements at that time.   His
grandson Thomas, the Senator's uncle, was in the Legislature
several terms, and in Congress from 1829 to 1833, being elected
as a Jackson Democrat.   His name is frequently mentioned in
the records of the church where he was choir-leader and where
he formed a class for instruction in sacred music.   He was also
selectman for many years, and held other positions in connection
with the town government.   He as well as his father "kept
tavern" on one of the main New England thoroughfares of
those days, and both were widely known through that region.
Samuel, the father of the Senator, played the first bass-viol ever
used in the church choir, and helped to stem the tide of indig-

nation with which the introduction of this "ungodly" instrument was met by the more rigid members of that orthodox Presbyterian body. His name often appears in the records as clerk of the church, selectman, and town clerk. He was for over twenty years consecutively a justice of the peace, and in his hands was usually placed such business as the settlement of estates. In the list of town officers the name of Chandler appears almost every

THE BIRTHPLACE OF ZACHARIAH CHANDLER.

year, and in almost all church and public gatherings for over a century some member of this family was present among the active and public-spirited citizens.

The first house built on the Chandler farm was on the east side of the river road, and not far from the present homestead. It was torn down many years ago, but the cellar was visible until within a comparatively recent period. The second house was built before the Revolutionary War, by the grandfather of the Senator, and this is still standing, though it has been remodeled and modernized. It was used as a tavern and court-house during that war.' In this the second Zachariah and his wife lived for many years, and in this they and their daughter Sarah died. During their declining years they were cared for there by the mother of Rodney M. Rollins, the present occupant and owner of the place, and the house, with forty acres of land, was willed to Mrs. Rollins by "Aunt Sarah" previous to her death. This was the first alienation from the possession of the family of any part of the Chandler farm. Although the house has been remodeled, it retains many of its old features, and one apartment at the northwest corner has been preserved nearly as it was at the time of the Revolution. It is called the Revolutionary room, and has still in its furniture some of the chairs that were there a hundred years ago, and among its fixtures an ancient buffet, carved by hand and unchanged except by paint since 1776.

On the opposite side of the road, fronting the east, and in sight of the Merrimack, where it takes its broad sweep above Goff's Falls, is the present Chandler homestead, which was built by Samuel Chandler in 1800, before his marriage. It remains to-day almost precisely as first constructed, and seems good for half a century more. Its rooms are large, and the ceilings unusually high for a farm-house of the earlier times. The front portion contains four large apartments on the lower floor, and in the rear are the dining-room, the kitchen, the pantry, and store-rooms. In the second story are five bed-rooms, with closets and additional store-room, and above these is a spacious attic. Among the furniture are chairs and chests of drawers of pre-revolutionary times, one of the ancient four-post bedsteads common a hundred years ago, and brass andirons which would delight the eyes of a lover of antique relics. Here still

lives the Senator's oldest sister, and here the family of seven
were born.

In the ancient family bible, printed in 1803 and preserved by
Mrs. Lee, is an entry of a birth, of which this is a fac-simile:

Zacharias Chandler
Born Dec.r 10 th 1813

It will be noticed that the given name is written Zacharias.
Mrs. Lee still speaks of her brother as Zacharias, and his name
is also so printed in the Chandler geneaology in the centennial
history of Bedford. The Senator in his signatures simply used
the initial of his first name, but he ultimately adopted the
ancestral Zachariah, and that was the name which he made
famous, and by which he will be known in this biography.

Zachariah Chandler's father and paternal grandfather, Samuel
and Zachariah, are described as spare men of medium stature,
but energetic and full of endurance. His mother, Margaret Orr,
was tall and powerful; her distinguished son resembled her in
face, and inherited from her many of his most vigorous traits.
She was a woman of great strength of character and robust sense,
and exercised a large influence over her children. Her family
was a remarkable one; her father was the conspicuous man of
his day in his part of New Hampshire; her brother, Benjamin
Orr, became the foremost lawyer of Maine early in the present
century, and served one term from that State in Congress; her
half-brother, the Rev. Isaac Orr, was a man of many accomplishments and a diverse scholarship, a prolific writer on scientific and
philosophical topics, and with a claim on the general gratitude as
the inventor of the application of the air-tight principle to the
common stove.

The boy Zachariah was healthy, strong, quick-tempered, and self-reliant, and the contrast was marked between his sturdiness and the constitutional feebleness of his short-lived brothers. The traditions of his childhood, still fondly cherished by his surviving sister, all show that from his cradle he was ready to fight his own battles, and that his "pluckiness" was innate. One juvenile anecdote related by Mrs. Lee will illustrate scores that might be repeated: His father's poultry-yard was ruled by a large and ill-tempered gander, the strokes of whose horny beak were the dread of the smaller children. The oldest brother was one day driven back by this fowl while attempting to cross the road, when the young "Zach.," then three years old, called out "Do, Sammy, do, I'll keep e' dander off," and rushed into a pitched and victorious battle with the "dander," during which his brother made good his escape.

His rudimentary education was obtained in the little brick school-house at Bedford, which remains substantially unchanged and is still used. Here he attended school regularly from the age of five or six until he was fourteen or fifteen. He had an excellent memory, and was a good scholar, standing well with others of his age. He was a leader in the boys' sports, always active, and entering with zest into every frolic. Of these days, one of his early playmates — now the Rev. S. G. Abbott, of Stamford, Conn. — thus writes: "The death of Mr. Chandler "revives the memories of half a century ago. The old brick "school-house where we were taught together the rudiments of "our education; the country store where his father sold such a "wonderful variety of merchandise for the wants of the inner "and outer man; the broad acres of field and forest in the "ancestral domain where we used to rove and hunt; his uncle's "'tavern,' the cheerful home of the traveler when there were no "railroads, situated on a great thoroughfare, constantly alive with "stages, teams, cattle, sheep, swine, turkeys, and pedestrian

THE SCHOOL - HOUSE AT BEDFORD, N. H.

"immigrants—all these form a picture as distinct to the mind's "eye as if a scene of the present. No unimportant feature of "that picture in my boyish memory was a rough-built, over-"grown, awkward, good-natured, popular boy, who went by the "never-forgotten, familiar sobriquet of 'Zach.' He never forgot "it. After more than forty years' separation, when I called on "him in the capitol, and apologized for calling him Zach, in "his old, rollicking way he said 'Oh, you can call me old Zach, "that's what they all call me out West.'"

In his fifteenth and sixteenth years he attended the academies at Pembroke and Derry, with his older brother, who was fitting for college. In the winter following he taught school one term in the Piscataquog or "Squog" district. As is the rule in country schools, many of the pupils were about as large as the teacher, and the "Squog" boys had the reputation of being especially unruly. The usual disorders commenced, but after some trouble the energetic young man from the Chandler farm established his supremacy, and the scholars recognized the fact that there was a head to the school. Mr. Chandler always spoke with interest of his brief experience in teaching, although he never claimed any particular success in that calling. While he was thus employed the teacher of the brick school, in which he had been so long a pupil, was a Dartmouth sophomore who in his "boarding around" was especially welcome at the house of Samuel Chandler. This was James F. Joy, who then formed with the young Zachariah an intimacy, which ranked among the causes that determined Mr. Joy's own selection of Detroit as a home, and lasted through life.

In the latter years of his school life young Chandler worked on the farm through the summer, and the last season that he was home he took entire charge, employing the help and superintending the labor. Thomas Kendall, who was with him during three summers, and who is still living in Bedford, says, "Zach.

was a good man to work and a good man to work for." He was just in his dealings with the men, but vigorous as an over-seer, and himself as good a "farm hand" as there was. Stories are still told of his achievements in mowing contests with the men. He had no liking, as had many of his fellows, for hunt-ing or fishing, but he was fond of athletic sports, and was the best wrestler in town. "Whoever took hold of Zach.," says Mr. Kendall, "had to go down."

During one of the last years of his residence at Bedford, Mr. Chandler was enrolled in the local militia company and turned out at the "general muster." He did not, however, succeed in bringing himself to perfect obedience to the orders of the young captain, whom he knew he could easily out-wrestle and out-mow, and was arrested for insubordination. He was kept under arrest through one afternoon, but the court-martial which had been ordered for his trial was recalled and he was released. He was afterwards for a short time on the staff of the command-ing officer, General Riddle, but his removal from New Hampshire took place at about this time. After his Janesville, Wis., speech, two days before his death, Mr. Chandler was called upon by the Captain Colley who had placed him under arrest nearly fifty years before. Mr. Colley is now a resident of Rock county, Wis., and had driven a long distance to listen to his old-time subordinate, or rather insubordinate, and to revive with him old memories.

In the year 1833 Zachariah Chandler entered the store of Kendrick & Foster of Nashua, and in September of that year, moved by the same impulse that has sent so many New Eng-landers into the growing territories, turned his face Westward, and in company with his brother-in-law, the late Franklin Moore, came to the city, which from that time to his death was his home. He had not then shown in any marked degree the qualities which made his future success so eminent, and was

apparently simply a good specimen out of thousands of the energetic, determined, and sagacious young men, who, leaving more
sterile New England, have subdued the forests, moulded the
politics and conducted the business of half a dozen Western
States.

For the old homestead and its occupants, and for the town
of Bedford, Mr. Chandler always entertained a warm affection.
He was a good correspondent, and ·his home letters, which until
his entrance into public life were frequent and long, breathed a
genuine feeling of filial and brotherly affection. After his election to the Senate, with the voluminous correspondence which
his official position involved, his letters to the old home became
less frequent, but to the last he kept up occasional communication
with the surviving friends at his birthplace. During his father's
life he visited Bedford twice or more each year, and after his
father's death made at least one annual journey there. In 1850,
when the centennial celebration of the incorporation of the township occurred, Mr. Chandler was among those invited to be
present, and sent the following letter of regret:

DETROIT, May 16, 1850.

GENTLEMEN :—I regret exceedingly my inability to accept your kind
invitation to be present at your Centennial Celebration of the settlement of
the good old town of Bedford.   It would have afforded me great pleasure to
meet my old friends upon that occasion, but circumstances beyond my own
control will prevent.   The ashes of the dead, as well as the loved faces of the
living, attract me strongly to my native town, and that attachment I find
increasing each day of my life.   Permit me, in conclusion, to offer: "*The
town of Bedford*—May her descendants (widely scattered through the land)
never dishonor their paternity."

Be pleased to accept, for yourselves and associates, my kind regards, and
believe me,   Truly yours,

Z. CHANDLER.

His later visits were looked forward to with much interest,
not only by his relatives, but by the neighbors, to whom a talk
with him was one of the events of the year. He was there

always genial and friendly, kept up his acquaintance with the old residents, and thoroughly enjoyed his association with them. His last visit to the homestead was after the close of his campaign in Maine, in August, 1879. He then met many of his boyhood friends, and enjoyed a ramble over the undulating fields which stretch from the central hills toward the banks of the Merrimack. And as he drove for the last time down the road from the house of his birth toward Manchester, he pointed to a pine grove which skirts the northern border of the Chandler farm, and said to his companion, " That, to me, is the most beautiful grove in the world."

New Hampshire has been prolific in strong men with the granite of its hills in the fibres of their characters. Bedford itself has been the birthplace of scores of the leading men of the thriving city of Manchester; of Joseph E. Worcester, the lexicographer; of Benjamin Orr, of Maine; of David Aiken, Isaac O. Barnes, and Jacob Bell, of the Massachusetts bar; of the Hon. David Atwood, of Wisconsin; of Judge A. S. Thurston, of Elmira, N. Y.; of Hugh Riddle, of the Rock Island Railroad, and Gen. George Stark, of the Northern Pacific; of the Rev. Silas Aiken, of the Boston pulpit; and of others of large influence in their generations. But upon no one of its sons was the impress of its peculiar history so indelibly stamped as upon the young man who left it to aid in founding a powerful State amid the Great Lakes, and who became the foremost representative of that State's vigorous political conviction and purpose.

CHAPTER III.

IN 1833 Zachariah Chandler, then still a minor, joined the current of Western emigration from New York and New England which had sprung up with the completion of the Erie canal, and in the fall of that year entered into the retail dry-goods business at Detroit. Franklin Moore (the husband of his sister Annis), who had already visited Michigan, came with him as a partner in the enterprise, and the original firm name was Moore & Chandler. At the outset the young merchant had some assistance from his father, who, the tradition is, offered him $1,000 in cash or the collegiate education which his brothers received, the money being chosen. Samuel Chandler also subsequently bought a store for his son's use, but it is understood that all such advances were speedily and fully repaid. The building in which the future Senator first laid the foundation of his ample fortune was located where the Biddle House now stands; it adjoined the mansion of Governor Hull, and was subsequently transformed into the American House. Upon its shelves Moore & Chandler displayed a small general stock, representing the ample assortment usual in frontier stores, and saw a promising business answer their invitations. In the following spring they removed to a brick store (on the site now occupied by S. P. Wilcox & Co.), near the main corner of the town (where Woodward and Jefferson avenues meet). In the summer of 1834 Detroit was visited by the Asiatic cholera, which appeared in malignant form, and was attended by an appalling death rate, and an almost entire suspension of general traffic. Mr. Chandler did not yield to the prevalent panic, but remained at his business and was indefatigable in his efforts to relieve the universal distress. His vigorous constitution and plain habits guarded his own health, and he cared for the sick and buried the dead without faltering amid the dreadful scenes of the pestilence. For weeks he and a clerk (Mr. William N. Carpenter, of Detroit) alternated in watching by sick beds, and, with others of like strength and courage, brightened with unassuming heroism the gloomy picture of a season of dreadful mortality.

On August 16, 1836, the firm of Moore & Chandler was dissolved, and the junior partner retained the established business, and continued its vigorous prosecution. Those who knew him then describe a fair-haired, awkward, tall, gaunt and wiry youth, blunt in his ways, simple in habits, diffident with others, but shrewd, tireless in labor, and of unlimited energy. He worked day and night, slept in the store, often on the counter or a bale of goods, acted as proprietor, salesman, or porter as was needed, lived on $300 a year, avoided society, and allowed only the Presbyterian church to divide his attention with business. He kept a good stock, especially strong in the staples, bought prudently, and there was no better salesman in the West. His trade became especially large with the farmers who used Detroit as a market, and the unaffected manners and homely good sense of the rising merchant soon gave him a popularity with his rural customers that foreshadowed the strong hold of his later life on the affectionate confidence of the yeomanry of the State.

The training which this intense application added to native vigor of judgment early made him a thorough business man, exact in dealings, strong in an intuitive knowledge of men, sound in his judgment of values, prudent in ventures, and of an unflagging energy which pushed his trade wherever an opening

could be found. As interior Michigan developed he added job-
bing to his retail department, and became known as a close and
prudent buyer, a shrewd judge of credits, and a most successful
collector. A business established at the commencement of an
era of marvelous growth, pushed with such industry, drawn upon
only for the meagre expenses of a young man living with the
closest economy, and unembarrassed by speculation, meant a
fortune, and at twenty-seven years of age Mr. Chandler found
himself with success assured and wealth only a matter of patience.
His nearest approach to financial disaster was in the ruinous
crash which swept "the wild-cat banks" and so many mercantile enterprises out of existence in Michigan in the year 1838.
Like others he found it almost impossible at that time to obtain
money, and the Bank of Michigan which had promised him
accommodations was compelled by its own straitened condition
to decline his paper. Thus it happened that a note for about
$5,000 given to Arthur Tappan & Co. of New York fell due
and went to protest. Mr. Chandler, accustomed to New England
strictness in business and exceedingly sensitive on the point of
meeting all engagements, was inclined to treat the protest as
bankruptcy itself, and called upon his Bedford friend, James F.
Joy, then a young lawyer in Detroit and for years afterwards
Mr. Chandler's counsel, to have a formal assignment drawn up.
What followed is given in Mr. Joy's language : " I looked care-
" fully into his affairs, and found them in what I believed to be
" a sound and healthy condition. I then said : ' I won't draw
" an assignment for you, Chandler ; there is no need of it.'
" ' What shall I do ? ' was his answer, ' I can't pay that note.'
" My reply was, ' Write to Tappan & Co. and say that you
" cannot get the discounts that have been promised, but that if
" they will renew the note you will be able to pay it when it
" next falls due.' He took my advice and went through, and
" never had any trouble with his finances after that. I reminded

" Mr. Chandler of that occurrence about two months before his
" death, when he said he remembered it perfectly, and added
" that if it had not been for that advice he might have been a
" clerk on a salary to this day."

Mr. Chandler's was the first business in Detroit whose sales
aggregated $50,000 in a single year, and the reaching of that
limit was hailed by the community as a great mercantile triumph.
He showed increasing commercial sagacity at every stage of his
active business life. He pushed his jobbing trade in all directions
and made his interior customers his personal friends. He invested
his surplus profits in productive real estate which grew rapidly
in value. He was never tempted into speculation, and he was
very reluctant to incur debt. As a result, ten years after he
landed at Detroit he had a reputation throughout the new
Northwest as a merchant of ample means, personal honesty,
large connections, and remarkable enterprise.

Between 1840 and 1850 Mr. Chandler reduced his business
to a purely wholesale basis and made himself independently and
permanently rich. He had opportunities and they were improved
to the full. [And it may be here said without exaggeration that
every dollar of the fortune with which he closed his career as an
active merchant represented legitimate business enterprise; it was
the product of personal industry and good judgment put forth
in a field wisely selected and with only slight aid at the outset.]
The wiry stripling had become a stalwart man, despite a family
consumptive tendency which at times caused alarm. Prosperity
did not affect the plainness of his manners and speech, nor the
simplicity of his character, and maturity added method to, without impairing, his powers of personal application. He was a man
alive with energy and thoroughly in earnest. He was active and
influential in all public matters in Detroit. Every year he drove
through the State, visited its cross-roads and its clearings, saw its
pioneer merchants at their homes and in their stores, made up

his estimate of men and their means, studied the growth of the State, and marked the course of the budding of its resources. He thus kept himself thoroughly informed as to the material develop-ment of Michigan, and acquired that intimate knowledge of the State and its representative men which formed such an important part of his equipment for public life. His companion in these numerous commercial journeys was the man who succeeded him in the Senate, the Hon. Henry P. Baldwin of Detroit, who came to Michigan largely through his solicitations, was engaged in business for years by his side, and remained his intimate associ-ate through life. This part of Mr. Chandler's career abounded in the making of friendships which endured until death. While strict in all his dealings, he was considerate and his sympathy was quick with struggling industry and honesty. He aided when they needed it many who afterwards rose to position and wealth, and these men became the most firmly attached of his supporters in his public career.

Shortly after 1850 political affairs commenced to receive Mr. Chandler's attention, and he gradually entrusted more and more of the actual management of his large business to others, though he still for some years directed in a general way the operations of the house. He had been already absent one winter on a trip to the West Indies for his health, and had made a brief and not wholly satisfactory experiment (about 1846) at establishing a job-bing fancy-goods trade in New York. With these exceptions he had made his Detroit dry-goods business his personal charge. The firm name had generally been Z. Chandler & Co., although it was for some time Chandler & Bradford, and some of his relatives had been and were associated with him in business. From his second location he had moved his stock to more com-modious quarters on the site now occupied by the Chandler Block, and in 1852 he again moved to the stores built jointly by himself and Mr. Baldwin on the southwest corner of Woodward avenue and Woodbridge street. In 1855, as outside matters commenced to press constantly upon Mr. Chandler's attention, there came into his employment as a clerk a young man of twenty-three from Kinderhook, N. Y., Allan Shelden. He showed

THE CHANDLER BLOCK.

an aptitude for business and a capacity for work that recalled to the head of the house his own earlier days, and Mr. Shelden's rise in his employer's confidence was rapid and permanent. On Feb. 1, 1857, just before Mr. Chandler took his seat as the suc-

4

cessor of Lewis Cass in the Senate, the firm name was changed
to Orr, Town & Smith, with Mr. Chandler as a special partner,
with an interest of $50,000. In the fall of that year, it became
Town, Smith & Shelden; in the fall of 1859 it was changed to
Town & Shelden; on Feb. 1, 1866, it was again changed to the
present name of Allan Shelden & Co. Three years later Mr.
Chandler ceased to be a special partner, and thus finally sundered
his formal connection with the business he had established. The
mercantile pre-eminence in Michigan of his house in its line of
trade has been maintained by his successors, and it now occupies
the magnificent Chandler Block, built for its accommodation by
its founder in 1878 on Jefferson avenue in Detroit. Mr. Shelden
himself continued in confidential relations with his predecessor,
and was entrusted in later years with the management of a large
share of his private affairs.

During his active business life no Northwestern merchant
surpassed Mr. Chandler in credit, in enterprise, or in success,
and he left the counter and office of his store with wealth and
with an unsullied mercantile character. His commercial integrity
and sagacity always remained among his marked characteristics.
He made profitable investments, became interested in remunerative enterprises, and, while he lived generously after his income
warranted it, saw his riches steadily increase under prudent and
shrewd management. At the time of his death, his estate which
was absolutely unincumbered was roughly estimated as exceeding,
at the least, two millions, representing valuable business property in Detroit, several farms, large tracts of timbered lands, the
marsh farm at Lansing, residences in Washington and Detroit,
bank stock, government and other securities, and investments in
railroad and like enterprises. His business habits remained in
full vigor to the last. He was punctuality itself in all appointments; he was rigid in his adherence to his engagements; he
hated debt, and never permitted the second presentation of an

account; he did business on business principles and with business exactitude; he spent money freely but knew where and for what it went; and always his counsel was sought and prized by men engaged in enterprises of the largest magnitude. Without being ostentatious or profuse in his charities he was a large giver, rarely refusing a meritorious application for aid, but he invariably satisfied himself that the object was worthy, and put a heartiness into his "no" when a refusal seemed to him to be in order.

His business instincts he never relaxed except for well-considered reasons. The ditching of the marsh farm he regarded as an experiment of far-reaching public importance, and he paid its cost cheerfully for the sake of settling the question of the possibility of reclaiming such lands. Some of his "imprudences" of this deliberate and well-weighed sort proved profitable. During the war and when the credit of the United States was at an alarmingly low ebb as shown in the ruling prices of its bonds, he visited the city of New York in company with Representative Rowland E. Trowbridge, of his State. On the way there he spoke, in private, in a tone of unusual depression of the financial difficulties of the government, and lamented the absence of any available remedy. The next day there was a decided improvement in the rates for "governments" on Wall street, and the firmer feeling it created never wholly disappeared but was followed by a gradual appreciation in this class of securities. Mr. Trowbridge called his attention to the advance on the day following, and the Senator answered, "I know all about it. "I gave my broker orders to buy heavily and the street, finding "that out, said 'Chandler is just over from Washington and "knows something,' and so they followed my lead, and there "was a rush which sent the market up." Years afterwards, Mr. Chandler was reminded by Mr. Trowbridge of the permanent character of the improvement in the government's credit which attended his speculation and of his own profit in the matter. He replied that while he had sold many of his bonds bought during the war, he still held those which came into his possession at that time, cherishing them for their associations with an investment which he made at some risk to help the treasury in its difficulties and which had proved very·remunerative.

During his public life information legitimately acquired and the broadening of his judgment by contact with men undoubtedly helped his investments, and thus added to his wealth, but individual pecuniary advantage he resolutely ignored in shaping his public career. And his sturdy incorruptibility as a legislator was proverbial at the capital. An illustration of this fact was shown in his strenuous resistance to and emphatic denunciation of the bills to remonetize and coin without limit the old silver dollar. While these measures were pending he had considerable investments in silver mining stocks, which would have been greatly increased in value by the proposed policy, but, showing one day to a friend a large draft representing a silver-mine dividend, he said, " I ought for personal reasons to favor these " bills, but I can't consent to make money at the expense of the " people." Another incident exemplifies this phase of his character : In February, 1873, the city of Manistee, on the shore of Lake Michigan, sent Gen. B. M. Cutcheon to Washington to secure an increased appropriation for the improvement of its harbor. Senator Chandler, as the chairman of the Committee on Commerce and with a reputation for vigilance in caring for Michigan interests, was naturally relied upon for valuable assistance. He received General Cutcheon cordially, gave his personal attention to the matter of introducing the representative of Manistee to influential Congressmen and to department officials, and then made an appointment for the consideration of what his own share in the work should be. At that private meeting he expressed to General Cutcheon his cordial sympathy with his

errand, but added, "My hands are tied; the fact is that I am
"interested in large tracts of pine on the Manistee river, and, if
"I should take charge of your appropriation, it would be said,
"'Chandler is feathering his own nest;' and if I am going to
"retain my influence for good here, I must keep clear of even
"the suspicion of a job."

The great multitude who knew Mr. Chandler as a public man
knew nothing of this early chapter of business life. It wholly
ante-dated his appearance at Washington, and the channels in
which his strong energies made themselves felt there and in his
younger days were widely distinct. But it is a fact that he was
a remarkable man of business and as thorough a merchant as
ever developed in the West a great trade from small beginnings.
His was a doubly successful career. Before he had reached
middle age he had won success in business and a fortune. Then
he entered public life and made himself a leader of men in a
historic era.

CHAPTER IV.

HE forty-six years of Zachariah Chandler's life in Michigan saw a vast material empire supplant an almost unbroken wilderness. His commercial enterprise and success and his labors as a legislator were among the influential agents in this marvelous development and give its story a title to a place in his biography.

As early as 1634 Jesuits Brebuef, Daniel and Davost, following a route explored by Samuel Champlain eighteen years before, passed up the River Ottawa, across Lake Nipissing, down French river and along the lonely shores of the great Georgian bay to the dark forests bordering Lake Huron. Brebuef reached there first; Daniel came later, weary and worn; Davost came last of all, half-dead with famine and fatigue.* Champlain had been before them, and other explorers preceded Champlain, but these three were the first Europeans who made a habitation by the shores of the great lakes which roll their tireless flood down through the gateway of Detroit. They erected a hut, and daily rang a bell to call the surrounding savages to prayers. Behind them was the tangled forest they had penetrated; at their feet were the broad waters of Lake Huron; beyond — toward the setting sun — was an abyss so soundless that no echo had ever come from it. And these three soldiers of the cross, converters of the heathen, unarmed and alone amid a multitude of savages, were the advance ripples of the mighty wave that two

---

* Parkman's "Jesuits in North America."

centuries later was to break across the lake at their feet and the rivers below them and surge over the trackless wilderness beyond.

Seven years later (September, 1641,) Charles Raymbault and Isaac Jaques embarked in a frail birch-bark canoe, paddling northwest from Georgian bay among the countless islands of the St. Marie river, amid scenery that filled them with delight. After seventeen days the Sault de St. Marie burst upon their enraptured vision. There they were welcomed "as brothers" by the Chippewas and there began the first known white settlement in Michigan.

On the 28th of August, 1660, Rene Mesnard left Quebec, resolved to make greater progress in the exploration of the Northwest. He ascended the Sault in a canoe, coasted along the northern shore of the upper peninsula of Michigan, and on the 15th of October of that year reached the head of Keweenaw bay to which he gave the name of St. Theresa. Eight years later (1668) a permanent mission was established at the Sault. In the autumn of 1678 occurred an event forever memorable in the annals of Michigan. There was then laid on the Niagara river the keel of the first large vessel built on the shores of the great lakes. It was completed and launched early in the following summer, and on the 7th of August, 1679 (200 years ago), amid the discharges of arquebuses and the sound of swelling *Te Deums* it began the first voyage ever made by Europeans upon the upper inland seas of North America. This was the "Griffin," sixty tons burden, carrying five guns, with La Salle commander, Hennepin missionary and journalist, and a crew of Canadian fur traders. Three days later (August 10), after many soundings, they reached the islands grouped at the entrance of Detroit river. They thus knew the lake was navigable by vessels of large size — this was one step toward solving the destiny of the West. Ascending the river, the explorers passed by a large number of

Indian villages; these had been visited years before by Jesuit missionaries and *coureurs des bois.* Some fix the date as early as 1610, but others make it later, no names being given in either case. Louis Hennepin gives the earliest description of the river: "The strait (De troit) is finer than Niagara, being one "league broad, excepting that part which forms the lake that "we have called St. Clair." The strait once voyaged and understood, its value was quickly appreciated by the French as a means of resisting the inroads of the persevering English (who from New York and New England were pressing upon their possessions in the East), and of preventing British interference with the valuable hunting privileges or with the Indian tribes dwelling upon the borders of the Northern lakes. With this in view the Marquis de Nonville, Governor-General of the Canadas, ordered (June 6, 1686) M. Du Lhut, who had been commandant at Michilimackinac, "to establish a post on the Detroit, near Lake Erie, with a garrison of fifty men," and the order added, "I desire you to choose an advantageous place to secure the "passage, which may protect our savages who go to the chase, "and serve them as an asylum against their enemies and ours." In obedience to these instructions, M. Du Lhut proceeded to the entrance of the strait from Lake Huron, where he built a fort and established a trading post (on the site of the present Fort Gratiot) which he called Fort St. Joseph. Thus (1686) was made the first settlement by Europeans in the lower peninsula of Michigan.

The misfortunes of the war with England which terminated with the peace of Ryswick (Sept. 1, 1697,) still further convinced the most sagacious of the leading French colonists of the importance of a fort on the Detroit river which would command this channel of communication with the great lakes above. Impressed with this fact, Antoine de la Mothe Cadillac, a Gascon sailor who amid a career of romantic adventure came to be commandant at Michilimackinac, crossed the Atlantic in person, and earnestly and repeatedly pressed upon the colonial minister, Count Ponchartrain, the necessity of the prompt establishment of a permanent post on the Detroit, where it would bring the French forces in closer proximity to the Iroquois and would give them command of the waters of the upper lakes and of the great fur trading regions about them. Cadillac did not urge this as a missionary enterprise but for its commercial and military advantages, and the force and vigor of his representations prevailed at the palace. He sailed from France with the royal order, "Take prompt possession of Detroit," with this supplement from Ponchartrain: "Prosecute vigorously; if the Jesuits obstruct, return and report." Cadillac arrived in Quebec early in the first year of the eighteenth century (March 8). Three months later (June 5) his preparations were made, and on that day he took his departure from La Chine. With him were Captain Tonti, Lieutenants Dugue and Chacornacle, fifty soldiers, and fifty Canadian traders and artisans. Nineteen days later he arrived upon the site of the present city of Detroit. In his memoir Cadillac wrote: "I arrived at Detroit, July 24 (1701), "and fortified myself there immediately. I had the necessary "huts made and cleared up the ground preparatory to its being "sowed in the autumn." When he touched the shore of Michigan, with pomp and ceremony he erected a cross, a cedar post beside it; then with a sword in one hand and a sod in the other he made solemn proclamation with many words of "possession taken" of all the country round about, from the great lakes to the south seas, in the name of the King of France.

Thus French Michigan began, and so it remained until Wolfe's victory gave new rulers to Canada and to all the French possessions beyond. On Nov. 29, 1760, the French flag floated for the last time over Detroit, as a part of the dominion of France. On that day Maj. Robert Rogers, an English provincial

officer, native of New Hampshire, took possession in the name
of another king, ran up the Cross of St. George, fired a salute,
gave some round British cheers, and (the Treaty of Paris con-
firming this occupation) Michigan was English. It so remained
until the Revolution and the treaty of 1783 made it American.
But it was not until thirteen years after (1796) that it was
evacuated by the British garrison; in June of that year Captain
Porter with a detachment of American troops entered the fort
and hoisted the Union flag for the first time, and took formal
possession in the name of the United States. The Hull surrender again swept Detroit and that part of Michigan lying within
its command under the Cross of St. George (Aug. 16, 1812,) to
remain until Perry's victory and the subsequent military successes
of General Harrison expelled the English and restored it permanently to the Union, on Sept. 28, 1813. During the Revolution
Detroit was the headquarters of British power in the Northwest,
and from it were sent out the expeditions which ravaged the
frontiers of Pennsylvania and Virginia.

The British captain, Rogers, who took possession in 1760,
afterwards reported the population (1765) as: Able-bodied men,
243; women, 164; children, 294 — total, 701. This was exclusive
of the garrison, who were sent away as prisoners of war, and
included the 60 men, women and children who were slaves. He
also reported that of the French families remaining in the settlement there were 23 men able to bear arms, 24 women, and 41
children. The others were probably English who had followed
upon the track of the troops. Captain Rogers's report gives
strength to th's supposition. It says: "There are in the fort
many English merchants, several of whom have bought houses."
Then it gives this insight into the industrial condition of the
settlement: "Of farms there are 40, and some fourscore
"acres in depth with a frontage on the river; of these several
"farms are at present in cultivation." The number of acres

under cultivation is given as 404;- number of bushels of wheat raised the preceding year, 670; bushels of corn, 1,884. The report quaintly adds: "The Indian corn would have been in " greater abundance, had proper care been taken of it; the most " part has been devoured by birds."

Here remote from the world, with the joyous sparkling of the great river at their feet, the luxuriance of the forest about them, the cottages of the settlers peeping out from the green foliage in which they were half hidden, these simple colonists lived uneventful lives, surrounded by the beauty and the bounties of nature. The forests teemed with game, the marshes with wild fowl, and the rivers with fish. The long winters were seasons of enjoyment. In summer and autumn traders, voyageurs, *coureurs des bois*, and half-breeds gathered from the distant Northwest, and the settlement was boisterous with rude frolic and gaiety. This was Detroit and Michigan in 1765.*

Between the French surrender and American occupancy, little was done toward the development of the peninsulas. In 1796 there were a few straggling settlements on the Detroit river, as also on Otter creek and on the rivers Rouge, Pointe aux Tremble, and other small streams flowing into Lake Erie. The French Canadians had extended their farms to a considerable distance along the banks of the St. Clair. Detroit was a small cluster of rude wooden houses, defended by a fort, and surrounded by pickets. Villages of the Ottawas and Pottawatamies stood on the present site of the city of Monroe, and near them were a few primitive cabins constructed of logs, erected by the French on either bank of the river Raisin; this was called Frenchtown, and is now part of Monroe. On the upper lakes there were the posts on the island of Mackinac, at St. Marie, and at St. Joseph (on the St. Joseph river). The transition from France to Eng-

---

* This is Parkman's picture in "The Conspiracy of Pontiac."

land had given the monopoly of the fur trade to the Hudson
Bay Company, thus changing the direction of its profits; otherwise the effect upon Michigan had been a change of masters,
flag and garrison, and little else. And the shifting from England
to the United States also meant only new faces and new colors
in the fort; otherwise it was for the time effectless.

The interior of the country was but little known except to
those engaged in the fur trade, and they were interested in
depreciating its value. Even as late as 1807 the Indian titles
had only been partially extinguished, and no portion of the public domain had been brought into the market. The opposite
shore was occupied by a vigilant and jealous foreign power. The
interior of the future State swarmed with the savages who yet
made it their home, and an Indian war was threatening. These
things repelled the tide of immigration that was already surging
over Ohio and the country bordering on the Ohio river. Fourteen years after American possession the population of Michigan
was given as: Whites, 4,384; free blacks, 120; slaves, 24—total,
4,528. Five years before the number of householders in the
lower peninsula was officially given as 525. There are antecedent
estimates of population and assertions, but no facts that can be
relied on. It is, however, probable that at the time of the British evacuation (1796) the population did not exceed 2,500 souls,
for two years afterwards (1798) Wayne county, then co-extensive
with the present State of Michigan, sent a representative to
Chillicothe, where it was claimed that the Northwest Territory
was entitled to a delegate in Congress because there were then
5,000 inhabitants within its boundaries. It can scarcely be possible that half of that aggregate was in Michigan alone, and that
its settlers then equaled in numbers those scattered over the
inviting and fertile region which now includes the powerful and
populous States of Ohio, Indiana and Illinois.

The growth of the decade succeeding 1810 was trifling. In 1820 the census showed but 9,048 souls in Michigan Territory, which included the present State and the region beyond the lakes north of Illinois. The war was over. Indian depredations had ceased and the Indian titles had been quieted. The perils of settlement were removed. The seeming obstacles of the toil and privations of frontier existence were mere cobwebs in the way of the hardy and adventurous. But there yet remained serious impediments to Michigan's growth. Distance was one, for the State was still difficult of access, and canals and railroads were yet in the future. A more serious impediment was a blunder. On May 6, 1812, Congress passed an act requiring that 2,000,000 acres of land should be surveyed in Michigan Territory. The surveyors went into the forest with their chains and poles, and the result was a report to Congress which may be thus summarized: "Many lakes of great extent; marshes on their "margins; marshes between; other places covered with coarse "high grass; this grass covered with water from six inches to "three feet; lakes and swamps over half the country; the inter- "mediate space poor, barren and sandy; the dry land composed "of sand-hills, with deep basins between and more water; the "margins of many of the streams and lakes literally afloat, or "thinly covered with a sward of grass with water and mud "underneath; the country altogether so bad that there would "not be more than one acre out of a hundred, if there would "be one out of a thousand, that would in any case admit of "cultivation." Official stupidity had its effect on Congress, and in 1816 (April 29) that body cancelled the survey order, and abandoned Michigan to the hunters and trappers and their game. For two years this continued; but the adventurous would plunge into the wilderness and would come back and talk of beautiful valleys, broad prairies and fertile soils. Explorations widened and a multitude of witnesses came with their facts to

prove that the curtain of forest concealed something more inviting than marsh and barren and sand-hill. Then the government
(1818) ordered a new survey and out of all this came part of
the truth, namely: There was in this wilderness an immense
variety of forest trees — oak, maple, ash, elm, sycamore, locust,
butternut, walnut, poplar, whitewood, beech, hemlock, spruce,
tamarack, chestnut, white, yellow, and Norway pine. There were
plains and natural parks; there were level prairies and hills rising
with gradual swell away to the center of the State. Of soils
there were deep sandy loams mixed with limestone pebbles, deep
vegetable moulds mingled with clay producing dense and luxuriant vegetation, brown loams mingled with clay, deep vegetable
moulds with a surface covering of black sands. There was water
in abundance, rivers and streams and creeks and beautiful lakes.
All these reports and more, confirmed and re-confirmed by
pioneers and surveyors, came back from the interior, until the
exceeding richness and great agricultural value of the Lower
Peninsula of Michigan was established.

But another event was to exercise a most important influence
upon the future State. In 1817 the first steamer upon the
Northern lakes, the "Ontario," was launched, and, amid bonfires,
illuminations and most lively demonstrations of joy, made her
first trip upon Lake Ontario. This heralded the dawn of a
material revolution. One year later, on the 27th day of August,
1818, the "Walk-in-the-water," the first steamer launched above
Niagara Falls, came up to the wharves of Detroit after a passage
of forty-four hours from Buffalo. This vessel, of only 340 tons,
and lost three years later, was a puny affair, but wise men saw
in her advent the promise of a future which time has more than
realized. Then in the wake of the steamer, Congress (1819)
ordered the public lands of Michigan placed in the market for
sale. At this time Detroit contained 250 houses, 1,415 inhabitants, and the entire territory a population of 8,896. In 1825

the Erie canal was completed, and its far-sighted projector, De Witt Clinton, sailed amid national acclamations from Lake Erie to tide-water. It completed the link of direct water communication with Michigan, and the stream of Western emigration was quickly swollen to a torrent.

Mr. Chandler first came to Michigan in 1833. Three years before (1830) the census of the entire territory, as it was constituted when Illinois was admitted to the Union, was 32,531. The growth during the preceding decade had been steady, not immense; that was to come after. It was in the year of 1833 that the first settlement was made in the present State of Iowa. And in that fall (September) the people of Detroit were rejoicing that "arrangements were in train for the establishment of a new "stage-line route to Chicago, by which travelers can go from "one place to the other in five days." There was not then a mile of railroad in the territory, and not until five years after (1838) was the first twenty-nine miles completed to Ypsilanti. Detroit was still a frontier post numbering less than 4,000 inhabitants. On all the Western lakes at the beginning of that year there were but eighteen steamers, ranging from fifty to 395 tons in burden, and aggregating but 3,710 tons, and with the best of these a voyage of thirty-nine hours from Buffalo to Detroit was a remarkable passage. All this was improvement; yet the Detroit merchant in that year could not expect to receive his purchases made in New York within less than from three to six months after the time of setting out to procure them. During the winter steamboats and river craft were ice-bound, and the settlements at Detroit, the River Raisin and elsewhere throughout the broad peninsula were shut out from the Eastern world, except as travelers braved the tedious and painful staging through Canada to Buffalo, with its week of continuous day and night journeying.

A year later (1834) Congress defined the boundaries of Michigan Territory. Let the finger trace on the atlas the northern borders of Ohio and Indiana, follow around the south shore of Lake Michigan to the boundary between Wisconsin and Illinois, pursue that line to the Mississippi river, then down its stream to the north line of the State of Missouri, along that westward to the Missouri, and up that river until between the 25th and 26th degrees of west longitude the finger reaches the faint line, coming down into the Missouri from the north, of the White Earth river—all the land and lakes between the Detroit straits and this little White Earth river and between the line so traced and the British possessions, was Michigan Territory in 1834 and until Michigan was admitted as a State into the Union. It was an imperial domain, larger than Sweden and Norway united; nearly three times greater than England, Wales, Scotland, Ireland, and the Channel islands; surpassing the united territories of France, Belgium, Switzerland, Denmark and The Netherlands; even exceeding the combined acreage of Italy and the German Empire. Yet in all this region, when Mr. Chandler displayed his first stock of goods in Detroit, there was not one mile of railroad or telegraph, not one steam mill or manufactory, but one city approaching 4,000 inhabitants and not one exceeding it, and not a single mile of paved street or sewerage. There was but one water-works, and no gas-works. There was not one daily newspaper, and but few of any kind. The valuable iron deposits of the Upper Peninsula were undiscovered. The wealth of pine timber was unknown. In the previous year (1832) the total value of foreign and domestic produce exported from Michigan amounted to but the trifling sum of $9,234, and in the preceding federal census (1830) the entire civilized population of this vast area of limitless possibilities was less than 33,000, although there were then in the Union twenty-four States with a population of 12,866,020.

DETROIT IN 1894.

5

Mr. Chandler came in with the first swell of the great tide of emigration which broke over Michigan Territory. Up to within a brief period preceding, that extensive and fertile region was scarcely known except as it appeared on maps. Its rich prairies, its fertile plains, its deep forests with all their wealth, were a *terra incognita* to all white men except the fur traders. But it was being rapidly known and understood. Its fame had rolled back over the East, and the fruits were seen in the new faces and sturdy forms swarming to Detroit as a point of departure to the new and beautiful land. In that year (1833) it was a matter of boasting that as many as "one hundred and seventy-five emigrants had landed in Detroit in one day." The next year *Niles' Register* had a report from Detroit that the arrivals had reached the magnificent proportions of "nine hundred and sixty in one day," and that "the streets of Detroit were full of wagons loading and departing for the West," principally for the region about Grand river. And the same journal said: "The "character of these emigrants is in every respect a subject of "felicitation. They will give Michigan a capital stock of wealth "and moral worth unequaled by any of the newly-formed States, "and scarcely approximated by Ohio."

In 1833 and for more than a year afterward the business part of Detroit was confined to the narrow space bounded by Wayne and Randolph streets, Jefferson avenue and the river, and at the same time there were but few buildings on Jefferson avenue above Rivard, and but one on Woodward avenue north of State street. Old wind-mills lined the shores; the little unsightly French carts clattered through the streets; ducks, geese and pigs were the only city scavengers. This sounds like another age — another continent — but it was the Detroit and Michigan of but forty-six years ago. Change came with population — slowly at first, then with increased speed, then with immense strides. Mr. Chandler lived to see it all and to be a part of it.

He came with the early tide of population; he saw the tide rising, at first languid, halting and uncertain; he saw it year by year gathering momentum and volume until it swelled and rolled over Michigan a mighty flood of brawn and brain, of enterprise and conscience.

On the fifth day of November, 1879, tens of thousands of people looked upon the dead face of the stalwart Senator and followed his body to its last resting place in the city to which he had come in 1833. Forty-six years and a few weeks had passed; no more. But in that time the city which he made his home had spread its wings until it covered an area of thirteen and a half square miles, with 300 miles of streets (seventy-six miles paved), and some of them among the broadest and most beautiful in the world, shaded by rows of graceful trees of luxuriant foliage, and adorned by stores and private residences rich in finish and architecture. It had 200 miles of water-mains and 150 miles of sewers, making it one of the most perfectly-drained cities on the continent. Its population had grown to be 120,000, and its taxable wealth to exceed $87,000,000. School buildings, representing a public investment of $650,000 and accommodating 15,000 pupils, were scattered through its wards, and numerous churches and abundant public and private charitable institutions made proclamation of the faith and philanthropy of its citizens. Great manufacturing enterprises lined its wharves and suburbs; scores of railroad trains arrived at and departed from its depots daily; and the commerce of the lakes was passing along its river front at the rate of thousands of tons hourly.

But the change in Michigan had been no less marvelous. The State has a representation in the present Congress of the United States exceeding that of any one of eight of the first States of the Union, equaling the representation of that of two others (Georgia and Virginia), and only exceeded by that of three of the original thirteen—Massachusetts, New York, and

Pennsylvania. In a single county of the Upper Peninsula, in
1833 supposed to be only a mass of barren, uninviting and unin-
habitable rocks, there are three cities either one of which has a
greater population than the Detroit of that day, and in Michigan out of its forty-three cities and 178 villages (April, 1879)
there are over thirty more populous than Detroit in 1833—some
of them with populations from five to eight times greater. The
people of the State are a million and a half in number, spread
over the greater part of the Lower Peninsula, about the Sault,
and from Marquette to Ontonagon and south to Menominee in
the Upper Peninsula. Its newspapers have grown to twenty-
three dailies and over 300 with less frequent issues. Its railroads
have developed from non-existence to 3,500 miles, owned by
thirty-six corporations, connecting Detroit and the principal cities
of Michigan with all portions of the State, penetrating to every
center of population and industry, costing over $160,000,000, and
paying in each year for salaries and operating expenses over
$13,000,000. Strong institutions for the care of the deaf and
dumb and the blind and for the insane, a thriving college for
agricultural education, and that noblest monument of the wisdom
and forethought of the latter-day founders of Michigan, the State
University, were all planted in these years. And with this, the
public school system was nourished until there are over 300
graded schools and over 6,000 public schools in the State, with
property valued at over $9,000,000, paying almost $2,000,000
yearly in teachers' wages, and with annual resources amounting
to nearly $4,000,000. In the mountains of the Upper Penin-
sula, so long reputed a barren wilderness, have been discovered
exhaustless mines of the richest iron ores and the most extensive
and valuable copper deposits known on the globe. The Saginaw
Valley has poured a briny stream of wealth upon the State
from its unfailing salt-wells, and from the forests about and
beyond to the westernmost limits of Michigan have been gathered

great treasures of pine and hard woods. And while nature was yielding its hidden stores to enrich the State its skilled citizens were not idle. Over 10,000 manufacturing establishments in Michigan now employ upward of 70,000 people, pay more than $25,000,000 annually in wages, make an infinite variety of wares, and turn out products each year amounting in value to more than $130,000,000. The statistics of agricultural development are equally remarkable. The log cabin and the clearings have yielded to ample farms. The marsh, the pine barren, even the hyperborean soil of the Upper Peninsula, have been transformed into productive wheat-fields. The cereals of Michigan exceed in their annual product 70,000,000 bushels, and $45,000,000 in their value. Highly cultivated and valuable farms (over 111,000 in number and with a total acreage of 10,000,000) cover the greater part of the Lower Peninsula. Comfortable, even stately, farm houses dot the landscape. School-houses, churches, villages, towns and cities stand where the forest was. The wilderness has fled away. Everywhere there are evidences of peace, prosperity, happiness and a high civilization. It is magic; courage, intelligence and industry have been the magicians.

The changes in the other parts of the Michigan Territory of 1833 have been no less marvelous. Four States have been carved out of that region whose boundaries in 1834 were traced on the atlas — Michigan, Wisconsin, Iowa and Minnesota — and the great wheat farms of Dakota will soon develop into a fifth. This entire territory to-day has eight Senators, twenty-nine Representatives and one Delegate in Congress, has over 11,000 miles of railroad, seventy-seven daily papers and over 1,100 weekly or monthly publications, and several great cities larger than Philadelphia and New York when the United States had taken its second census. It has a population greater than that of the thirteen colonies which successfully defied the power of Great Britain during the Revolution, greater than that of the

six New England States in the present day. It produces a larger
amount of breadstuffs than the whole Union yielded when Mr.
Chandler first came to the territory, and contains more wealth
than did all the States fifty years ago.

This is a marvelous story of growth. Nothing in the Old
World has equaled it. Nothing the New has exceeded it. It
has confounded prophecy. It has outrun imagination. It is the
achievement of a stalwart race. It is the triumph of faith, of
zeal, of courage. It dazzles the men of to-day. And it will
stand for centuries to excite the admiration of the historian and
the wonder of the future.

CHAPTER V.

HE conspicuous figure in Michigan politics, when Zachariah Chandler landed at Detroit and for twenty-five years afterward, was Lewis Cass. He was a man of ability and many accomplishments, irreproachable in private life, and with a claim upon the enduring gratitude of the people of the Northwest for his large share in the founding of mighty States about the shores of the great lakes. He came to Michigan with military distinction, and had added to his laurels civic honors as a territorial ruler, as a skilful negotiator with the Indians, and as an intrepid explorer. General Cass was a warm political and personal friend of Andrew Jackson, and his influence made Michigan a strongly Democratic territory and State. In 1831 he had been appointed Secretary of War in President Jackson's cabinet, and in 1836 he was sent to Paris as the United States Minister at the court of Louis Phillippe. The courage, vigor and skill of his attack upon the "Quintuple Treaty," which embodied Great Britain's theories on the then delicate topic of the right of search on the high seas, and which was defeated by the refusal of France to ratify the preliminary negotiations, made his ambassadorship an event in European diplomacy, and gave him a national reputation on this continent. His return to Detroit in 1843 was attended by unusual popular demonstrations at every important point in his Westward journey. In 1845 Michigan sent him to the Senate, and in 1848 the Democracy nominated him as its candidate for the presidency. That a man

who thus made a new commonwealth influential in national politics should call about him a strong following and mould public
sentiment at his own home was natural, and the State of Lewis
Cass was long regarded as staunchly Democratic. His party held
control for years of the main avenues of political preferment,
and not a few young men of parts and ambition who came to
Michigan as Whigs were led into the ranks of the Democracy
by the fact that it was the only organization which had honors
and offices to bestow.

General Cass was a courtly gentleman, dignified in manners,
who, with a natural boldness of character which never lost
wholly its power of self-assertion, gradually became ultra-con-
servative in his Democracy. Originally he had anti-slavery
tendencies, but the Southern drift of his party, which became
apparent about the time of his return from France, carried him
with it, and he grew to be one of the most assiduous originators
and supporters of the series of compromises which so long
defeated justice and encouraged the aggressions of the slave
power. The result was that in time the hammer of his personal
influence in Michigan was broken on the anvil of New England
ideas, while his name became the symbol of "hunkerism" in the
Northwest; but in December, 1860, his octogenarian patriotism
flamed up in the presence of armed treason and executive imbecility, and he branded the administration of James Buchanan as
it deserved by indignantly resigning the portfolio of the department of state. No political contrast could well be more vivid
than that between Lewis Cass and the man who succeeded
him in the Senate, and replaced him in the political leadership of Michigan, representing a greater State, a nobler political
cause, and instead of the make-shifts of compromise ideas which
are to-day embodied in the fabric of American civilization.

Zachariah Chandler's father was originally a Federalist, and
then a Whig. The son brought with him to Detroit Whig

sympathies and anti-slavery convictions, but no predisposition to political activity. For many years he refused to divert his energies from his mercantile pursuits, and took no share in party contests, except such as would be natural in the case of any enterprising citizen with a lively interest in public questions. He was known as a staunch Whig, and he thoroughly identified himself with that party when in both Michigan and the Union its victories seemed accidental, and its defeats certain. Between 1837 and 1848 his name frequently appears among the officers of Whig meetings, or as a member of the election day vigilance committees of his party, and (very rarely) as a ward delegate to Whig conventions. He was a regular contributor to the campaign fund, and he did his share of work at the polls. At that time the labors of election day were not those of persuasion merely. Partisan feeling was bitter, and in the population of the growing frontier city, there was a strong ruffianly element, which was as a rule Democratic in its sympathies. In close contests mobs sometimes gathered about the voting places, and sought by jostling and occasional assaults to keep away from the ballot-boxes the more timid or fastidious of the Whigs. On these occasions Mr. Chandler was among the men of strong frames, sinewy arms, and pugnacity of spirit, who furnished the Whig muscle to defeat this variety of "Loco-foco trick." He and Alanson Sheley (now a well-known Detroit merchant) were, with a few others of like strength and stature, the Whig body-guard who forced a way for voters through the dense crowd, and interposed for the rescue of the threatened. There is no lack of amusing anecdotes of this species of service rendered by Mr. Chandler to the Whig party; and it was at times attended by serious danger. In later years he credited Mr. Sheley with having saved his life in one of these election disturbances, and frequently recalled reminiscences of the muscular exploits of those days. It was not until Mr Chandler

was a Whig of nearly twenty years' standing, that he became
that party's candidate for any office, or that he actively interested himself in its committee work and practical management.
He cast a void vote for Harrison in 1836, before Michigan had
been formally admitted; he attended the monster meetings and
sang campaign songs in the log cabins of 1840, and gave
then a valid vote to Harrison; he denounced Tyler's political
treason, and in 1844 cheered for Clay and Frelinghuysen; he
opposed General Cass in 1848, and at that time delivered his
maiden speech, in support of "Zach." Taylor; but it was not
until 1851 that he manifested any especial taste for or skill in
politics, or that he allowed his name to be used as a candidate
for position.

The Whigs of Michigan were as a rule of New England
extraction, and the masses of the party were always staunchly
anti-slavery in sentiment. They charged General Cass's denunciation of the "Quintuple Treaty" to a disposition to seek
Southern approval by indirectly shielding the slave trade; they
opposed the annexation of Texas, applauded the Wilmot Proviso,
and were restive under Southern aggression and slave-holding
arrogance at the capital. The few Congressmen whom they
were able to elect voted uniformly for free institutions and
against the extension of human bondage. Michigan's first Whig
Senator, Augustus S. Porter, while still new in his seat, opposed
alone Calhoun's resolutions in "the Enterprise case" (a vessel
employed in the coastwise slave trade had touched at Port Hamilton in the British West Indies, and some negro chattels who
formed part of her cargo had taken advantage of English law
to assert their manhood and freedom), and cast a solitary vote
to lay them upon the table. Of this act Joshua R. Giddings
wrote: "Seeing that eminent Senators around him interposed
"no objection to the passage of the resolutions, Mr. Porter,
"obeying the dictates of his own judgment and conscience,

" heroically met the overwhelming influence arrayed against him,
" and showed the most cogent reasons for rejecting the resolu-
" tions, by exhibiting the absurdity of the attempt to induce the
" British government to acknowledge the laws of slavery and the
" slave trade to exist and be enforced within her ports." Both
Mr. Porter and William Woodbridge voted against the resolution
for the annexation of Texas. In the House of the Twenty-sev-
enth Congress Jacob M. Howard acted with the friends of
freedom on questions involving that issue, and in the Thirtieth
Congress William Sprague, the second Whig Representative, was
openly classified as a Free Soiler. In 1849 the Whigs and Free
Soilers united to support Flavius J. Littlejohn for Governor, and
the Whigs of Michigan as a whole were a body of intelligent
and conscientious anti-slavery men, and made their political
weight felt on the side of free institutions.

Mr. Chandler was from his boyhood radical in his opposition
to human bondage, and for a time hoped that the Whig party
of the North could be used to effectually resist the conspiracy
of the slave power against the territories. His anti-slavery
activity preceded his appearance in politics. Detroit was an
important terminus of the "Underground Railroad," that mysterious organization which so skilfully and quickly transported
colored fugitives from the Ohio to Canadian soil, and Mr.
Chandler, while still absorbed in business, was a frequent and
liberal contributor to the fund for its operating expenses. He
manifested an especial interest in the Crosswhite case, which
played a conspicuous part in the fugitive slave law agitation
preceding the compromises of 1850. Adam Crosswhite was the
mulatto son of a slave mother who was owned by his father, a
white farmer in Bourbon county, Kentucky. While a boy he
was given as a servant to his half-sister, a Miss Crosswhite, who
married a slave-dealer named Stone. Her husband subsequently
sold her brother for $200, and Crosswhite ultimately became the

chattel of a Kentucky planter named Giltner living in Carroll county. When he had reached the age of forty-four and had become the father of four children, he learned that his master was planning to sell a portion of his family. The parental instinct drove this man to a step which he had not taken through any desire for personal freedom, and he determined upon flight. He succeeded in getting his entire family across the Ohio in a skiff, and into the hands of the "Underground Railway" managers in Indiana. There was a vigorous pursuit, and at Newport the fugitives were nearly captured, but Quaker shrewdness concealed and protected them, and after weeks of stirring adventure, during which the father and mother were compelled to separate, they reached Michigan, and became the occupants of a little cabin in the eastern part of the present city of Marshall. They were quiet and industrious citizens, and by thrift and unremitting labor commenced making payments on their homestead. In time the history of the fugitives became known to their neighbors, and finally some one with the genuine spirit of the slave-driver sent to Kentucky information concerning their hiding-place. In December, 1846, Francis Troutman came to Marshall, ostensibly as a young lawyer in search of business, but in fact as Giltner's representative in identifying his fugitive slaves and planning their recapture. He did his work well, through artifice and with the help of aid which he hired at Marshall, but did not succeed in perfectly concealing his plans. Crosswhite received warning of the impending danger, and both armed himself and arranged with sympathizing friends for prompt assistance. The abduction was finally attempted early on the morning of Jan. 27, 1847. Troutman was assisted by David Giltner, Franklin Ford, and John S. Lee, all Kentuckians, and the four men were well armed. Crosswhite saw their approach, and succeeded in giving the alarm, but before his friends commenced to assemble the Kentuckians broke in the door of his cabin and informed the negroes that they must go at once before a magistrate where it was proposed to prove the fact of their escape from slavery. While the preparation of the children for the winter's ride to the justice's office was in progress, a crowd, at first largely composed of colored men but soon including many whites, gathered about the cabin, and promptly made the fact apparent that they were in no mood to permit the proposed restoration of human property to its Kentucky owners. The courage of the slave-hunters did not prove equal to the occasion, and finally Troutman resorted to argument. He harangued the jeering crowd on the sanctity of the fugitive slave law and the legality of Giltner's claim, even offering as proof of his law-abiding spirit not to take back to slavery a child born to the Crosswhites since their escape. The response to this proposition to do exact justice by separating an infant from its mother may be imagined, and in the end the Kentuckians abandoned their attempt. Crosswhite had meanwhile complained against them for trespass, and they were then arrested, convicted and fined $100. Money was also at once raised in Marshall by which the negroes were sent to Detroit and thence to Canada. While the excitement was at its hight some of the prominent citizens of Marshall joined the crowd, and endeavored to restrain them from violence and to convince the slave-hunters of the folly of attempting to defy the aroused indignation of the community; they were careful, however, to avoid any violation of the law. Troutman met their remonstrances by a demand for their names. One of them replied, " Charles T. Gorham; write it in capital letters." The answer of another was, " Oliver Cromwell Comstock, Jr.; take it in " full so that my father may not be held responsible for what I " do." Troutman also obtained the name of Jarvis Hurd, these three being well-known residents of Marshall and gentlemen of pecuniary responsibility. Nothing further took place at the time, and in a few days the Kentuckians returned to their State, which was soon aflame with wrath at this "Northern outrage." Public meetings were held to denounce the "abolition rioters," the most exaggerated accounts of the Marshall release were circulated and believed, the event received Congressional attention, and finally the State of Kentucky made an appropriation for the prosecution of all who were concerned in the escape of the Crosswhite family. Troutman returned to Michigan in the summer of 1847, and brought an action to recover the value of the rescued slaves, in the United States Circuit Court, against a large number of defendants; the case as tried, however, was practically a prosecution of Messrs. Gorham, Comstock, and Hurd. The Kentuckians retained a large array of counsel, including John Norvell, the veteran Democratic leader, while the defense was represented by Theodore Romeyn, Wells & Cook, and Hovey K. Clarke, with Halmer H. Emmons (subsequently United States Circuit Judge) and James F. Joy as counsel. Gerrit Smith also came from New York to argue the constitutional question involved, but the defendants' attorneys did not deem it prudent in a jury trial at that time to ally themselves with so radical an abolitionist. The case was taken up before Justice John MacLean, in 1848, and attracted national attention. The first trial took place in the June term and resulted in a disagreement of the jury. A second trial followed in November and December of the same year and ended in a verdict for the plaintiffs of $1,926 and costs; the expenses of defending the suits had also imposed heavy pecuniary burdens upon the Marshall gentlemen. Mr. Gorham was then a Democrat, and found among his party friends a strong feeling that it was important at that time and in so conspicuous a case that Michigan should manifest a disposition to rigidly enforce the fugitive slave law, as these were the years when General Cass's presidential aspirations culminated, and when it was essential that his hold upon

Southern confidence should be preserved. There was no lack of private expressions of Democratic sympathy with the defendants, and assurances were given that they should not be left to meet alone the heavy expenses involved, but among the Democratic leaders there was an unmistakable wish that the prosecution should be vigorously pushed for the sake of its political effect, and this secret pressure had a powerful influence. This case interested Mr. Chandler from the outset, and he watched every development closely. Early in the proceedings he met Mr. Gorham, with whom his acquaintance was then but slight, and said to him, "I am satisfied from what I have seen and learned "that this case is being manipulated in the interest of the Dem- "ocratic party, and that you are to be sacrificed to appease the . "slave power of the South, so that Cass may not be damaged "by the result. Offer no compromise; fight them through to "the end; I will stand by you, and see that you do not suffer." He was as good as his word, gave and helped to raise money for the defense, and attended the trial to the close. Mr. Gorham, who received no Democratic aid of importance, became one of his firmest and most intimate friends, and when Mr. Chandler was appointed Secretary of the Interior Mr. Gorham (who had then served five years as United States Minister at The Hague) became the Assistant Secretary of that department. Of the same period of Mr. Chandler's life this characteristic anecdote is told: John Sumner, one of his Jackson customers, passed Sunday as his guest in Detroit, and at church listened with him to a sermon of pro-slavery flavor, followed by a prayer by a visiting clergyman in which the Divine blessing was earnestly invoked upon the down-trodden and the oppressed. At the conclusion of the services Mr. Chandler stepped to the foot of the pulpit, sought an introduction to the utterer of the prayer, and said: "Thank you for that prayer! It was all that I have heard this morning that was worth hearing."

Throughout the days of Mr. Chandler's earnest attachment. to the Whig party, his anti-slavery feeling was pronounced.

In 1848 Mr. Chandler fleshed his political broadsword with one or more speeches in behalf of General Taylor. He had been an occasional participant in the debates of the Young Men's Society, the training-school for not a few of Detroit's eminent men, but in that year for the first time he addressed a miscellaneous audience on public questions. His earlier speeches showed the strength of the man, and despite some ruggedness were effective. In the State election of 1849 Mr. Chandler took no active part. In 1850 he was one of the Wayne county delegates to the Whig State convention, which met at Jackson on the 18th of September, and nominated a ticket headed by George Martin, of Kent, for Secretary of State; the following campaign was a local one, arousing but little interest, and in it Mr. Chandler did not prominently share. On February 19, 1851, the Whigs of Detroit held a convention to select a city ticket for the charter election in March, and after one informal ballot Mr. Chandler was unanimously nominated by them for Mayor. This event marks the commencement of his career as a popular, shrewd, and successful political leader. The Democratic candidate for the Mayoralty was Gen. John R. Williams, a native and one of the foremost citizens of Detroit, the president of the Michigan constitutional convention of 1835, and the senior officer of the State militia. He had been the first Mayor of the city, and had held that place for six terms, and was a man of practical ability, the owner of a large estate, and popular with the people. His personal strength made him a formidable candidate, and his defeat not easy of accomplishment. Mr. Chandler's answer to the delegation who waited upon him with the question, "Will you run on the Whig ticket against John R. Williams?" was, "I will and I will beat him too," and he put all his energy into the campaign which followed. The Whig convention by resolution presented his name to the people of Detroit as that of "a man "identified with its improvements, prominent in its welfare, and "interested in its prosperity," and in the Whig journals he was warmly commended as "known to every man, woman, and child "in the city as a man of strict integrity, active and industrious "business habits, of great liberality of views, both in person and "sentiment, and of the purest moral character; eminently popular "and affable in his habits of intercourse with his fellow- citizens, "his extensive business operations have brought him in daily "contact with all, through a long course of years." His election was also urged on the ground that he was the only candidate "known to be in favor of extending the various enterprises "of sewerage, pure water, pavements and sidewalks, just as "fast as the needs of a young city shall require," and because his "course in his own business, and in relation to the public "interest, has been an energetic, discreet and efficient prose- "cution of everything upon which he has laid his hands." During this canvass Mr. Chandler gave what is believed to be the only lecture of his life, and its marked success undoubtedly helped him at the ballot - box. It was delivered before the Young Men's Society upon February 25, 1851, its theme being "The Element of Success in Character." The newspaper report of it was as follows :

The theme chosen by Mr. Chandler. "The Element of Success in Character," though much worn, was most successfully treated. Intending only to discourse from his own observations and experience, his views were as philosophical as they were practical. Therein was the charm and *takingness* of the lecture. Without rhetorical flourish the composition was excellent, severe in its simplicity and directness, nevertheless abounding in beauty. For originality, aptness of quotation and illustration, and felicitous use of lan- guage, it ranks with the choicest productions before the society. In his own person he furnished the very best illustration and proof of success. Such a lecture from any one would do good, but how much greater its influence when enforced by the living example the lecturer himself affords of the truths of his teaching.

6

Mr. Chandler organized his first political battle with characteristic thoroughness and system, visited every ward, called upon
the voters, and made a remarkable personal canvass. The result
was that when the ballots were counted it was found that he had
carried every precinct in Detroit and had defeated his opponent
by 349 majority in a total vote of less than 3,500. He led by
nearly 400 the average vote of his ticket, and the Democrats
elected at the same time a large proportion of their candidates.
The victory was celebrated by a Whig serenade, at which the
Mayor-elect made a modest and brief speech of thanks. This
manifestation of personal strength and political skill at once
attracted State attention, and it became the source of new Whig
hope.

Mr. Chandler's term as Mayor continued for one year, but
was devoid of especial incident, although even now some
interest will be felt in this official letter to Kossuth, which the
Hungarian patriot answered with a note of regretful declination:

DETROIT, January 10, 1852.

To his Excellency Louis Kossuth:

DEAR SIR : By resolution of the Common Council, it becomes my pleasing
duty to invite you to visit the city of Detroit and partake of its hospitalities.
Much as we esteem you personally, highly as we appreciate your public and
private worth, it is not to these alone that we do homage, but to the great
principles which you advocate. We hail you as the champion of republicanism in Europe, as God's instrument in arousing throughout the world a hatred
of despotism, as a man who has sacrificed his all, and offers his life upon
the altar of liberty, as a teacher of "even bayonets to think." We, sir, have
not been disinterested spectators of your glorious struggle for Hungarian independence. We watched with most intense interest the commencement and
progress of that sanguinary conflict. When we saw the people rising in
their might, the nobleman and citizen vieing with each other in devotion to
their country's cause, emulous in sufferings and sacrifices, under such a
leader, we felt that victory must crown your exertions ; and when we saw the
elements of Despotism uniting to crush this (to them) detested spirit of
Freedom, when we saw the temporary triumphs of your oppressors, we felt
that all was not lost — that the Almighty Ruler of the Universe would neither
leave nor forsake you in your low estate, that the days of despotism were
numbered.

Again would I invite you to visit Detroit and partake of its hospitalities. Again would I assure you of our deep sympathy for your down-trodden country, and I hazard nothing by the assertion that that sympathy will manifest itself in a tangible form. Whether our government will act in your behalf as a government, is not for me to say ; whether it would be proper for it to do so, is not for me to discuss at this time. But that you have the deep sympathy of our entire population is manifest to all.

With great respect, I have the honor to be your obedient servant,

ZACHARIAH CHANDLER,

Mayor of the City of Detroit.

At the conclusion of Mr. Chandler's term as Mayor the Common Council of Detroit, by unanimous vote, spread upon its records this resolution :

Resolved by the Common Council of the City of Detroit, That in retiring from the office of chief magistrate of this city the Hon. Zachariah Chandler, by his urbanity, fidelity and zeal in the discharge of his official duties for the past year, merits the admiration and respect of the Council, and that in retiring to private life he carries with him our cordial wishes for his happiness and prosperity.

In November, 1852, occurred Michigan's first general election under the constitution of 1850. The Democratic candidate for Governor was Robert McClelland, who had already held that office during the preceding short term. General Cass alone surpassed this gentleman in personal strength with his party in the State. Mr. McClelland was an upright and able man, who had served with distinction in Congress, and had held many important offices in Michigan; he subsequently became Secretary of the Interior in the cabinet of President Pierce. While a member of the House of Representatives he had assisted in drafting the original Wilmot Proviso, but he had grown conservative with his party, and in 1852 came before the people as a warm champion of the compromises of 1850. Personally he was a man of some reserve, but affable with acquaintances and respected everywhere. He was renominated enthusiastically and with every prospect of an easy re-election. With the single exception of William Woodbridge, who was borne into office on the Whig tidal-wave of 1839 and 1840, Michigan had chosen an unbroken line of Democratic Governors. At the first election after its admission to the Union, Stevens T. Mason had a majority of 237 in a total poll of 22,299. The term for which Governor Woodbridge was chosen (he resigned to take a seat in the Senate) was followed by six successive Democratic victories. John S. Barry was elected in 1841 with 5,326 majority over his Whig competitor, Philo C. Fuller, and two years later he defeated Dr. Zina Pitcher by 6,493 votes. Alpheus Felch in 1845 had 3,807 majority over Stephen Vickery, Whig, and in 1847 Epaphroditus Ransom was chosen over James M. Edmunds by 5,649 votes. In 1849 John S. Barry was again elected, defeating Flavius J. Littlejohn, Whig and Free Soiler, by 4,297 votes in a total poll of 51,377. In 1851, which was the last election under the old constitution, Robert McClelland led Townsend E. Gidley 6,926 votes. The Liberty party, as a distinct organization, also existed six years in Michigan, beginning in 1841 with 1,214 votes and ending in 1847 with 2,585, Thus from 1841 to 1852 not only did the Democrats control Michigan but at every State election had a clear majority over all shades of opposition.

In 1852 the chronic difficulties of the Whig situation in Michigan were aggravated by the fact that the Baltimore convention which nominated Scott and Graham had condemned that anti-slavery sentiment of the party, which gave it all its virility in the West. The greater portion of the Northern Whigs with Mr. Greeley supported the ticket and "spat upon the platform," but some of them abandoned old party affiliations and joined the Free Soil Democrats, who put up Hale and Julian as their national candidates and in Michigan nominated a full State ticket headed by Isaac P. Christiancy. The Whig State convention of 1852 met at Marshall on July 1, and was called to order by Henry T. Backus as chairman of the State Central Committee, and presided over by Cyrus Lovell of Ionia. In the preliminary consultations Mr. Chandler's was the name chiefly urged for the head of the ticket, on account of his acquaintance throughout the State and the political strength and capacity he had shown as a candidate in Detroit. This is an extract from the official record of the convention:

On motion of W. A. Howard of Detroit a ballot was taken for Governor and was announced by the tellers as follows:

Z. Chandler, ...	76	H. R. Williams, ... 1
H. G. Wells, ...	7	J. R. Williams, ... 1
G. A. Coe, ...	2	George R. Pomeroy, . . . 2

On motion of Mr. DeLand of Jackson a formal ballot was had as follows:

Z. Chandler, ...	95	J. R. Williams, . . 1
H. G. Wells, . . .	2	Blank, ... 1

Mr. Chandler was not present and inquiry was made if it was known whether he would accept the nomination. Mr. Wm. A. Howard of Detroit, chairman of the delegation from that city, said on the part of that delegation that he had seen Mr. Chandler previous to leaving Detroit, and Mr. Chandler had said to him that he was not a candidate for any of the offices under consideration, that he preferred working in the ranks, but that should the convention see fit to nominate him he was with them.

The result was hailed with hearty cheering, and Mr. Chandler soon formally accepted this nomination and commenced a most energetic personal canvass of the State. The Temperance party made up a ticket in that year from the Democratic and Whig candidates, and Mr. Chandler was also retained as its nominee for Governor, but this action was without practical importance in the campaign or at the polls. During the fall of 1852 the Whig nominee for Governor labored unremittingly. He visited all the leading towns in the State, and spoke constantly from the middle of September until the week before election. The list of his appointments included Jonesville, Coldwater, Constantine, Cassopolis, Howell, Lansing, Eaton Rapids, Hastings, Allegan, Grand Rapids, Ionia, DeWitt, Corunna, Flint, Saginaw, Lapeer, Almont, Romeo, Mt. Clemens, Ann Arbor, Jackson, Marshall, Battle Creek, St. Clair, and Detroit. His addresses were vigorous, entertaining and telling, and while he neither then nor afterward sought for the polished sentence or rounded period, he showed that capacity for plainness and force of reasoning and for hard-hitting which ultimately made his oratory so characteristic and effective. In this series of speeches he dealt largely with the national questions of Protection and Internal Improvements, and also with the business aspects of the State administration. His friends laid especial stress upon his strength as " a " business man of energy, " integrity and success," and urged his election because he bore " the reputation, " well earned by a long " course of business experi- " ence, of being a keen and " shrewd business man of

Temperance Ticket.

For Governor,
Zachariah Chandler.
For Lieut. Governor,
Andrew Parsons.
For Secretary of State,
George E. Pomeroy.
For State Treasurer,
Bernard C. Whittemore.
For Auditor General,
Whitney Jones.
For Attorney General,
Nathaniel Bacon.
For Sup't of Pub. Instruction,
U. Tracy Howe.
For Com'r of State Land Office,
Nathan Power.
For State Board of Education.
Isaac E. Crary, for the term of six years.
Grove Spencer, for the term of four years.
Chauncey Joslin, for a term of two years.
For Member of Congress 1st District,
William A. Howard.
For Member of Senate.

For Representative,

For Sheriff,
Henry B. Holbrook.
For Clerk.
Jeremiah Van Rensselaer.
For Prosecuting Attorney.
D. Bethune Duffield.
For Judge of Probate,
Rufus Hosmer.
Circuit Court Commissioner,
John S. Newberry.
For Register,
Robert E. Roberts.

FAC-SIMILE OF ONE OF THE STATE TICKETS OF
MICHIGAN IN 1852.

"the highest moral tone," and because he was "endowed with remarkable business talent," and had been "identified with the growth and interests of the State." Mr. Chandler was also helped in this contest by his mercantile friendships throughout Michigan, and by the natural pleasure with which his fellow merchants saw one of their own guild fighting his way to political distinction along the paths so largely occupied by men of professional callings. As part of the organization of this canvass he mailed large quantities of gummed "slips" bearing his name to acquaintances in all parts of the State, and this is believed to be the first instance in which this now common weapon of political warfare was used in the Northwest. The Democrats found themselves compelled by this unprecedentedly vigorous attack to put forth most strenuous efforts, and General Cass labored assiduously to prevent the loss of his own State. So pronounced did the opposition of the veteran Democratic leader to the head of the Whig ticket become, that Mr. Chandler laughingly said to friends by way of comment upon it, "I am "afraid that it will take General Cass's Senatorial seat to balance "the account between us."

But the national tide was then overwhelmingly against the Whigs, and Southern distrust of General Scott and Northern wrath at the circumstances of his nomination brought that party to the Waterloo defeat from which it never recovered. Michigan cast 41,842 votes for Pierce, 33,859 for Scott, and 7,237 for Hale. Mr. Chandler received 34,660 votes for Governor against 42,798 for McClelland, and 5,850 for Christiancy. He thus received 801 more votes than Scott; he also led the entire Whig State ticket by from 500 to 4,000 votes, and received over 11,000 more votes than had ever been given to any Whig candidate for Governor. He had made a resolute fight, and again strikingly manifested his personal strength with the people and his political ability.

In the Michigan Legislature of 1853, which was chosen at the same State election, the Democrats had a majority on joint ballot of forty-eight, and the Whig minority included but seven Senators and twenty-one Representatives. The term of Alpheus Felch as United States Senator expired on March 3, 1853, and Charles E. Stuart was chosen as his successor. The Whigs gave expression to their high estimate of the value of Mr. Chandler's services in the preceding campaign by complimenting him with their united vote for the Senate, and the footings of the Legislative ballot for that office were:

SENATE.		HOUSE.	
C. E. Stuart,	27	C. E. Stuart,	49
Z. Chandler,	7	Z. Chandler,	21
		H. K. Clarke,	1

This was the last important political action of the Whig party of Michigan. Before another State election its formal dissolution had been pronounced, and the great body of its members had gathered around the cradle of infant Republicanism.

CHAPTER VI.

H E darkest hour for the anti-slavery cause preceded the dawn of 1854. The compromises of 1850 had closed that long series of so-called bargains, by which the South had forced surrender after surrender from the North in the vain hope of preserving by such artificial devices its traditional preponderance in the government, so constantly threatened by the rapid development of the free States and the marvelous settlement of free territory. Behind the Louisiana purchase from Bonaparte was slavery's demand for new States to re-inforce its political strength. Florida was bought from Spain for the same reasons. The Missouri compromise of 1820 involved the admission of a new slave State to the Union, and the organization of Arkansas as a slave territory; it was the work of the advocates of slavery extension, and was practically a surrender of free territory to bondage, the only consideration being the exclusion of slavery' from soil on which (judging from all the experience of American settlement up to that time) it could not be established nor maintained. The annexation of Texas had been forced to add to the Union an enormous expanse of slave territory, capable, it was hoped, of early division into several slave States. The Mexican War was a peculiarly Southern scheme, having as its real aim the conquest of an empire which was to include human bondage among its established institutions. The futile plans for the annexation of Cuba came from the same prolific source, and were inspired by the same need of forcing the expansion of the political power of the slave South to prevent its being outstripped by the magnificent growth of the free North. But the forces of nature prove more potent than human devices, and the last speech of John C. Calhoun (read for him in the Senate on March 4, 1850,) showed how clearly this fact had impressed itself on the ablest and acutest of the Southern statesmen. That farewell address sketched minutely the history and condition of the steadily - growing disparity between the North and the South, declared in effect that the South with its institutions could not permit Northern ascendancy, demanded from the North constitutional amendments " which would restore " to the South in substance the power she possessed of protect- " ing herself before the equilibrium between the sections was " destroyed," added that on no other basis could the South safe'y remain in the Union, and said that, if this demand was refused, " we would be blind not to perceive that your real objects are " power and aggrandizement, and infatuated not to act accord- " ingly." To this candid avowal of the Southern programme (ten years later it became evident that Mr. Calhoun had stated then the slave power's ultimatum) the answer was the final surrender of 1850. The compromise measures of that year pledged the United States to the subdivision of Texas into new (slave) States, organized Utah and New Mexico without any prohibition of slavery within their boundaries, forbade the abolition of slavery in the District of Columbia, and set the odious machinery of the Fugitive Slave law in operation throughout the North. The consideration Freedom received for these concessions was the admission of California to the Union (it was evident that noth- ing but invasion and conquest could ever make it a slave State) and the abolition of the slave trade in the District of Columbia, amounting to a removal of the auction blocks of slave dealers from the shadow of the Capitol to the narrow streets of decay- ing Alexandria.

The opiate of compromise sufficed to keep still dormant the conscience of the North, and the national acquiescence in this adjustment was emphatic. The Whig and the Democratic parties in 1852 both formally accepted in their platforms the legislation of 1850 as a decisive and just settlement of the slavery question, and they polled almost 3,000,000 votes, while for the Free Soil ticket, representing hostility to slavery extension and to pro-slavery compromises, but 155,000 votes were cast. The victory of the Democrats, who embodied in much the fullest degree the spirit of concession to Southern demands, was an overwhelming one. They carried 27 out of the 31 States, and had 254 electoral votes out of 296, with a clear popular majority over the entire opposition. In the Senate they had 14 majority out of a membership of 62, and in the House a majority of 84 in a total membership of 234. The condition of public sentiment then is thus described by the most accurate and graphic historian of that era:

Whatever theoretic or practical objections may be justly made to the compromise of 1850, there can be no doubt that it was accepted and ratified by a great majority of the American people, whether in the North or in the South. They were intent on business — then remarkably prosperous — on plant-ing, building, trading and getting gain — and they hailed with general joy the announcement that all the differences between the diverse "sections" had been adjusted and settled. The terms of settlement were, to that majority, of quite subordinate consequence; they wanted peace and prosperity, and were no wise inclined to cut each other's throats and burn each other's houses in a quarrel concerning (as they regarded it) only the *status* of negroes. The compromise had taken no money from their pockets ; it had imposed upon them no pecun-iary burdens ; it had exposed them to no personal and palpable dangers ; it had rather repelled the gaunt spectre of civil war and disunion (habitually conjured up when slavery had a point to carry), and increased the facilities for making money, while opening a boundless vista of national greatness, security and internal harmony. Especially by the trading class, and the great majority of the dwellers in seaboard cities, was this view cherished with intense, intolerant vehemence. . . . Whatever else the election of 1852 might have meant, there was no doubt that the popular verdict was against "slavery agitation" and in favor of maintaining the compromises of 1850. . . . The finances were healthy and the public credit unimpaired. Industry and trade were signally prosperous. The tariff had ceased to be a theme of parti-san or sectional strife. The immense yield of gold in California during the four preceding years had stimulated enterprise and quickened the euergies of labor, and its volume as yet showed no signs of diminution. And though the Fugitive Slave law was still denounced, and occasionally resisted by aboli tionists in the free States, while disunionists still plotted in secret and more openly prepared in Southern commercial conventions (having for their ostensi ble object the establishment of a general exchange of the great Southern staples directly from their own harbors with the principal European marts, instead of circuitously by way of New York and other Northern Atlantic ports) there was still a goodly majority in the South, with a still larger in the North and Northwest, in favor of maintaining the Union and preserving the greatest practical measure of cordiality and fraternity between the free and slave States, substantially on the basis of the compromise of 1850.

This was the blackest chapter in the history of the agitation for Freedom on this continent. The era seemed to have been at last reached of national surrender to slavery's demands, and of the purchase of peace by the abandonment of (with the promise never to resume) resistance to "the sum of all vil lainies." John Quincy Adams had said that up to his day "the preservation, propagation, and perpetuation of slavery" had ever been "the animating spirit" of the American government. Daniel Webster had bitterly declared in 1848 that there was no North in American politics, and that the South absolutely con trolled the government. Certainly, in 1853, the surface of the political situation fully justified the indignant words of Gerrit Smith: "Were this government despotic and her religion "heathen, there might be some hope of republicanizing her "politics and Christianizing her religion; but now that she has "turned into darkness the greatest of all political lights and the "greatest of all religious lights, what hope is left for her?"

It was at this juncture, when its triumph appeared to be complete, that slavery fatally overreached itself. The Missouri compromise of 1820, which *forever* prohibited slavery in all of the original Louisiana territory north of 36 degrees, 30 minutes of north latitude, had remained unquestioned upon the statute books for a generation. The South had received the full benefits of its share of that bargain, which added Arkansas and Missouri to the ranks of the slave States. In the interminable discussions of 1850 there had been no suggestion that the compromise measures of that year were intended to either disturb or supersede the Missouri compact, and the first message of Franklin Pierce congratulated the country on the sense of repose and security in the public mind which the compromise measures had restored, and added the pledge, "this repose is to suffer no shock during my official term, if I have power to avert it." Before two months had elapsed, the North heard with astonishment and indignation the doctrine laid down in Congress by the representatives of the slave power that the Missouri compromise had been abrogated by the measures of 1850, and that the vast domain between the Missouri and the Rocky Mountains, rich in all material and political possibilities, was open to slaveholding settlement. A few days more passed, and it was discovered that this claim was receiving the powerful support of the administration, and that it would also be championed by Stephen A Douglas, with his formidable energy, personal influence, and rare skill in debate, as a step towards the vindication of his dogma of "Popular Sovereignty." Of the memorable four months' struggle over this issue, the following is a sketch in outline:

Soon after the Thirty-third Congress assembled, in December, 1853, Senator A. C. Dodge, of Iowa, introduced a bill to organize the Territory of Nebraska out of the magnificent region between Missouri and Iowa and the Rocky Mountains. It was referred to the Committee on Territories, and was reported back by Senator Douglas with amendments, none of which, however, proposed to repeal the prohibition of slavery included in the Missouri compromise. Upon this, Senator Archibald Dixon, of Kentucky, a Whig who declared that on the question of slavery he knew no Whiggery and no Democracy, but was a pro-slavery man, gave notice that he should offer an amendment, providing that the act of 1820 should not be so construed as to apply to the territory contemplated by this act, nor to any other territory of the United States. Senator Douglas thereupon had the bill recommitted, and subsequently reported in an entirely different form, creating *two* territories, Kansas and Nebraska, instead of one, and including the provision that all questions pertaining to slavery in the territories and in the new States to be formed therefrom should be left to the action of the people thereof through their appropriate representatives, and that the provisions of the constitution and laws of the United States in respect to fugitives from service should be carried into faithful execution in all the organized territories the same as in the States. This was, equally with Senator Dixon's proposition, a direct violation of the provision of the Missouri compromise, which was in these words (Section 8): "That in all that territory ceded by France "to the United States under the name of Louisiana, which lies "north of 36 degrees and 30 minutes of north latitude, not "included within the limits of the State contemplated by this "act, slavery and involuntary servitude, otherwise than as the "punishment of crime, shall be and is hereby forever pro- "hibited." In the last report, however, the pill was sugar-coated with Mr. Douglas's catch-word of "Popular Sovereignty."

The territory which the Kansas-Nebraska bill was intended to organize was included in this quoted prohibition. That bill as introduced, in the section that provided for the election of a delegate to Congress from Kansas, had the stipulation :

That the constitution and all laws of the United States, which are not locally inapplicable, shall have the same force and effect within said territory as elsewhere in the United States.

To this the amended bill added the following reservation :

Except the section of the act preparatory to the admission of Missouri into the Union, approved March 6, 1820, which was superseded by the principles of the legislation of 1850, commonly called the compromise measure, and is declared inoperative.

A similar provision with a like reservation was added to the section providing for the election of a delegate from Nebraska. A prolonged and brilliant debate followed in the Senate, and finally in place of the original reservation the following was adopted, on motion of Senator Stephen A. Douglas, by a vote of 35 to 10:

Except the section of the act preparatory to the admission of Missouri into the Union, approved March 6, 1820, which, being inconsistent with the principle of non-intervention by Congress with slavery in the States and territories, as recognized by the legislation in 1850 (commonly called the compromise measure), is hereby declared inoperative and void, it being the true intent and meaning of this act not to legislate slavery into any territory or State, nor to exclude it therefrom, but to leave the people thereof perfectly free to form and regulate their domestic institutions in their own way, subject only to the constitution of the United States.

Senator Chase then moved to add to the above the following:

Under which the people of the territory, through their appropriate representatives, may, if they see fit, prohibit the existence of slavery therein.

· This amendment was voted down, yeas 10, nays 36, the Senate thus declaring its understanding that the people of the new territories should *not* be allowed to prohibit slavery previous to their admission as a State. The bill passed on the morning of March 4th, by a vote of 37 to 14. In the House a separate bill had been introduced, but when it came up for consideration the Senate bill was substituted for it — by a parliamentary trick its opponents were prevented from offering amendments — and the bill was passed, yeas 113, nays 100. It went back to the Senate, in form as an original measure, but in effect the Senate bill, and on May 26 was finally passed by that body and was approved by President Pierce on May 30. The debate had been a memorable one; for the friends of Liberty, while they resisted to the last the surrender of what had been once bought for Freedom, joyfully recognized the fact that this act would in its logic make every compromise repealable, and thus kill in the womb all future political bargainings. Benjamin F. Wade said in the

Senate that "the violation of the plighted faith of the nation " would precipitate a conflict between liberty and slavery; and " that, in such a conflict, it will not be liberty that will die in " the nineteenth century. You may call me an Abolitionist if " you will; I care little for that, for if an undying hatred to " slavery constitutes an Abolitionist, I am that Abolitionist. If " man's determination at all times and at all hazards, to the last " extremity, to resist the extension of slavery, or any other " tyranny, constitutes an Abolitionist, I before God believe my- " self to be that Abolitionist." William H. Seward said: "You " are setting an example which abrogates all compromises. . . . " It has been no proposition of mine to abrogate them now; " but the proposition has come from another quarter — from an " adverse one. It is about to prevail. The shifting sands of " compromise are passing from under my feet, and they are " now, without agency of my own, taking hold again on the " rock of the constitution. It shall be no fault of mine if they " do not remain firm." Charles Sumner closed his protest against this removal of " the landmarks of freedom " by declaring the measure to be " at once the worst and best bill on which Con- " gress ever acted — the worst inasmuch as it is a present victory " for slavery, and the best bill because it prepares the way for " the 'All hail hereafter,' when slavery must disappear. Sorrow- " fully I bend before the wrong you are about to perpetrate. " Joyfully I welcome all the promises of the future."

The response of the North to the abrogation of the Missouri compromise justified these predictions. To this overthrow of a solemn compact for the purpose of opening a vast empire to attempts at slave colonization, men of every shade of anti-slavery conviction made answer by eagerly seeking ways of uniting in effective resistance to such a crime against civilization. Amid an excitement, which grew profounder as the contest progressed, and which was fed by the press, the pulpit, and the lyceum, and was organized by public meetings, the demand became daily stronger for political action on the basis of uncompromising hostility to the aggressions of the slave power. Before the Kansas-Nebraska controversy was finished the Whig party had ceased to exist, the Democracy had become a pro-slavery organization, the era of compromise had passed away, and the young giant of Republicanism stood on the threshold of the territories commanding slavery to stand back. This vast and far-reaching political revolution was accomplished through the wholesale sacrifice of cherished ties by the friends of free institutions and through their hearty union in the new party of Freedom. The State in which this fusion of anti-slavery opinion into Republicanism was first accomplished was Michigan, and the Republican party as a distinct organization was born and christened under the oaks of Jackson on the 6th of July, 1854. Political opinion in that State was peculiarly ripe for this step. Its Whigs were with but rare exceptions staunch anti-slavery men. Even Senator Cass's great influence had failed to keep all the Democrats submissive to pro-slavery compromises. The Free Soilers were strong in character and several thousands in number. Thus when the opportunity came for decisive action it found the men ready.

The Free Democrats of Michigan, encouraged by the increase in their vote in 1852, and responding to an appeal of the "Independent Democrats in Congress" (signed by Salmon P. Chase, Charles Sumner, Joshua R. Giddings, Gerrit Smith, Edward Wade, and Alexander De Witt) for popular resistance to the attack on the Missouri compact, held the first political convention of 1854 in that State. It met in Jackson, on February 22d, under a call issued at Detroit on January 12, and signed by U. Tracy Howe, Hovey K. Clarke, Samuel Zug, Silas M. Holmes, S. A. Baker, S. B. Thayer, S. P. Mead, J. W. Childs, and Erastus Hussey, forming the state central committee of that party. The convention was called to order by Hovey K. Clarke, and it organized
7

with Wm. T. Howell of Hillsdale as president. The committee
on resolutions consisted of Hovey K. Clarke, Fernando C. Beaman,
Kinsley S. Bingham, E. Hussey, Nathan Power, D. C. Leach,
and L. Moore, and a committee of twenty-four was appointed to
nominate a State ticket. The committee on resolutions reported
a platform prepared by Hovey K. Clarke, declaring freedom
national and slavery sectional, and denouncing the attempt to
repeal the Missouri compromise as an infamous outrage upon
justice, humanity and good faith. The nominating committee
submitted this list of candidates for the State offices:

Governor — Kinsley S. Bingham.
Lieutenant-Governor - Nathan Pierce.
Secretary of State — Lovell Moore.
State Treasurer — Silas M. Holmes.
Auditor-General — Philotus Hayden.
Attorney-General — Hovey K. Clarke.
Commissioner of Land Office — Seymour B. Treadwell.
Superintendent of Public Instruction — Elijah II. Pilcher.
Member of Board of Education — Isaac P. Christiancy.

Kinsley S. Bingham was a pioneer farmer of Central Michigan, one of the very best representatives of his influential class,
and a man of sterling sense, strong convictions, and excellent
abilities. He had served with honor in the State Legislature,
and had as a Democratic Congressman sustained alone in his
State delegation the Wilmot Proviso. His nomination was in
itself the strongest possible appeal to the anti-slavery Democrats
of the State. The ticket also had upon it the names of gentlemen who had in the past acted with the Whigs. The convention ratified the reports of its committees, and after listening to
a few speeches adjourned. It was a significant fact that two
of the speakers were conspicuous Whigs, Henry Barns of the
Detroit *Tribune*, and Halmer H. Emmons; Mr. Emmons was
especially emphatic in his expression of the hope that before the

day of election "all the friends of freedom would be able to "stand upon a common platform against the party and platform "of the slave propagandists."

Cotemporaneously with this organized action of the Free Soilers, but outside of it and of all party lines, there were held many public meetings throughout Michigan to denounce the Kansas-Nebraska act. Some of these were county conventions in form, and others were local mass-meetings. One of the latter took place at Detroit on the 18th of February; Zachariah Chandler was among the many prominent citizens who signed its call, and was one of the five speakers from its platform (the others were Jonathan Kearsley, Samuel Barstow, James A. Van Dyke, and D. Bethune Duffield). The tone of all the speeches was wholesomely defiant, and this was also true of the resolutions adopted which were reported by a committee consisting of Samuel Barstow, Jacob M. Howard, Joseph Warren, James M. Edmunds, and Henry H. Le Roy. The effect of this demonstration in the metropolis of the State upon public opinion was marked, and it and like non-partisan action did much to pave the way for the fusion of July. Powerful contributions to the same movement came also from the strong and growing current of sentiment in that direction throughout the entire North, and from the significant results of many of the spring elections. Both New Hampshire and Connecticut elected anti-administration candidates in March and April, and in Michigan anti-slavery coalitions were successful in quite a number of municipal contests, notably in the important city of Grand Rapids which chose Wilder D. Foster mayor on that issue.

Throughout the spring of 1854 many private conferences (Mr. Chandler sharing in them) were held in Michigan among representative men of the Whigs, Free Soilers, and Anti-Nebraska Democrats to discuss the feasibility of union and consider plans for its accomplishment. The early action of the

Free Soilers was in fact a practical obstacle in the way. That party represented but a small element of the anti-slavery sentiment of Michigan, and neither the sincerity of its purpose, nor its tender of the olive branch by placing Whig names on its State ticket, nor the soundness of its platform on the slavery question could counterbalance the many reasons why the Whigs would not surrender a time-honored organization and march bodily into the camp of what they had always regarded as a faction of impracticables. There was also much in the State situation to encourage Whig hope, for the party there was almost solidly anti-slavery and certain to profit by the weakening of the enemy through the revolt of the Anti-Nebraska Democrats. But there was a vigor of principle and an intelligence of sentiment in the Whig party of Michigan which encouraged the belief that it would not subordinate essentials to a name, and that it would assent to an anti-slavery union under conditions not involving any seeming self-degradation. In fact it was called upon to make the only real sacrifice involved in the desired coalition. The Free Soilers were powerless, and had nothing to lose and everything to gain in the new movement; the Anti-Nebraska Democrats were condemned by, and without influence in, their own party; but the Whigs were strong in numbers, and were asked to surrender a historic name, honorable traditions and reviving hope for a doubtful experiment. But that the hour demanded precisely this act of self-denial was clear, and men of resolution and principle grappled with the problem of making it possible. Altogether the most important work in that direction was done by Joseph Warren, editor of the Detroit *Tribune*, then an influential Whig paper, which began the publication in its columns of a series of vigorous and well-considered articles advocating the organization of a new party composed of all the opponents of slavery extension. This policy accorded with the drift of public opinion, and, involving as it did the disbanding of both the Whig and Free Soil organizations, avoided any appearance of surrender and humiliation. Public and private discussion made its wisdom plainer, and the proof of its feasibility was followed by steps for its accomplishment. An indispensable preliminary was the withdrawal of the "Free Democrat" ticket, as this would remove the chief stumbling-block in the path of the anti-slavery Whigs. Mr. Warren, whose personal labors at this juncture were of the utmost value, writes with reference to the spirit with which the Free Soil leaders met the demand for this step :

One of the first and chiefest obstacles to be overcome in order to ensure the co-operation of all the opponents of slavery extension in the movement looking to the organization of a new party, was to induce the Free Soilers to consent to the withdrawal of their ticket from the field, thus placing themselves on the same footing as the Whigs (who as yet had made no nominations), free from all entangling alliances and in a position to act in a way likely to prove most effectual. But formidable as this obstacle seemed to be in the beginning, it was promptly removed through the wisely directed and patriotic efforts of the prominent leaders of the party. Such men as Hovey K. Clarke, Silas M. Holmes, Kinsley S. Bingham, Seymour Treadwell, all on the Free Soil ticket, F. C. Beaman, S. P. Mead, I. P. Christiancy, W. W. Murphy, Whitney Jones, U. Tracy Howe, Jacob S. Farrand, Rev. S. A. Baker, proprietor, and Rev. Jabez Fox, editor of the Detroit *Free Democrat*, were especially active and influential in preparing the way for this necessary preliminary step.

This readiness of the Free Soil leaders to make the sacrifices required on their part bore prompt fruit. The Kansas-Nebraska bill was passed by the House on the 22d of May, and three days after a stirring call was issued for a mass convention of the Free Democrats of Michigan at Kalamazoo on June 21st. The village of Kalamazoo had long been a center of anti-slavery sentiment, and the agitation against the pending bill had been especially vigorous there and in the surrounding counties. The call was full of fiery denunciation of the slavery propagandists, and its vigor and *vim* showed how thoroughly the people were aroused. The convention itself, owing to bad weather and other

inauspicious circumstances, was not a large one, but its character
and action were significant and important. Among those in
attendance were four of the candidates on the "Free Democrat" ticket, including Kinsley S. Bingham. M. A. McNaughton
was made president, and Hovey K. Clarke, from the committee
for that purpose, reported a series of resolutions reviewing the
disgraceful proceedings of the session of Congress, denouncing the
Kansas-Nebraska bill as the crowning act of a series of aggressions by which slavery had become the great national interest of
the country, and appealing to the virtue of the people "to
"declare in an unmistakable tone their will that slavery aggres-
"sion upon their rights shall go no further, that there shall be
"no compromise with slavery, that there shall be no more slave
"States, that there shall be no slave territory, that the Fugitive-
"Slave law shall be repealed, that the abominations of slavery
"shall no longer be perpetrated under the sanctions of the federal
"constitution, and that they will make their will effective by
"driving from every place of official power the public servants
"who have so shamelessly betrayed their trust, and by putting
"in their places men who are honest and capable, men who
"will be faithful to the constitution and the great claims of
"humanity." A final resolution directed the appointment of a
committee of sixteen, two from each judicial district, to consult
with others for the organization of a new party animated and
guided by the principles expressed in the resolutions, and it
empowered that committee, in case of the establishment of an
"efficient organization" of such a character, to surrender the
"distinctive organization" of the "Free Democrats" and withdraw the State ticket nominated on the 22d of February. This
action, reached after a vigorous discussion, cleared the way for
the coalition.

A few days before the meeting of the Kalamazoo convention,
but after its probable course had become apparent, a call had

appeared in the columns of the Detroit *Tribune* (it was copied, after the Kalamazoo action, by the Detroit *Free Democrat* also) for a mass-meeting at Jackson, on July 6, of all the opponents of slavery extension. This was signed by several thousand leading citizens of Michigan, in all parts of the State, including Zachariah Chandler, Jacob M. Howard, H. P. Baldwin, H. K. Clarke, Franklin Moore, John Owen, Jacob S. Farrand, Shubael Conant, J. J. Bagley, E. B. Ward, R. W. King, James Burns, Charles M. Croswell, Allen Potter, Austin Blair, Isaac P. Christiancy, Chas. T. Gorham, and others. The signatures filled two newspaper columns in close type, and it was announced on the last day that several hundred names had been received too late for publication. The text of this document was as follows:

TO THE PEOPLE OF MICHIGAN.

A great wrong has been perpetrated. The slave power of this country has triumphed. Liberty is trampled under foot. The Missouri compromise, a solemn compact, entered into by our fathers, has been violated, and a vast territory dedicated to freedom has been opened to slavery.

This act, so unjust to the North, has been perpetrated under circumstances which deepen its perfidy. An administration placed in power by Northern votes has brought to bear all the resources of executive corruption in its support.

Northern Senators and Representatives, in the face of the overwhelming public sentiment of the North, expressed in the proceedings of public meetings and solemn remonstrances, without a single petition in its favor on their table, and not daring to submit this great question to the people, have yielded to the seductions of executive patronage, and, Judas-like, betrayed the cause of liberty; while the South, inspired by a dominant and grasping ambition, has, without distinction of party, and with a unanimity almost entire, deliberately trampled under foot the solemn compact entered into in the midst of a crisis threatening to the peace of the Union, sanctioned by the greatest names of our history, and the binding force of which has, for a period of more than thirty years, been recognized and declared by numerous acts of legislation. Such an outrage upon liberty, such a violation of plighted faith, cannot be submitted to. This great wrong must be righted, or there is no longer a North in the councils of the nation. The extension of slavery, under the folds of the American flag, is a stigma upon liberty. The indefinite increase of slave representation in Congress is destructive to that equality between freemen which is essential to the permanency of the Union.

The safety of the Union — the rights of the North — the interests of free labor — the destiny of a vast territory and its untold millions for all coming time — and finally, the high aspirations of humanity for universal freedom, all are involved in the issue forced upon the country by the slave power and its plastic Northern tools.

In view, therefore, of the recent action of Congress upon this subject, and the evident designs of the slave power to attempt still further aggressions upon freedom — we invite all our fellow citizens, without reference to former political associations, who think that the time has arrived for a *union* at the North to protect liberty from being overthrown and downtrodden, to assemble in mass convention on Thursday, the 6th of July next, at 4 o'clock, P. M., at Jackson, there to take such measures as shall be thought best to concentrate the popular sentiment of this State against the aggression of the slave power.

The response to this appeal was the gathering at Jackson, on a bright mid-summer day, of hundreds of influential men from all parts of Michigan, representing every shade of anti-slavery feeling, and thoroughly alive to the importance of the occasion and the difficulty of the task projected. The convention far outstripped in numbers the preparations for its accommodation, and, after filling to excess the largest hall in the town, it adjourned to meet in a beautiful oak grove, situated between the village and the county race-course, on a tract of land then known as "Morgan's Forty." The growth of Jackson has since covered this historic ground with buildings, and the spacious grove has dwindled to a few scattered oaks shading the city's busy streets. A rude platform erected for speakers was appropriated by the officers of the convention, and about it thronged a mass of earnest men, the vanguard of the Republican host. In a body so incongruous and unwieldy, confused purposes, discordant views, and conflicting interests were unavoidable, but the universal fervor of the fusion sentiment formed a broad foundation for harmonious action, and the convention did not lack for shrewd and sagacious political managers with the skill to direct earnest effort into practical channels. Such differences of opinion as there were on questions of policy and as to candidates exhausted themselves in private conferences and secret committee deliberations, and the convention itself did its business with promptness, without discord, and amid a genuine enthusiasm.

Its temporary chairman was the Hon. Levi Baxter, of Jonesville, a pioneer settler of Southern Michigan, and the founder of a family of marked prominence in that State. He was well known as the master spirit of many important business enterprises, had been a Whig and then a Free Soiler, and had been elected to the State Senate by a local coalition of both those parties in his own county. After a brief address by Mr. Baxter, Jeremiah Van Renselaer was chosen temporary secretary, and this committee on permanent organization was appointed: Samuel Barstow, C. H. Van Cleeck, Isaac P. Christiancy, G. W. Burchard, Lovell Moore, James W. Hill, Henry W. Lord, and Newell Avery. While they were deliberating, the convention adjourned to the oak grove, and there listened to brief speeches until a permanent organization was effected with the following gentlemen as officers of the first Republican State convention ever held:

President — David S. Walbridge, of Kalamazoo.

Vice - Presidents — F. C. Beamau, Oliver Johnson, Rudolph Diepenbeck, Thomas Curtis, C. T. Gorham, Pliny Power, Emanuel Mann, Charles Draper, George Winslow, Norman Little, John McKinney, W. W. Murphy.

Secretaries — J. Van Renselaer, J. F. Conover, A. B. Turner.

Mr. Walbridge was a prominent merchant of Central Michigan, and an exceedingly active and earnest Whig. He had already served several terms in the Legislature and was afterward a Republican Congressman for four years from Michigan. His selection as president of the convention was a wise recognition of the important Whig element in its membership. The great throng next separated into representatives of the four congressional districts, and chose the following committee on resolutions: Jacob M. Howard, Austin Blair, Donald McIntyre, John Hilsendegen, Charles Noble, Alfred R. Metcalf, John W.

Turner, Levi Baxter, Marsh Giddings, E. Hussey, A. Williams, John McKinney, Chas. Draper, M. L. Higgins, J. E. Simmonds, Z. B. Knight. The chairmanship of this important committee naturally fell to Jacob M. Howard, of Detroit, a lawyer of eminence and rare powers, the first Whig Congressman from Michigan, and a man of deservedly high reputation for intellectual vigor and personal integrity. He was afterward for nine years a Republican Senator, and at Washington earned national distinction as the author of the Thirteenth Amendment and by much able and laborious public service. Mr. Howard had prepared a draft of a platform in advance of the convention, and the committee met to consider it under a clump of trees on the outskirts of the grove (at the present intersection of Franklin and Second streets in the city of Jackson). No material modifications were made in the document, which was adopted substantially as written by Mr. Howard, except that Austin Blair proposed to add two resolutions relating to State affairs purely. As to the expediency of this action there was some difference of opinion, and finally Mr. Blair submitted his propositions as a minority report, and the convention adopted and thus added them to the main platform. Over the resolution formally christening the new party "Republican," there was no especial discussion. There had already been suggestions made throughout the country that, for the new organization evidently about to be born, it might be expedient to revive " the name of that wise conservative party, " whose aim and purpose were the welfare of the whole Union " and the stainless honor of the American name." * The history of this resolution in the Howard platform has been thus given with undoubted correctness by Mr. Joseph Warren in a published letter: " The honor of having named and christened " the party the writer has always claimed and now insists " belongs jointly to Jacob M. Howard, Horace Greeley and him-

---

* Israel Washburn in an address at Bangor, Me.

" self. Soon after the writer began to advocate, through the
" columns of the *Tribune*, the organization of all opponents
" of slavery into a single party, Horace Greeley voluntarily
" opened a correspondence with him in regard to this movement,
" in which he frankly communicated his views and gave him
" many valuable suggestions as to the wisest course to be
" pursued. This correspondence was necessarily very short, as
" it began and ended in June, it being only five weeks from
" the repeal of the compromise, May 30, to the Jackson con-
" vention. In his last letter, received only a day or two before
" it was to assemble, Mr. Greeley suggested to him 'Republican,'
" according to his recollection, but, as Mr. Howard contended,
" ' Democrat - Republican,' as an appropriate name for the pro-
" posed new party. But this is of comparatively little conse-
" quence. The material fact is, that this meeting the writer's
" cordial approval, he gave Mr. Greeley's letter containing the
" suggestions to Mr. Howard on the day of the convention,
" after he had been appointed chairman of the committee on
" resolutions, and strongly advised its adoption. This was done
" and the platform adopted."

While the committee on resolutions was absent, the convention was addressed by Zachariah Chandler, Kinsley S. Bingham,
and a number of others. No complete record was made of Mr.
Chandler's remarks upon this occasion, but the report of the
convention in the Detroit *Free Democrat*, prepared by its secretary, contains this: "We would say in parenthesis that an
" allusion most generously made by Mr. Chandler to Mr. Bing-
" ham drew from the crowd three rousing cheers for the latter
" gentleman." The Jackson *Citizen* also gave the following
reference to Mr. Chandler's remarks: "When in the course of
" his speech he gave a brief history of the Wilmot Proviso in
" Michigan, alluding to the anti-slavery resolutions passed by a
" Democratic State convention in 1849, and the resolutions of

"instructions to our Senators and Representatives in Congress
"by the Legislature on the same subject, and then exclaimed
"that 'not one of our Representatives had ever been *honest*
"enough to carry them out except Kinsley S. Bingham,' a spark
"of enthusiasm fired the crowd, the shout of approbation ran
"through the vast assembly, and, if any doubt had previously
"existed as to who should be the man, that doubt was then
"removed." These addresses were followed by the report of the
committee on resolutions, which was read by Mr. Howard amid
frequent outbursts of applause, and was as follows:

The freemen of Michigan, assembled in convention in pursuance of a
spontaneous call, emanating from various parts of the State, to consider upon
the measures which duty demands of us, as citizens of a free State, to take in
reference to the late acts of Congress on the subject of slavery and its antici-
pated further extension, do

Resolve, That the institution of slavery except in punishment of crime is
a great moral, social and political evil; that it was so regarded by the fathers
of the republic, the founders and best friends of the Union, by the heroes and
sages of the Revolution who contemplated and intended its gradual and peaceful extinction as an element hostile to the liberties for which they toiled; that
its history in the United States, the experience of men best acquainted with
its workings, the dispassionate confession of those who are interested in it; its
tendency to relax the vigor of industry and enterprise inherited in the white
man; the very surface of the earth where it subsists; the vices and immorali-
ties which are its natural growth; the stringent police, often wanting in
humanity and revolting to the sentiments of every generous heart, which it
demands; the danger it has already wrought and the future danger which it
portends to the security of the Union and our constitutional liberties — all
incontestably prove it to be such evil. Surely that institution is not to be
strengthened and encouraged against which Washington, the calmest and wisest
of our nation, bore unequivocal testimony; as to which Jefferson, filled with
a love of liberty, exclaimed: "Can the liberties of a nation be ever thought
"secure when we have removed their only firm basis, a conviction in the
"minds of the people that their liberties are THE GIFT OF GOD; that they are
"not to be violated but with His wrath? Indeed, I tremble for my country
"when I reflect that God is just; that His justice cannot sleep forever; that,
"considering numbers, nature and natural means only, a revolution of the
"wheel of fortune, an exchange of situation is among possible events; that it
"may become probable by supernatural interference! The Almighty has no
"attribute which can take sides with us in such a contest!" And as to which

another eminent patriot in Virginia, on the close of the Revolution, also exclaimed: "Had we turned our eyes inwardly when we supplicated the Father "of Mercies to aid the injured and oppressed, when we invoked the Author "of Righteousness to attest the purity of our motives and the justice of our "cause, and implored the God of battles to aid our exertions in its defense, "should we not have stood more self-convicted than the contrite publican ? " We believe these sentiments to be as true now as they were then.

Resolved, That slavery is a violation of the rights of man as man; that the law of nature, which is the law of liberty, gives to no man rights superior to those of another; that God and nature have secured to each individual the inalienable right of equality, any violation of which must be the result of superior force; and that slavery therefore is a perpetual war upon its victims; that whether we regard the institution as first originating in captures made in war, or the subjection of the debtor as the slave of his creditor, or the forcible seizure and sale of children by their parents or subjects by their king, and whether it be viewed in this country as a *"necessary evil"* or otherwise, we find it to be, like imprisonment for debt, but a relic of barbarism as well as an element of weakness in the midst of the State, inviting the attack of external enemies, and a ceaseless cause of internal apprehension and alarm. Such are the lessons taught us, not only by the histories of other commonwealths, but by that of our own beloved country.

Resolved, That the history of the formation of the constitution, and particularly the enactment of the ordinance of July 13, 1787, prohibiting slavery north of the Ohio, abundantly shows it to have been the purpose of our fathers not to promote but to prevent the spread of slavery. And we, reverencing their memories and cherishing free republican faith as our richest inheritance, which we vow, at whatever expense, to defend, thus publicly proclaim our determination to oppose by all the powerful and honorable means in our power, now and henceforth, all attempts, direct or indirect, to extend slavery in this country, or to permit it to extend into any region or locality in which it does not now exist by positive law, or to admit new slave States into the Union.

Resolved, That the constitution of the United States gives to Congress full and complete power for the municipal government of the territories thereof, a power which from its nature cannot be either alienated or abdicated without yielding up to the territory an absolute political independence, which involves an absurdity. That the exercise of this power necessarily looks to the formation of States to be admitted into the Union; and on the question whether they shall be admitted as *free* or *slave* States Congress has a right to adopt such prudential and preventive measures as the principles of liberty and the interests of the whole country require. That this question is one of the gravest importance to the free States, inasmuch as the constitution itself creates an inequality in the apportionment of representatives, greatly to the detriment of the free and to the advantage of the slave States. This question, so vital to the interests of the free States (but which we are told by certain political doctors of modern times is to be treated with utter indifference) is one which we hold it to be our right to *discuss;* which we hold it the duty of Congress in every instance to determine in unequivocal language, and in a manner to *prevent* the spread of slavery and the increase of such unequal representation. In short, we claim that the North is a *party to the new bargain, and is entitled to have a voice and influence in settling its terms.* And in view of the ambitious designs of the slave power, we regard the man or the party who would forego this right, as untrue to the honor and interest of the North and unworthy of its support.

Resolved, That the repeal of the "Missouri Compromise," contained in the recent act of Congress for the creation of the territories of Nebraska and Kansas, thus admitting slavery into a region till then sealed against it by law, equal in extent to the thirteen old States, is an act unprecedented in the history of the country, and one which must engage the earnest and serious attention of every Northern man. And as Northern freemen, independent of all former parties, we here hold this measure up to the public execration, for the following reasons:

That it is a plain departure from the policy of the fathers of the republic in regard to slavery, and a wanton and dangerous frustration of their purposes and their hopes.

That it actually admits *and was intended to admit* slavery into said territories, and thus (to use the words applied by Judge Tucker, of Virginia, to the fathers of that commonwealth) "sows the seeds of an evil which like "a leprosy hath descended upon their posterity with accumulated rancor, "visiting the sins of the fathers upon succeeding generations." That it was sprung upon the country stealthily and by surprise, without necessity, without petition, and without previous discussion, thus violating the cardinal principle of republican government, which requires all legislation to accord with the opinions and sentiments of the people.

That on the part of the South it is an open and undisguised breach of faith, as contracted between the North and South in the settlement of the Missouri question in 1820, by which the tranquillity of the two sections was restored; a compromise binding upon all honorable men.

That it is also an open violation of the compromise of 1850, by which, for the sake of peace, and to calm the distempered pulse of certain enemies of the Union at the South, the North accepted and acquiesced in the odious "fugitive slave law" of that year.

That it is also an undisguised and unmanly contempt of the pledge given to the country by the present dominant party at their national convention in 1852, not to "*agitate the subject of slavery in or out of Congress,*" being the same convention that nominated Franklin Pierce to the Presidency.

That it is greatly injurious to the free States, and to the Territories themselves, tending to retard the settlement and to prevent the improvement of the country by means of free labor, and to discourage foreign immigrants resorting thither for their homes.

THE FIRST REPUBLICAN STATE CONVENTION.
"Under the Oaks," Jackson, Mich., July 6, 1854.

That one of its principal aims is to give to the slave States such a decided and practical preponderance in all the measures of government as shall reduce the North, with all her industry, wealth and enterprise, to be the mere province of a few slave - holding oligarchs of the South — a condition too shameful to be contemplated.

Because, as openly avowed by its Southern friends, it is intended as an entering wedge to the still further augmentation of the slave power by the acquisition of the other Territories, cursed with the same ."leprosy."

Resolved, That the obnoxious measure to which we have alluded ought to be *repealed*, and a provision substituted for it, prohibiting slavery in said Territories, and each of them.

Resolved, That after this gross breach of faith and wanton affront to us as Northern men, we hold ourselves absolved from all *"compromises"* (except those expressed in the constitution) for the protection of slavery and slave-owners ; that we now demand measures of protection and immunity for ourselves; and among them we demand the *repeal of the fugitive slave law*, and an act to abolish slavery in the District of Columbia.

Resolved, That we notice without dismay certain popular indications by slaveholders on the frontier of said Territories of a purpose on their part to prevent by violence the settlement of the country by non - slaveholding men. To the latter we say : Be of good cheer, persevere in the right, remember the Republican motto, "THE NORTH WILL DEFEND YOU."

Resolved, That postponing and suspending all differences with regard to political economy or administrative policy, in view of the imminent danger that Kansas and Nebraska will be grasped by slavery, and a thousand miles of slave soil be thus interposed between the free States of the Atlantic and those of the Pacific, we will act cordially and faithfully in unison to avert and repeal this gigantic wrong and shame.

Resolved, That in view of the necessity of battling for the first principles of republican government, and against the schemes of an aristocracy, the most revolting and oppressive .with which the earth was ever cursed, or man debased, we will co - operate and be known as REPUBLICANS until the contest be terminated.

Resolved, That we earnestly recommend the calling of a general convention of the free States, and such of the slaveholding States, or portions thereof, as may desire to be there represented, with a view to the adoption of other more extended and effectual measures in resistance to the encroachments of slavery; and that a committee of five persons be appointed to correspond and co-operate with our friends in other States on the subject.

Resolved, That in relation to the domestic affairs of the State we urge a more economical administration of the government and a more rigid accountability of the public officers: a speedy payment of the balance of the public debt, and the lessening of the amount of taxation ; a careful preservation of the primary school and university funds, and their diligent application to the

great objects for which they were created ; and also further legislation to prevent the unnecessary or imprudent sale of the lands belonging to the State.

Resolved, That in our opinion the commercial wants of Michigan require
the enactment of a general railroad law, which, while it shall secure the
investment and encourage the enterprise of stockholders, shall also guard and
protect the rights of the public and of individuals, and that the preparation
of such a measure requires the first talents of the State.

The resolutions were adopted almost unanimously, and thereupon Isaac P. Christiancy, as chairman of the committee of
sixteen appointed by the Kalamazoo convention, came forward
and announced the absolute abandonment of the State ticket and
organization of the Free Democracy — an act which was greeted
with loud and prolonged applause. A committee of ninety,
consisting of three from each Senatorial district in the State,
and including the names of Jacob M. Howard, Moses Wisner,
Charles M. Croswell, Fernando C. Beaman, and Chas. T. Gorham, was next appointed to nominate a State ticket, and the
convention adjourned until evening. At that session, which was
held in one of the village halls, a State central committee was
chosen, and the committee on nominations reported the following
ticket which was unanimously endorsed by the convention, this
closing its formal proceedings :

Governor — Kinsley S. Bingham, of Livingston.
Lieutenant - Governor — George A. Coe, of Branch.
Secretary of State — John McKinney, of Van Buren.
State Treasurer — Silas M. Holmes, of Wayne.
Attorney - General — Jacob M. Howard, of Wayne.
Auditor - General — Whitney Jones, of Ingham.
Commissioner of Land Office — Seymour B. Treadwell, of Jackson.
Superintendent of Public Instruction — Ira Mayhew, of Monroe.
Member Board of Education — John R. Kellogg, of Allegan.
(To fill vacancy) — Hiram L. Miller, of Saginaw.

The response of the anti - slavery masses to the action of the
convention was prompt and cordial. Some of the more earnest
and enthusiastic Whigs who had hoped that the Northern wing

8

of their party could be transformed into an efficient champion of slavery restriction — Mr. Chandler had shared in this feeling — at first doubted the wisdom of what had been done. They found themselves called upon to make large sacrifices of cherished traditions and ties, and felt that their representation upon the fusion State ticket was not in due proportion to the number of votes they would be expected to contribute to its election. But this not unnatural feeling of early disappointment had but a brief existence among the Whigs of strong anti-slavery convictions. As the good faith of the movement, the spontaneous character of the popular uprising, and the possibility of accomplishing anti-slavery union throughout the North became clear, they laid aside all hesitation and joined with sincere ardor in the work of Republican organization. Before the close of the summer of 1854 the strong leaders and the intelligent rank and file of the Michigan Whigs had accepted the new fellowship, and the action of the Jackson convention received their hearty acquiescence and loyal support. Mr. Chandler rendered valuable service the following campaign as an organizer of Republicanism throughout Michigan, and put into this work enough of his characteristic vigor to earn from the Democratic papers the title of the "traveling agent" of the "new Abolition party."

There was still among the Whigs a small conservative minority who, chiefly through the inspiration of pro-slavery sentiment and under the leadership of the Detroit *Advertiser*, made a desperate effort to prevent the abandonment of their party organization. They procured the signing of a circular addressed to the Whig committee asking that a State convention should be held, and in compliance with this request a call was issued for a convention to meet at Marshall on October 4. When it assembled it was found that the great majority of its delegates favored union with the Republicans. They controlled its proceedings throughout, and put in the chair Rufus Hosmer who was then the head of the new Republican State central committee, elected a State central committee composed of ardent fusionists, defeated the schemes for the nomination of a ticket, and issued an address urging the Whigs of Michigan to unite in this campaign with all other opponents of the spread of slavery. This decisive action made the Michigan election of 1854 a contest between Republicanism and the Democracy (which held its convention at Detroit on September 14, and placed John S. Barry at the head of its State ticket).

The local result of the Jackson convention was a permanent political revolution. In November the Republicans elected their entire State ticket (giving Mr. Bingham 43,652 votes to 38,675 for Mr. Barry), three of the four Congressmen, and a Legislature with an overwhelming majority in both branches against the Kansas-Nebraska policy. The Republican ascendancy thus established in Michigan has never been impaired. That party has been victorious in every State election since 1854; and of the Governors since chosen every one who was at that time a resident of the State (Henry H. Crapo did not settle in Michigan until 1856) was a member of the Jackson convention. Michigan has also since sent only Republicans to the Senate; every one of them except Thomas W. Ferry (who had barely attained his majority in 1854) was a prominent actor in the scenes "under the oaks." It has sent seventy-six Republicans and only seven Democrats to the House of Representatives, and the Republicans have controlled both branches of every Legislature since 1854. Iowa is the only State which can point to a similar record of uninterrupted Republican victory. In Vermont the Democrats have been uniformly defeated, but the opposition ticket in 1854 was not called Republican. Of the States which have been admitted since 1854, three (Kansas, Nebraska and Minnesota) have been steadfastly Republican, but Michigan surpasses them in the duration, while she equals them in the quality, of her fidelity to the party of Freedom. Each of the other Northern States has at least once chosen an anti-Republican Governor, while Michigan (with Iowa) has been uniformly Republican.

The claim that Michigan was the first State to organize and name the Republican party cannot be successfully disputed.* The convention "under the oaks" of Jackson ante-dates by a week or more all similar bodies. The first Republican convention in Wisconsin was held at Madison on July 13, 1854. Its call was issued (July 9) after a number of Anti-Nebraska meetings had been held in different parts of the State, and invited "all men "opposed to the repeal of the Missouri compromise and the "extension of the slave power" to take part. This convention adopted the following as one of its resolutions:

Resolved, That we accept the issue forced upon us by the slave power, and in defense of Freedom will co-operate and be known as Republicans.

The Anti-Nebraska men of Massachusetts met in convention on July 19 of the same year, and organized the Republican party in that State by adopting the following resolution:

Resolved, That in co-operation with the friends of Freedom in sister States, we hereby form the Republican party of Massachusetts.

But the Republicans did not carry Massachusetts that year, the Anti-Nebraska vote being cast almost solidly for the successful Know-Nothing ticket. In Vermont, on July 13, 1854,

---

* The Senator from Virginia has stated that the Republican party originated in New England, from Know Nothingism. It is not true, sir; it had no such origin; it originated in no such place and from no such source. The Republican party was born in Michigan, on the sixth day of July, 1854. It had no origin from Know Nothingism or any other thing, except the outrageous, the infamous repeal of the time-honored Missouri compromise by the Congress of that year. It was christened the Republican party at its birth. It is perfectly evident the Senator from Virginia knows nothing at all about the Republican party, its origin, its ends, or its aims. He does not know anything about its birth or its principles I merely wish to correct the misapprehension on his part that it was born in New England or anywhere else out of the State of Michigan. There is where it was born, sir, and we glory in the production of such a child. — *Mr. Chandler in the Senate, December 14, 1859, in reply to Senator Mason, of Virginia.*

a mass convention was held of persons "in favor of resisting, "by all constitutional means, the usurpations of the propagandists "of slavery." Among the resolutions there adopted was one which closed with these words: "We propose and respectfully "recommend to the friends of Freedom in other States to "co-operate and be known as Republicans." A State ticket was nominated, but, the State committees of the various parties being empowered "to fill vacancies," a fusion ticket was afterward placed in the field, voted for and elected under the name of Fusion. On the same day a convention was held in Columbus, O., which organized a canvass which swept that State at the fall elections; during this campaign most of the Anti-Nebraska candidates called themselves Republicans, and the party formally adopted that name at the State convention in 1855 which nominated Salmon P. Chase for Governor. It will be seen that the Jackson convention preceded all these kindred gatherings. To this statement may be profitably added the testimony of Henry Wilson, who, after thoroughly investigating the whole subject of the origin of Republicanism, wrote:*

But whatever suggestions others may have made, or whatever action may have been taken elsewhere, to Michigan belongs the honor of being the first State to form and christen the Republican party. More than three months before the passage of the Kansas-Nebraska bill the Free Soil convention had adopted a mixed ticket, made up of Free-Soilers and Whigs, in order that there might be a combination of the anti-slavery elements of the State. Immediately on the passage of the Nebraska bill, Joseph Warren, editor of the Detroit *Tribune*, entered upon a course of measures that resulted in bringing the Whig and Free Soil parties together, not by a mere coalition of the two, but by a fusion of the elements of which the two were composed. In his own language, he "took ground in favor of disbanding the Whig and "Free Soil parties and of the organization of a new party, composed of all "the opponents of slavery extension." Among the first steps taken toward the accomplishment of this vitally important object was the withdrawal of the Free Soil ticket. This having been effected, a call for a mass convention was issued signed by more than 10,000 names. The convention met on the 6th day of July, and was largely attended.

---

* Wilson's "Rise and Fall of the Slave Power in America," volume 2, page 412.

A platform drawn by the Hon. Jacob M. Howard, afterward United States Senator from Michigan, was adopted, not only opposing the extension of slavery, but declaring in favor of its abolition in the District of Columbia. The report also proposed the name of "Republican" for the new party, which was adopted by the convention. Kinsley S. Bingham was nominated for Governor, and was triumphantly elected; and Michigan, thus early to enter the ranks of the Republican party, has remained steadfast to its then publicly-avowed principles and faith.

It is true that the Michigan convention of July 6, 1854, was only one development of a vast national agitation. The forces that gave it being were at work throughout the continent. Like movements were on foot in every Northern State. Kindred bodies met in the same month to take the same action. But to the men who gathered on that mid-summer day in the oak grove at Jackson belongs the honor of being the first to comprehend a great opportunity; they were wise enough to improve all its possibilities, and there founded and named the party of the future.

CHAPTER VII.

II E abrogation of the Missouri compromise was followed by the arbitrary enforcement of the Fugitive Slave act in important Northern cities, and by a determined struggle between freedom and slavery for the possession of the virgin soil of Kansas. These phases of "the irrepressible conflict" were attended by many exciting incidents which constantly strengthened the new anti-slavery party in the North and in the end made it the main competitor of the Democracy in the presidential election of 1856. The decisive character of its victory in Michigan in 1854 made Republicanism especially strong in that State, and the events of each successive month of 1855 and 1856 added to its power both in numbers and in sentiment. Throughout this period Mr. Chandler labored, in public and in private, and with earnestness and effect, to inspire the new party with vigor of conviction and unflinching firmness of purpose. No man did more than he to make it thoroughly "radical," and his former prominence as a Whig rendered his efforts especially fruitful. His earliest Republican speeches did not differ from his latest in courage of opinion, in plainness of expression, or in manifest sincerity of conviction. On September 12, 1855, he addressed, with Henry Wilson, an immense mass-meeting at Kalamazoo, and denounced the border-ruffian crimes in Kansas in the strongest terms. On the 30th of May, 1856, he was one of the speakers at a large meeting held in the city of Detroit to consider the assault of Preston Brooks upon Charles Sumner. He there gave expression to Republican indig-

nation in the plainest language. After fitly describing the era
of pro-slavery murder in Kansas, and the recent crime of
"a cowardly assassin on the very floor of the Senate of the
United States," he offered two resolutions, one demanding the
impeachment of Franklin Pierce for his action in relation to
Kansas, and a second to expel Rust, of Arkansas, for his attack
upon Horace Greeley, and Preston Brooks for his assault on Mr.
Sumner. Then he said in substance:

> This is not a time for argument. It is a time for action, for speaking
> boldly and fearlessly. . . . This assault is upon the entire North. So
> long have craven doughface representatives sat in her places in Congress that
> the South has come to doubt our manhood. . . . We should uphold the
> hands of our representatives, and tell them that an indignity offered to them
> is an indignity offered to us. [Applause.] . . . The resolution calling for
> the impeachment of the President is one proper to be offered. He has con-
> nived at and aided all this Kansas treachery and wrong. He supports the
> bogus Legislature of Kansas and orders its odious laws enforced. If Thomas
> Jefferson was to read his preamble to the Declaration of Independence in
> Kansas, he could be condemned by those laws to imprisonment in the peni-
> tentiary for two years. . . . What the British did at Lexington, the United
> States troops, under the orders of President Pierce, did at Lawrence. Our
> fathers resisted by all means in their power. We should imitate their exam-
> ple. What should we do? . . . We should send enough men there to put
> Kansas in a peaceable condition.

Mr. Chandler also said: "Had I been on the floor of the
"Senate when that assault occurred, so help me God, that
"ruffian's blood would have flowed," and he closed by declaring
that Detroit should send one hundred men to Kansas, and by
pledging himself, if that was done, to devote his entire income
while they were there to aiding in their maintenance. He also
made a forcible speech at a Kansas relief meeting, held in
Detroit, to greet Gov. Andrew H. Reeder, on June 2, 1856, and
then headed a subscription paper for the aid of the struggling
Free State men of that territory with the sum of $10,000.
Actions and utterances of this kind in the plastic days of Michigan Republicanism gave to it that resolute and robust character
which has been the source of its power.

The first national convention of the Republican party was held at Pittsburg on the 22d of February, 1856, under a call issued by the chairmen of the Republican committees of Ohio, Massachusetts, Pennsylvania, Vermont, Wisconsin, and Michigan. It was attended by delegates representing twenty - seven States and territories, and provided for the national organization of the Republican party by creating a general executive committee and calling a convention, to meet at Philadelphia on June 17, to nominate a presidential ticket. Michigan was represented at Pittsburg by a delegation of eighteen, headed by Zachariah Chandler, and including Kinsley S. Bingham, Jacob M. Howard, and Fernando C. Beaman. Mr. Chandler was also a member of the committee which reported the plan for the national organization of the Republican party, and he participated briefly in the debates of that important gathering. The Michigan convention to elect delegates to Philadelphia was held at Ann Arbor, on March 8, 1856, and was addressed by Mr. Chandler and other prominent Republicans. He was a member of the Philadelphia convention, acting as an alternate for Charles T. Gorham, and, after Fremont was nominated, formally promised that the electoral vote of Michigan should be given for the ticket. He was there made the member for his State of the first Republican National Committee. The Michigan delegation at Philadelphia originally supported Mr. Seward for the presidency, but finally joined in the movement to nominate General Fremont on the first ballot. For the vice - presidency the majority of the delegation supported William L. Dayton, but Mr. Chandler, with four others, voted for Abraham Lincoln.

In the following campaign Mr. Chandler was among the most active of the Republican leaders. He aided liberally in the work of organizing the party throughout the State, and spoke at Detroit several times, and at Kalamazoo, Lapeer, Port Huron, Adrian, Coldwater, and other of the important cities and towns of Michigan. He also held one joint discussion with Alpheus Felch, at Olivet, on October 16. The tone of his public utterances in 1856 will appear from these extracts from his speech at Kalamazoo (on August 27) before an immense mass-meeting, which was also addressed by Abraham Lincoln and Jacob M. Howard:

The Republicans of Michigan stand by the constitution, and when their defamers proclaim that they are a disunion party, as they do so often, they publish what they know to be a falsehood. . . . We are determined to stand by the constitution in all its parts, and, more than that, to make our adversaries stand by it in all and every part. . . . Our opponents have ignored this constitution with but a single exception. And what is that exception ? It is the key to their character and their principles. In this whole instrument they acknowledge but one clause, and that is the right to reclaim fugitive slaves from their hard-earned freedom !

We intend to make our opponents stand by this clause : "The citizens of each State shall be entitled to the privileges of all the States." But how is this at present on the Missouri ? The citizens of Massachusetts, of New Jersey, of Pennsylvania or of Michigan, if they but presume to enter Kansas, are sent back with a guard or murdered in cold blood, while the citizens of the South are aided on their way to plant in that beautiful territory the accursed blight of slavery. We will make them stand by the constitution in all its parts, or, by the Eternal, we will have a different state of things here. The oak shall bear other fruit than acorns if the constitution be not upheld.

Here is another clause of that instrument : "Congress shall make no law abridging the freedom of speech or the press." How is it in Kansas to-day regarding this ? If any man shall dare to deny the right to hold slaves in that territory he is imprisoned for a term of five years.

Our opponents must also stand by this clause of the constitution : "A "well-regulated militia being necessary of a free state, the right of the people "to keep and bear arms shall not be infringed." That clause of the constitution is trampled under foot, and the Democratic platform in sustaining Pierce's administration virtually sustains and endorses the disgraceful outrage.

Here is another clause : "No person shall be deprived of life, liberty or property without due process of law." The whole history of the Kansas matter shows how shamefully this clause has been rejected by those who uphold the administration.

There are but two candidates for the Presidency and but two platforms. The issue — the only issue — is : Shall slavery be national ? Shall it be under our protection, or shall it be under the protection of the slave States only ? The whole question of platforms is in that. It is the only question. . . . The policy of this government for twenty-five years has been pro-slavery.

The first act toward breaking that policy was the election of Banks as Speaker last winter. It was the first of what I hope will be a series of victories.

A few years ago there was great commotion in the land. We were told "the Union is in danger." "What shall be done?" That was the first question. What was the answer of the men in power? "Use the utmost power of the government; the Union must be saved." Armed men went through the streets of Boston. Troops were ordered there in great numbers. Ships of war were sent to Massachusetts Bay. What was the terrible danger of the Union? There was a Negro lost! A slave had run away! A poor African had escaped from his master and—lo, the Union was in danger! "Use all the power of the government; the laws must be enforced." Other troops were ordered there. The militia were called out. They surrounded the jail. A sloop of war was sent. Burns was borne back to his master and the Union was saved!

There came a later cry, "the Union is in danger." This time it was heard from bleeding Kansas. Armed bands were committing daily depredations. This appeal reached the government, and what answer is made by the party in power? "I see nothing to call for executive interference." "Nothing?" Yet an empire is being crushed. "Nothing?" Yet houses are being robbed and burned, and helpless women and children murdered! "No cause for interference?" The reason is plain. There was no Negro lost.

Michigan fulfilled the pledge made in her behalf at Philadelphia by Mr. Chandler, and gave to the Fremont electors 71,762 votes, while the Buchanan ticket received but 52,136 and the Fillmore strength was only 1,660. The Republicans thus more than trebled their majority of 1854, and in this year carried all of the four Congressional districts of the State. Their victory in the legislative districts was overwhelming, and they elected twenty-nine of the thirty-one Senators, and sixty-three of the eighty Representatives. The term of Lewis Cass as Senator of the United States expired on the 4th of the following March, and his State had thus decided that he should give place to a representative of its earnest and aggressive Republican sentiment. Mr. Chandler was at once recognized as the leading candidate for the position by reason of his positive qualities, his personal strength with the business classes of the State and the masses of the people, and his prominence as a

representative of the strong Whig element in the Republican
ranks.   The senatorial canvass was an earnest one, but it was
from the outset clear that Mr. Chandler was the first choice of
decidedly the largest number of legislators, and that no other
man possessed his popular following.   Some unavailing efforts
were made to combine against him the friends of all other candidates, but the fact that he was also "the second choice"
of many members defeated this plan, and the Republican caucus
met at Lansing on January 8, 1857, with his marked lead in
the contest still unimpaired.   Three ballots were taken at its first
session, the third giving Mr. Chandler a clear majority of all
the votes cast.   The caucus then adjourned until the following
day, when he received a still stronger support on the fourth
ballot and was formally nominated on the fifth.   The following
is the record of the balloting:

	FIRST SESSION.			SECOND SESSION.	
	First Informal Ballot.	Second Informal Ballot.	Third Informal Ballot.	Fourth Informal Ballot.	First Formal Ballot.
Zachariah Chandler, . . .	37	45	49	54	80
Isaac P. Christiancy, . . .	17	21	22	33	..
Austin Blair, ...	18	7	6	..	..
Moses Wisner, ...	12	9	10	..	..
Jacob M. Howard, ...	..	6	6	3	..
Kinsley S. Bingham, . . .	3	7	2	..	..
George A. Coe, . . . : . .	4	..	..	..	..
James V. Campbell, ...	1	..	..	..	..
Halmer H Emmons, ...	..	..	..	1	..
Blank, ...	..	..	1	..	..
Scattering, ...	..	..	..	..	8
TOTAL, ...	92	95	96	91	88

This result was received with the heartiest enthusiasm by
the Republicans, and the caucus greeted its nominee, when he
came before it to return his thanks, with prolonged cheering.
The scene which followed has been thus described by an eye-
witness: " This was the only time in an acquaintance of nearly

"thirty years that I ever saw Mr. Chandler abashed. When "brought before the caucus he trembled with emotion, and it "was several minutes before he could compose himself to even "briefly return his thanks. He has often said that it was the "only time that his courage and nerve absolutely failed him "and that he completely broke down. The rejoicing was so "hearty and unselfish that it overcame him, and he trembled "like a child." On the 10th of January the two branches of the Legislature voted for Senator, the Democrats complimenting General Cass with their ineffectual votes. The record of the balloting was as follows:

	SENATE.	HOUSE.	TOTAL.
Zachariah Chandler,	27	62	89
Lewis Cass,	2	14	16
Blank,	..	1	1

In the following joint convention of the two Houses the resolution, reciting the action taken separately and finally recording Mr. Chandler's election, was adopted without any dissent. Among the members of the Legislature whose votes made him the first Republican Senator from Michigan were Thomas W. Ferry, in later years his colleague in the Senate, Omar D. Conger, who became afterward a Republican leader in the lower branch of Congress, and George Jerome, a most intimate political and personal friend throughout life.

The Senate of the Thirty-fifth Congress met in special session at Washington, on March 4, 1857, Franklin Pierce having convened it at the request of his successor, who was inaugurated on that day. The names upon its rolls were these:

Clement C. Clay, Jr., and Benj. Fitzpatrick, of Alabama; Robert W. Johnson and Wm. K. Sebastian, of Arkansas; David C. Broderick and Wm. M. Gwin, of California; James Dixon and Lafayette S. Foster, of Connecticut; Martin W. Bates and James A. Bayard, of Delaware;

Stephen R. Mallory and David L. Yulee, of Florida;
Alfred Iverson and Robert Toombs, of Georgia;
Stephen A. Douglas and Lyman Trumbull, of Illinois;
Jesse D. Bright and Graham N. Fitch, of Indiana;
James Harlan and Geo. W. Jones, of Iowa;
John J. Crittenden and John B. Thompson, of Kentucky;
Judah P. Benjamin and John Slidell, of Louisiana;
W. P. Fessenden and Hannibal Hamlin, of Maine;
Anthony Kennedy and James A. Pearce, of Maryland;
Charles Sumner and Henry Wilson, of Massachusetts;
Zachariah Chandler and Chas. E. Stuart, of Michigan;
Albert G. Brown and Jefferson Davis, of Mississippi;
James S. Green and Trusten Polk, of Missouri;
James Bell and John P. Hale, of New Hampshire;
John R. Thomson and William Wright, of New Jersey;
Preston King and William H. Seward, of New York;
Asa Biggs and David S. Reid, of North Carolina;
Geo. E. Pugh and Benj. F. Wade, of Ohio;
William Bigler and Simon Cameron, of Pennsylvania;
Philip Allen and James F. Simmons, of Rhode Island;
Josiah J. Evans and Andrew P. Butler, of South Carolina;
John Bell and Andrew Johnson, of Tennessee;
Samuel Houston and Thos. J. Rusk, of Texas;
Jacob Collamer and Solomon Foot, of Vermont;
R. M. T. Hunter and James M. Mason, of Virginia;
James R. Doolittle and Charles Durkee, of Wisconsin.

This Senate met in the old chamber now occupied by the Supreme Court, but around which then clustered fresh memories of Clay, Webster, Calhoun and their cotemporaries. The Secretary, Asbury Dickins, called the body to order, and in the absence of John C. Breckenridge, Vice-President elect, James M. Mason of Virginia was chosen to preside temporarily. After the roll was called of the members with unexpired terms, the

THE NATIONAL CAPITOL AT WASHINGTON.

list of newly-elected Senators was read. As they responded to
their names they advanced to the front of the presiding officer's
desk, in groups of four, to take the oath of office. The first
group were Bates, Bayard, Bright and Broderick; the second
consisted of Simon Cameron, Zachariah Chandler, Jefferson Davis
and James Dixon. This scene was the subject, twenty-two
years later,* of the most effective speech ever delivered by Mr.
Chandler; probably no speech ever uttered in the Senate more
thoroughly touched the popular heart or was more widely read.
Of the men who were then United States Senators, parts and
witnesses of this scene, Fitzpatrick, Sebastian, Broderick, Dixon,
Bates, Mallory, Iverson, Douglas, Bright, Crittenden, Thompson,
Slidell, Fessenden, Kennedy, Pearce, Sumner, Wilson, Green,
Hale, Thomson, Wright, King, Seward, Pugh, Wade, Allen,
Simmons, Evans, Butler, John Bell, Jas. Bell, Andrew Johnson,
Houston, Rusk, Collamer, Foot, Mason and Durkee (perhaps
others) preceded Mr. Chandler to the grave. Of this number,
one (Broderick) was killed in a duel and two committed sui-
cide (Rusk killed himself at Nacogdoches, Tex.; on July 29,
1857, and Preston King on August 15, 1865, and while collector
of the port of New York, jumped heavily weighted into the
Hudson river).

Of the members of this Senate Hamlin, Wilson (his original
name was Jeremiah Jones Colbath) and Johnson became Vice-
Presidents, and Johnson, on the death of Abraham Lincoln,
became President. Mr. Hamlin was the only one still in the
Senate at the time of Mr. Chandler's death, and his service had
not been continuous but was broken by his Vice-Presidential
term. Sons of Cameron and Bayard were in 1879 in the seats
occupied by their fathers in 1857. Seward became Secretary of
State, Cameron Secretary of War, Fessenden Secretary of the
Treasury, and Harlan and Chandler Secretaries of the Interior.

---

* "The Jeff. Davis speech," March 3, 1879.

Durkee became Governor of Utah, Jones Minister to Colombia and Cameron Minister to Russia. Jones was, on his return from Colombia, arrested ˙for treason and confined in Fort Warren. Bright was expelled for treasonable correspondence with the enemy; Polk was expelled for treason, and Sebastian, who retired from the Senate when Arkansas seceded from the Union, was also expelled, but after the war, ample proof being furnished that he was and always remained true to the Union, the resolution of expulsion was rescinded. Doolittle, Trumbull, Dixon and Foster, who were Republicans in 1857, afterward joined the Democracy, and Mr. Seward also ceased to be in sympathy with the party to which he was indebted for his greatest honors. Gwin identified himself with the Confederacy, then became *aide* to the unfortunate Maximilian, by whom he was created "Duke of Sonora," and is back again at Washington as a lobbyist. Douglas and John Bell were defeated candidates for the Presidency in 1860. Houston was Governor of Texas when the ordinance of secession passed and was deposed from his office by the disunion convention.

Jefferson Davis, who swore to support the constitution and the Union at the same instant with Mr. Chandler, within four years rebelled against the government and became President of the so-called "Southern Confederacy." Slidell, the most skilful of the disunion leaders, and Mason were appointed by the rebel government Commissioners to Great Britain, and while on their way across the ocean were seized by Captain Wilkes, commanding the United States steamer San Jacinto, taken from the British vessel Trent, and carried to Boston harbor, where they were confined in Fort Warren on a charge of treason. This seizure the Department of State declined to uphold, and on the demand of Great Britain the "embassadors" were released. Slidell died abroad in merited obscurity. Benjamin became Secretary of War of the Confederacy, and after its downfall emigrated to England,

9

became a British citizen, and is a prosperous lawyer in London. Toombs was Confederate Secretary of State, and is still living in Georgia, crying as he did in 1861 "death to the Union." Mallory was Confederate Secretary of the Navy, and for a time after the war was imprisoned in Fort Lafayette. Hunter was also Secretary of State of the Confederacy; since the war he has been Treasurer of Virginia, but with the political revolution of 1879 retired to private life and poverty. Clay was a Confederate Senator and diplomatic agent; in 1865 he was imprisoned in Fortress Monroe. Fitzpatrick was the original nominee for Vice-President on the Douglas ticket in 1860, but declined; he became a rebel but without prominence. Robert W. Johnson was a Confederate Senator and afterward practiced law in Washington. Yulee (whose original name was David Levy) retired from the Senate to join the Confederacy, ceased to be conspicuous, and is now president of a railroad in Florida. Iverson was a Brigadier-General in the rebel army, as was also Toombs. Brown was Captain in the Confederate army and a member of the Confederate Senate. Butler died during the following recess of Congress, and Evans, his colleague, died before the war. All of these Southern Senators, who retired with their States in 1861 were afterward formally expelled from the Senate.

When Mr. Chandler entered the Senate the House of Representatives was controlled by the Democrats, but out of 234 members ninety-two were filled with the fresh blood of the Republican party. Some of these men were then distinguished, and others have become so since, but of the entire number of Representatives only twelve yet remain in either branch of Congress. Henry L. Dawes is a Senator from Massachusetts, Lafayette Grover from Oregon, Justin S. Morrill from Vermont, Zebulon B. Vance from North Carolina, George H. Pendleton from Ohio, and L. Q. C. Lamar from Mississippi. Samuel S. Cox, a Representative from Ohio in 1857, is now a Representative from New York. Alex. H. Stephens of Georgia, Alfred M. Scales of North Carolina, John H. Reagan of Texas, Otho R. Singleton of Mississippi, and John D. C. Atkins of Tennessee are again members of the House. Stephens was Vice-President of the Confederacy; Scales was Captain, Colonel and Brigadier-General in the rebel army; Singleton was Aid-de-camp to Gen. Robert E. Lee; and Atkins was Lieutenant-Colonel of the Fifth Confederate Tennessee regiment, and afterward a member of the Confederate Congress.

Others who were members of the House in 1857 afterward added to the reputations they then enjoyed. Schuyler Colfax has been Vice-President. A. H. Cragin, R. E. Fenton, Thomas L. Clingman, Frank P. Blair, Jr., John W. Stevenson, Edwin D. Morgan, Joshua Hill, and George S. Houston have been United States Senators. Israel Washburn has been Governor of Maine, John Letcher of Virginia, and C. C. Washburn of Wisconsin. N. P. Banks was a General in the Union army, and is United States Marshal of Massachusetts. Daniel E. Sickles was also a General in the Union army and afterward Minister to Spain. Francis E. Spinner was for many years Treasurer of the United States. John Sherman has been a Senator, and is Secretary of the Treasury. Elihu B. Washburne was Minister to France. John A. Bingham is Minister to Japan, and Horace Maynard to Turkey. Anson Burlingame was Minister to China, and afterward the embassador of that empire to negotiate treaties with foreign powers. William A. Howard is Governor of Dakota, and John S. Phelps of Missouri. The roll of the dead of the Thirty-fifth House of Representatives far exceeds that of the living.

Zachariah Chandler entered the Senate of the United States with an abiding faith in Northern civilization and its right to supremacy, with a wise distrust of Southern professions, with a just hatred of institutions poisoned by slavery, with a determination to attack treason wherever found, with an unquestioning belief that his cause was right and its defeat impossible, and with as resolute a spirit as ever crossed the threshold of the Senate chamber. His nature was without an atom of compromise, and was strong in the rugged qualities of courage, honesty, sincerity, firmness, and moral intrepidity.

CHAPTER VIII.

MR. CHANDLER became a Senator of the United States at the time when the Southern followers of John C. Calhoun had determined that the preservation of slavery was impossible without disunion, and had commenced preparations for that desperate measure of defense. The heavy vote given to Fremont in the North, the failure of the attempt to plant slavery in Kansas, the widening schism in the Democracy itself on the issue of slavery - extension, and the certainty that the census of 1860 would greatly increase the voting power in Congress of the North and Northwest — all made it plain that the South could not re-inforce its waning strength with new slave States. Its leaders saw that the alternative before them was a systematic repression of slavery pointing toward its ultimate extinction, or the creation of a new government pretending to be a republic but "with its foundations laid, its corner-stone "resting upon, the great truth that the negro is not equal to "the white man, that slavery, subordination to the superior race, "is his natural and normal condition." * Every civilized instinct urged them to assent to peaceful and gradual emancipation, but they chose the alternative of disunion from a belief that in no other way could the political ascendancy so long enjoyed by the ruling classes of the South be maintained. The administration of James Buchanan was their period of preparation. Whatever of needed assistance his sympathy failed to supply was furnished

---

*Speech of Alexander H. Stephens at Savannah on March 21, 1861, after his election to the rebel Vice-Presidency.

by his imbecility of purpose. In his Cabinet and in federal
offices throughout the South active disunionists plotted and
labored to make all things ready for rebellion and unready for
its suppression. Chronic compromisers, Northern believers in
slavery, and State Rights theorists were their useful allies. In
Congress they threatened and bullied, and month by month
made the demands of slavery more arrogant and exacting,
scheming to kindle the war spirit of the South and to widen
the breach between the sections, until they could offer to the
North the ultimatum of abject surrender to the slave power or
disunion and civil strife. The representatives of the North at
Washington met these early developments of treason in various
moods; there was no lack among them of those who were inclined
to submit; there were many who disbelieved in the reality of
the purpose underlying Southern vaporing and bluster, and this
class included earnest and able Republicans; but there were
also some who did not doubt that the slave power would try
secession before accepting defeat, and who, yielding not one inch
of the right to menaces, proposed to treat disunion, whether
threatened or attempted, as treason and to denounce and resist
it as such.

Early in his Senatorial career Mr. Chandler became convinced
that the purpose of rebellion was a well-defined one at the
South, that preparations to make it successful were in active
progress, and that the longer the crisis was delayed the more
difficult would be the task of its suppression. Between 1857
and 1861 his comments to his intimate friends on the outlook
were exceedingly gloomy, and he often declared that he saw no
possible escape from war. If the government was to be maintained on the basis on which it was founded and was not to be
revolutionized in the interest of slavery, he believed that an
armed conflict with the men who had determined to change its
character was inevitable. He did not underestimate their ambition, their desperateness of purpose, or their readiness for

violence. But neither in public nor in private did he quail
before them in any degree, and his only plan of action was the
simple, straight-forward and characteristic one of meeting their
threats with defiance and their treason with all the force required
for its punishment. In a time of vacillation, feebleness and
moral cowardice, and while he was still new in the Senate and
hampered by his own inexperience and the usages of that body,
what he did say and all his acts and influence were important
contributions to that invigorating of Northern sentiment which
the times so greatly demanded and which alone made possible
the national uprising of 1861.

As a matter of record, the first time Zachariah Chandler's
voice was heard in the Senate chamber, he asked that " Cornelius
" O'Flynn have leave to withdraw his memorial and papers from
" the files of the Senate." The first caucus he attended was that
in which the Republican minority decided to make a vigorous
protest against the unfairness of its treatment in the appointment
of the Senate committees of the Thirty-fifth Congress. In his
first speech he added, on the floor of the Senate, to the protest
of his party an equally vigorous remonstrance against the complete ignoring of the commercial importance of the Northwest in
the selection of members of the Committee on Commerce. In
his second speech (on the proposition to increase the army) he
said in significant language: " If they will show to me that they
" require a force in Utah to put down rebellion I will vote for
" it, I care not whether it be one regiment or one hundred
" regiments." His first prepared address in the Senate was
delivered on the 12th day of March, 1858, and had as its theme
that most reckless of the slave power's efforts at self-extension,
the attempt to force upon Kansas what was known as the
Lecompton constitution.

This was a pro-slavery instrument, framed by a constitutional
convention elected and controlled by Border-Ruffians, apparently
ratified at an election whose managers · allowed no one to vote

against it but only to vote for it with slavery or for it without slavery (even the "without" was fraudulent, because property in slaves already in Kansas was in any event guaranteed until 1864), and overwhelmingly rejected at the only election which in any degree fairly represented the opinions of the genuine settlers of the territory. Mr. Chandler's speech on this topic, the absorbing one of that day, was prepared with much care and delivered from manuscript. Portions of it were read to Senators Cameron, Wade and Hamlin before it was uttered. While it was spoken with the impulsive manner that generally characterized his speeches, it was the result of long deliberation and of such careful study of phraseology as was necessary to make it explicit and forcible. It was listened to by a large audience. Mr. Chandler had in private conversation spoken with much vigor of the duty of the Republican party in case the Lecompton constitution of Kansas was accepted and the new State admitted under that instrument, and his remarks had been freely quoted. His reputation for radicalism of opinion and plainness of speech had also reached Washington, and there was a general interest felt in his first prepared address. He began speaking about fifteen minutes after the Senate was called to order (in the chamber now occupied by the Supreme Court) and held the floor for nearly three hours. The spectators included many members of the House, among them John Sherman, since Senator and Secretary of the Treasury, Alexander H. Stephens, afterward Vice-President of the Confederacy, and John A. Logan, now well-known as both soldier and Senator. The address was one of power and was attended by marked effect.* It con-

---

* Of this speech the New York *Courier and Enquirer* said: "The speech of Mr. "Chandler on the 12th places him among the first debaters of the country. No more "unanswerable exposition of the usurpation in Kansas has been made." The Chicago *Tribune* said: "Mr. Chandler made his first formal speech in the Senate to-day. That "body paid him the compliment of unwavering attention through the whole of his able "and effective speech. The passage in which he described the murder of Brown, Barbour "and Gay . . . excited the sympathies and passions of his audience to a pitch rarely "observed in parliamentary debate."

tained this description of the fate of three Michigan emigrants to Kansas:

Men have been hunted down by sheriffs and by *posses* from other States, by border-ruffians—everywhere under the color of law. Sir, the State of Michigan has over a thousand of her people in Kansas to-day. Three of her citizens, and many other good men, have been murdered in cold blood. Two of them, Barbour and Brown, I know were as good men as can be found on the face of the earth. The other—Gay—was Mr. Pierce's Land Agent for the territory. He was a Nebraska pro-slavery Democrat. He was met one day, with his son, on the road, and asked whether he was for Free-State or pro-slavery. He had become a little Free-Statish in his views, and, not dreaming of danger, he said: "I am a Free-State man," and he was shot down, and his son, in attempting to defend his father, received a bullet in his hip, and is now a cripple in Michigan. I speak with some feeling. My own constituents, my own people, have been brutally murdered, and I should be recreant to my trust if I did not speak with feeling on this subject. I know the men from Michigan who are in Kansas to be as good men as can be found within these United States, and when any one says the emigrants from Michigan to the territory of Kansas are picked from the purlieus of cities I tell him he knows nothing about the subject and that it is not true. They are as good men as the State of Michigan produces: they are honest and brave; they know their rights and, knowing, dare defend them.

But those parts of the speech which most thoroughly stirred his hearers and fell with unaccustomed force on ears which rarely heard such defiant tones, were these:

I cannot permit this bill to pass without protest. It was conceived and executed in fraud. . . . It is one of the series of aggressions on the part of the slave power which, if permitted to be consummated, must end in the subversion of the constitution and the Union. . . . It strikes a death-blow at State sovereignty and popular rights. . . . When Missouri applied for admission as a slave State . . . the North objected. They declared it was agreed to that no more slave States should be admitted into the Union. . . . Agitation ran high. The South then as now threatened a dissolution of the Union. The North then as now denied her power to dissolve it. . . . During this excitement the hearts of brave men quailed. . . . A new compromise was made. . . . As a part of this compromise slavery was forever prohibited north of 36° 30'. . . . The compromise was acquiesced in. . . . Peace again reigned through the land, . . . and this peace continued until the discovery of the new doctrine of popular sovereignty. . . . This is called a new compromise. . . . We are told we must accept it because the Union is in danger. . . . But that set of people who have been in labor and suffering and trial for so long a time on account of the Union have passed off the stage. In their places are men who love this glorious Union and love it as it was made by the fathers; men who will not whine "danger to the Union," but brave men who will fight for this Union to the death. . . . The old women of the North who have been in the habit of crying out "the Union is in danger" have passed off the stage. They are dead. Their places will never be supplied, but in their stead we have a race of men who are devoted to this Union and devoted to it as Jefferson and the fathers made it and bequeathed it to us.

Any aggression upon the constitution has been submitted to by the race who have gone off the stage. They were ready to compromise any principle, any thing. The men of the present day are a different race. They will compromise nothing; they are Union-loving men; they love all portions of the Union; and they will sacrifice anything but principle to save it. They will, however, make no sacrifice of principle. Never! Never! No more compromises will ever be submitted to to save the Union! If it is worth saving, it will be saved; but if you sap and undermine its foundations it must topple. It will be the legitimate result of your own action. The only way that we ever shall save this Union and make it as permanent as the everlasting hills will be by restoring it to the original foundations upon which the fathers placed it. . . .

The people of Kansas are almost unanimously opposed to this constitution; yet you propose to force it upon them without their consent. It cannot be done. The government has not bayonets enough to force a constitution upon the necks of any unwilling people. . . . It is our purpose to avoid the shedding of blood upon the soil of the United States by civil war. While I will not charge on the supporters of the Lecompton constitution the purpose, in civil war, of shedding blood upon the soil of the United States, I do charge that they, and they alone, will be responsible for every drop of blood that may be shed in consequence of the adoption of that constitution. I trust in God civil war will never come; but if it should come, upon their heads, and theirs alone, will rest the responsibility of every drop that may flow. I trust in God that this question will never be pushed to that extremity, for I would have less respect for the people of Kansas than I now have if I supposed they would tamely submit to have a constitution thrust down their throats without authority of law, and against law, without making resistance. I would disown them as the descendants of the men who fought our revolutionary battles if I did not think they would resist any illegal attempts to force a constitution upon them.

A speech of such vigor of opinion was not without marked effect. There was a disposition among the less radical Republicans to rate it as imprudent, and there were some attempts at rebuking Mr. Chandler for being so outspoken. He received these criticisms good-humoredly, but felt confident of his position and constantly defended it. The effect of his demonstration on the Democratic side was marked; the new Senator from Michigan surprised his political opponents by the directness and force of his attack, but won from them the respect always accorded to boldness and candor. Mr. Chandler also showed spirit on little as well as great occasions. In the latter part of the following April, the Democrats attempted to coerce the Republicans into voting upon the same bill for the admission of Kansas. Without any ill-temper, but with no lack of earnestness, Mr. Chandler arose, and said : " I understand gentlemen on the other side to "say that no adjournment shall take place until this question is " disposed of. If that is their determination I can assure them "that no adjournment will take place until the 7th of June. " When I say that no adjournment will take place until that "time, I mean what I say. I propose to take a recess until 9 " o'clock, and I advise gentlemen to bid farewell to their families " for thirty days at least."

In 1858 fuel was added to the anti-slavery flame by the Dred Scott decision, in which the majority of the Judges of the Supreme Court affirmed, that as a matter of history the negroes at the time of the formation of the constitution "had no rights which the white man was bound to respect," that as a principle of law neither emancipated slaves nor the emancipated descendants of slaves were entitled to claim the rights and privileges which the constitution provides for and secures to citizens of the United States, and that under a correct constitutional construction acts excluding slavery from the territories were without validity. This utterance was rendered especially obnoxious by the fact that the court, while leaving Dred Scott in slavery on the ground that the United States tribunals had no jurisdiction in his case, practically asserted jurisdiction for the purpose of deciding (outside of the real issues of the trial as limited by its own finding) that Congress could not exclude slavery from the territories. In reference to this decision Mr. Chandler said in the Senate on the 17th of February, 1859:

> What did General Jackson do when the Supreme Court declared the United States Bank constitutional? Did he bow in deference to the opinion of the court? No, . . . he said he would construe the constitution for himself, that he was sworn to do it. I shall do the same thing. I have sworn to support the Constitution of the United States, and I have sworn to support it as the fathers made it and not as the Supreme Court have altered it. And I never will swear allegiance to that.

In October, 1859, "Old John Brown" made his memorable attempt to liberate the enslaved negroes of the South by the descent upon Harper's Ferry. The rashness of his unaided attack on a giant wrong is protected from ridicule by a heroism worthy of Thermopylæ and by a death which Sidney's last hours did not surpass in moral grandeur. Mr. Chandler, with deep respect for Brown's motives and the unique simplicity of his character, was earnest in condemnation of his methods and of the utter foolhardiness of his effort. Congress was not in session when Brown seized Harper's Ferry and convulsed Virginia with fright, and Mr. Chandler was not in Washington. When Congress did meet in December, Brown had just been hanged, and the excitement was still feverish. A Senate committee, consisting of Mason of Virginia, Jefferson Davis, Fitch of Indiana, Democrats, and Collamer and Doolittle, Republicans, was at once appointed to investigate the raid, and while the resolution providing for it was under consideration Mr. Chandler made one of his telling speeches. In it he thus ridiculed "the reign of terror" at the South:

> Senators ask us why we have no sympathy with Virginia in this instance. Sir, we do not understand this case at all. What are the facts? Seventeen white men and five unwilling negroes surround and capture a town of 2,000 people, with a United States armory, any quantity of arms and ammunition, and with 300 men employed in it—as I am informed, employed in it under a civil officer—and hold it for two days. These I understand to be

the facts, and you ask, Why have we not sympathy ? We do not understand
any such case as that. The Senator from Mississippi (Mr. Brown) asks, What
would we say if North Carolina and Virginia were to attack the armory at
Springfield ? I do not know what is the population of Springfield, but I will
guarantee if any seventeen or twenty-two of the Generals . . . of the States
of Virginia and North Carolina were to attack Springfield, if there was not a
man within five miles of there, the women would bind them in thirty minutes
and would not ask sympathy and the matter would not be deemed of sufficient
importance to ask for a committee of investigation on the part of the corpora-
tion. Why, sir, Governor Wise compared the people of Harper's Ferry to
sheep, as the public press state. That is a libel on the sheep. For I never saw
a flock of fifty or a hundred sheep in my life that had not a belligerent ram
among them. We do not understand any such panic as this. If seventeen or
one hundred men were to attack a town of the size of Harper's Ferry anywhere throughout the region with which I am acquainted, they would simply
be put in jail in thirty minutes, and then they would be tried for their crimes
and they would be punished and there would be no row made about it.

The pointed passage of the speech was the one in which he
thanked a Southern Governor for demonstrating so conspicuously
that treason was a crime punishable by death. He said.

I am in favor of the resolution because the first execution for treason
that has ever occurred in the United States has just taken place. John Brown
has been executed as a traitor in the State of Virginia, and I want it to go
upon the records of the Senate in the most solemn manner to be held up as
a warning to traitors, come they from the North, South, East or West. Dare
to raise your impious hands against this government, its constitution and its
laws—and you hang ! . . . Threats have been made year after year for
the last thirty years, that if certain events happen this Union will be dissolved.
It is no small matter to dissolve this Union. It means a bloody revolution
or it means a halter. It means the successful overturn of this government or
it means the fate of John Brown, and I want that to go solemnly on the
record of this Senate !

These were the speeches of a man untried in public life and
still in the early years of his first Congressional term. The
Senate which he thus addressed listened also to Charles Sumner's
magnificent philippics — blows "struck with the club of Hercules
entwined with flowers," to the philosophic eloquence of Seward
in his moral prime, to Wade's sturdy fearlessness of speech, to
the wit of Hale, and to the vigorous oratory of Fessenden. But

no man measured more accurately than Zachariah Chandler the political forces of that day, no man branded the hatching treason with his blunt precision and homely power, and no man asserted with more boldness the courage and the purpose of the North. In that hour resolute words were useful in themselves; but the lapse of twenty years has shown that Mr. Chandler was then as clear-sighted as he was intrepid in spirit and plain in speech.

This unsparing denunciation of treason to plotting traitors was not without personal peril. Mr. Chandler became a Senator at a time when the South had unleashed its brutality at Washington and regarded resistance to its demands as justifying violence and insult. Horace Greeley, while visiting Washington, was assaulted and injured in the Capitol grounds by Rust of Arkansas, on account of some criticisms in the *Tribune* on Congressional action. Preston Brooks committed (on the 22d of May, 1856) his assault on Charles Sumner in the Senate chamber, a crime which was publicly upheld by Toombs, Slidell, Davis and other Southern leaders, and which led South Carolina to unanimously re-elect the ruffian to the House when he resigned after the adoption of a vote of censure. Henry Wilson's denunciation of this attack upon his colleague as "brutal, murderous, and cowardly" was followed by a challenge from Brooks, to which he responded by arming himself and by a note declaring that while he repudiated the duelling code he "religiously believed in the right of self-defense in the broadest sense." John Woodruff, a Connecticut Representative, having stigmatized Brooks's act as a "mean achievement of cowardice," was tendered a duelling challenge which he declined to receive. Anson Burlingame pursued another course. Of the assault on the Massachusetts Senator, he said: "I denounce it in the name of the "constitution it violates. I denounce it in the name of the "sovereignty of Massachusetts, which was stricken down by the "blow. I denounce it in the name of humanity. I denounce it "in the name of civilization, which it outraged. I denounce it "in the name of that fair play which bullies and prize-fighters "respect." To this the response was a challenge from Brooks, which Mr. Burlingame accepted, and, selecting Canada as the spot for the meeting, had the satisfaction of seeing the representative of South Carolina chivalry refuse to abide by the code he had himself invoked. William McKee Dunn, of Indiana, was challenged by Rust, of Arkansas, for words spoken in the House, and, naming "rifles at sixty paces" as the weapons, learned that such was not the "satisfaction" desired by Southern "gentlemen." Owen Lovejoy denounced the crimes of slavery in front of the Speaker's desk in the House, with the fists of angry Southerners shaking in his face, and amid their yells and threats. Potter, of Wisconsin, cooled off the hot blood of Roger A. Pryor by accepting his duelling challenge and selecting bowie-knives as the weapons. Amid all this there was much chronic servility among Northern members to Southern insolence, which gave pungent force to Thaddeus Stevens's sarcasm (uttered during the prolonged contest over the Speakership of the Thirty-sixth Congress) that he could not blame the South for trying intimidation, for they had "tried it fifty times and fifty times, and had always found weak and recreant tremblers in the North." Mr. Chandler entered the Senate with the firm resolution that he would not be bullied, that he would not submit to bluster, and that if occasion came he would fight without hesitation. His decision did not spring from love of quarrel or mere passion, but was the fruit of mature reflection and was based upon a clear purpose. He saw that the Southerners in Congress vapored and threatened for effect; that they believed that Northern men would not fight, and that they would be permitted to offer unlimited insults without arousing resentment. The public sentiment of the North was against duelling or fisticuffs, and the

Southerners supposed — and sincerely — that this was the result
of cowardice and not of conscience. This condition of opinion
was of decided assistance to the conspirators who were plotting
disunion at the South, and the stigma of pusillanimity was the
source of no little practical weakness with the North. Under these
circumstances Mr. Chandler fully determined — as did Mr. Wade,
Mr. Hamlin, Mr. Cameron, and one or two other Senators —
that if occasion offered, so that justice should be clearly upon
his side, he would fight. This was a deliberate purpose, not
reached through any admiration for fighting men, nor through
belief in force as a method of argument, but from a conviction that the moral effect of such a demonstration of the personal
courage of Northern representatives would be of service to the
nation. Mr. Chandler knew himself to be physically capable of
meeting almost any assailant; he prepared himself for a collision
by muscular exercise and the practice of marksmanship, and,
while he did not seek, he made no effort to avoid, an encounter.

On February 5, 1858, there was a personal altercation in the
House of Representatives between Galusha A. Grow, of Pennsylvania, afterward Speaker, and Lawrence M. Keitt, of South
Carolina, who was killed in battle, during the rebellion, at the
head of a Confederate brigade. Mr. Harris of Illinois, an Anti-
Nebraska Democrat, had offered a resolution for the appointment
of a committee to ascertain by an investigation whether the
Lecompton constitution was the work in any just sense of the
people of Kansas. Coming from such a source, the resolution
would have received a majority of votes in the House, but its
opponents resorted to parliamentary stratagem to prevent its
passage, " filibustering " for several hours. Amid the attending
excitement there was a very heated colloquy between Grow and
Keitt, which ended in blows on both sides, Keitt being the first
to strike. Grow resisted, and a general melee followed which
was participated in by many members. The affair was afterward

adjusted, and both apologized to the House but without apologizing to each other. This occurrence impressed Mr. Chandler deeply, and, as soon as he heard of it, he went to the Hall of Representatives, and assured Mr. Grow of his approval and his readiness to render any desired aid. It was the first outbreak of the kind which came within his personal observation, and confirmed him in his belief that it was the duty of the Northern minority to resist all encroachments upon their personal and official rights. Not long afterward a colloquy occurred in the Senate between Simon Cameron and Senator Green of Missouri, in which the lie was given, and only the prompt interference of Vice-President Breckenridge, who was in the chair, prevented a personal altercation. The Democrats were insisting upon a vote upon the bill to admit Kansas under the Lecompton constitution, while the Republicans were endeavoring to secure longer time for debate. It was about 4 o'clock in the morning when the offensive words were exchanged. Vice-President Breckenridge at once rapped with his gavel, and commanded both Green and Cameron to take their seats. After order had been restored, Senator Green continued his remarks, and, referring to Cameron, said: "I will not use a harsh word now; it will be out of "order. But if I get out of this Senate chamber I shall use a "harsh word in his (Cameron's) teeth, for there no rule of order "will correct me. . . . As to any question of veracity "between that Senator and myself, in five minutes after the "Senate adjourns we can settle it." Mr. Cameron's reply was: "I desire to say, if these remarks are intended as a threat, they have no effect upon me." The debate was continued at length, but a small group of Senators was soon after seen in earnest conference in a cloak-room. It was composed of Senators Chandler, Cameron, Wade and Broderick, and the result of the consultation was, that by the advice of his friends Mr. Cameron armed himself, and prepared for self-defense in case he was

10

attacked by Green. The Senate remained in continuous session for over eighteen hours, and for some time after the quarrel. Meanwhile Mr. Green's passion cooled, and the expected collision did not take place (explanations were ultimately made by both in the Senate chamber). But when the Senate adjourned, Mr. Chandler accompanied Mr. Cameron to his lodgings, as a measure of precaution. Out of this affair grew a formal agreement between Mr. Chandler, Mr. Cameron and Mr. Wade, which was reduced to writing, and sealed with the understanding that its contents should not be made public until after the death of all the signers. His copy of this historic document is still among Mr. Chandler's papers, but it will not be made public while Mr. Cameron lives. Of its purport one,* who knew intimately the men and the circumstances and motives of this act, has written :

The assaults of the violent Southern leaders upon some of the ablest and purest Republicans in the Senate, known to be non-combatants, finally became unbearable to some of the less scrupulous Republicans, until, in the midst of one of the most denunciatory tirades of one of the fire-eaters, there was noticed a little group of the lately-admitted Republicans in a side consultation on the floor of the Senate   Precisely what was said in consultation is not known to the writer, nor is it likely that it will transpire during the lifetime of either of the three gentlemen engaged. It is, however, known that the group was composed of Senators Wade, Cameron, and Chandler ; that it was agreed between them substantially that the business of insulting Republican Senators on the floor of the Senate had gone far enough, and that it must cease ; and further, that, in case of any renewed insolence to any other Republican Senator of the character which had been practiced, it should be the duty of one of the three to take up the quarrel and make it his own to the full extent of the code—to the death if it need be. The compact was not only made, but signed and sealed, and remains sealed to this day. Its import, however, became known, and the demeanor of the Southern fire-eaters, though still violent and disloyal, soon after became courteous personally toward Republican Senators.

They did, however, feel around a little to ascertain whether the whisperings as to the fighting Senators could be relied on. They had a scheme to assault Senator Chandler in the street, but a little inquiry as to his strength

---

* The Hon. James M. Edmunds, for many years Commissioner of the Land Office, and afterward postmaster of the Senate and of Washington City.

and skill led to its sudden abandonment. A blustering Southerner took offense at the remarks of Senator Wade, who had said in relation to an assertion made by him, that such a statement would only come from a liar or a coward. Of course this could not be borne by the high - toned cavalier, and his friend, or agent, or servitor called on Senator Wade, not with a formal challenge, but to ascertain how Wade would probably act in the event of a challenge. As soon as Wade pierced the diplomacy of the agent so far as to become aware of his purpose, he told him to tell the old coward that he dare not fight. This was not quite satisfactory. The agent or spy seemed anxious to know what kind of weapons Wade would choose in case of a contest. On learning this, Wade said, "rifles at twenty paces, with a white paper the size of a "dollar pinned over the heart of each combatant; and tell him, if I do not "hit the one on his breast at the first shot, he may fire at me all day."

These inquiries seemed to, cure all further desire on the part of the chivalry for personal combats. Threats, however, continued to be made of street - assaults and caning, generally pointing to the more prominent of the non - combatants in the Republican ranks.

Certain of the Republicans went thoroughly armed all the time, and these, for weeks together, took turns in walking with their non - belligerent colleagues to and from the Capitol, to protect them from personal assault.

The decided practical value of Mr. Chandler's bearing at that time and of his known determination to maintain his official and personal rights at all physical hazards cannot be doubted. It made itself felt among his associates on both sides of the Senate chamber, and earned for him early recognition at Washington as a bold and staunch leader of his party. Personal influence was the natural outgrowth of positive qualities so fearlessly displayed, and he became a man whose opinions were sought and whose energy in execution was prized by his fellow-Senators. A close personal intimacy with Mr. Wade, Mr. Hamlin and Mr. Cameron sprang up at this time, and general agreement of opinion on public questions led them into concerted action as representatives of the more "radical" element. Much of their work was beneath the surface and is not a matter of record, but the results of their efforts at that crisis to infuse vigor by all possible means into the lifeless national sentiment of the North and to prepare the people for the coming struggle were important and durable.

Mr. Chandler was heard with interest during the sessions of 1858–59–60 on other questions than those connected with the conflict over slavery. His speech (on Feb. 17, 1859) in opposition to the bill appropriating $30,000,000 to "facilitate the acquisition of Cuba by negotiation" attracted some attention. Its scope and tenor will appear from this extract:

This is a most extraordinary proposition to be presented to the Congress of the United States at this time. With a Treasury bankrupt, and the government borrowing money to pay its expenses, and no efficient remedy proposed for that state of things ; with your great national works in the Northwest going to decay, and no money to repair them ; without harbors of refuge for your commerce, and no money to construct them ; with a national debt of $70,000,000, which is increasing, in a time of profound peace, at the rate of $30,000,000 per annum — the Senate of the United States is startled by a proposition to borrow $30,000,000. And for what, sir ? To pay just claims against the government, which have been long deferred ? No, sir ; you have no money for any such purpose as that. Is it to repair your national works on the Northwestern lakes, to repair your harbors, to rebuild your lighthouses ? No, sir ; you have no money for that. Is it to build a railroad to the Pacific, connecting the Eastern and Western slopes of this Continent by bands of iron, and open up the vast interior of the Continent to settlement ? No, sir ; you say that is unconstitutional. What, then, do you propose to do with this $30,000,000 ? Is it to purchase the island of Cuba ? No, sir ; for you are already advised in advance that Spain will not sell the island ; more, sir, you are advised in advance that she will take a proposition for its purchase as a national insult, to be rejected with scorn and contempt. The action of her Cortes and of her government, on the reception of the President's message, proves this beyond all controversy ? What, then, do you propose to do with this $30,000,000 ? . . . It is a great corruption fund for bribery and for bribery only. . . . But let us admit for the sake of argument that this proposition is brought forward in good faith and will be successfully terminated. What do any of the Northwestern States gain by the purchase of this island of Cuba ? I know something of Cuba, something of its soil, something of the climate, something of its people, their manners and customs, something of their religion and something of their crimes. I spent a winter in the interior of the island of Cuba a few years since and can, therefore, speak from personal knowledge. . . . Much of the soil of the island is rich and exceedingly productive, but it is in no way comparable to the prairies and bottom lands of the great West. You can go into almost any of your territories and select an equal number of acres and you will have a more valuable State than you can possibly make out of Cuba. . . . You propose to pay $200,000,000 for the island, $10 an acre for every acre of land on

It. . . . You are selling infinitely better lands, and have millions upon millions of acres of them, at $1.25 per acre. You propose to pay $200,000,000 — nearly $200 a head for every man, woman and child, including negroes, on the island. And for what? For the right to govern one million of the refuse of the earth.

During this same period Mr. Chandler was very active in helping on the work of Republican organization throughout the country. In the campaign of 1858 in Michigan, he spoke repeatedly in the larger towns of that State, great audiences gathering to hear him, and answering with growing enthusiasm his vigorous attacks on the administration and its master, the slave power. The result was that Moses Wisner, Republican, was elected Governor by a vote of 65,202 to 56,067 for Charles E. Stuart, Democrat. The Republicans also carried every Congressional district (William A. Howard obtained his seat after a contest with George B. Cooper) and had a large majority in both branches of the Legislature. That body, on meeting in January, 1859, elected Kinsley S. Bingham to the Senate, and Michigan has always since that year been represented in the upper branch of Congress by two Republicans. Charles E. Stuart, whom Mr. Bingham succeeded, was a man of ability who had manfully refused to support the Lecompton outrage, and with Stephen A. Douglas and David C. Broderick had been classed as an Anti-Nebraska Democrat. Mr. Bingham was a thorough Republican, and during his brief Senatorial term (he died in October, 1861,) stood side by side with his colleague on all political questions.

In the Presidential campaign of 1860 Mr. Chandler labored with untiring zeal to secure Mr. Lincoln's election. Early in the fall he spoke with marked effect in the State of New York. Throughout August, September, and October he addressed a series of great mass-meetings at different points in Michigan (at Hillsdale 8,000 people gathered to hear him, at Cassopolis 10,000, at Paw Paw 5,000, and at Kalamazoo 20,000). In October he visited Illinois, speaking at Mr. Lincoln's home

(Springfield) on the 17th of that month.* His last speech in that campaign was made in the Republican wigwam at Detroit on November 1, and was alive with the spirit of victory and the firm purpose to secure its rewards. On the day of election his State answered his appeals with an increased Republican majority, giving Lincoln 88,480 votes to 65,057 for Douglas, 805 for Breckenridge, and 405 for Bell.

---

* The Springfield *Journal* of October 18 said : "Senator Chandler, of Michigan, made "yesterday one of the best speeches to which our citizens have had the pleasure of "listening during the campaign. . . . The meeting was a magnificent one and the "greatest enthusiasm prevailed."

CHAPTER IX.

ACHARIAH CHANDLER as a Republican Senator was a thorough Whig in both his advocacy of an enlightened national system of Internal Improvements and his constant and efficient championship of the cause of the Protection of American Industries. It has been justly said that "the Great West of to-day owes its unequaled growth "and progress, its population, productiveness and wealth, pri- "marily, to the framers of the federal constitution, by which its "development was rendered possible, but more immediately and "palpably to the sagacity and statesmanship of Jefferson, the "purchaser of Louisiana; to the genius of Fitch and Fulton, "the projector and achiever, respectively, of steam navigation; "to De Witt Clinton, the early, unswerving and successful "champion of artificial inland navigation; and to Henry Clay, "the eminent, eloquent, and effective champion of the diversi- "fication of our national industry through the Protection of "Home Manufactures." No man knew better or acknowledged more fully the truth of this analysis than Mr. Chandler. His own State abounded with evidences of its justice, and his firm faith in the protective principle was also strengthened by the teachings of his practical mercantile experience and by his general commercial sagacity. No State presents to-day more abundant proofs of the beneficence of "the American system" than Michigan, and no personal contributions to the protection of its interests and the diversification of its industries equaled those given on every possible occasion by Mr. Chandler through-out his prolonged Senatorial service.

Political economy has been well defined as "the science of "labor-saving applied to the action of communities, its aim "being to save labor from waste, from misapplication, and from "loss through constrained idleness." The objects of Protection are the ennobling of labor and the enhancing of its productiveness, and its method is interdicting an unwholesome competition which looks no farther than securing mere cheapness of production at whatever cost of human energy, comfort and enlightenment. There has never been an intelligent and sincere protectionist without a thorough faith in the vast importance and inherent nobility of Labor. On this as on all great questions Mr. Chandler's convictions were radical, and he was right fundamentally. He had been himself a laborer. The store, the farm, the factory, the work-shop, are all one in this — their duties are labor. Mr. Chandler knew the worth of free labor. He had witnessed its seed-planting and wonderful fruitage of development in Michigan, and he honored the strong, hardy, intelligent and self-reliant race who were the laborers there, and of whom he was one. He had early opportunity to make this plain in the Senate. Hammond of South Carolina, a true representative of that turbulent, rebellious State and of the embodied insolence of its master class and of the man-owner's contempt for free labor, made at this time his notorious "mud-sill" speech. "There must be laborers "in every community, a low, degenerate class, who hew the "wood and draw the water, . . . the mud-sills of society, in "effect they are slaves;" this was its idea. It was a frank avowal of the estimate put by the slave-holding oligarchy upon the Northern laborers, upon the men who have made this country what it is. Mr. Chandler was then young in the Senate, and had spoken but rarely, but to this insult to his constituency he was quick to reply. In his speech of March 12, 1858, the first in which he addressed the Senate at any length, he said:

It is an attack upon my constituents. Under the Senator's version, under his exposition of slavery, nine-tenths of the people of the North are or have been at some time slaves; for nine-tenths of the people of the North have at some time been hirelings and laborers. We do not feel degraded by being laborers. We believe it to be respectable. . . . Travel on any road in the State of Michigan, and you will find flourishing farms on almost every 160 acres, with comfortable dwellings, and a high state of improvement and cultivation. . . . You will find the owners of these farms with four or five sons of their neighboring farmers hired out by the day or the month or the year. . . . These young men go to service or labor until they get money enough to buy a farm; then they, too, become the employers of labor. . . . These men are never degraded by labor. . . . They are the foundations of society there. Some of these men who are at work by the month during the summer on farms are in the Legislature making laws for us in the winter

There was more of it to the same effect — honest, indignant words in defense of free Northern labor, and in eulogy of the men who toiled. And the tone of these portions of the speech was wholesomely defiant, without a shade of truckling to Southern insolence. Nine years later, in discussing proposed tariff amendments in 1867, Mr. Chandler said in the Senate, "I thank God we are able to pay good prices to our laborers." These utterances indicate the vein in which he always made his voice heard and influence felt whenever the interests and rights of labor were challenged either by speech or attempted legislation.

The tariff controversy in the United States dates back half a century. This republic in its colonial days was agricultural. There were no mines nor manufactures. Each house did its own spinning and weaving. There were small shops for the making and repairing of a few articles, and luxuries and fine goods for the rich were imported from the factories of Europe. The great labor-saving appliances of the nineteenth century did not exist even in imagination. The water power of the country was unused and its boundless wealth of minerals unknown. The people were farmers or traders. For them the government was founded, and apparently there was no contemplation of anything beyond. It was years before a change came, but, once begun, it hurried with rapid stride, until to-day more than one-twentieth of the entire population of the United States are engaged in manufacturing, as many more are employed in occupations connected with and dependent upon such enterprises, and the capital invested in productive industries exceeds by millions of dollars the entire national debt.

.These changes as they progressed made new demands upon the government. After the development of the steam engine, and after later inventions and contrivances had cheapened the production of cotton, woolen and other goods, household spinning - wheels and looms were silent, and the United States imported nearly every manufactured article needed by its people, sending out in return the products of its farms and plantations, its tobacco, cotton and grain. Year after year this draining process went on, the manufacturing towns of Europe growing great and prosperous, the United States widening and increasing in population, but adding little to its wealth. The mill - owners of Europe bought their cotton in South Carolina or Georgia, transported it across the Atlantic, made it into cloths, and returned them to New York or Charleston. The American purchaser paid the cost of both transportations, the cost and profit of manufacture abroad, all the profits of middle - men who handled the goods, and all the cost of exchanges. By this process America toiled, while England and the other manufacturing States of Europe reaped the harvest. Thoughtful people, knowing that capital employed in production feeds, clothes and lodges the industrious workman, adds to the wealth of the nation, adds to its strength, adds to its power of resistance, and lessens the individual burden of taxation, and comprehending the inevitable result of the drain in progress, asked, Is there no way of preventing this? They saw the raw material produced in bountiful profusion, saw the water power of the country running away to the sea unvexed by use, and naturally asked, Is it not possible to bring the miners and smelters, the founders, machinists and laborers, the mechanic and manufacturer of every description, here, to place them beside the raw material, to utilize this wasted power, and to save the losses and attrition that are impoverishing the country? When these thoughts took shape in the active brains of Americans, the change began. Mills and factories sprang up by the water-courses. Tall chimneys, clouds of smoke and glowing furnaces came after. Thus American manufacturing was born.

But as the first mills and factories were established, these discoveries were made: In building a mill in England the laborers and mechanics could be hired at wages from twenty to forty per cent. lower than prevailed on this continent. The cost of machinery, most of it being brought from Europe, was also greater. Foreign manufacturers could hire their capital from the immense reservoir of Europe, where it had been accumulating for centuries, at from four to six per cent. interest. Here the borrower must pay eight or ten per cent. or even higher. There was another and even graver matter presented to the consideration of the pioneer manufacturer. Labor in Europe was cheap —so cheap that, combined with abundant capital and low interest, it enabled the foreign manufacturer to pay two ocean transportations and yet undersell an American competitor at the very door of his own mill. Should the American mechanic be asked to toil for the pauper wages of Europe? Should it be the policy of this government to gather about its factories the hungry-eyed, ill-clad, impoverished, ignorant and hopeless crowds which are found in the manufacturing towns of the old world? Could American institutions endure this? Where the people are all agriculturists, except under very extraordinary circumstances they need never want for food, and such circumstances are rarely chargeable to misgovernment or to bad laws. The farming classes are widely scattered; they are conservative and self-reliant, not given to mobs and outbreaks, nor to obeying the will of self-constituted leaders as do men gathered in great masses. But the men of mills and shops and factories, unless they are well paid, must suffer; and when they suffer their discontent threatens society itself. Despotic governments may apply the gag of a bayonet or the silence of a musket ball, but this is not possible in a republic resting upon the uncompelled support of all the people. Plainly, if a government, constituted as is this, is to be preserved, the mechanics, the laborers in mills and mines, in shops and factories, must be paid enough to support themselves and their families in comfort, to educate their children and to permit the thrifty to make savings. If the time ever comes when the millions of American workers upon whose assent this government exists are reduced to the condition of the pauper labor of Europe, this republic and its golden promises of freedom will most certainly ignobly perish from the face of the earth. From such circumstances and ideas as these sprang the doctrine, accepted by almost all of the earlier statesmen of the republic, that the revenue system of the United States must be so modeled as to stimulate domestic manufactures, protect them from ruinous foreign competition, and promote that diversification of industry which is so essential to the prosperity and independence of free labor.

The first tariff measure (passed by the First Congress and approved by George Washington) imposed but low duties, but in some of its details practically recognized the protective principle, and in its preamble declared one of its purposes to be "the protection and encouragement of Domestic Manufacture." From 1807 to 1815 the United States was in a great degree driven from the ocean. A part of that time it was involved in a war with Great Britain, with an embargo laid upon its ports. During these years the home manufacturer had no foreign competition to fear, and factories sprang up to meet the local demands, drawing about them laborers and their families, making

a quick market for the productions of the soil, and placing consumer and producer side by side. But this was the result of
accident and not of deliberate policy. The scene changed when
the raising of the embargo brought into the country a flood of
manufactured articles representing cheap labor, cheap interest and
cheap capital. Then came the demand for the levying of such
duties on the products of foreign labor as would protect the American manufacturer and enable him to pay a suitable compensation
to the American workman. The first response to this was the
tariff of 1816, justly styled "The Planters' and Farmers' Tariff,"
because it gave protection to coarser commodities which least
required it, and withheld it from those articles in whose production others were to be used. Eight years afterward came
a third tariff varying little in its general features, but with rates
of duties slightly increased. Four years later (in 1828) was
enacted the first thoroughly American protective tariff, but it was
soon destroyed by the act of July 12, 1832 (the outcome of the
Nullification controversy), which completely abolished its protective features. Within a few months, through the exertions of
Mr. Clay, this measure was modified by what was known as the
compromise tariff act, which continued in force until the passage of the protective tariff of 1842. This was in time displaced
by the free-trade tariff, which went into force four years later,
in June, 1847. It was followed in 1861 (March 23) by the
Morrill tariff, a thoroughly protective measure, which with some
modifications yet remains on the statute books.

In 1816, notwithstanding it had just emerged from war, the
country's industrial condition was at least hopeful, but the consequences of the tariff of that year promptly manifested themselves.
The American manufacturer was undersold at the door of his
mill by the foreigner; factories closed, wages shrunk and the
demand for labor diminished. Prices of all kinds of planter's and
farmer's produce declined in turn, and to industrial prostration

was speedily added agricultural depression. Henry Clay pronounced the seven years preceding 1824 the most disastrous this
nation had ever known. But almost from the moment of its
passage the country felt the impetus of the protective tariff of
1828. Furnace doors were thrown open; foundries were built;
the cobwebs that had gathered about factory machinery disappeared in the whir of busy wheels; labor came again into
demand; immigration increased; the products of farms and plantations brought good prices; and the public revenue grew until
the national debt was extinguished. Prosperity thus became
universal throughout the land. When this protective tariff of
1828 gave way to the gradual reductions in duties of the compromise measure of 1832, there followed a repetition of the
scenes that succeeded the tariff of 1816. From 1837 to 1842
mills and furnaces were closed, wages were reduced, laborers
sought in vain for employment, the poor-houses were filled and
manufacturers, farmers and planters became bankrupts together.
Even the public treasury was unable to borrow at home as small
a sum as $1,000,000 at any rate of interest, and the great bank-
ing houses of Europe refused it credit, so that it was forced to
the humiliation of selling its securities at ruinous discounts. The
passage of the protective tariff of 1842 marks the date of another
business revival. Old mines were re-worked and new ones were
opened. Mill-fires were re-lighted and new mills sprang up in
all directions. Money became abundant, and public and private
incomes exceeded all precedent. Farmers and planters secured
easy markets and ample prices for their produce, and laborers'
homes grew bright with plenty. Then came the Free-Trade
tariff of 1846 and the commercial decadence which culminated
in the disasters of 1857. California and its gold delayed the
catastrophe but could not avert it. From the moment of the
repeal of the protective tariff, the inflow of British iron and
cloth began and the receding tide carried back American gold,

impoverishing the country. Industry was stricken to the earth, and day by day saw the dependence of the United States on foreign markets growing until when the crash came it was complete. The vast flood of gold from California had gone into European vaults and in its stead could only be shown receipts for foreign goods consumed and the wrecks of American industries. The Morrill tariff was followed by an unparalleled mercantile and manufacturing development, which not even the disastrous effects of an inflated currency (in 1873-76) could more than briefly check.

Mr. Chandler, who knew well these facts, and had learned "the American doctrine" in the days of Clay, had taken his seat in the Senate when the crash of 1857 came, and was active in demanding and shaping that revolution in the revenue system which has made the United States one of the great manufacturing nations of the world. He was an ardent champion of the Morrill tariff (of 1861), and aided materially in perfecting its details, watching with special vigilance those of its provisions which affected the vast interests of the Northwest. He believed in the largest possible application of the protective principle, and favored aiding every American producer and every American manufacturer who could complain on valid grounds of foreign competition. Every demand for protection, which gave reasonable promise of increasing the yield of any staple or of developing a new industry, received his energetic support. To any revenue measure or proposition, which seemed to him calculated to advance foreign at the expense of American interests, he was uncompromisingly hostile. The abrogation of the Reciprocity treaty with Canada he labored most assiduously to bring about, and he resisted with all his characteristic pertinacity each successive effort to restore a compact which imposed such heavy burdens upon the lumbermen, salt manufacturers, and farmers of the Northwest. Throughout his Senatorial term all measures

affecting duties in any form or proposing any modification in
their schedules found him alert, well - informed, and determined
to maintain the protective policy against any assault.* Very
much the greater, and undoubtedly the most effective, part of
his labors for an American tariff was put forth in committee-
rooms and in the earnest use of argument and influence with
fellow - Congressmen ; he relied much more upon this work than
upon speech - making for results — and results he always ranked
far above display or mere publicity. Still he spoke not unfre-
quently on tariff questions, and a few quotations will illustrate
satisfactorily his positions and methods. This passage shows how
radical was his protectionism :

> This nation to - day should be an exporter of iron instead of an importer.
> There is no valid reason why we should buy one single pound of iron from
> any other nation on the globe. Our mountains are filled with the purest ores
> on the face of the earth. . . . If I had my way I would absolutely pro-
> hibit the introduction of foreign iron.

* The following letter is written by a gentleman thoroughly familiar with the history
of tariff legislation at Washington for many years:

WASHINGTON, D. C., Jan. 6, 1880.

Some eight years ago, when a serious reduction in the copper tariff was proposed, I
know that Mr. Chandler rendered valuable aid in bringing the facts before the Senate in
his clear, terse way — going straight to the mark. Then, as always in practical matters,
his prompt manner, his business knowledge, and his immense power of will made him the
man to be called on, and he ever responded to the call, and had a power wonderful indeed
to "push things." When the act to reduce internal revenue taxes—which had passed the
House almost unanimously, and had been perfected by the mutual labors of Congressional
committees and representative business men — was before the Senate for final action in
March, 1868, an effort was made by Senator Fessenden, of Maine, to add to it as a "rider"
a clause affecting the copper tariff, which would surely have delayed if not defeated the
measure. Senator Chandler spoke ten minutes, putting concentrated power in his words,
and showing the great importance of passing the act and the needless mischief that must
come of saddling it with another question. He succeeded in defeating the Fessenden
amendment, the act passed without it, and it reduced the annual burden of internal revenue taxation some $60,000,000 (all this internal).

The Senator's views on tariff legislation were broad and comprehensive, recognizing
the interdependence of all branches of industry and the importance of such action as
should bear with equal justice on all ; knowing no East, nor West, nor South—no petty
and narrow jealousy between farmer and merchant and manufacturer—but seeking the
wise care and healthy growth of a varied home industry all over the land.

On these subjects he showed practical sagacity and the same moral courage and
bold vigor that marked his great efforts for freedom and justice to all in the last and
grandest year, which so nobly closed a public career which will live and grow in the minds
of future generations. Very truly yours,   GILES B. STEBBINS.

The context does not sustain an absolutely literal construction of the last sentence. Mr. Chandler had seen Michigan when its copper mines were unworked, its limitless riches of iron undiscovered, its salt deposits unknown, and its pine forests unfelled. He had seen these industries passing through various stages of prosperity and disaster as they were affected by prevailing tariffs, now shielded by a wise policy of protection and now at the mercy of foreign producers, who at times (to use their own admission) "voluntarily incur immense losses in order to destroy "American competition and to gain and keep control of Ameri- "can markets." He saw these industries grow from nothing, until the annual yield of Michigan's copper mines became 20,266 tons, of its iron mines 1,125,231 tons, and of its salt wells 1,885,884 barrels, and until its lumber product expanded to the enormous total of 2,700,000,000 feet in one season. They thus became powerful interests, employing a great host of laborers and offering support to thousands of families. These facts and the tone of what Mr. Chandler said on kindred topics make it plain that by the absolute prohibition of the introduction of foreign iron he meant not an embargo, but the affording of such ample protection to the iron industries of the entire country as would make it impossible for the products of foreign cheap labor to compete in its markets with those of American labor, and as would make the United States a seller and not a buyer of iron and its wares.

With all his earnestness as a protectionist, he kept the interests of labor predominant in his consideration of this subject. For instance, in some remarks upon the lumber tariff, he said: "It is perfectly well known that the great value of lumber is "in the labor and the transportation, and while we in the United "States are paying our laborers (in lumber) $2 a day, they are "in the British Provinces paying but from 75 cents to $1 per "day." And he steadily voted for such protection of the lumber trade as would enable producers engaged in that business to

11

pay large wages, and opposed every suggestion which looked to impoverishing or pauperizing the American artisan. He uniformly upheld American industry and labor of every kind against the competition of the world. He felt that the highest civilization can only be secured through that policy of industrial diversification which brings consumer and producer side by side, and he favored giving it the widest possible scope. He frequently declared, "I cannot vote to discriminate against any particular branch," and he firmly believed in protecting everything his country could produce. His vigilance in caring for all interests and his grasp of the practical details of tariff legislation will appear from one or two brief citations from speeches made in 1867 on proposed modifications of the Morrill tariff. The duty on pig-metal was then $9 per ton, and it was proposed in the new bill to admit scrap-iron on the payment of a duty of $3. On this proposition Mr. Chandler said :

The effect of this tariff will be to admit all the rails in the world into the United States at a duty of $3 a ton. We will become the recipients of all the scrap-iron in the world. . . . And the effect will be to put out every blast-furnace in the United States, and stop the mining in every mountain in the country. . . . The expense of re-rolling bars is only about $30 a ton. You admit scrap-iron at this nominal duty, and the result will be to utterly destroy the revenue you now receive from iron — you will import nothing but at the duty of $3 per ton. This scrap-iron is worth two or three times as much as pig-metal. Pig-metal has to be puddled once. It costs to-day $28 per ton to put pig-metal into scrap, and yet you put a duty of $9 per ton on pig-metal and propose a mere nominal duty of $3 per ton on scrap. . . . This is absolutely abandoning the whole iron interests of the United States, save and excepting the rolling-mills. . . . The State of Pennsylvania takes about 300,000 tons of Lake Superior ore to mix with her inferior ore, and transports it by water 700 or 800 miles, and afterward by land carriage — a very expensive carriage — from 50 to 300 miles. This ore is mixed with the Pennsylvania ores, and transported then a long distance at very great expense. The demand for pig-iron is for rolling. . . . Calling material nothing, it costs the manufacturers $60 per ton of scrap-iron to take the ore and the coal from the mine and deliver at the works, every cent of which is labor. . . . There are in the world 100,000 miles of railroads, of which 36,000 are in the United States, and 64,000 in the rest of the world. These railroads are laid, on an average, with rails weighing 56 pounds to the yard, and use 40,000 tons net to the mile. This gives the 64,000 miles abroad

3,136,000 tons of iron. This has to be re-rolled on an average once in ten years ; consequently one-tenth of this amount is let loose upon some country every year in the shape of scrap-iron. That would make the amount of railroad scrap alone 313,600 tons per annum, which it is proposed to admit at a duty of $3 a ton, and which it costs to-day $60 a ton to put in the form of scrap in the United States. This is Free Trade in the broadest sense. It is worse than that. . . . It will build up rolling-mills, but it will break down every forge in the United States. . . . It will stop our mines in Michigan that yield ores richer than any other in the world. . . . It will make this country the entrepôt for the scrap-iron of the world.

He would not build up the rolling-mill at the expense of the mine and the blast-furnace. He would not build up one industry upon the ruins of any other. His many speeches and his more numerous votes in the Senate all indicated the same clear purpose to avoid discrimination against home interests where possible, and to protect everything American against everything of foreign production.

One phase of this many-sided question which made a deep impression upon Mr. Chandler remains to be mentioned. In common with all thoughtful Americans, during the course of the rebellion he realized the priceless value of the large-brained, energetic and highly-skilled American mechanic. He had marked these men in every brigade, upon every field of the war, enabling commanders to overcome obstacles which without them would have been insurmountable. He had seen mills and factories and shops pouring into the storehouses of the government the multitudinous articles without which a successful prosecution of the war would have been impossible, and that, too, with a rapidity which was as amazing as it was unexampled. He was from his early manhood a strong protectionist. But when he realized what the American working-men had done for the country and for freedom, and how its protected trades had served the government in its hour of trial, he became still firmer in his faith in the wisdom of the system which fosters American industry and secures to the country the priceless heritage of prosperous and intelligent laborers and mechanics.

CHAPTER X.

PON the day following that on which Mr. Chandler first took his seat in the Senate Judah P. Benjamin of Louisiana offered a resolution, from a special committee in regard to the formation of committees, amending the thirty-fourth rule of the Senate by providing that thereafter the standing committees of that body (their members are selected by the Senate itself and not by its presiding officer) should be appointed at the commencement of each session of Congress. The Committee on Commerce then, and from that time until the special session in the spring of 1875, consisted of seven members. Mr. Benjamin's resolution was adopted, and on March 9th the standing committees for the special session were, on motion of Mr. Seward of New York, announced. The Committee on Commerce was composed of Messrs. Clay of Alabama, chairman, Benjamin of Louisiana, Bigler of Pennsylvania, Toombs of Georgia, Reid of North Carolina, Bright of Indiana, and Hamlin of Maine. Mr. Chandler was assigned to the Committee on the District of Columbia, of which Mr. Brown of Mississippi was chairman. Mr. Hamlin of Maine was also appointed on this inferior committee, giving it two Republican members, while the Committee on Commerce had but one. The general assignment of places to the minority was so inadequate and unfair that a Republican caucus (the first Mr. Chandler attended) had been called to consider the matter. Mr. Chandler, although a new member, was one of its speakers and gave strong expression to his sense of the injustice with which both his party and the Northwest had been treated. It was decided to make a formal protest against the constitution of the committees, and, as a result of this consultation, when Mr. Seward's motion was made, Mr. Fessenden of Maine, as the spokesman of the Republicans, denounced the unfairness of the majority with force and vigor. In his remarks he said "that there was not an individual "member of the Republican party in the Senate who deemed "that a just and fair division had been made in the appointment "of the committees, especially two or three of them." He also declared that there was not a just and fair division with reference to questions coming before the committees, and then gave this illustration: "Take, for instance, the Committee on Com-"merce. On that committee the Republican party, numbering "twenty out of the sixty-one members of the Senate, is assigned, "of the whole number of seven, one member. . . . The "interests of the whole lake region, the interests of New England "and of New York, involving, as those large portions of the "country do, such an infinite superiority of all its commerce, "are found with only two members out of the seven." Mr. Hamlin here corrected Mr. Fessenden's statement, by saying, "My colleague is mistaken. . . . The interests of which he speaks have only *one* member on that committee, not two." Mr. Hamlin was right; there was but one member of the Committee on Commerce to represent the immense interests of the country of the Great Lakes of the Northwest and of the whole of New England and New York, and that single member was himself. But the Republican protest, well-grounded as it was, proved then unavailing.

At the first regular session of the Thirty-fifth Congress, beginning in December, 1857, Mr. Allen, of Rhode Island, presented under the rule a new list of the standing committees of the Senate for adoption. That on Commerce was only changed by the substitution of Mr. Allen for Mr. Bright of Indiana, increasing its New England but diminishing its Western member-ship. Messrs. Hamlin, Chandler and Wilson again made vigorous remonstrances against the unjust formation of the standing com-mittees as a whole. This was Mr. Chandler's first speech in the Senate, and it was as follows:

I find in the "Globe" of yesterday the following announcement: "The "caucus of all parties in the Senate has agreed to constitute the committees "as follows." And then follows a list in detail. This announcement, as I understand it, is incorrect. I believe that no such caucus has been held. I am informed that a Democratic caucus was held, and the committees made up, leaving certain blanks to be submitted to the Republicans for them to fill. They saw fit to fill these blanks, under protest. No such caucus as is announced in the statement which I have read was ever held. No assent has ever been given by the Republicans of this Senate to any such formation of committees as is there announced.

I rise, sir, to protest against this list of committees as presented here. Never before, in the whole course of my observation, have I seen a large minority virtually ignored in a legislative body upon important committees. This is the first time that I have ever witnessed such a total, or almost total, ignoring of a large and influential minority. But, sir, whom and what does this minority represent? It represents — I believe I am correct in saying — more than half — certainly nearly one-half — of all the free white inhabitants of these United States; it represents two-thirds of all the commerce of the United States; and more than two-thirds of the revenues of the United States; and yet this minority, representing the commerce and revenues of the nation, is expected to be satisfied with one place upon the tail end of a com-mittee of seven on Commerce. I may almost say that that committee is of more importance to the Northwest than all the other committees of this body; but the great Northwest is totally ignored upon a committee in which it takes so deep an interest. Not a solitary member of this body from that portion of the country is honored with a position on that committee, and yet you have been told of the hundreds of millions of dollars' worth of commerce which is there looking for protection to this body.

Sir, we are not satisfied, and we desire to enter our protest against any such formation of committees as is here presented. But we would say to the gentlemen on the other side of the chamber: You have the power to-day; you can elect your committees as you see fit; you can give us one represent-ative on a committee of five, or one on a committee of seven, or none on any of the committees, if you think proper. Exercise that power in your own discretion; but, gentlemen, beware! for the time is not far distant when the measure you mete out to us to-day shall be meted to you again.

Senators Pugh, Bayard, Gwin and Brown, from the Democratic side, defended the list as presented by Mr. Allen, and his resolution for its appointment was adopted by a strict party vote of thirty to nineteen. The Republican protests were again unheeded by the Senate, but in less than four years Mr. Chandler's prediction, that the situation would be reversed, was fulfilled.

Before Mr. Chandler entered the Senate there had been some work done by the United States upon the most serious natural obstacle to the navigation of the Great Lakes, the tortuous channels and extensive shoals at the mouth of the St. Clair river, known as the "St. Clair Flats." Largely through Senator Cass's efforts an appropriation of $45,000 had been made in the Thirty-fourth Congress (it was passed over Franklin Pierce's veto) for this work, and this sum had been expended under the supervision of Major Whipple in the clearing out of a channel through the shoals of about 6,000 feet in length, 150 feet in width, and nine feet in depth at low water. This improvement, valuable as it was, did not prove at all adequate, and was made much less useful in the few following years by a lessening in the depth of the water of Lake St. Clair. The rapidly-growing commerce of the lakes manifestly demanded the early construction and permanent maintenance through these shoals of a first-class ship canal, which could be safely used in all conditions of water and weather by vessels of the largest class. Mr. Chandler clearly perceived the necessity for this important national work, determined to rest not until its completion, and commenced at once his attack on the great obstacles in its way — namely, the disposition of the older States to undervalue the commercial importance of the Northwest, and the traditional hostility of the Democracy to all internal improvements. The first measure, which (on January 14, 1858) Mr. Chandler gave notice of his intention to introduce, was a bill "making an additional appropriation for deepening the channel of the St. Clair Flats;" when introduced it was referred to the Committee on Commerce. There an effort was made to strangle it by persistent inaction. Accordingly, on April 24, Mr. Chandler introduced in the Senate a resolution instructing the Committee on Commerce to report back this bill for action by the Senate. This resolution not receiving immediate consideration, on May 3 he called it up and demanded a vote. Mr. Clay, the chairman of the committee, opposed it with much temper, and moved to lay it on the table, but this motion was lost by one vote. Mr. Clay then attacked Mr. Chandler's resolution as insulting to the Committee on Commerce, and said he spurned the idea that the committee could be instructed to report in favor of a certain appropriation for a certain work, and that he should despise himself if he was capable of obeying such instructions. Mr. Hamlin, the sole Republican member, expressed his gratification at the fact that the Senator from Michigan (Mr. Chandler) had offered this resolution; he thought that it was appropriate, and that the action of the committee called for such instructions. Mr. Clay having inquired, "What "is the use of having a Cabinet or an engineer corps, if the "Senate is to take these matters into its own hands?" Mr. Hamlin replied, "What is the use of a Senate, if the Com- "mittee on Commerce, or the Cabinet officers, or the engineer "corps, are to control these matters?" and insisted that the Committee on Commerce was a creature of the Senate, within its control, and that if it differed from the Senate in regard to any proposition before it, that body had the right to instruct the committee what action to take. He added that because the committee had agreed to make no appropriation excepting for certain specific matters, it did not follow that the Senate must adopt its views, and be controlled thereby; that the servant had no right nor authority to bind the master, and that the committee was the servant of the Senate. Mr. Clay finally yielded the point that the Senate had the right to order a committee to report back the bill, but still objected to the proposition to have it instructed to specify a certain amount to be appropriated, and Mr. Chandler consented to modify his resolution so as to instruct the committee to report back the bill for the action of the Senate without recommendation as to the amount of the appropriation. Mr. Benjamin, at this point, moved, as a substitute for the pending resolution, a general order to the committee to report on all public works upon which there had been any expenditure, and this motion prevailed. Mr. Chandler, who was after a specific point and not a mere generality, accepted this as a defeat, and began anew by giving notice on the spot that he should ask leave at a subsequent day to introduce a bill for the improvement of the St. Clair Flats, making an appropriation of $55,000, this being the amount estimated by the United States engineers as necessary at that time. On May 10 he presented this bill, but the Senate refused to refer it, and adopted a motion to lay it upon the table. Mr. Chandler met this second defeat without discouragement, and later in the session did succeed after two efforts in procuring the addition of this item of $55,000 to the civil appropriation bill. But the threat of an executive veto of the whole measure, if this appropriation was not omitted, proved potent with the Senate, and it was ultimately stricken out. Mr. Chandler closed his last speech on this measure at that session, with a demand for a vote by yeas and nays, and these words:

I want to see who is friendly to the great Northwest, and who is not — for we are about making our last prayer here. The time is not far distant when, instead of coming here and begging for our rights, we shall extend our hands and *take* the blessing. After 1860 we shall not be here as beggars.

Of this resolute struggle of his first Congressional session, Mr. Chandler said in an address at St. Johns, in Michigan, on Oct. 17, 1858:

When I took my seat in the Senate I supposed every section of the country would be fairly heard in the details of business. There were twenty

Republican Senators representing two-thirds the revenue, business and wealth of the country. How were they placed on committees? Out of seven in the Committee on Commerce they had one. I call attention to this fact. It bears the mark of design. How does this work? . . . I introduced at an early day a bill appropriating money for the St. Clair Flats, and it went to this Southern Committee on Commerce. I procured all the necessary maps and plans and estimates, and gave them into their charge. One hundred days rolled away and they had not deigned to examine them. I then introduced a resolution instructing them to report. Subsequently I introduced a bill myself which was laid on the table. By the most untiring efforts I succeeded in getting the desired appropriation tacked upon an appropriation bill and passed. But the President's friends threatened a veto of the whole bill unless this was stricken out — and that was done. Thus committees were packed against us and we were thwarted at every turn. Thousands of dollars can be obtained for almost any creek in the South, while the inland seas of the North are denied a dollar, and we are left to take care of ourselves the best we can.

The second session of the Thirty-fifth Congress began in December, 1858, and on the 21st of that month Mr. Chandler moved to take his St. Clair Flats bill from the table. This time it was passed by a vote of 29 to 22, and sent to the House where it encountered a vigorous opposition but was finally passed, its introducer working for it with the utmost energy in the committee-rooms, on the floor, and by private solicitation. It reached Mr. Buchanan in the last days of that Congress, and he killed it by withholding his signature but without a formal veto. The Thirty-sixth Congress met in December, 1859, and on the 4th of January Mr. Chandler's bill to deepen the St. Clair Flats channel made its appearance. On February 2 Mr. Buchanan informed Congress, in a special message, of his reasons for "pocketing" the measure at the last session. This veto took the position that the improvement of harbors and the deepening of the channels of rivers should be done by the respective States, and suggested that Michigan in conjunction with Upper Canada should provide the necessary means to carry out the contemplated improvements in the channels of commerce between those two countries, whereas the plain fact was that the interest of that State in such works was a mere tithe of that of the whole

Northwest. Mr. Chandler reviewed this message at length in the Senate on February 6, exposing Mr. Buchanan's misstatements in detail, and denouncing the Democratic construction of the constitution. Jefferson Davis at once came to the defense of the veto on constitutional grounds, and a running debate followed on the subject between Messrs. Chandler and Bingham of Michigan, Hamlin, Crittenden, Davis, Toombs, Wigfall and others. Mr. Crittenden condemned the veto, while Toombs and Wigfall joined Davis in its defense. Thus the plotters of rebellion assumed a hypocritical attitude as defenders of the constitution. Their treasonable daggers were yet concealed beneath their Senatorial togas, as they stood in their high places and assumed a virtue that they never had, that of being patriots with a deep regard for the fundamental law of the land. No action followed this debate, but on February 20 Mr. Chandler moved that his bill be made the special order for the 23d. This motion prevailed, but when that day arrived the Senate refused to proceed with its consideration, Mr. Chandler protesting against this delay in a speech pointing out the necessity for prompt action. On March 13 he moved to take the bill from the table but the Senate refused. Six days later he renewed the motion with the same result. Eleven days after that he did succeed in getting the measure made the special order for April 10, but again other business displaced it, and so no action was taken before adjournment. The second session of this Congress commenced in December, 1861, with civil war imminent and no chance for the consideration of any project of internal improvement. At the meeting of the next Congress the Democracy found itself in a petty minority, and remained powerless at Washington for many years. As soon as it became plain that rebellion could not destroy the life of the nation, Mr. Chandler brought forward again his bill for the improvement of the channels at the head of Lake St. Clair, and with the powerful support of his col-

leagues and the commercial interests of the Northwest obtained
without difficulty from Republican Congresses such appropriations as were required for the prompt construction of a great
ship-canal, ranking to-day among the most important and useful
of the public works of this continent. Its history and statistics
are given in this extract from an official report for the year
ending June 30, 1879:

This canal (according to its present plan) was projected by Col. T. J.
Cram, of the Corps of Engineers, in August, 1866, as the best method of
improving navigation at the mouth of the St. Clair river. He proposed open
ing the lower tortuous reach of the south channel, and making a direct cut
from its mouth proper to deep water in Lake St. Clair. His project was
approved, and construction began on the 20th of August, 1867, under contract
with Mr. John Brown of Thorold, Canada. The original plan was a straight
canal 300 feet wide in the clear, and 13 feet deep at low stage of water, protected by dykes 5 feet in height and 58 feet wide on top, built of the material
dredged from the channel and thrown behind a pile and timber revetment.
The canal was completed in the autumn of 1871, and turned over to the
charge of Maj. O. M. Poe, Corps of Engineers, on the 11th of December. As
completed, the banks are 7,221 feet in length, and constructed mostly of
dredged sand thrown behind a revetment consisting of piling in two rows
driven 13 feet apart and parallel, and capped with a timber superstructure
5 feet high, the front row being supplemented with a single row of sheath-
piling to prevent the sand bank from washing back into the canal. As originally planned, the reverse faces of the embankment were to be permitted to
take their natural slope, but as it was found that the banks if left so would
be gradually washed away, they were secured eventually by a pile and plank
revetment. The timbers in the superstructure were carbolized to prevent
rotting, but the process proved a disastrous failure, owing to its imperfect
application, and the timbers thus treated are as a general rule at this date
a mere shell with a core of dry rot. The banks were planted with willows
and sodded in some places. The history of the work since Major Poe took
charge, excepting as regards the deepening of the channel for 200 feet of its
width to a depth of 16 feet, as projected by that officer, has been a monoto-
nous routine of stopping leaks on the canal face, due to the imperfection of the
single row of sheath-piling, which permits the sand to be sucked through by
passing vessels, and propeller-wheels working near the revetment. These
leaks have been stopped from time to time at various points by various devices,
such as marsh sod, etc. . . . The deepening of the canal was begun under
Major Poe's direction by contract with Mr. John Brown of Thorold, Canada,
in June, 1873, and finished September 23, 1878, under the direction of Major
Weitzel, who had in the meanwhile relieved Major Poe.

THE SHIP-CANAL AT THE ST. CLAIR FLATS.

WESTERN ENG. CO. DETROIT.

Up to the time when the canal was turned over as completed to Major
Poe, it cost in construction and repair $472,837.84. There was subsequently
expended by Majors Poe and Weitzel $101,533.63, partly in repairs, but mainly
in deepening the canal ; and afterward, up to the close of the present fiscal
year, $19,162.78 were expended in repairs and protection. It will thus be seen
that the canal has thus far cost $586,111.56 in construction, improvement and
repair. . . . Colonel Cram's original estimate of the cost of this work
was $428,754. The whole amount appropriated has been $590,000. The
annual cost of maintenance is $5,000. There are two light-houses on the
banks.

The value of the commerce which annually passes between
the willow-clad piers of the canal is estimated by hundreds of
millions, and in every season its cost has been more than made
good by the disasters and delays it has averted. Mr. Chandler
regarded his efforts to secure its construction as the hardest fight
of his Congressional service, and there is nothing in his public
life more thoroughly characteristic of the man than the skill,
energy, and persistence with which he championed this measure
in the face of the strongest obstacles, and in spite of repeated
defeats, session after session and Congress after Congress, until
entire success crowned his labors. Many others co-operated with
him and aided in securing the ultimate victory; but circumstances and his indomitable will placed him at the front in the
decisive struggle, and this great public work is an enduring
monument of the value of his services to the vast commercial
interests of the Northwest.

At the second session of the Thirty-fifth Congress the
earnest protests of the year before bore fruit, and the Committee
on Commerce then appointed was composed of Senators Clay of
Alabama, chairman, Bigler of Pennsylvania, Toombs of Georgia,
Reid of North Carolina, Allen of Rhode Island, Hamlin of
Maine, and Chandler of Michigan. This commenced Mr. Chandler's connection with that committee; he remained a member of
it throughout all his Senatorial terms, and was its chairman and
inspiring spirit during the years of its greatest activity and use-

fulness. It is one of the most important standing committees of the Senate of the United States, and during Mr. Chandler's chairmanship its labors were gradually increased, partly through the growing business and commerce of the country, and partly by having new topics assigned for its consideration and action, because of the prompt attention and rigid scrutiny given to all matters coming under the supervision of Mr. Chandler as its head. To this committee are referred under the rules nominations of collectors of customs, appraisers of merchandise, surveyors of customs, of officers appointed to or promoted in the revenue marine service, of the chief officers in the life-saving service, and of all incumbents of consular positions. It also considers bills fixing the compensation of such officers; bills relating to marine hospitals and the customs, consular and life-saving services; bills concerning the interests of the commercial marine of the country, including the registry, enrollment and license of vessels, their inspection and measurement, tonnage-tax, entrance and clearance fees, names and official numbers, the lights to be carried, the steam pressure allowed, the providing of small boats and life-saving apparatus on passenger steamers, and restrictions upon the number of passengers or kind of freight; and bills granting medals for heroic service in saving life in case of shipwreck or similar disaster. To it are referred all measures for the improvement of rivers and harbors in the interests of commerce; for the construction of breakwaters, harbors of refuge, ship-canals, and locks for slack-water navigation; for the building of bridges across navigable rivers, or other waters of the United States; for the establishment of ports of entry and ports of delivery; for the establishment of customs collection districts or changing the boundaries thereof; granting American registers to foreign vessels (usually passed where a wreck of a foreign vessel has been purchased and rebuilt by an American citizen); and relating to the duties and districts of supervising

and subordinate inspectors of steam craft. There is hardly any
conceivable question relating to vessels of the United States that
Congress has not power to act upon, and such matters, unless
pertaining to the naval service, are always referred to the respective committees on commerce of the Senate and House, Congress as a rule following their recommendations where no
political question is involved. In addition to an immense mass
of measures coming under the classes enumerated, the Senate
Committee on Commerce, during Mr. Chandler's connection with
it, considered and reported bills to admit ship-building material
free of duty, to prevent the extermination of the fur-bearing
seals of Alaska, authorizing the appointment of shipping commissioners, and defining a gross of matches. All these facts are
recited to show the great variety of questions that are referred
to the Senate Committee on Commerce — greater than are sent
to any other Congressional committee.

No particular changes took place in the *personnel* of this
committee as already given until in the last year of Buchanan's
administration. At the closing session of the Thirty-sixth Congress it consisted of C. C. Clay, chairman, Bigler, Toombs,
Clingman, Saulsbury, Hamlin, and Chandler. Senator Hamlin
having been elected Vice-President, resigned (in January, 1861)
his Senatorship, and Mr. Baker of Oregon was appointed to fill
the vacancy thus caused on this committee. In the middle of
January Mr. Clay resigned to join the rebellion, and A. O. P.
Nicholson of Tennessee was made a member of the committee
in his place. On the 24th of January, 1861, by the unanimous
consent of the Senate, the Vice-President filled all the vacancies
on the standing committees caused by the retiring of the Southern
Senators, and the Committee on Commerce then, as re-consti-
tuted, consisted of Senators Bigler, chairman, Clingman, Saulsbury, Chandler, Baker, and Nicholson.

At the special session of the Thirty-seventh Congress (in
March, 1861) the Senate committees were radically re-organized,

and the new Committee on Commerce, the first appointed by
the Republican party, consisted of Zachariah Chandler, chairman,
Preston King, Lot M. Morrill, Henry Wilson, Thomas L. Clingman, Willard Saulsbury, and Andrew Johnson.   Mr. Chandler
continued in the chairmanship until he ceased to be a member
of the Senate in 1875.   Mr. Clingman soon joined the rebels,
and his place on the committee was filled by Mr. Ten Eyck of
New Jersey.   From session to session changes were made in its
membership, and among the names on its rolls during the fourteen
years that Mr. Chandler sat at the head of its table were Edwin
D. Morgan, James H. Lane, Solomon Foot, Timothy O. Howe,
James W. Nesmith, Justin S. Morrill, John A. J. Creswell,
George F. Edmunds, James R. Doolittle, William P. Kellogg,
George E. Spencer, Roscoe Conkling, William A. Buckingham,
J. R. West, John H. Mitchell, John B. Gordon, George R.
Dennis, and George S. Boutwell.   Mr. Chandler was succeeded
in the chairmanship when he left the Senate by Roscoe Conkling
of New York; soon after he was re-elected in 1879 the Demo-
crats regained control, and the Committee on Commerce of
the Forty-sixth Senate was organized by them.   Mr. Chandler
was made a member of it, and at the time of his death it
consisted of Senator Gordon of Georgia, chairman, Ransom of
North Carolina, Randolph of New Jersey, Hereford of West
Virginia, Coke of Texas, Conkling of New York, McMillan of
Minnesota, Jones of Nevada, and Chandler of Michigan.

Mr. Chandler's business principles were carried out in his
committee work as thoroughly as they had been in his mercantile career.   He believed that what was worth doing at all was
worth doing well.   It was the custom of the Senate Committee
on Commerce to assemble formally once a week, for the consideration of such petitions and bills as had been referred to it
for action.   Whenever the appointed hour for meeting arrived
Mr. Chandler was always in his seat, while its other members but

12

rarely displayed anything like his promptitude. It annoyed the
chairman to have any one late, and it was his custom to proceed
with business as soon as a quorum was present, or if no quorum
appeared within fifteen or twenty minutes, to assume that there
was one and commence work; no protests against this course
were ever made by the tardy or absent members. The location
of the room of the Senate Committee on Commerce during Mr.
Chandler's whole term of Senatorial service was in the northwest corner of the capitol, on the floor leading to the galleries.
Its windows look down upon the city of Washington, with the
broad, historic Potomac and the forest-crowned Virginia hills in
the distance, and the sunset view from them — including the blue
glimmering river, the golden gossamer clouds, the green foliage
upon the brow of the hills in the extreme horizon — could never
be excelled in an artist's most vivid conception.

The first bill reported by Mr. Chandler as chairman of the
Committee on Commerce was one to provide for the collection
of duties on imports and for other purposes. He brought it in
five days after the appointment of the committee at the first
session of the Thirty-seventh Congress, and asked that it should
be put upon its passage at once. A single objection carried it
over under the rules until the next day, when it was passed by
a vote of 36 to 6. The scope of the bill was extensive. It
provided for confiscating to the United States all vessels belonging to rebels, for closing ports of entry in rebellious States, and
for the employment of additional revenue cutters. It also authorized the President under certain circumstances to declare by
proclamation States, sections, or parts of States, in insurrection
against the United States, and prohibited all commercial intercourse between such insurrectionary States, or parts of States,
and the rest of the Union so long as the insurrection should
continue. It was thus among the earliest and most important of
the war measures.

It is not necessary to occupy space with the details* of the enormous mass of business transacted by the Senate Committee on Commerce during Mr. Chandler's chairmanship. It was in those years that the sentiment of every section, in favor of extending the fostering care of the government to the aid of internal commerce, was consolidated and organized until it bore down all opposition and completely reversed the general policy and practice of the United States. How important and complete this revolution was will appear from the table of the appropriations for river, harbor and kindred improvements made at successive Congressional sessions since the foundation of the republic.

Mr. Chandler was the firm friend of an intelligently - planned and general system of internal improvements. His labors, and those of men like him, have borne fruit in manifold aids to commerce scattered over river, lake and ocean — light - houses, break - waters, harbors of refuge, straightened and deepened chan-

---

* Mr. Chandler entered the Senate when Congress was under the control of Democratic majorities. He was in the minority, but he never feared to assert his views, and denounce measures of doubtful advantage to the best interests of the country. The policy of the dominant party had been uniformly adverse to internal improvements — especially to making appropriations for harbor and river improvements. Soon after taking his seat, Mr. Chandler brought this important subject before the Senate, and insisted upon the necessity of fostering and aiding internal commerce. He introduced several measures, with this object in view. . . These improvements were not then considered ; but his vigorous speeches and persistent efforts subsequently compelled their partial recognition, and Mr. Chandler was placed on the Committee of Commerce, of which he was made chairman when the Republican party came into power, and so continued to the end of his Senatorial labors. It is not too much to say, for it is only the truth, that to Mr. Chandler's untiring zeal in this capacity, the country is indebted for many of those magnificent harbor and river improvements, which have been made since the Republican party came into power. Says a recent writer — an excellent authority : "The evidences of their "utility are seen on every hand, scattered along our seaboard, along our extended lake "coast, and upon all our rivers. The beneficent effects of these improvements are demon "strated by our vastly - increased and increasing commerce, its greater safety, the economy "with which the work is performed, the extraordinary development of our agricultural "and mineral resources and the increased compensation of productive labor." . . . Reference is thus made to Mr. Chandler's efforts in behalf of those great internal improve ments in aid of the commerce and internal development of the country, in order to demonstrate his peculiar fitness for the position which he has just been commissioned to fill. — *Editorial of the Washington Chronicle of Oct. 20, 1875, announcing the appointment of Zachariah Chandler as Secretary of the Interior.*

TABLE GIVING THE TOTAL AMOUNT OF MONEY APPROPRIATIONS BY CONGRESS FOR THE IMPROVEMENT OF RIVERS AND HARBORS AND THE CONSTRUCTION OF SHIP-CANALS SINCE THE BEGINNING OF THE GOVERNMENT:

	YEARS.	AMOUNT.		YEARS.		AMOUNT.
Monroe	1822*	$34,200	Pierce	1853		$000
	1823	6,150		1854		140,000
	1824	145,000		1855		....
J. Q. Adams	1825	40,600		1856†		775,000
	1826	88,900	Buchanan	1857		....
	1827	160,200		1858		....
	1828	565,300		1859		....
Jackson	1829	254,200		1860		....
	1830	377,600	Lincoln	1861		....
	1831	637,000		1862		....
	1832	693,500		1863		....
	1833	546,300		1864		537,500
	1834	791,200	Johnson	1865		23,000
	1835	505,200		1866		3,579,700
	1836	1,198,200		1867		4,816,300
Van Buren	1837	1,681,700		1868		1,601,500
	1838	1,467,200	Grant	1869		2,200,000
	1839	18,000		1870		4,173,900
	1840	....		1871		5,047,000
Tyler	1841	17,500		1872		5,603,000
	1842	....		1873		6,102,900
	1843	233,000		1874		5,282,500
	1844	701,500		1875		6,643,500
Polk	1845	7,000		1876		5,213,000
	1846	....	Hayes	1877		....
	1847	14,220		1878		8,337,000
	1848	....		1879		7,912,600
Taylor-Fillmore	1849	20,000				
	1850	....				
	1851	....		TOTAL,		$80,292,270
	1852	2,099,300				

(Bracket spanning 1861–1875: Term of Z. Chandler as Chairman of the Senate Committee on Commerce.)

NOTES.

This table only includes $750,000 of the $5,250,000 appropriated to pay Capt. James B. Eads for the jetty improvements at the mouth of the Mississippi.

The total of these appropriations during the years of Mr. Chandler's term as chairman was $45,610,800, or more than one-half of the entire amount.

* There were no appropriations for these purposes prior to 1822.

† This sum was contained in bills which were passed over the President's veto and included the first appropriation for the St. Clair Flats

nels, ship - canals and improved natural highways. He was prompt to recognize the claims of all sections, but was especially vigilant in regard to the necessities of the Northwest, and his memory will long be cherished throughout the region of the Great Lakes as that of the most ardent and efficient champion of its commercial development.

CHAPTER XI

THE news of the election of Abraham Lincoln to the Presidency of the United States — through strictly constitutional methods, by a large majority of the electoral vote and by a plurality of over half a million in the popular vote — was received with cheering and expressions of joy in many of the Southern cities. The men who exulted there were those who believed that with this pretext sectional passion could be kindled into instant rebellion, and they at once set about the work of consummating disunion before the close of the term of the traitorous and imbecile administration of James Buchanan. On Nov. 12, 1860, South Carolina ordered the election of a convention to take the formal step of secession, and the other cotton States promptly followed its example. Congress met on the 3d of December, and listened to a message from President Buchanan, in which he said: "After much serious reflection I "have arrived at the conclusion that no power to coerce into "submission a State which is attempting to withdraw, or has "actually withdrawn, from the confederacy, has been delegated "to Congress or to any other department of the Federal govern- "ment. It is manifest upon an inspection of the constitution "that this is not among the specific and enumerated powers "granted to Congress; and it is equally apparent that its exer- "cise is not 'necessary and proper for carrying into execution' "any one of these powers." On December 20 South Carolina adopted its ordinance of secession. Mississippi did likewise on

Jan. 9, 1861, Florida on January 10, Alabama on January 11, Georgia on January 18, Louisiana on January 26, and Texas on February 1. On Feb. 4, 1861, a convention of delegates from the seceding States met in the city of Montgomery and proceeded to form and organize the "Southern Confederacy." These events were attended by popular demonstrations throughout the South, in which the Union was denounced with unstinted bitterness and its power defied with the utmost audacity, and by the active drilling of the local militia and the organization of large bodies of armed men. More than all this, the officers of the United States in that section abandoned their positions, and sub-treasuries, post-offices, large sums of money, arsenals, arms, ammunition, fortifications, and vessels of the United States were seized in all the leading cities of the South, and used to prepare for war upon the power from which they had been stolen. The value of the government property thus confiscated by the rebels before the nation fired a shot was not less than $30,000,000. On Jan. 5, 1861, the United States steamer Star of the West was fired upon in the harbor of Charleston and driven out to sea, and within that month a bloodless siege of Fort McRae at Pensacola compelled its surrender to rebel forces by a United States garrison. Amid these events the traitors in Buchanan's Cabinet boldly resigned their portfolios, and Southern Congressmen with insolent words left their seats at the capitol "to join their States." The President himself was fitly described by Henry Winter Davis as "standing paralyzed and stupefied amid "the crash of the falling republic, still muttering, 'Not in my "time; not in my time; after me the deluge.'"

There were three ways of meeting these overt acts of high treason, namely: (1.) Submitting, either by sympathy and connivance, by frank surrender, or by an equally effective supineness. (2.) Meekly offering to rampant rebellion the bribe of fresh concessions to slavery. (3.) Treating armed secession as treason and its promoters as traitors, and dealing with it and them as such. The first method did not lack for supporters outside of the South. Thousands of Northern Democrats justified secession and promised the cotton States support. Their papers predicted that in case of war "it would be fought in the North,"* that "no Democrat would be found to raise an arm against his brethren of the South," † and that "if troops should be raised "in the North to march against the people of the South, a fire "in the rear would be opened upon such troops which would "either stop their march altogether or wonderfully accelerate it."* The Mayor of the great city of New York suggested in his annual message that that metropolis might well consider if the time did not seem to be at hand when it could profitably throw off allegiance to the United States and erect itself into "a free city." In public meetings and in party conventions like utterances were heard and applauded, all justifying the declaration of Lawrence M. Keitt in the city of Charleston that "there are a "million of Democrats in the North who, when the Black "Republicans attempt to march upon the South, will be found a "wall of fire in their front." These sympathizers with rebellion were reinforced by the holders of anti-coercion theories, by commercial timidity, and — most unexpectedly — by some Republican sentiment in favor of permitting peaceful separation rather than facing civil war. This sentiment was fortunately short-lived and not cowardly in its origin, but it found an advocate in, and was given public expression by, the most influential Republican journalist of that period, Horace Greeley, and it did much to encourage rebel arrogance and to distract the national councils. But that was the most numerous class which comprised the men who proposed to meet actual civil war with servile tenders to traitors in arms of new guarantees for slavery and with humble petitions for their acceptance. With the meeting

---

* Detroit, Mich. "Free Press." † Bangor, Me., "Union."

of Congress in December, 1860, these gentlemen became the conspicuous figures at Washington, and for three months labored industriously upon compromise schemes, every one of which was, in its essence, a proposition that Freedom should do homage to Slavery, and that the verdict of the people at the polls should be shamefully reversed to placate men who had deliberately plotted treason, and who again and again rejected with frank contempt offers of "conciliation." There were some who co-operated in these movements for the sake of gaining time and keeping the border States out of rebellion until Abraham Lincoln was inaugurated, but the great source of the compromise clamor of that winter was either some feeling of friendliness to the slave power or moral flaccidity.

It need not be said that Mr. Chandler was not found in either of these classes. For three years he had regarded this crisis as imminent. He did not believe that the South would now abandon its cherished dream of independent empire for any compromise. He did not propose to shrink back one inch before armed rebellion or to surrender one iota of principle to traitorous threats. He went to Washington determined to maintain the supremacy of the government at every cost, to listen to no plans of concession, to offer to disunionists only the alternative of obedience to the constitution or the penalties of treason, and to labor incessantly to stir into indignant action the slumbering sentiment of nationality in the hearts of the Northern people. It is in such hours that men of his indomitable stamp step to the front, and he became at once a pioneer leader of that uncompromising and tireless spirit which was the citadel of the Union cause. He spoke but rarely on political questions during the last session of the Thirty-sixth Congress, but was active in all the Republican consultations of that eventful period. In them he steadfastly opposed any policy that savored of bending to or temporizing with rebellion, and in the face of not a little

Republican demoralization urged that the crisis should be met with the spirit of Jackson and of Cromwell. Speaking of this session he afterward said: "If I could have had my way, when "treason was proclaimed on the floor of the Senate the traitor "would never have gone free from the capitol." With the Southern leaders he was frank in his denunciations of their course and plans. In a chance conversation at this time with the craftiest of their number, Slidell of Louisiana, he asked how the pending struggle would end, and Slidell replied, "Oh, we will all go out, and the Union will be broken up."

"And what are you going to do with the mouth of the Mississippi?" said Mr. Chandler.

"We will, of course, have to seize and hold that," was the answer, "but we will not tax your commerce."

To this, Mr. Chandler's indignant response was, "We own "that river, Mr. Slidell; we bought and paid for it; and, by "the Eternal, we are going to keep it. It was a desert when "we bought it, and we will make it a desert again before we "will let you steal it from us."

Mr. Chandler labored assiduously to thwart the plots of the rebel leaders, and to make such preparation as was possible for the coming strife. It was at this time that he formed that close intimacy with Edwin M. Stanton, which continued until the death of "the Carnot of the United States." Mr. Stanton, as the Attorney-General of the Buchanan Cabinet in its closing months, rendered service of the largest value to the nation by urging vigorous measures on his imbecile chief, by boldly confronting the traitors who were among his colleagues, and by secretly and promptly informing the Republican leaders of each new development of the disunion conspiracy as revealed in Cabinet consultations. His information and counsels furnished sure guidance at a time of the greatest peril, and, this it was that led to the early appointment by Mr. Lincoln to the Secretaryship of

War of a man whom the public then chiefly knew as a minor Cabinet officer in a detested administration. Mr. Chandler always rated Mr. Stanton's services to the Union cause in the early months of 1861 as second only in value to his herculean labors in the War Department; placed the highest estimate upon his ability, vigor, and patriotism; aided greatly in securing his appointment and confirmation as one of Mr. Lincoln's Cabinet; remained his firm friend and counselor, and was largely instrumental in obtaining from President Grant the nomination to the justiceship of the Supreme Court which so shortly preceded his death. It was also at this time that Mr. Chandler began to distrust the political fidelity of Mr. Seward, whose spoken suggestions of compromise and whose persistent negotiations with rebel emissaries, however diplomatic in origin and intent, were fruitful sources of Southern hope and Northern weakness. Time increased rather than diminished this dislike, and Mr. Chandler was always an impatient critic of Mr. Seward's influence upon the Lincoln administration, and saw in the course of the Secretary of State of Andrew Johnson's Cabinet only the fulfillment of his own suspicions and predictions.

The secret history of these exciting days, teeming with incident and concealing many startling revelations, has yet been but sparingly written; it is doubtful if the veil will ever be more than slightly lifted. Mr. Chandler himself guarded scrupulously from public knowledge much that was well known to him and a few associates and would have shed light on the hidden springs of actions of vast moment. This class of information he treated as state secrets, whose perishing with the actors in the great drama was desirable for public reasons. A well-known Washington journalist, who dined one day with Mr. Chandler and Mr. Wade, and listened with interest to their reminiscences of "war times," suggested to these gentlemen that their recollections should be recorded while they were still fresh for the

benefit of history, and did succeed at first in obtaining their
consent to an arrangement by which the two "war Senators"
were to devote one evening in each week to the relation of the
inside history of the period between the fall of 1860 and the
end of Johnson's administration. These narratives were to be
taken down by a stenographer, whose notes were to be written
out, carefully compiled, and subjected to the revision of Messrs.
Chandler and Wade. The manuscript was then to be sealed and
placed in such keeping as should make it certain that it would
not be published until the lapse of many years. On the
following Saturday night the literary gentleman was promptly at
Mr. Chandler's residence with the stenographer. Mr. Wade
shortly afterward came in, and at once said: "I have been
"thinking this matter over, Chandler, and you must allow me to
"decline. There is no use in telling what we know unless we
"tell *the whole truth*, and if I tell the whole truth I shall blast
"too many reputations. These things would be interesting and
"valuable if they were preserved in a book, but they would not
"be as valuable as the reputations that would be destroyed. The
"days we were going to talk about were exciting days, when
"good men made mistakes, and their mistakes ought to be for-
"gotten." Mr. Chandler promptly assented, and the reminiscences were never written.

In the Senate at this time Mr. Chandler's course was bold
and straightforward. On Feb. 19, 1861, he denounced on its
floor "traitors in the Cabinet and imbeciles in the Presidential
chair." He steadfastly opposed the Crittenden Compromise, well
described by Charles Sumner as "the great surrender to slavery,"
and the circumstances of his opposition to "the Peace Congress"
attracted national attention then and afterward. The Legislature of Virginia in January, 1861, adopted resolutions inviting
a conference of delegates from the various States to meet at
Washington on February 4, and consider how the pending

"unhappy controversy" could be adjusted by (of course) some plan giving "to the people of the slaveholding States adequate guarantees for the security of their rights." Twenty-two States answered this invitation, and their representatives, presided over by John Tyler, deliberated in Washington for nineteen days, and in the end recommended to Congress a so-called "compromise measure," which was thus justly characterized at the time: "Forbearing all details, it will be enough to say that they under- "took to give to slavery positive protection in the constitution, "with new sanction and immunity — making it, notwithstanding "the determination of the fathers, national instead of sectional; "and, even more than this, making it one of the essential and "permanent parts of our republican system." Its origin and its avowed object made this body distrusted from the outset by the sincere anti-slavery men, who did not believe that it could accomplish anything except to still farther debauch the public mind of the North. The result proved that it was called in the interest of slavery, and was designed to strengthen that system. Mr. Chandler from the outset opposed all Republican participation in this Congress, and, through the urgent recommendations of its Senators, Michigan was one of the five Northern States which did not send delegates. But after the Congress had met and was at work, it was thought that the friends of freedom on its floor might be able to accomplish something if they were increased in numbers, and accordingly application was made to Mr. Chandler and Mr. Bingham to procure the appointment by their State of delegates who could take their seats before final action was reached. Under such circumstances those gentlemen telegraphed to Lansing a request for the appointment of a delegation, and followed the message up with letters of the same tenor, which, although in the nature of private communications to Governor Blair, were shown at Lansing, and soon appeared in the newspapers; they were as follows:

WASHINGTON, Feb. 11, 1861.

MY DEAR GOVERNOR : Governor Bingham and myself telegraphed you on Saturday, at the request of Massachusetts and New York, to send delegates to the Peace or Compromise Congress. They admit that we were right and that they were wrong; that no Republican States should have sent delegates but they are here, and cannot get away. Ohio, Indiana and Rhode Island are caving in, and there is danger of Illinois; and now they beg of us for God's sake to come to their rescue, and save the Republican party from rupture. I hope you will send *stiff-backed* men or none. The whole thing was gotten up against my judgment and advice, and will end in thin smoke. Still I hope as a matter of courtesy to some of our erring brethren, that you will send the delegates. Truly your friend,   Z. CHANDLER.

His Excellency Austin Blair.

P. S. Some of the manufacturing States think a fight would be awful. Without a little blood-letting, this Union will not, in my estimation, be worth a rush.

WASHINGTON, Feb. 10, 1861.

DEAR SIR : When Virginia proposed a convention in Washington, in reference to the disturbed condition of the country, I regarded it as another effort to debauch the public mind and a step toward obtaining that concession which the imperious slave power so insolently demands. I have no doubt, at present, but that was the design. I was therefore pleased that the Legislature of Michigan was not disposed to put herself in a position to be controlled by such influences. The convention has met here, and within a few days the aspect of things has materially changed. Every free State, I think, except Michigan and Wisconsin, is represented, and we have been assured by friends upon whom we can rely, that, if those two States should send delegations of true, unflinching men, there would probably be a majority in favor of the constitution as it is, who would frown down the rebellion by the enforcement of laws. These friends have urged us to recommend the appointment of delegates from our State, and in compliance with their request, Mr. Chandler and myself telegraphed to you last night. It cannot be doubted that the recommendations of this convention will have a very considerable influence upon the public mind and upon the action of Congress. I have a great disinclination to any interference with what should properly be submitted to the wisdom and discretion of the Legislature, in which I place great reliance. But I hope I shall be pardoned for suggesting that it may be justifiable and proper by any honorable means to avert the lasting disgrace which will attach to a free people who, by the peaceful exercise of the ballot, have just released themselves from the tyranny of slavery, if they should now succumb to treasonable threats, and again submit to a degrading thraldom. If it should be deemed proper to send delegates, I think if they could be here by the 20th it would be in time. I have the honor, with much respect, to be, Yours truly,

K. S. BINGHAM.

The Legislature of Michigan refused to follow even these recommendations (although an effort to make the two Senators themselves delegates received a strong support), and that State was not represented at any stage of the abortive Peace Congress. On the 27th of February Senator Powell of Kentucky presented to the Senate newspaper copies of these letters, and then moved to lay aside the army appropriation bill which was pending, in order that the Senate could proceed at once to amend the constitution. He added that it might "better be at that than be "appropriating money to support an army that is to be engaged, "it seems, in the work of blood-letting." Mr. Chandler followed by stating that the letter was a private one of which no copy had been preserved, but that whether the printed copy was accurate or not he adopted it as his, and would at another time speak on the questions it involved. He added: "The people of "Michigan are opposed to all compromises. They do not believe "that any compromise is necessary; nor do I. They are pre- "pared to stand by the constitution of the United States as it "is, to stand by the government as it is; aye, sir, to stand by "it to blood if necessary." On the 2d of March Mr. Chandler made his promised speech in reply to Mr. Powell. He com- menced: "I desire to ask the Senator whether, after we have "adopted this or any other compromise, he is prepared to go "with me, and with the Union-loving men of this nation, for "enforcing the laws of the United States in the thirty-four "States of this Union." Powell's response was: "I am for "enforcing the laws in all the States that are within the "Union, but I am opposed to making war on the States that "are without the Union. I am opposed to coercing the seceded "States. . . . We have no right, under the constitution, to "make war on those States." Upon this frank admission from one of its most ardent advocates of the utter fruitlessness of compromise, this confession that it would be a sale without consideration, Mr. Chandler's comment was: "That is just what I "expected; it is just what I want the North to know; that "those men who profess to be for the Union with an 'if' are "against it under all circumstances." He then quoted the letter of Thomas Jefferson written at Paris on Nov. 13, 1787, to Colonel Smith, and closing as follows:

> And what country can preserve its liberties if the rulers are not warned from time to time that the people preserve the spirit of resistance ? Let them take up arms ! The remedy is to set them right as to facts ; pardon and pacify them. What signify a few lives lost in a century or two ? The Tree of Liberty must be refreshed from time to time with the blood of patriots and tyrants. It is its natural manure.

And with this authority of Thomas Jefferson on "a little blood-letting" as his text, Mr. Chandler spoke nearly an hour, denouncing the treason about him with unsparing vigor and branding the Democracy as responsible for the impending crime against the nation. In the face of such distempers he did not hesitate to pronounce war for the suppression of rebellion the only adequate remedy. The tone and style of this speech will appear from these extracts:

> This is not a question of compromise. It is a question whether we have or have not a government. If we have a government it is capable of making itself respected abroad and at home. If we have not a government, let this miserable rope of sand which purports to be a government perish, and I will shed no tears over its destruction. Sir, General Washington reasoned not so when the whisky rebellion broke out in Pennsylvania ; he called out the *posse comitatus* and enforced the laws. General Jackson reasoned not so when South Carolina in 1832 raised the black flag of rebellion ; he said : "By the Eternal, I will hang them;" and he would have done it.
>
> After these illustrious examples, we are told that six States have seceded, and the Union is broken up, and all we can do is to send commissioners to treat with traitors with arms in their hands ; treat with men who have fired upon your flag ; treat with men who have seized your custom-houses, who have erected batteries upon your great navigable waters, and who now stand defying your authority ! What will be the result of such a treaty ? You would stand disgraced before the nations of the earth, your naval officers would be insulted by the Algerines, your bonds would not be worth the paper on which they are written, to-morrow. If you submitted to this degradation

your government would stand upon a par with the governments of South America and the Central American States.

Sir, I will never submit to this degradation. If the right is conceded to any State to secede from the Union, without the consent of the other States, I am for immediate dissolution ; and if the State which I have the honor in part to represent will not follow that advice, I, for one, upon my own responsibility and alone, will resign my seat in this body, and leave this government, so soon as I can prepare the small matters I shall have to arrange, *for emigration to some country where they have a government.* I would rather join the Comanches ; *I will never live under a government that has not the power to enforce its laws.* . . . I see before me some of those men who have been fighting this corrupt organization (the Democratic party) for the last twenty years, who now turn about in dismay at the threatened disruption of the government. Why are they terror - stricken ? Why do they not stand firm and denounce you as infamously connected with a plundered treasury instead of cowering before your threats ? This thing has gone far enough. . . . Sir, this Union is to stand ; it will stand when your great - grandchildren and mine shall have grown gray ; aye, when they shall have gone to their last account, and their great - grandchildren shall have grown gray. But the traitors who are to - day plotting against this Union are to die. I do not say, literally, that they are all to die personally and absolutely ; but they are soon to pass from the stage, and better and purer men are to take their places. God grant that that consummation, "so devoutly to be wished," may be early accomplished ! . . .

For the Union - loving men of this nation, for the true patriots of the land, there is no reasonable concession that I would not most cheerfully make; but for those men who profess to be Union men and who are Union men with an "if" ; who will take all the concessions we will give them — all that they demand — and then turn about and say "your Union is dissolved," I have no respect ; and for them I will do nothing. For the men who love this Union, who are prepared to march to the support of the Union, who will stand up in defense of the old flag under which their fathers fought and gloriously triumphed, I have not only the most profound respect, but to their demands I can scarce conceive anything that I would not yield. But, sir, when traitorous States come here and say, unless you yield this or that established principle or right, we will dissolve the Union, I would answer in brief words — no concession, no compromise ; aye, give us strife even to blood before yielding to the demands of traitorous insolence.

This "blood letter" (as it was commonly termed) Mr. Chandler was often called upon to meet in the course of his subsequent public life, and he never failed to justify its writing or to stand by its language. In the extra session of the Senate

13

in March, 1861, John C. Breckenridge alluded to "Senatorial threats of blood-letting," and Mr. Chandler retorted by re-reading Jefferson's letter and re-asserting the purpose to meet attempted treason with force. In the last session of the Thirty-seventh Congress (on Feb. 13, 1863) William A. Richardson of Illinois said in a debate upon a war loan measure:

> The Senator from Michigan, at the outset of this controversy, declared in a letter to the Governor of the State of Michigan, that this government was not worth a rush without some blood-letting. Standing in array against all our history for seventy years, standing in array against the peace of the country for seventy years, the constitution itself in every proceeding from that time to this being but compromise, he declared at the outset against any compromise for the peace of the country, and he is responsible to a very large extent for the arbitrament of war that is now upon us. He is responsible for those consequences that are now flowing to us from the position assumed then strongly by him at the head of a dominant party in the country.

Mr. Chandler was prompt in meeting this attack, and said:

> Mr. President: I do not propose to-day to go over my record. It has been made before the country and the world. There let it stand. So far as my loyalty and devotion to the country are concerned, I doubt if any man ever seriously attempted to cast suspicion on them. But, as I said before, my record is made. I stand upon it and am proud of it in all its entirety. The Senator alluded to the blood-letting letter, as it is called in Michigan. That letter has been discussed before the people of that State. Thousands and tens of thousands, and, for aught I know, hundreds of thousands of copies of it, were scattered broadcast throughout that State. What were the circumstances under which that letter was written? We had traitors in this body proclaiming from day to day that this government was then destroyed, and there was no rebuke from the Senator of Illinois or his friends. There was no rebuke from the administration then in power, whom he aided in placing there. They proclaimed that the government was entirely destroyed; and that it should never be restored. Senators proclaimed on this floor that you might give them a blank sheet of paper and allow them to fill it as they pleased, and still they would not live with us under the same government. . . . Here in this hall and in the other chamber, and on the streets wherever you went, you heard traitors declare that the government was ended, declare that if you attempted to coerce the rebel States it would lead to war. I believed then, as I believe now, that they intended to break up this government; that they intended a disruption of the nation. And I believed then, as I believe now, that without the intervention of armed force to put down armed rebels and traitors, your government was destroyed. Believing it, I so wrote to the

governor of a sovereign State—a confidential note, it is true, but that is of no account. I stand by that letter precisely as it was written. A majority of the people of this nation believe to-day, as I believed then, that there was and could be but one way to save the nation, and that was by putting down armed rebels by force. That is what I believed then, what I believe now.

Another thing the Senator says: Nobody is more responsible for this bloody and wicked war than myself. Mr. President, let us look a little into the matter of responsibility. There is a responsibility somewhere, and a fearful responsibility, for this rebellion and this dreadful war, but that responsibility is not upon my soul. . . . You may go through all the ranks of rebeldom, aye, sir, you may take all the officers of your regular army, who have deserted by hundreds and violated their oath, and gone into the ranks of the enemy, and are fighting to overturn the government; go and poll the whole of them, and you cannot find one that ever co-operated with me politically. They are all Democrats, every man. Yes, sir, and go among the officers of the navy who have deserted and gone over to the enemy, and are now fighting against their flag and attempting to overturn this government; poll them, and among all the hundreds of them you cannot find a single Republican—not one. No, sir, they are all Democrats, every man. You may go and poll the whole four or five hundred thousand men the rebels have now in arms against this government, and you cannot find a man who was ever a Republican or who even sympathized with the Republicans. They are all Democrats or "Union men" such as we had here two years ago, men who had professed to be for the Union when their hearts were with the enemies of the government. Sir, go among the Northern sympathizers with the rebellion, the men who are proclaiming to-day that this government is overturned, and that it will never be restored, who are to-day denouncing your currency and saying that your money is not worth the paper upon which it is written; search through all the sympathizers with this rebellion, and you cannot find a man who ever co-operated with me politically—not one. They are Democrats, but yet, forsooth, I am responsible for this war. . . . I have no responsibility for this rebellion, nor have the party with which I act. We have with perfect unanimity, in every instance, come up to the support of the government. When the government demanded 400,000 men, every single individual on this side of the house voted to give them 500,000 men. And when they demanded $400,000,000 to support the government, every man on this side of the house voted to give them $500,000,000 to save the nation. Sir, we have been ready under all circumstances to make any and every sacrifice so that this nation might be saved. Our armies are in large force and ably commanded; they are ready to advance and crush the hydra-headed monster of rebellion. Aye, sir, but we have an enemy insidious and dangerous. The seat of the rebellion is to-day not in Richmond, it is among the copper-headed traitors of the North, and if this government is overturned, if we should fail in saving the government, it will be, not from the force of rebels in our front, but because of the accursed traitors in our rear.

In the course of a debate in the Senate on Feb. 16, 1866, upon reconstruction topics, Thomas A. Hendricks of Indiana said:

When the good and the patriotic, North and South, representing the yearning hearts of the people at home, came here in the winter and spring of 1861, in a peace congress, if possible to avoid this dreadful war, then the Senator from Michigan announced to his Governor and the country that this Union was scarcely worth preserving without some blood-letting. His cry before the war was for blood. Allow me to say that when the Senator's name is forgotten because of anything he says or does in this body, in future times it will be borne down upon the pages of history as the author of the terrible sentiment that the Union of the people that our fathers had cemented by the blood of the Revolution and by the love of the people; that that Union, resting upon compromise and concession, resting upon the doctrine of equality to all sections of the country; that that Union which brought us so much greatness and power in the three-quarters of a century of our life; that that Union which had brought us so much prosperity and greatness until we were the mightiest and proudest nation on God's footstool; that that grand Union was not worth preserving unless we had some blood-letting. Mr. President, it is not the sentiment of the Senator's own heart; it is the expression of a bitter political hostility; but it will carry him down to immortality; he is sure of living in history; he has gained that much by it.

To this Mr. Chandler's response was instant. He said:

The Senator from Indiana has arraigned me upon an old indictment for having written a certain letter in 1861. It is not the first time I have been arraigned on that indictment of "blood-letting." I was arraigned for it upon this floor by the traitor John C. Breckenridge, and I answered the traitor John C. Breckenridge, and after I gave him his answer he went out to the rebel ranks and fought against our flag. I was arraigned by another Senator from Kentucky, and by other traitors upon this floor; I expect to be arraigned again. I wrote the letter, and I stand by the letter and what is in it. What was the position of the country when the letter was written? The Democratic party as an organization had arrayed itself against this government—a Democratic traitor in the Presidential chair, and Democratic traitors in every department of this government, Democratic traitors preaching treason upon this floor and preaching treason in the hall of the other House, Democratic traitors in your army and in your navy, Democratic traitors controlling every branch of this government. Your flag was fired upon and there was no response. The Democratic party had ordained that this government should be over-thrown, and I, a Senator from the State of Michigan, wrote to the Governor of that State "unless you are prepared to shed blood for the preservation of this great government the government is overthrown." That is all there was in that letter. That I said, and that I say again. And I tell that Senator, if he is prepared to go down in history with the Democratic traitors who then co-operated with him, I am prepared to go down on that "blood-letting" letter, and I stand by the record as made.

Because I wrote to the Governor of my State that unless he was prepared to shed blood for the preservation of this government it was overthrown, now I am to be arraigned as going down to be remembered in history! Yes, sir, I shall be remembered, and I am proud of the record. May it stand, and stand as long as this government stands! When that Senator and the men who co-operated with him shall have gone, down to eternal infamy my record will be brilliant.

In the closing session of Mr. Chandler's Congressional service Senator Benjamin H. Hill of Georgia, in the course of a reply (on May 10, 1879) to a declaration of his on the previous day that "there were twelve Senators on the other side whose seats were obtained and are held by fraud and violence," again read and commented upon "the blood letter." Mr. Chandler promptly answered as follows:

Mr. President, this is the fourth time since 1861 that allusion has been made to a letter written by me to the Governor of the State of Michigan; first it appeared in a newspaper published in Detroit; a copy was sent to me and a copy was likewise sent to the late Senator Powell. The letter was a private note written to the Governor and no copy retained. Senator Powell approached me with his copy of the letter and asked if it was correct. I told him I did not know; I had written to the Governor of Michigan a private note and had kept no copy and could not say whether this was correct or not. He told me that if it was a correct copy he would wish to make use of it, and if it was not he did not propose to make use of it. I said, "Sir, I will adopt it, and you may make any use of it you please." So to-day that is my letter. If not originally written by me, it is mine by adoption.

And, Mr. President, what were the circumstances under which that letter was written? I had been in this body then nearly four years listening to treason day by day and hour by hour. The threat, the universal threat daily, hourly, was, "Do this or we will dissolve the Union; if you do not do that we will dissolve the Union." Treason was in the White House, treason in the Cabinet, treason in the Senate, and treason in the House of Representatives; bold, outspoken, rampant treason was daily and hourly uttered. The threat was made upon this floor in my presence by a Senator, "You may "give us a blank sheet of paper and let us fill it up as we please, and then "we will not live with you." And another Senator stood here beside that Senator from Texas and said, "I stand by the Senator from Texas." Treason was applauded in the galleries of this body, and treason was talked on the streets, in the street cars, in private circles; everywhere it was treason — treason in your departments, traitors in the White House, traitors around these galleries, traitors everywhere!

The flag of rebellion had been raised; the Union was already dissolved, we were told; the rebel government was already established with its capital in Alabama; "and now we will negotiate with you," was said to us. Upon what basis would you negotiate? Upon what basis did you call your peace convention? With rampant rebellion staring us in the face! Sir, it was no time to negotiate. The time for negotiation was past.

Sir, this was the condition of affairs when that letter was written; and after Mr. Powell had made his assault upon me in this body for it I responded, relating what I have related here now with regard to it, and I said, "I stand by that letter," and I stand by it now. What was there in it then, and what is there in it now? The State of Michigan was known to be in favor of the constitution and the Union and the enforcement of the laws, even to the letting of blood if need be, and that was all there was and all there is in that letter. Make the most of it!

The Senator from Georgia says that I did not shed any blood. How much blood did he shed?* [Laughter.] Will somebody inform us the exact quantity of blood that the Senator from Georgia shed?

Mr. HILL, of Georgia: The difference between us is that I was not in favor of shedding anybody's blood.

Mr. CHANDLER: Nor I, except to punish treason and traitors. Sir, the Senator is not the man to stand up on this floor and talk about other men saving their own blood. He took good care to put his blood in Fort Lafayette where he was out of the way of rebel bullets as well as Union bullets. He is the last man to stand up here and talk to me about letting the blood of others be shed.

Mr. President, I was then, as I am now, in favor of the government of the United States. Then, as now, I abhorred the idea of State sovereignty over National sovereignty. Then, as now, I was prepared even to shed blood to save this glorious government. Then, as now, I stood up for the constitution and the Union. Then, as now, I was in favor of the perpetuity of this glorious government. But the Senator from Georgia, was, as he testified before a committee, "a Union secessionist." I have the testimony here before me. Will somebody explain what that means—"a Union secessionist?" Mr. President, I should like to see the dictionary wherein a definition can be found of "a Union secessionist!" I do not understand the term. He says they have the right to have a solid South, but a solid North will destroy the government. Why, Mr. President, the South is no more solid to·day than it was in 1857. . . . It has been solid ever since, and it was no quarrel with

---

*An allusion to the common report that, during a secret session of the Confederate Senate, William L. Yancey received injuries in a personal encounter with B. H. Hill from which he finally died.

the North that made it solid. It was solid because it was determined either to "rule or ruin" this nation. It tried the "ruin" scheme with arms ; and now, having failed to ruin this government with arms, it comes back to ruin it by withholding supplies to carry on the government. Sir, the men have changed since 1857. There is now but one member on this floor who stood here with me on the 4th of March, 1857. The men have changed, the measures not all. You then fought for the overthrow of this government, and now you vote and talk fo. the same purpose. You are to-.day, as you were then, determined either to rule or ruin this government, and you cannot do either.

This letter was also for years constantly quoted and denounced by the Democratic press of Michigan with the hope of by this means breaking the Senator's hold upon the confidence of the people of his State. He uniformly met these attacks, not only without the shadow of apology, but with the most emphatic defiance. On the stump he repeatedly declared that "that letter was a good one," that he would not qualify a sentence nor retract a word of it, that he "stood by it" without reservation, and that he believed when he wrote it and knew afterward that it pointed out the only path in which the nation could then walk with honor and with safety. Time has shown that Mr. Chandler was right and that the men who deprecated his boldness were wrong, and that the real statesmanship of the winter of 1860 – 61 was that which proposed not to parley with, but to draw the sword upon, "foul treason." The paper which at that time first printed "the blood letter" and made it the text for unsparing and constant denunciation of its author was edited by a man who grew to be one of the foremost of American journalists, and — always hostile to Republicanism — published in 1879 the chief Northwestern organ of Independent opinion, which said, in announcing Mr. Chandler's sudden death in its city: "To "superior intellectual endowments he united a force of will and "resolution of purpose that hesitated at no obstacle. Few men "ever displayed in a more remarkable degree the courage of "opinions. No dread of unpopularity, no fear of consequences,

"ever troubled him. His famous 'blood-letting letter,' written
"near the opening of the Southern rebellion, was a faithful
"manifestation of the man. When frightened party chiefs of
"the North were running up and down with peace propositions
"to placate Southern fire-eaters and patch up a new truce
"between free civilization and slave barbarism, Zach. Chandler
"stood up in his place in the Senate and in terms of intense,
"bitter scorn, denounced all such efforts as the pitiful manifesta-
"tions of political cowardice and folly. He had no word of
"regret to utter upon the departure of the Southern Senators;
"but told them that the North would whip them back, and that
"in their humiliation the bond of nationality would be strength-
"ened. He had no dread of the threatened blood-letting, but
"believed it to be the only way of curing the Southern ulcer,
"and that the nation would afterward be the healthier for it."
And

"Thus the whirligig of Time brings in his revenges."

CHAPTER XII.

ABRAHAM LINCOLN reached Washington on the 23d of February, 1861, having come from Harrisburg *incognito*, and in advance of the announced time, because of threats of assassination. Mr. Chandler was one of the first persons informed of his arrival, called upon him at once, and was in frequent consultation with him thereafter with reference to the formation of his Cabinet and the policy to be pursued toward the South. Mr. Chandler earnestly opposed placing any but the most uncompromising Union men at the head of the departments, urged bold and decisive measures toward armed traitors for the sake of the moral effect of such a course, and advised the most emphatic declarations in the inaugural of the President's intention to enforce the laws at all hazards. Mr Lincoln had seriously thought of inviting two gentlemen from the Southern States to seats in his Cabinet, the names chiefly considered by him being those of Alexander H. Stephens of Georgia, and James Guthrie of Kentucky. Mr. Chandler strongly opposed any such concession to the rampant disunionism of the slave States, and the hostility of the wing of the party with which he acted finally led Mr. Lincoln to abandon his original plan and select Edward Bates of Missouri and Montgomery Blair as the Southern members of the Cabinet. Mr. Chandler also advised that Breckenridge, Wigfall, and other avowedly disloyal Congressmen should be arrested at once, and urged that the "Secession Commissioners," when they came to Washington, should be dealt with summarily as traitors and not be permitted to even informally negotiate with the Administration.

He always believed that this summary treatment of rebellion at the outset would have greatly curtailed its dimensions, but the President was guided by Mr. Seward and others, whose counsels were different and who hoped to prevent the impending war by mildness. Accordingly the inaugural was almost apologetic in tone toward the South; throughout March, men like Stephen A. Douglas inquired whether the Administration meant peace or war; flagrant treason was still defiantly uttered on the floor of Congress, and John Forsyth and M. J. Crawford, embassadors from the "Confederacy," spent weeks in Washington holding relations with the new Secretary of State which, if not "official," looked like a concession in fact of the practical independence of the seceded States. The first official favor Mr. Chandler asked from President Lincoln was the appointment of his life-long friend, James M. Edmunds, as Commissioner of the General Land Office, and Mr. Edmunds was promptly nominated to that position and confirmed by the Senate.

At noon on March 4, 1861, Vice-President Hamlin took the chair of the Senate and directed the secretary to read this proclamation convening an extra session of that body:

BY THE PRESIDENT OF THE UNITED STATES:

A PROCLAMATION.

WHEREAS, Objects of interest to the United States require that the Senate should be convened at twelve o'clock on the 4th of March next, to receive and act upon such communications as may be made to it on the part of the Executive: Now, therefore, I, James Buchanan, President of the United States, have considered it to be my duty to issue this, my proclamation, declaring that an extraordinary occasion requires the Senate of the United States to convene for the transaction of business, at the capitol in the city of Washington, on the 4th day of March next, at twelve o'clock at noon on that day, of which all who shall at that time be entitled to act as members of that body are hereby required to take notice.

Given under my hand and the seal of the United States at Washington, the 11th day of February, in the year of our Lord one thousand eight hundred and sixty-one, and of the independence of the United States of America the eighty-fifth.   JAMES BUCHANAN.

[L. S.]

By the President: J. S. BLACK, *Secretary of State.*

Sixteen new Senators then took the oath of office, and at fifteen minutes past one o'clock James Buchanan and Abraham Lincoln entered the Senate chamber, arm in arm, accompanied by Senators Foote, Baker and Pearce, members of the Committee of Arrangements, and were conducted to seats in front of the secretary's desk. In a few moments afterward, those assembled in the Senate chamber proceeded to the platform on the central portico of the eastern front of the capitol, to listen to the inaugural address of the President elect. Then the oath of office was administered to him by the Chief Justice of the Supreme Court, and the administration of the government by the Republican party had commenced. The business of this extra session of the Senate was chiefly limited to the confirmation of executive appointments, although there were some exciting discussions upon the political situation. Mr. Chandler, on taking possession (as the new chairman) of the room of the Committee on Commerce, had his righteous wrath at the men who had availed themselves of their official positions to plot treason against the government still further stimulated by finding in one of the drawers of the large committee table the original draft of the secession ordinance of Alabama, which had been prepared in the national capitol by Senator Clement C. Clay, his predecessor in the chairmanship of the committee.* This illustration of Southern perfidy Mr. Chandler carefully kept, and at his death it was among his private papers. The executive session of the Senate closed on March 28, 1861, and Mr. Chandler at once returned to Detroit.

At 5.20 A. M. on April 12, 1861, a mortar in the rebel battery on Sullivan's Island in the harbor of Charleston fired a

---

* Mr. Clay (C. C. Clay, Jr., of Alabama), chairman of the Committee on Commerce, drew up in the room of that committee the original ordinance of secession for the State of Alabama, while he, a rebel traitor, was drawing the pay of this government. It was drawn upon government paper, written with government ink, and copied by a clerk drawing $6 a day from this government. I found it in that room and I have it now.—*Zachariah Chandler in the Senate, April 12, 1864.*

shell into Fort Sumter. This was the announcement to the world of the decision of the rebels to delay no longer, but to at once

"ope
"The purple testament of bleeding war."

On the 13th Major Anderson abandoned the unequal contest, and surrendered the blazing ruins of his fortress to Beauregard; on the 14th his garrison marched out with the honors of war; and on the 15th Abraham Lincoln called for 75,000 volunteers, a force which it was believed would trample out rebellion in ninety days. The North answered Charleston's cannon and the President's appeal with a magnificent assertion of its latent patriotism, and the war spirit flamed up in every State. On April 17 the business men of Detroit held a public meeting at the invitation of its Board of Trade, at which the firm purpose to support the government in its contest with treason was emphatically declared, and all needed assistance in troops and money was pledged. Senator Chandler escorted General Cass to this gathering, and their entrance, arm in arm, typifying as it did the solidification of the Union sentiment of the North, was followed by long-continued cheering. Both gentlemen spoke in tones of earnest loyalty and amid constant applause. That night the following letter was mailed to Washington:

DETROIT, April 17, 1861.

Hon. Simon Cameron.

DEAR SIR: One of the most distinguished Democrats in this country * says: "Don't defend Washington. Don't put batteries on Georgetown Heights, but shove your troops directly into Virginia, and quarter them there."

Stand by the Union men in Virginia and you will find plenty of them.

By this bold policy you will save Virginia to the Union as well as the other border States.

There is but one sentiment here. We will give you all the troops you can use. We will send you two regiments in thirty days, and 50,000 in thirty days more if you want them. General Cass subscribed $3,000 to equip the regiments.

_____

* This undoubtedly refers to Lewis Cass.

There are no sympathizers here with treason, and if there were we would dispense with their company forthwith. Your friend, Z. CHANDLER.

Michigan justified her Senator's pledges by promptly raising and equipping many more troops than the State was required to furnish under the call for 75,000 volunteers, and this correspondence soon followed:

DETROIT, April 21, 1861.

Hon. Simon Cameron.

MY DEAR CAMERON: . . . I will esteem it a very great favor if you will officially call for at least one more regiment to go to the front immediately from this State. You did not call for but one, but we have got two all ready, and have raised $100,000 by private subscription to equip them. Truly yours, Z. CHANDLER.

[REPLY.]

WASHINGTON, April 29, 1861.

Hon. Z. Chandler.

DEAR SIR: . . . It would give me great pleasure to gratify your wishes, but this can only be done in one way. The President has determined to accept no more for three months' service, but to add to the regular army twenty-five more regiments whose members shall agree to serve two years unless sooner discharged. This will enable the Department to accept another regiment from your State. Truly yours,

SIMON CAMERON, *Secretary of War.*

To this suggestion the response was prompt, and the enlistment of men and formation of companies for three years' service went briskly on, Michigan sending only one three-months' regiment to the field. Mr. Chandler was active in stimulating and organizing the war movements at home, both by untiring personal labor and by liberal subscriptions of money, until the first regiments were ready for marching orders. He was one of the speakers at an imposing Union meeting held in Detroit on April 25, with Lewis Cass in the chair, and he there said: " A " greater contest than the Revolutionary war is now about to " take place. It is to be tested whether a republican government " can stand or not. The eyes of all Europe are upon us, and we " will convince them that ours is the strongest government on

" earth." He also made an earnest, and in the end successful, effort to procure from the War Department such orders as should obtain for the Michigan men an opportunity for prompt service against the enemy. It was originally intended to send the regiments from his State to Cairo, but his influence accomplished a change in this plan and they were directed to report to Washington for immediate duty. In May Mr. Chandler went to the capital to aid in preparing for their reception and to urge upon the authorities, who were then declining the profuse offers of troops, the importance of accepting all the regiments tendered by his own and other States and of promptly attacking the constantly growing rebellion by invading its territory and interfering with the organization of its armies. On the 17th of May, 1861, the First Regiment of Michigan Volunteers arrived in Washington, Col. O. B. Willcox commanding. They were met at the depot by Senator Chandler and escorted to quarters he had aided in securing for them in a business block on Pennsylvania avenue. Mr. Chandler was active in providing for their comfort, purchased supplies for them out of his own private purse, was present at their parade when they were formally mustered into the service of the United States by Adjutant-General Thomas, and asked the Secretary of War to send them at once to the front for active duty. His request was complied with and this regiment was prominent in the ·first important military movement of the war.

After he had seen the Michigan troops well cared for, Mr. Chandler, on the 19th of May, in company with Senators Wade and Morrill and John G. Nicolay, the private secretary of President Lincoln, sailed for Fortress Monroe to visit General Butler, and see the condition of his newly-organized army. On the following day the party started to return on the steamer Freeborn, and as they were passing through Hampton Roads heard heavy cannonading, which proved to be an artillery duel between the steamer Monticello and a battery erected by the rebels at Sewell's Point, where the Elizabeth river empties into Hampton Roads. The Freeborn went at once to the assistance of the Monticello, and being of light draft approached within 300 yards of the battery and opened fire with her guns. The columbiads of the Virginians were soon disabled, and the rebels were scattered in every direction, Mr. Chandler pronouncing the spectacle "the best ball-playing he had ever seen." On her voyage up the Potomac the Freeborn seized two suspicious boats, and found them loaded with a company of fifty rebel soldiers on their way to join "the Confederate army." Both vessels were brought to the Navy Yard at Washington and they were the first prizes taken during the war, and the men on board were the first rebel prisoners captured.

On the night of the 23d of May, the Union forces at Washington crossed the Potomac and proceeded to seize and fortify advantageous positions on Virginia soil. The First Michigan accompanied the famous Zouave regiment by ferry-boats to Alexandria, taking possession of that city in the night. Mr. Chandler went with the Michigan men, and was the only civilian who was allowed to accompany this wing of the expedition. He was with a detachment of soldiers who surprised and captured a party of forty rebel dragoons, including four officers, and he was in Alexandria when Colonel Ellsworth fell and private Brownell instantly avenged his death. Of this event, since obscured by four years of carnage, but which then first brought to excited millions some sense of the dreadful realities of war, he was the first to bear the news to the authorities at Washington.

Mr. Chandler remained at the capital some weeks, working industriously in helping on the preparations for war, and urging the most vigorous and sweeping measures upon the Administration. He believed and said repeatedly that the call for 75,000 men for three months was a mistake. He was no opti-

mist, and never thought that a rebellion, so carefully organized
and left so long undisturbed, could be subdued without a
desperate and bloody struggle. He thought that 500,000 rather
than 75,000 volunteers should have been called for to serve
through the war, and judged that the effect of such a proclamation upon the country, and particularly upon the South,
would have been salutary, as showing the determination of
the government to crush the rebellion at once and forever.
While the raw levies of volunteers were massing in Washington
in May and June, there was a lamentable lack of discipline and
organization. The commissary department of the army was
feeble and inefficient, and there was a want of proper and sufficient food for the soldiers. Mr. Chandler's executive capacity
was very useful then to the Secretary of War in assisting in
the organization of a commissariat and in procuring supplies and
equipments, and he spent no small sum in obtaining food for
the soldiers when the regular rations were not forthcoming.
Although entirely without military training, Mr. Chandler's business experience, his quick perception, and his clear judgment
made his services at this period of confusion and mismanagement
of great value to the country. In June he returned to Michigan
for a few days, and on the 21st of that month spoke (with the
Hon. Charles M. Croswell) at Adrian, on the occasion of the
presentation by the ladies of that city of a stand of colors to a
volunteer regiment in camp there.

On the 4th of July, 1861, the Thirty-seventh Congress met
in extra session, and adjourned on the 6th of August, after
having enacted laws to increase the army and navy, and to
provide the means and authority necessary for the vigorous prose
cution of the war. The scope of the work undertaken by this
Congress was far greater than that of any preceding session.
Many of the members had but little experience in legislative
matters, but their patriotism was sincere and ardent, and their

acts embodied the national purpose to maintain the integrity of the republic at any cost. On the second day of the session Mr. Chandler said in the Senate:

I desire to give notice that I shall to-morrow or on some subsequent day introduce a bill to confiscate the property of all Governors of States, members of the Legislature, Judges of Courts, and all military officers above the rank of lieutenant who shall take up arms against the United States, or aid or abet treason against the government of the United States, and that said individual shall be forever disqualified from holding any office of honor, emolument or trust under this government.

This bill was introduced on July 15, and was referred to the Committee on the Judiciary; it reported back a measure of much narrower scope, which was passed, and is known as the confiscation act of 1861. The origin of Mr. Chandler's bill was the fact that John Y. Mason of Virginia, who had been expelled from the Senate for treason, owned a large amount of property in Pennsylvania, and so indignant were the people of the county in which it was located at his treachery, that a guard was kept over it constantly to prevent its destruction by a mob. Mr. Chandler believed it was important that the government should be enabled to legally seize for its own use such property as this; there were also many officers of the army and navy who were undecided whether to go with the rebellion or remain at their posts. He wished to add to the penalties of treason to affect them, as well as those wealthy citizens of Washington and Maryland who had formerly been in office and who sympathized with the rebellion and gave the South as much encouragement as they dared. His proposition proved then too vigorous to obtain the endorsement of his colleagues, but within a year its principle received Congressional sanction. During this session (on July 18) Mr. Chandler said in the Senate with characteristic force:

The Senator from Indiana says there are three parties in the country. I deny it, sir. There are but two parties, patriots and traitors — none others in

14

this body nor in the country. I care not what proposition may be brought up to save the Union, to preserve its integrity, patriots will vote for it; and I care not what proposition you may bring up to dissolve the Union, to break up this government, traitors will vote for that. And those are the only two parties there are in the Senate or the country.

It is not necessary to add that Mr. Chandler voted at this session for every measure to organize armies and to raise means for their maintenance, and that he favored at all times vigorous and summary measures in dealing with the enemies of the republic.

General McDowell's "invasion of Virginia" on May 23 was followed by several weeks of military inactivity on the Potomac, broken only by a dash of the Union cavalry into Fairfax Courthouse and the skirmish at Vienna, where a regiment of Ohio troops, who were backed on a railroad train into a rebel ambuscade, lost twenty men. On July 16 the Union army began a forward movement against the rebels who were found in position about and along a creek known as Bull Run. After a short and indecisive engagement on that day, General McDowell commenced to concentrate his forces for an attack on Beauregard's line, but various delays prevented any definite movement until Sunday, July 21. On that date was fought the battle of Bull Run, ending in a complete Union defeat, attended by severe losses and a panic-stricken retreat by many regiments, and followed by great national dismay and alarm. An inquiry into the blundering strategy, political half-heartedness, and poor generalship, which were the causes of this unnecessary and most serious reverse, are foreign to the purpose of this work. Mr. Chandler was one of a large number of members of Congress who joined the army on the eve of battle, and watched its progress to the final disaster. The First Michigan was among the regiments engaged in the thickest of the fight, and the Second and Third were in the brigade of Gen. I. B. Richardson, which acted as a rear-guard in the retreat of the army and prevented defeat from becoming a total rout. Mr. Chandler himself aided in halting and rallying the panic-stricken fugitives,* and reached Washington late at night, covered with mud and wearied with travel and hunger. He drove at once to the White House, where he found Mr. Lincoln despondent, exhausted with his labors, and greatly depressed by the defeat and the loss of life involved. Mr. Chandler urged upon the President the necessity of vigorous measures, the wisdom of calling for more troops, and the certainty that the North would follow the Administration in meeting a reverse with undismayed and redoubled energies. He asked Mr. Lincoln to issue an order for the enrolling of 500,000 men at once, "to show to the country and the rebels that the govern-" ment was not discouraged a whit, but was just beginning to "get mad." Mr. Chandler's vitality, the timely vigor of his bold words, and his overwhelming earnestness acted as a tonic upon the over-burdened Executive, and he left Mr. Lincoln cheered, encouraged and resolute. The governors of the loyal States were at once appealed to for more troops, and the answer of the North to Bull Run was the rush of tens of thousands of men into camp and the organization of great armies along the Potomac, the Ohio and the Mississippi. Secretary Stanton, who knew of this midnight interview, estimated its effect upon the course of events as of the utmost importance, and repeatedly said that Mr. Chandler's opportunely-manifested courage and vigor then saved the Union from a great peril.

In the task of re-organizing the army after Bull Run, of clearing Washington of fugitives, and of extracting order from

---

* Whatever credit there was in stopping the rout (at this point) is due wholly to Senators Chandler and Wade. and Representatives Blake. Riddle, and Morris. These gentle men, armed with Maynard rifles and navy revolvers, sprang from their carriages some three miles this side of Centreville. and, presenting their weapons. in loud voices commanded the fugitives to halt and turn back. Their bold and determined manner brought most at that point to a stand-still Many on horseback. who attempted to dash by them, had their horses seized by the bits. Some of the fugitives wno were armed menaced these gentle men. None. however. were permitted to pass until the arrival of the Second New Jersey Regiment, on its way to the battle-ground, turned back the flying soldiers and teamsters. —*Washington Intelligencer. July 22. 1861.*

chaos, Mr. Chandler rendered important aid to the authorities, and after the adjournment returned to Michigan and threw his strong energies into the work of raising and equipping troops. This letter (which was not followed by any practical results, owing to various causes) is of interest as showing the spirit of those days:

DETROIT, Aug. 27, 1861.

Hon. Simon Cameron, Secretary of War.

MY DEAR CAMERON : A Colonel Elliott, member of the Canadian Parliament, is desirous of raising a regiment of Canadian cavalry for the war against treason. I don't know how the Administration may look upon this proposition, but there are many reasons in favor of its acceptance.

1. Colonel Elliott is a brave and experienced officer.

2. He is in favor of the closest union between the Canadas and the United States, and believes that this fraternal union upon the battle-field would tend strongly to cement a yet closer connection.

3. It would satisfy England that hands-off was her best policy.

The moment it is proven that black men are used in the Southern army *against us*, I propose to recruit a few regiments of negroes in Canada myself to meet that enemy, and I think this would be an opening wedge for the movement of emancipation.

My colleague will introduce Colonel Elliott to you and explain more at length. Truly, your friend,   Z. CHANDLER.

To this same period also belongs this characteristic defense of his State and the Northwest against what Mr. Chandler believed — and with reason — to be an unjust statement:

To the Editor of the New York World:

My attention has been called to an article in your valuable and patriotic paper in which you say: "The extreme Northern States, from Maine to Mich- "igan, have not done their duty, and it is high time that State pride aroused "them to emulate the noble example of New York, Massachusetts, and Rhode "Island." As I am sure you would not willingly do injustice to Michigan, I ask you to state editorially, the population and the number of regiments in the field for the war from each of the States whose example is to be emulated. Michigan had at Bull Run one three-months' regiment (now recruiting and in for the war) and three regiments for the war, *and not a private soldier in camp in the State.* Since that time she has sent seven regiments for the war, making ten regiments now present in the army, in addition to which she furnished to other States over 2,000 men, *now in the field,* for the reason that the government would accept no more men from Michigan at that time, and the patriotic ardor of our citizens could not be restrained. We have now in camp nearly 4,000 men, and shall send two regiments this week and two more within a few days.

The Northwest has done her whole duty; how is it with the East? The Northwest has exceeded every call made upon her, and yet you lack men and are denuding over 2,000 miles of border territory of troops for the defense of Washington. If New York, Pennsylvania, New Jersey, and the New England States cannot defend Washington, in God's name what can they do? The Northwest will defend the lines from the mountains of Virginia to the Rocky Mountains. She will sweep secession and treason from the valley of the Mississippi, aye, *and will defend the Potomac, too, if she must.* But is not this Union worth as much to New York, Pennsylvania, and Massachusetts as to the Northwest? Why, then, so tardy in supplying troops? Had five of the forty Northwestern regiments now on the Potomac been with Lyon he would have won the battle and cleared Missouri! Had five been with Mulligan he would now be in possession of Lexington! Could ten of them be sent into Kentucky to-morrow (in addition to what they have) they would clear the State of secession in ten days, and threaten Tennessee! Could ten be sent to Rosecrans he would clear the mountains of Virginia and threaten the rear of the grand army! But, no; this cannot be done — because the East will not do her duty. If she does not at once, the whole world will cry shame. Respectfully, your obedient servant, Z. CHANDLER.

DETROIT, Sept. 30, 1861.

During the Congressional recess he also sent this letter of characteristic suggestions to the Secretary of War:

DETROIT, Nov. 15, 1861.

Hon. Simon Cameron, Secretary of War.

MY DEAR SIR: The time for delivering a battle upon the Potomac has now passed, and something *must and can be done*. In my opinion the following plan is still feasible, and will close the war:

Let Rosecrans be ordered immediately to Kentucky with his army of veteran Northwestern troops. Substitute an equal or larger number of Eastern troops with an Eastern general, who will act strictly upon the defensive. Send your Northwestern troops now upon the Potomac to Cairo *at once*. Send Pope (if he is the man) to Missouri with sufficient arms to supply all the Northwestern regiments in readiness to march on the 1st day of December. Let an abundance of transports and material be provided at Cairo and St. Louis, by that date (December 1st).

Give the order, "Forward," and *then cut the wires*.

Stop all official communication with the Army of the Northwest. That army, if thus untrammeled, will *spend New Year's day in New Orleans, via* Memphis, and will reach Washington *via* Richmond by the 1st of May next.

In the meantime Sherman, Butler, and Burnside can take care of South Carolina, Georgia, and Alabama, and North Carolina will fall of itself with Virginia and the Gulf States.

Is this plan feasible ?

None but a traitor will say you Nay, for you and I know that 200,000 Northwestern soldiers, with Rosecrans's and Lyon's veterans, *can* and *will* go *wherever they are ordered*, and *on time*.

As to your Army of the Potomac, select 100,000 men of your city regiments which look well on parade, and keep them for reviews. Send the balance to the Gulf States. We want none of them out West.

We will, by recruiting during the winter, keep our Grand Army up to 200,000 men, and furnish garrisons as fast as needed for captured towns.

Very truly yours,   Z. CHANDLER.

Congress re-assembled for its regular session in December, 1861, and Mr. Chandler was called upon (on Jan. 17, 1862) to present the credentials of the Hon. Jacob M. Howard as his colleague from Michigan, *vice* Kinsley S. Bingham, who had died suddenly in the preceding October. Mr. Howard remained a Senator for ten years, winning distinction in that position. Throughout his term his relations with his colleague were intimate and cordial, and the foremost merchant and the first lawyer of Michigan stood side by side in the Senate in the support of every important measure which had for its object the encouragement of loyal sentiment, or the strengthening of the military and financial arms of the government, or the prompt suppression of the rebellion.

CHAPTER XIII.

URING the Congressional recess of the autumn of 1861 gross mismanagement led to the annihilation at Ball's Bluff of a brigade of Union troops, led by Senator Edward D. Baker of Oregon. They had been sent across the Potomac in flat-boats and skiffs, were left without adequate support, and, being surrounded by a vastly superior force of rebels, were driven to the edge of the river, and there either killed, wounded, captured, or driven into hiding places along the banks. Their commanding officer, who displayed throughout a high order of personal courage, was shot at the head of his line before the final rout. General Baker was a man of eloquence and many gallant qualities, and his death created a profound impression; that he was sacrificed by military incapacity cannot be doubted.

Congress met on Dec. 2, 1861, and on the first business day of the session Mr. Chandler offered a motion for the expulsion of John C. Breckenridge, who had at last joined the rebels, and it was unanimously adopted. On December 5 he introduced this resolution :

Resolved, That a committee of three be appointed to inquire into the disasters at Bull Run and Edward's Ferry (subsequently changed to Ball's Bluff), with power to send for persons and papers.

Mr. Chandler said, in explanation of his motion, that these reverses had been attributed to politicians, to civilians, to everything but the right cause, and that it was due to the Senate and to the country that they should be investigated and that the blame should rest where it belonged. After some discussion the Senate adopted the resolution with only three dissenting votes, first amending it by providing for a joint committee of both branches, and by enlarging the scope of its inquiries so as to include "the conduct of the war." The House concurred in the action, and the famous "Committee on the Conduct of the War" was thus created. On December 17, Mr. Chandler moved that the Vice-President should appoint the Senate members, adding: "I do not know what the parliamentary usage may be in a case "of this kind. If that usage would give me the position of "chairman, I wish to say that, under the circumstances, I do not "wish to accept it." Mr. Chandler had also privately requested Mr. Hamlin to appoint Senator Wade to the chairmanship, saying it was important that a lawyer should be given that place, and his desires were followed in both respects. The first committee, as announced at that time, consisted of the following Congressmen: On the part of the Senate, Benjamin F. Wade, Zachariah Chandler and Andrew Johnson; on the part of the House, Daniel W. Gooch of Massachusetts, John Covode of Pennsylvania, George W. Julian of Indiana, and Moses F. Odell of New York. Of the original committee, George W. Julian is the only one who survived Mr. Chandler. When Andrew Johnson was appointed Military Governor of Tennessee, he resigned his position upon the committee, and Senator Joseph A. Wright of Indiana took his place. Mr. Wright served but a year, and after the expiration of his term the Senate branch of the committee in the Thirty-seventh Congress consisted of only Mr. Chandler and Mr. Wade. William Blair Lord, now one of the official reporters of the House of Representatives, was appointed its clerk and stenographer.

The tone of the Congressional discussion upon Mr. Chandler's proposition shows that this was regarded as an exceedingly important step, for the resolution clothed the committee with powers of very unusual magnitude, which, if abused, must have seriously embarrassed the Administration. Mr. Lincoln and Secretary Cameron, as well as General Scott and General McClellan, opposed its appointment at the outset, but Mr. Chandler took prompt and successful measures to assure the President that, if

ZACHARIAH CHANDLER IN 1862.

the plans of its projectors were carried out, the committee would be used only to strengthen the hands of the Executive, and promised that it should be made a help and not a hindrance to the vigorous prosecution of the war. On this point the Hon. James M. Edmunds, who was thoroughly informed as to the secret history of that period, has said:

The writer knows that the Administration was not without fear that this was an unfriendly measure. A member of the Cabinet expressed such fears

to him, and said that the President had not only expressed doubts as to the
wisdom of the movement, but also fears that the committee might, by
unfriendly action, greatly embarrass the Executive. On being told by the
writer that the measure was not so intended, but, on the contrary, that it was
the intention of the mover to bring the committee to the aid of the Administration, he expressed much gratification, and said it was of the utmost
importance to bring such purpose to the knowledge of the President in some
authoritative way, and at the earliest moment possible. This conversation was
at once reported to Senator Chandler, whereupon both he and Senator Wade
went immediately to the President and the Secretary of War, and assured
them that it was their purpose to bring the whole power of the committee to
the aid of the Executive. From this moment the most cordial relations existed
between the committee and the Administration.*

President Lincoln and Secretaries Cameron and Stanton ultimately placed great reliance upon the committee, and constantly,
throughout the war, it gave them the most valuable assistance.
Mr. Wade and Mr. Chandler were deeper in the confidence of
Secretary Stanton, from their connection with it, than were any
other members of Congress, and differences of aim and opinion
between them were exceedingly rare.

Upon organizing for work the committee found itself confronted with an enormous task, inquiries into every phase of the
organization and management of the Union armies being referred
to it for consideration. "Upon the conduct of the war," to quote
from its own report, "depended the issue of the experiment
"inaugurated by our fathers, after the expenditure of so much
"blood and treasure — the establishment of a nation founded
"upon the capacity of man for self-government. The nation
"was engaged in a struggle for its existence; a rebellion,
"unparalleled in history, threatened the overthrow of our free
"institutions, and the most prompt and vigorous measures were
"demanded by every consideration of honor, patriotism, and a
"due regard for the prosperity and happiness of the people."
And its sphere of duty was the constant watching of the details

---

* In "The Republic" magazine of April, 1877.

of movements, upon whose result depended such vast interests, as well as the safety of thousands of lives. The committee, in laying out its work, followed the suggestion of Mr. Chandler, which was, first, to obtain such information in respect to the conduct of the war as would best enable them to point out the mistakes which had been made in the past, and the course that promised to ensure the avoidance of their repetition; second, to collect such information as the many and laborious duties of the President and Secretary of War prevented them from obtaining, and to lay it before them with those recommendations and suggestions which the circumstances seemed to demand. Working in such a field, the committee soon became a second Cabinet council, and its proceedings were constantly at the President's hand. Its sessions were nearly perpetual, and almost daily its members were in consultation with the President or the Secretary of War. Many of its transactions were never committed to paper, and, as the members were sworn to the strictest secrecy, will never be revealed. Secretary Stanton was frequently present while the committee was in session, and its door was always open to him. There was never any lack of harmony between him and its chief members, but, on the contrary, the utmost confidence was exchanged, and this committee was the right arm of the War Department in the darkest days of the rebellion. Repeatedly, after the examination of some important witness, did Mr. Chandler or Mr. Wade go at once to the White House with the official stenographer, when Mr. Stanton would be sent for and the stenographic notes of the evidence would be read to the President and Secretary of War for their information and guidance. From such conferences there sprang many important decisions, and the files and records of the committee were constantly referred to and relied upon as sources of exceedingly useful knowledge and hints both at the White House and at the War Department.

Many subjects presented themselves for investigation, any one of which would, in ordinary times, have required the exclusive attention of a separate committee, and to follow out every line of inquiry suggested was manifestly a practical impossibility. Therefore the committee decided not to undertake any investigations into what might be considered side issues, but to keep their attention directed entirely to the essential features of the war, so that they could ascertain and comprehend the necessities of the armies and the causes of disaster or complaint, and the methods of supplying the one and remedying the other. Attempts were made repeatedly to use its power to punish enemies or to avenge private grievances, but its members adhered resolutely to the straightforward course originally marked out as the path of its duty.

The first subject which the committee carefully inquired into was the defeat at Bull Run. Many witnesses were examined, chiefly officers who were engaged in the battle — Generals Scott, McDowell, Meigs, Heintzelman, Butterfield, Fitz - John Porter, and others. The testimony was very voluminous, but the committee reached an early and unanimous opinion as to the causes of the disaster. Their report, written by Mr. Wade, said: "That "which now appears to have been the great error was the "failure to occupy Centreville and Manassas at the time Alex- "andria was occupied, in May. The position at Manassas "controlled the railroad connections in all that section of the "country. . . . The next cause of disaster was the delay in "proceeding against the enemy until the time of the three "months' men was nearly expired. The enemy were allowed "time to collect their forces and strengthen their position by "defensive works. . . . There had been but little time "devoted to disciplining the troops and instructing them, even "in regiments; hardly any instruction had been given them in "brigade movements, and none at all as divisions." General

McDowell prepared a plan of campaign, which was approved by the Cabinet, and the 9th of July was fixed upon as the day for the advance; but the movement did not commence until a week later than the appointed time. Transportation was deficient, and there was much delay resulting from lack of discipline among the troops, and when the battle came the Union forces were fatigued and not in good fighting condition. "But," said the report, "the principal cause of the defeat was the failure of "General Patterson to hold the troops of General Johnston in "the valley of the Shenandoah." Patterson had 23,000 men, while Johnston had but 12,000. Still, Patterson disobeyed the orders of General Scott, which were to make offensive demonstrations against General Johnston so as to detain his army at Winchester, and if he retreated to follow him and keep up the fight. Those orders were repeated every day for more than a week in the telegraphic correspondence between Scott and Patterson. Finally, General Scott heard of a large force moving from Patterson's front, and telegraphed, " Has not the enemy stolen a march on you?" To this Patterson replied, "The enemy has stolen no march upon me," while at that very time his large army was watching an empty camp and Johnston was far on his way to reinforce the rebels at Manassas. Patterson did not discover that Johnston had gone until he was miles distant, and the consequence was that McDowell had both Beauregard and Johnston to fight, while Patterson, with 23,000 men, was lying idle in his camp. This is the substance of the report of the Committee on the Conduct of the War on the battle of Bull Run, and was the official announcement to the country of the inefficiency of the organization and generalship of the Army of the Potomac.

But before the committee was organized the men who were responsible for this failure had been displaced, and General McClellan had been made the commander-in-chief. He had taken the reins of authority amid national acclamations, and was then at the height of a remarkable popularity, which it is now known was adroitly stimulated for political purposes by the conservative press. But on the investigation into the second subject taken up by the committee (the disaster at Edward's Ferry or Ball's Bluff) facts came to the knowledge of its members which created the suspicion in their minds that General Stone, who was charged with the blame of that defeat, and who, as the scape-goat, was arrested and imprisoned in Fort Lafayette, was not alone responsible for the calamity, but that the real fault would be found higher up. This suspicion they were never able to substantiate by absolute proof, and it was not expressed in any of their reports.

The third topic taken up by the committee was the military management of the Western Department, under General Fremont. This was an inquiry of special importance, for the reason that that officer, upon taking command at St. Louis, issued a proclamation declaring free all slaves whose masters were engaged in rebellion against the United States. This order caused a great excitement throughout the country, and the Republican party was widely divided in opinion as to its legality and propriety. President Lincoln was conservative on the question, and revoked the Fremont order, much to the disappointment of Mr. Chandler and the other more "advanced" Republicans. Hence the committee approached the subject with unusual interest, and, after a thorough investigation, made an elaborate report. That part of this document which relates to General Fremont's order in regard to slaves was signed by Messrs. Wade, Chandler, Julian, and Covode, and showed the ground on which these gentlemen then stood with regard to emancipation; it was as follows:

But that feature of General Fremont's administration which attracted the most attention, and which will ever be most prominent among the many points of interest connected with the history of that department, is his proclamation of emancipation. Whatever opinion may be entertained with reference to the time when the policy of emancipation should be inaugurated, there can be no doubt that General Fremont at that early day rightly judged in regard to the most effective means of subduing this rebellion. In proof of that, it is only necessary to state that his successor, when transferred to another department, issued a proclamation embodying the same principle, and the President of the United States has since applied the same principle to all the rebellious States; and few will deny that it must be adhered to until the last vestige of treason and rebellion is destroyed.

The committee heartily endorsed General Fremont's administration, declaring it to have been "eminently characterized by earnestness, ability, and the most unquestionable loyalty." They also examined into various minor military matters and movements, including, particularly, rebel barbarities and the return of slaves to their masters by the army.

It was as a member of the Committee on the Conduct of the War in the Thirty-seventh Congress, and from the evidence taken in its inquiries, that Mr. Chandler obtained the mass of information which enabled him to make the most important of his war speeches, that of July 16, 1862, in which he exposed so conclusively General McClellan's utter incompetence. Ample as was the foundation of facts upon which rested this effective arraignment of conspicuous incapacity, the attack was one requiring genuine boldness, for it defiantly invited a storm of denunciation and, if it had failed of justification by the event, would have certainly ended its maker's political career. Notwithstanding his tardiness, his timidity, his inefficiency as a commander in the field, and his political sympathy with the more unpatriotic classes of the Northern people, General McClellan was still strong with the people and entrusted with great powers. The Democracy warmly commended his sentiments and methods, and labored incessantly to prevent any diminution of his hold upon the public confidence. The Army of the Potomac yet regarded him as "the young Napoleon," and its corps commanders were, with but few exceptions, his personal adherents.

The long-suffering President was submitting with patience to his unjust complaints, after having labored incessantly to stimulate into activity his chronic sluggishness, fearful, with characteristic over-caution, lest his summary removal should divide the North and breed a dangerous disaffection in the face of the enemy among his troops. Many who did not believe in the sincerity or ability of the man also smothered their distrust, for fear that criticism would only weaken the common cause and with the hope that even in his nerveless hands the mighty weapon of the national resources would at last fall—even if by its own weight only—on the enemy with decisive force. At this juncture, and under these circumstances, Mr. Chandler, with characteristic vigor of statement and plainness of speech, placed before the Senate and the country the demonstration of McClellan's imbecility.

Originally Mr. Chandler believed that McClellan's selection as the practical successor of General Scott was a wise one, and hoped to see his organizing capacity in camp supplemented by enterprise and courage in the field. Distrust first sprang up with the persistent inaction of the Army of the Potomac throughout the last months of 1861, and it was strengthened by contact with the man himself and the study of his character and his plans. An illustration of how this change of opinion was brought about is given in an incident which occurred in the room of the Committee on the Conduct of the War. That committee sent for General McClellan as soon as they took up matters relating to his command, in order to consult with him informally as to the situation. This was in January, 1861, while he was in Washington "organizing" his army, and while there was no little impatience felt because he did not move. He was not formally summoned before the committee then, but simply called in for general consultation. After the regular business was finished, Mr. Chandler asked him bluntly why he did not attack the rebels. General McClellan replied that it was because there were not sufficient means of communication with Washington; he then called attention to the fact that there were only two bridges and no other means of transportation across the Potomac.

Mr. Chandler asked what the number of bridges had to do with an advance movement, and McClellan explained with much detail that it was one of the most important features of skillful strategy that a commander should have plenty of room to retreat before making an attack. To this Mr. Chandler's response was:

"General McClellan, if I understand you correctly, before "you strike at the rebels you want to be sure of plenty of room "so that you can run in case they strike back!"

"Or in case you get scared," added Senator Wade.

The commander of the Army of the Potomac manifested indignation at this blunt way of putting the case, and then proceeded at length to explain the art of war and the science of generalship, laying special stress upon the necessity of having lines of retreat, as well as lines of communication and supply, always open. He labored hard to make clear all the methods and counter-methods upon which campaigns are managed and battles fought, and, as he was an accomplished master of the theory of war, succeeded in rendering himself at least interesting. After he had concluded, Mr. Wade said:

"General, you have all the troops you have called for, and "if you haven't enough, you shall have more. They are well "organized and equipped, and the loyal people of this country "expect that you will make a short and decisive campaign. Is "it really necessary for you to have more bridges over the Poto- "mac before you move?"

"Not that," was the answer, "not that exactly, but we must "bear in mind the necessity of having everything ready in case "of a defeat, and keep our lines of retreat open."

15

With this remark General McClellan left the room, whereupon Mr. Wade asked:

"Chandler, what do you think of the science of generalship?"

"I don't know much about war," was the reply, "but it seems to me that this is infernal, unmitigated cowardice."

The committee, after this interview, made a careful inquiry into the strength of the rebel forces confronting the elaborate intrenchments about Washington, and became convinced that the army at and about Manassas was a handful compared with the magnificent body of troops under McClellan's command. They submitted these facts to the President and his Cabinet at a special session held for that purpose, and urged the importance of an instant advance. With one single exception (a Cabinet officer) the heads of the departments and the committee agreed that an offensive movement from the line of the Potomac into Virginia was important and must be made. General McClellan promised that his army should start, but it did not. Toward the close of the winter the President ordered a general advance, but the Army of the Potomac still remained immobile. Finally, on March 10, under the peremptory orders of the President, it did advance to Centreville and found there deserted camps, wooden guns, weak intrenchments, and traces of the retreat of not more than a single full corps of rebel troops. It was during this most aggravating delay that members of the committee had another characteristic interview with General McClellan. On the 19th of February a sub-committee waited upon the Secretary of War* to ask why the army was idle, and why the city of Washington and the North side of the Potomac river were crowded with troops when the enemy was all in Virginia. Mr. Wade said that it was a disgrace to the nation that Washington was thus allowed to remain to all intents and purposes in a state of siege.

---

* Edwin M. Stanton had succeeded Simon Cameron on Jan. 13, 1862.

To this Secretary Stanton replied that the committee could not feel more keenly upon this subject than did he, that he did not go to bed at night without his cheek burning with shame at this disgrace, and that the subject had received his earnest attention, but he had not been able to change the situation as he wished. General McClellan was then sent for, and Secretary Stanton stated to him the object of the visit, and repeated the inquiries as to why an advance movement was not made into Virginia, the rebels driven away from Washington, and the soldiers who were idle in their camps in and around the city sent to active duty.

General McClellan answered that he was considering the matter, but that instant action was impossible, although he hoped that he would soon be able to decide what ought to be done. The committee asked what time he would require to reach a decision. He replied that it depended upon circumstances; that he would not give his consent to have the troops about Washington sent over to the Virginia side of the Potomac without having their rear protected more fully, and better lines of retreat open; that he designed throwing a temporary bridge across the river as soon as possible, and making a permanent structure of it at his leisure. That would make three bridges, and then the requisite precautions would be completed.

Mr. Wade replied, with great impatience, that with 150,000 of the best troops the world ever saw, there was no need of more bridges; that the rebels were inferior in numbers and condition, and that retreat would be treason. "These 150,000 men," Mr. Wade said, "could whip the whole Confederacy if they were "given a chance; if I was their commander I would lead them "across the Potomac, and they should not come back until they "had won a victory and the war was ended, or they came in "their coffins." Mr. Wade spoke strongly and plainly throughout the interview, and the Secretary of War endorsed every word he uttered. The committee had another conference with Secretary Stanton on the following day at his residence, at which it was decided that they should co-operate with him in an effort to persuade President Lincoln either to displace McClellan or to compel him to commence an active campaign at once. On the 25th of February this conference with the President was held, and it was followed by others, Senators Chandler and Wade finally threatening to make the laggardness of the commander of the Army of the Potomac a subject of debate in the Senate, and to offer a resolution directing the President to order an advance forthwith. The first result was what the committee were so anxious to accomplish. In March, the armies commenced to move, and McClellan, at last taking the field in person, pushed out to Centreville, and then followed up this delayed advance by his flank movement to the Peninsula, driving the rebels out of Yorktown by a month's work with the shovel, and following General Johnston up to Williamsburg, where a bloody victory was won, but its fruits were left ungathered. This campaign was short, bloody, and blundering, ending with the battle of Malvern Hill, which was also deprived of its proper importance by McClellan's failure to follow up his advantage with a prompt advance upon Richmond, and which thus in the end amounted to but little more than another Union reverse. Mr. Chandler always firmly believed that had McClellan moved toward the rebel capital and not toward his gunboats after Malvern Hill, the war would have been shortened by two years.

When it first became evident that General McClellan was, by sullenness and incapacity, throwing away advantages gained by the heroism of his troops on the Peninsula, Mr. Chandler determined to denounce him on the floor of the Senate, but was restrained by Mr. Stanton, who urged that, while the campaign was still in active progress, there was yet some hope of a change for the better, and that to destroy confidence in a commanding officer under such circumstances might injure the army in the field. After Malvern Hill these reasons ceased to have force, and Mr. Chandler commenced the careful preparation of his speech. This time the Secretary of War endorsed the timeliness as well as the truth of the *expose*, and the Committee on the Conduct of the War by formal vote authorized the use of the testimony taken before it and not yet made public. After he had gathered and grouped the facts which formed the basis of his arraignment, Mr. Chandler submitted them to a friend upon whose good judgment and sincerity he greatly relied, and asked:

"Knowing all these facts, as I do, what is my duty?"

The answer was: "Beyond all question, these facts ought " to be laid before the country, for the knowledge of them is " essential to its safety. But they will create a storm that will " sweep either you or McClellan from public life, and it is more " than probable that you will be the victim."

Mr. Chandler said: "I did not ask your opinion of the consequences, but of my duty."

To this it was replied: "The speech ought to be made, and no one else will make it."

Mr. Chandler simply said: "It will be made to-day; come and hear it." And he did make it, in the midst of a running discussion on a bill "to provide for the discharge of state prisoners and others," which was the special order in the Senate for that day (July 16, 1862).

Mr. Chandler commenced by briefly reciting the history of the appointment of the committee, and then gave from the evidence taken at its sessions a compact summary of the causes of the Bull Run disaster, fortifying each point with citations from the testimony. After closing this part of his speech he proceeded to review the Ball's Bluff catastrophe, saying:

Were the people discouraged, depressed? Not at all. Untold thousands rushed into the shattered ranks, eager to wipe out the stain and stigma of

that defeat (Bull Run). From the East, the West, the North, and the Middle
States, thousands and tens of thousands and hundreds of thousands came
pouring in, until the government said, "Hold, enough." The Army of the
Potomac, denuded in August of three-months' men and scarcely numbering
50,000 efficient men, swelled in September to over 100,000, in October to
150,000, in November to 175,000 and upward, until, on the 10th day of
December, the morning rolls showed 195,400 men, and thirteen regiments
not reported, chiefly intended for the Burnside expedition, but all under
the command of General McClellan. During the months of October, November, and December, the weather was delightful and the roads fine. The
question began to be asked in October, when will the advance take place?
All had the most unbounded confidence in the army and its young general, and were anxiously waiting for a Napoleonic stroke. It came, but
such a stroke! That a general movement was being prepared the whole
country had known for weeks; but when the terrific blow was to be struck
no one knew save the commander of the Army of the Potomac. The nation
believed in its young commander; the President relied upon him, and all,
myself included, had the most unbounded confidence in the result of the
intended movement. It came! On the 21st of October, McCall's division,
12,000 strong, was ordered to Drainesville upon a reconnoissance. Smith's
division, 12,000 strong, was ordered to support him. McCall's reconnoissance
extended four miles beyond Drainesville, and to within nine miles of Leesburg.
Stone, on Sunday, was informed of McCall's and Smith's advance, and directed
to make a slight demonstration upon Leesburg. How? He could do it in
but one way, and that was by crossing the river and moving upon it. [Mr.
Chandler here introduced a mass of testimony and official orders to show that
Col. E. D. Baker, whom General Stone sent across the Potomac at Ball's
Bluff, had ample reasons to believe that he would be sustained in that advance,
and reinforced if necessary. He proceeded :] Thus it is shown that Colonel
Baker had reason to expect reinforcements, for the enemy were to be pushed
upon their flank by General Gorman.

At two o'clock on Monday morning Colonel Devens crossed the river upon
a reconnoissance with 400 men at Ball's Bluff, opposite Harrison's Island, as
directed by General Stone. At daylight Colonel Baker was ordered to cross
to the support of Colonel Devens. I have read his orders. One scow and
two small boats were their only means of transportation. At eight o'clock on
Monday morning the fight commenced by Colonel Devens, and Colonel Baker
was placed in command, as is alleged, with discretionary orders. Colonel
Baker knew that Smith and McCall were at Drainesville, or within striking
distance, that our troops were crossing at Edward's Ferry, or, in other words,
that 40,000 effective men were within twelve miles of him, and that at least
30,000 were upon the Virginia side of the Potomac, and that, in the nature of
things, he must be reinforced. He did not know that at half-past ten A. M.,
of Monday, or two and one-half hours after Colonel Devens commenced the

fight, the divisions of Smith and McCall commenced their retreat by the express orders of General McClellan. He knew that Colonel Devens was contending with greatly superior forces, and, like a gallant soldier as he was, he hastened to his relief with all the force he could cross with his inadequate means of transportation.

Colonel Baker has been charged with imprudence and rashness; but neither the facts nor the testimony support the charge. Instead of rashly or imprudently advancing into the enemy's lines, as was alleged, he did not move ten rods from the Bluff, and the only sustaining witness to this charge was one officer, who swore that he thought Colonel Baker imprudently exposed himself to the enemy's bullets. This kind of rashness is usually pardoned after the death of the perpetrator. At two o'clock P. M. Colonel Baker found himself in command of about 1,800 men upon Ball's Bluff, including Devens's men and three guns, and the fighting commenced. The alternatives were fight and conquer, surrender, or be captured. That noble band of heroes and their gallant commander understood these terrible alternatives as well upon that bloody field as we do now, and nobly did they vindicate their manhood. During all those long hours, from two o'clock P. M. until the early dusk of evening, the gallant Baker continued the unequal contest, when he fell pierced by three bullets and instantly expired. A council of war was called (after the frightful death-struggle over his lifeless remains and for them), and it was decided that the only chance of an escape was by cutting through the enemy and reaching Edward's Ferry, which was at once decided upon; but, while forming for the desperate encounter, the enemy rushed upon our little band of heroes in overpowering numbers, and the rout was perfect. . . . How many were killed in battle, how many drowned in the relentless river, will never be correctly known; suffice it to say, our little force was destroyed. Why was this little band permitted to be destroyed by a force little more than double its numbers in presence of 40,000 splendid troops? Why were McCall and Smith ordered back at the very moment that Baker was ordered to cross? If we wanted Leesburg, McCall could have taken it without the loss of a man, as his movement in mass had already caused its evacuation, and the enemy did not return in force until after McCall had retreated. If we did not wish to capture Leesburg, why did we cross at all? Of what use is "a slight demonstration" even, without results? These are questions which the people will ask, and no man can satisfactorily answer. Why were not reinforcements sent from Edward's Ferry to Colonel Baker? The distance was only three-and-a-half miles. We had 1,500 men across at two o'clock on Monday, and the universal concurrent testimony of officers and men is that a reinforcement of even 1,000 men — some say 500, and one gallant captain swears that with 100 men he could have struck them upon the flank, — would have changed the result of the day. Why were not reinforcements sent? Stone swears, as I have already shown, that there were batteries between Edward's Ferry and Ball's Bluff which would have utterly destroyed any force he could have sent to Baker's relief, and that Baker knew it. But Stone was not sustained by a single witness; on the contrary, all swear that there were not, to their knowledge, and that they did not believe there were any, and a civilian living upon the spot, and in the habit of passing over the ground frequently, swears there were none; and again, Stone, when questioned as to the erection of forts under the range of his guns upon his second examination, swears positively that there is not a gun now between Edward's Ferry and Ball's Bluff, and never has been. Why, then, were not reinforcements sent from Edward's Ferry? Let the men who executed and planned this horrible slaughter answer to God and an outraged country. General Banks swears that his orders were such from General McClellan, that, upon his arrival at Edward's Ferry, although his judgment was against crossing, he did not feel himself at liberty to decline crossing, and he remained upon the Virginia side until Thursday. . . . So much for the wholesale murder at Ball's Bluff.

Mr. Chandler next attacked General McClellan's disastrous procrastination. Describing the lapse of an army of 150,000 men into a state of chronic inaction in its intrenchments about Washington after the Ball's Bluff disaster, he laid before the Senate and the country documents which proved these facts: In October, 1861, the Navy Department requested that 4,000 men might be detailed to hold Matthias Point on the lower Potomac, after the gunboats should have shelled out the rebels, who were then in possession, and thus in control of the navigation of that important river. General McClellan agreed to furnish the infantry; twice the Navy Department prepared its vessels for the expedition, but the troops did not report for duty, so that, finally, the gunboats were necessarily detailed for other service, and the unnecessary, expensive and humiliating blockade of the Potomac continued for months. Mr. Chandler then proceeded:

Why was this disgrace so long submitted to? No man knows or attempts to explain. . Month after month one of the most splendid armies the world had ever seen, of 200,000 men, permitted itself and the national capital to be besieged by a force *never* exceeding one-half its own number.

During the month of December, the nation became impatient. The time had arrived and passed when we were promised a forward movement. The roads were good, the weather splendid, the army in high condition, and eager for the fray. How long the roads and weather would permit the movement, no man could predict ; still there was no movement. The generals, with great unanimity, declared that the army had reached its maximum of proficiency as volunteers, but still there was no movement. Under these circumstances, the Committee on the Conduct of the War asked an interview with the President and Cabinet, and urged that the winter should not be permitted to pass without action, as it would lead to an incalculable loss of life and treasure by forcing our brave troops into a summer campaign, in a hot and to them inhospitable climate. The President and Cabinet were united in the desire that an immediate advance should be made, but it was not made, although we were assured by General McClellan that it would be very soon, that he had no intention of going into winter quarters, and he did not ! While the enemy erected comfortable huts at Centreville and Manassas for their winter quarters, our brave and eager troops spent the most uncomfortable winter ever known in this climate under canvas, as thousands and tens of thousands of invalid soldiers throughout the length and breadth of the land will attest. Why did not the army move in all December, or why did it not go into winter quarters ? No man knows, nor is any reason assigned.

On the 1st day of January, 1862, and for months previous to that date, the armies of the republic were occupying a purely defensive position upon the whole line from Missouri to the Atlantic, until on or about the 27th of January the President and Secretary of War issued the order *forward.* Then the brave Foote took the initiative, soliciting 2,000 men from Halleck to hold Fort Henry after he had captured it with his gunboats. They were promptly furnished, and Henry fell ; then Donelson, with its 15,000 prisoners ; then Newbern, and the country was electrified. Credit was given where credit was due. Do-nothing strategy gave way to an "immediate advance upon the enemy's works," and the days of spades and pickaxes seemed to be ended. On the 22d of February a forward movement upon our whole line was ordered, but did not take place. The Army of the Potomac was not ready ; but on the 10th of March it moved, against the protest of the commanding general and eight out of twelve of the commanders of divisions; but the President was inexorable, and the movement must be made It proceeded to Centreville, and there found deserted huts, wooden artillery, and intrenchments which could and can be successfully charged by cavalry. It proceeded to Manassas, and found no fortifications worthy of the name, a deserted, abandoned camp, and dead horses for trophies. The enemy, less than 40,000 men, had leisurely escaped, carrying away all their artillery, baggage, arms, and stores. Our Army of the Potomac, on that 10th day of March, showed by its muster-roll a force of 230,000 men. Comment is needless ! The Grand Army of the Potomac proceeded toward Gordonsville, found no enemy, repaired the railroad, and then marched back again.

Why this Grand Army of the Potomac did not march upon Richmond has never been satisfactorily explained, and probably never will be. One reason assigned was lack of transportation ; but there were two railroads, one by way of Acquia Creek and Fredericksburg, the other via Manassas and Gordonsville, which could have been repaired at the rate of ten miles per day, and our army was ample to guard it. Had this overwhelming force proceeded directly to Richmond by these lines, it would have spent the 1st day of May in Richmond, and ere this the rebellion would have been ended. This grand army, *ably* commanded, was superior to any army the world has seen for five hundred years. Napoleon I. never fought 130,000 men upon one battle-field. Yet this noble army was divided and virtually sacrificed by some one. Who is the culprit?

Before the advance upon Manassas, General McClellan changed his plans, and demanded to be permitted to leave the enemy intrenched at Centreville and Manassas, to leave the Potomac blockaded, and to take his army to Annapolis by land, and there embark them for the rear of the enemy to surprise him. In the council of war called upon this proposition, the commanding general and eight out of twelve of the commanders of divisions (and here permit me to say that I am informed that seven out of the eight generals were appointed upon the recommendation of General McClellan) voted that it was not safe to advance upon the wooden guns of Centreville, and to adopt the new plan of campaign. The President and the Secretary of War overruled this pusillanimous decision, and compelled McClellan to "move immediately upon the enemy's works." He marched, and the trophies of that memorable campaign are known to the Senate and the country.

At Fairfax, General McClellan changed his plan and decided not to advance upon the rebels with his whole force, but to return to Alexandria, divide his army, and embark for Fortress Monroe and Yorktown. It was decided that 45,000 men should be left for the defense of the capital, and he was permitted to embark. After much delay (unavoidable in the movement of so vast a force, with its enormous material) the general-in-chief himself embarked. Soon after he sailed it came to the knowledge of the Committee on the Conduct of the War that the capital, with its vast accumulation of material of war, had been left by General McClellan virtually without defense, and the enemy's whole force, large or small, was untouched in front. [Mr. Chandler here introduced the official testimony to prove that General McClellan had so denuded Washington as to compel the President to interpose and detain General McDowell's corps for its adequate defense. He then said:] The country has been deceived. It has been led to believe that the Secretary of War or somebody else has interfered with General McClellan's plans, when he had an army that could have crushed any other army on the face of the earth. One hundred and fifty-eight thousand of the best troops that ever stood on God's footstool were sent down to the Peninsula and placed under command of General McClellan; and yet the whole treasonable press of the country has been howling after the Secretary of War because of his alleged refusal to send reinforcements to General McClellan. As I said the other day, he has sent every man, every sabre, every bayonet, every horse, that could be spared from any source whatever to increase that grand army under General McClellan in front of Richmond. Why did he not enter Richmond? We shall see. . . . It is not for me, sir, to state the strength of McClellan's army at this time; but I know it is 158,000 men, less the number lost by sickness and casualties. Does any man doubt that this army, ably handled, was sufficiently strong to have captured Richmond and crushed the rebel army? I think not, if promptly led against the enemy; but instead of that, it sat down in malarious swamps and awaited the drafting, arming. drilling, and making soldiers of an army to fight it, and in the meantime our own army was rapidly wasting away. Unwholesome water, inadequate food, over-work, and sleeping in marshes, were rapidly filling the hospitals, and overloading the return boats with the sick. Sir, we have lost more men by the spade than the bullet, five to one, since the army started from Yorktown under McClellan. Had the soldiers been relieved from digging and menial labor by the substitution of negro laborers, the Army of the Potomac would to-day, in my estimation, contain 30,000 more brave and efficient soldiers than it does. Had it been relieved from guarding the property of rebels in arms, many valuable lives would have been saved. Yorktown was evacuated after a sacrifice of more men by sickness than the enemy had in their works when our army landed at Fortress Monroe. The battle of Williamsburg was fought by a small fraction of our army, and the enemy routed. During the battle, General McClellan wrote a dispatch, miles from the field of battle, saying he should try to "hold them in check" there. . . . He would try to "hold them in check!" He could not hold them. He could not stop his eager troops from chasing them. After a small fraction of his army had whipped their entire force and had been chasing them for hours, he penned that dispatch and sent it to the Secretary of War, and, if I remember aright, it was read in one of the two houses of Congress. As you may suppose from that dispatch, there was no great eagerness in following up that victory. Three Michigan regiments were not only decimated, they were divided in twain, in that bloody battle at Williamsburg. They fought there all day without reinforcements. One Michigan regiment went into the trenches and left sixty-three dead rebels, killed by the bayonet, weltering in their blood. But who has ever heard, by any official communication from the head of the army, that a Michigan regiment was in the fight at Williamsburg? I do not blame him for not giving credit where credit is due, for I do not believe he knew anything more of that fight than you or I.

When that battle was fought and won, all the enemy's works were cleared away, and we had an open road to Richmond. There was not a single fortification between Richmond and Williamsburg. All we had to do was to get through those infernal swamps, march up, and take possession of Richmond. What did we do? We found the worst swamp there was between Richmond and Williamsburg, and sat right down in the center of it and went to digging. We sacrificed thousands and tens of thousands of the bravest troops that ever stood on the face of God's earth, digging in front of no intrenchments, and before a whipped army of the enemy. We waited for them to recruit; we waited for them to get another army. They had a levy *en masse*. They were taking all the men and boys between the ages of fifteen and fifty-five, and magnanimously we waited weeks and weeks and weeks for them to bring these forced levies into some sort of consistency as an army. The battle of Fair Oaks was fought. There the enemy found again a little fraction of our army, very much less than half, and they brought out their entire force. I have it from the best authority that they had not a solitary regiment in or about Richmond that was fit to put in front of an enemy that they did not bring to Fair Oaks and hurl upon our decimated army. Again the indomitable bravery of our troops (of the men, of private soldiers, the indomitable energy of Michigan men and New Jersey men—but I will not particularize, for all the troops fought like lions), and the fighting capacity of our army not only saved it from being utterly destroyed by an overwhelming force, but gave us a triumphant victory. The enemy went back to Richmond pell-mell. I have been informed by a man who was there at the time, that two brigades of fresh troops could have chased the whole Confederate army through the city of Richmond and into the James river, so utter was their rout and confusion.

And what did we do then? We found another big swamp, and we sat down in the center of it and went to digging. We began to throw up intrenchments when there were no intrenchments in our front, no enemy that was not utterly broken. We never took advantage of the battle of Fair Oaks. Again Michigan soldiers were cut to pieces by hundreds. Go into the Judiciary square hospital in this city, and you will find more than half the occupants are Michigan men who were shot at Fair Oaks and Williamsburg, men who stood until a regiment of 1,000 men was reduced to 105, and even then did not run. Sir, these men have been sacrificed, uselessly sacrificed. They have been put to hard digging, and hard fare, and hard sleeping, and if there was any hard fighting to do they have been put to that; and, besides all this, at night they have had to guard the property of rebels in arms. They have been so sacrificed that two or three of the Michigan regiments to-day cannot bring into the field 250 men each out of 1,000 with whom they started.

Fair Oaks was lost; that is to say, we won a brilliant victory, but it did us no good; we did not take advantage of it. Of course it would have been very unfair to take advantage of a routed army [laughter]; it would not have been according to our "strategy." We magnanimously stopped, and commenced digging. There was no army in our front; there were no intrenchments in our front; but we did not know what else to do, and so we began to dig and ditch, and we kept digging and ditching until the rebels had impressed and drilled and armed and made soldiers of their entire population. But that was not enough; they sent Jackson up on his raid to Winchester, and we waited for him to come back with his twenty or thirty thousand men.

We heard that Corinth was being evacuated, and of course it would have been very unfair to commence an attack until they brought their troops from Corinth, and so we waited for the army at Corinth to get to Richmond. After the rebels had got all the troops they ever hoped to raise from any source, we did not attack them, but they attacked us, as we had reason to suppose they would. They attacked our right wing, and, as I am informed upon what I must deem reliable authority, they hurled the majority of their entire force upon our right wing of 30,000 men, and during the whole of that Thursday our right wing of 30,000 men held their ground, and repulsed that vast horde of the enemy over and over again, and held their ground at night. Of course you will say a reinforcement of twenty or thirty thousand men was sent to these brave troops that they might not only hold their ground the next day, but send this dastardly army into Richmond a second time, as at Fair Oaks. No, sir, nothing of the sort was done.

At night, instead of sending them reinforcements, they were ordered to retreat. That was "strategy!" The moment they commenced their retreat, as is said in the dispatches, the enemy fought like demons. Of course they would. Who ever heard of a retreating army that was not pursued by the victors like demons, except in the case of rebel retreats? No other nation but ours was ever guilty of stopping immediately after a victory. Other armies fight like demons after a victory, and annihilate the enemy, but we do not. Our left wing and center remained intact. A feint was made upon the left and center, and I have here, not the sworn testimony, but the statement of one of the bravest men in the whole Army of the Potomac—I will not give his name, but a more highly honorable man lives not—that when his regiment was ordered under arms, he had no doubt that he was going to march into Richmond. He believed the whole force of the enemy had attacked our right wing; he believed there was nothing but a screen of pickets in front; and he thought that now our great triumph was to come off. His men sprang into line with avidity, prepared to rush into Richmond and take it at the point of the bayonet. He never discovered his error until he saw a million and a half dollars' worth of property burned in front of his regiment, and then he began to think that an advance upon Richmond was not intended. And it was not! We had been at work there and had lost 10,000 men in digging intrenchments; we had spent months in bringing up siege guns, and we abandoned those intrenchments without firing one gun. Our army was ordered to advance on the gunboats instead of on Richmond. This colonel told me that his regiment fought three days and whipped the enemy each day, and retreated each night. The left wing and center were untouched until they were ordered to retreat. No portion of our vast force had been fought except the right wing under Porter, and they whipped the enemy the first day.

This is called strategy! Again, sir, I ask, Why was this great Army of the Potomac of 230,000 men divided? Human ingenuity could not have devised any other way to defeat that army ; Divine wisdom could scarcely have devised any other way to defeat it than that which was adopted. There is no army in Europe to - day that could meet the Army of the Potomac when it was 230,000 strong, the best fighting material ever put into an army on the face of the earth. Why was that grand army divided ? I simply charge that grave and serious errors have been committed, and, as I have said, no other way could have been devised to defeat that army. If the 158,000 men that were sent to General McClellan had been marched upon the enemy, they could have whipped all the armies the Confederates have, and all they are likely to have for six months. One hundred and fifty - eight thousand men are about as many as can be fought on any one battle - field. One hundred and fifty - eight thousand men are a vast army, a great deal larger army than that with which Napoleon destroyed 600,000 of the Austrians in a single year. One hundred and fifty - eight thousand men ably handled can defeat any force the Confederates can raise ; and that is the force that went down to the Peninsula. But, sir, it lay in ditches, digging, drinking rotten water, and eating bad food, and sleeping in the mud, until it became greatly reduced in numbers, and of those that were left very many were injured in health. Still they fought ; still they conquered in every fight , and still they retreated, because they were ordered to retreat

Sir, I have deemed it my duty to present this statement of facts to the Senate and the country. I know that I am to be denounced for so doing, and I tell you who will denounce me. There are two classes of men who are sure to denounce me, and no one else, and they are traitors and fools. The traitors have been denouncing every man who did not sing pæans to "strategy," when it led to defeat every time. The traitors North are worse than the traitors South, and sometimes I think we have as many of them in the aggregate. They are meaner men ; they are men who will come behind you and cut your throat in the dark. I have great respect for Southern traitors who shoulder their muskets and come out and take the chances of the bullets and the halter ; but I have the most superlative contempt for the Northern traitors, who, under the pretended guise of patriotism, are stabbing their country in the dark.

The effect of this speech was profound. It enraged McClellan's friends to the highest pitch; it was not supported at the time by any like utterance in Congress, and at first many who believed it to be true condemned, or at least deprecated, the fierceness of the attack; but those who knew that "the young Napoleon" at heart preferred a pro-slavery compromise to the conquest of a durable and honorable peace, and who had marked with righteous indignation the attempt of his *claquers* to make the Secretary of War the scape-goat for his own blunders, greeted with enthusiasm the signal courage of the man who, in the face of abuse, prejudice, and popular blindness, dared to tell with words of rugged force this story of disastrous imbecility. Mr. Chandler disregarded the remonstrances of weak friends, and met without quailing the storm of vituperation he had invited. Events made themselves his justifiers and within four months* President Lincoln, with the full approval of the patriotic masses of the North, relieved General McClellan from all command and abruptly terminated his military career. Nothing contributed more to this salutary change than Mr. Chandler's arraignment, of which it has been well said, that "with words resembling battles "he told the American people that they were leaning upon a "broken reed, that 'the idol of the soldiers' was as incapable of "helping them as the idols of the heathen, and that McClellan "was only digging graves for the brave men who followed him "and a last ditch for the cause he defended; he shocked by his "language the mass of the people into a right comprehension of "the death's dance this military Jack-o'-lantern was leading "them through the swamps of Virginia."

Mr. Chandler, who took this step after full deliberation and not from any passing impulse, rated the McClellan speech as his most important public service, alike in its necessity, its timeliness, and its results. He also felt that it involved more real hazard, and made larger demands upon his courage, than any other act of his Senatorial career, for such relentless invective could scarcely fail to mortally wound either its object or its maker. Had time shown that he had uttered calumnies and not the sober truth, he would have been inevitably driven from public life; and even when he spoke, the men who thoroughly doubted McClellan were still a small minority. History has

* On Nov. 7, 1862.

shown that his indictment was as true in substance as it was unsparing in terms and bold in spirit.

Two other matters naturally group themselves with this speech: Mr. Chandler distrusted McClellanism in the Army of the Potomac as thoroughly as he did McClellan. The investigations of this committee convinced him that General Pope's campaign was so unfortunate because of the insubordination of General McClellan's friends among the corps commanders, and led him to believe that the same cause crippled the movements of both Burnside and Hooker, who, if faithfully supported, would have won decisive victories. So strong were his convictions on these points, that when General Grant became commander-in-chief he called upon the Secretary of War and requested him to make out a list of the incompetent, suspected and insubordinate generals of the Army of the Potomac, to be furnished to that officer so that he would be able to place them where they could do the least harm in the service. This Secretary Stanton promised to do. A few days afterward Mr. Chandler called again at the War Department, and, learning that this had not yet been done, said, " I will make out the list myself and send it to Grant ; " and he did so, Major-Gen. C. C. Washburn being its bearer. Mr. Chandler carefully studied and vigilantly watched the Fitz-John Porter case, and approved of the findings of the court-martial, except the failure to inflict the death penalty, which he believed that the character and consequences of Porter's action fully merited. The attempt to secure the reversal of this verdict and the re-instatement in the army of the dismissed officer aroused his sternest indignation, and he fought it resolutely at every stage — and successfully, while he remained in the Senate. He spoke at length on this subject in that body on Feb. 21, 1870, declaring that he did so in fulfillment of a voluntary pledge given some years before in the same chamber to General Pope, " that justice should be done to him and to his campaign

" in the valley of Virginia, even although I were called upon to " vindicate him from my seat in the Senate." After rehearsing the facts connected with Pope's movement, which was planned to create a diversion of Lee's army for the extrication of McClellan's forces from the Peninsula, in conformity with the suggestion of Gen. James S. Wadsworth, and showing that Pope had frequently requested to be relieved from the hazardous work laid out for him and that he had only a force of 42,000 men scattered betweer Harper's Ferry and Acquia Creek, Mr. Chandler said :

I asked him in the presence of the committee: "What is to prevent you from being struck by a superior force of the enemy and overwhelmed?" Said he: "Nothing on earth is more probable than that I shall be struck by a "superior force and shall be whipped; but I will keep my troops near the "mountains, and there are no ten miles where there is not a gulch up which "I can take my men and small-arms, and, by abandoning my artillery and "baggage, save my men; I shall probably be whipped, but it must be done." Any military man can see and appreciate the difficulties and responsibilities of so desperate a campaign. "Yet," said he, "it must be done."

Well, sir, General Pope started on that campaign. Had he announced to the newspaper press of Washington, or of the North, the number of his men or his object, the object itself would have been defeated. General Pope did what I believe is allowable in war: he perpetrated a *ruse de guerre*. He sent his scouts all through the mountains of Virginia proclaiming that he had an army of 120,000 men. And, sir, he fooled the newspaper correspondents of the city of Washington and of the whole North. General Pope, when he started on that campaign, had no more idea of going to Richmond than he had of following Elijah to Heaven in a chariot of fire without seeing death. He started with one single object, and that was to save the army of McClellan, or to do all that was in his power to save it. He massed his troops, and that terrible battle of Cedar Mountain was fought; and by that battle he not only fooled the people of this country, but he fooled the rebels. The rebels believed that he had 120,000 men, and that, unless they fought him and crushed him before he could unite with the Army of the Potomac, their cause was lost; and he drew upon his shoulders with that little force the whole rebel army, so that, when McClellan started for Yorktown, there was not even a popgun fired at his troops. The *ruse* was a perfect success, and, as I told General Pope then, "I consider that your campaign has been one of the most brilliant that has been fought up to this time"—which was February, 1863—"you saved two armies.; you first saved the Army of the Potomac, and then you saved your own."

16

Sir, General Pope fought for eleven days, fought night and day, fought the whole rebel army with his little force, his force never having exceeded 70,000 men,—comprising not simply his own army, but also General Burnside's forces, and the 20,000 men who had in thirty days been brought up from the Army of the Potomac, and of whom Porter's corps was part. The force which he had met with these was that originally in his front, but overwhelmingly augmented by that rebel force from which McClellan, with his 90,000 men, had to be delivered by a demonstration in their rear. He fought for time. He defended every brook, every barn, every piece of woods, every ravine. He fought for time for the Army of the Potomac to reach him and unite with him, so as to crush the advancing and overwhelming force of the rebels.

Mr. Chandler then reviewed at length (and with copious citations from the testimony of eye-witnesses and the official orders) the facts as to Fitz-John Porter's course in Pope's campaign, adding extracts from the reports of rebel officers which had come into the possession of the government since the war, and closed as follows:

Mr. President, if I had more time I should like to go more fully into this subject; but I cannot. The court, after forty-five days spent in careful investigation, brought in unanimously the verdict against Porter. Many of the members of that court were in favor of sentencing him to suffer death. It is rumored, and many believe, that the only reason the death-penalty was not inflicted was the fear that Mr. Lincoln, whose kindness of heart was so well-known, would not execute the sentence; and, hence, they unanimously brought in the verdict they did. It was first carefully examined *seriatim* by the then Secretary of War and the President. No more just tribunal ever investigated a case, I presume to assert, than this tribunal, and there its finding stands.

It may be asked, How came it that a misunderstanding, almost as universal as complete, was suffered to be put upon the country? General Pope himself says: "The next day it (my report) was delivered to General Hal- "leck; but by that time influences of questionable character, and transactions "of most unquestionable impropriety, which were well known at the time, "had entirely changed the purposes of the authorities. It is not necessary, "and, perhaps, would scarcely be in place, for me to recount these things."

It is as well known to others present as to me that, during that gloomy, eventful Sunday which succeeded the last battle on Saturday, the 30th of August, the President and Mr. Stanton were overrun and overcome with statements that, unless McClellan was restored to command "the army would not fight." These statements came from men who did not mean it should fight, who could not in the exigency of the moment be displaced. The President was able afterward to relieve McClellan and court-martial Porter. Had he lived, he would have seen justice to General Pope awarded also. It remains for me, while I live, to do my portion of that duty.

There is one other point to which I wish to allude. During this very trial —during the very pendency of the trial—Fitz-John Porter said, in the presence of my informant, who is a man whom most of you know, and who is to-day in the employment of Congress, and whose word I would take as soon as I would most men's—though I told him I would not use his name, but I will give his sworn testimony, taken down within two minutes after the utterance was made—Fitz-John Porter said in his presence: "I was not true to Pope, and there is no use in denying it." Mr. President, what was "not true to Pope"? If he was not true to Pope, whom was he true to? Being true to Pope was being true to the country; "not true to Pope" was being a traitor to the country. Sir, "not true to Pope" meant the terrible fight of the 30th of August, with all the blood and all the horrors of that bitter day; "not true to Pope" meant the battle of Antietam, with its thousands of slain and its other thousands maimed: "not true to Pope" meant the first battle of Fredericksburg, with its 20,000 slain and maimed; "not true to Pope" covered the battles of the Wilderness and Cold Harbor, and all the dreadful battles that followed. Had F z-John Porter been true to his government, Jackson would have been destroyed on the 29th of August, and on the 30th the rebels could scarcely have offered any resistance to our victorious army. "Not true to Pope" meant 300,000 slain and 2,000,000,000 of additional dollars expended.

Sir, I wish to put this on the record for all time, that it may remain. Let Fitz-John Porter thank God that he yet lives, and that he was not living at that time under a military government. I told General Pope, in the first interview I had with him, that I had but one fault to find in the whole conduct of the campaign. He asked, "What is that?" Said I, "That you ever allowed Fitz-John Porter to leave the battle-field alive!"

In 1877 Porter at last succeeded, by the most persistent effort, in obtaining the order for the re-examination of his case, and when Mr. Chandler re-entered the Senate in 1879, he found himself confronting an organized movement to secure that officer's restoration to his old rank with full pay since the date of his dishonorable dismissal from the army. To this contemplated action he proposed to offer the most strenuous resistance, and the last volumes he drew from the Congressional Library were authorities he wished to consult in the preparation of his argument against the reversal of the Porter finding.

Mr. Chandler's positive opinions in the McClellan and Porter cases were shared by his colleagues of the Committee on the Conduct of the War of the Thirty-seventh Congress, and are justified by their elaborate reports covering the history of the Army of the Potomac from the battle of Ball's Bluff to the close of the Fredericksburg campaign. The Thirty-eighth Senate adopted a resolution continuing the existence of this committee, and, the House concurring, the old members, so far as they were in Congress, were re-appointed. Senator Harding of Oregon took the place of Mr. Wright, and afterward Mr. Buckalew of Pennsylvania succeeded Mr. Harding. From the House, Mr. B. F. Loan of Missouri was appointed as the successor of Mr. Covode. Wm. Blair Lord was re-elected clerk and stenographer. This committee also devoted much of its time to the troubles of the Army of the Potomac. General Burnside had resigned the command because of a misunderstanding with the President, brought about by the interference of Gens. John Cochrane and John Newton, and General Hooker was appointed in his place, with General Halleck as commander-in-chief But Halleck disliked Hooker, and forced his resignation by overruling his plans and countermanding his orders, General Meade succeeding. The committee examined closely into this matter, reaching the conclusion that Hooker had not been fairly dealt with, and incidentally disposing of the false statement then current that that officer was intoxicated at the battle of Chancellorsville, and was defeated from that cause. The committee condemned Hooker's removal, and Mr. Chandler firmly believed in his courage, patriotism and ability, and regarded him as the victim of circumstances. These facts make it an interesting coincidence that these two men — both bold, frank and positive in their respective spheres of public activity — should have died sudden and painless deaths within the same week.

The committee did not believe that the selection of General Meade for the command of the Army of the Potomac was a fortunate one, and doubted his ability to properly control his subordinates. While there is no reference to the matter in their report on this subject, it is a fact that they recommended the removal of General Meade from command, and the re-instatement of Hooker. On the 4th of March, 1864, Mr. Chandler and Mr. Wade called upon the President, and told him that they believed it to be their duty, impressed as they were with the testimony the committee had taken, to lay a copy of it before him, and in behalf of the army and the country demand the removal of General Meade, and the appointment of some one more competent to command. The President asked what general they could recommend; they said that for themselves they would be content with General Hooker, believing him to be competent, but not being advocates of any particular officer, they would say that if there was any one whom the President considered more competent, then let him be appointed. They added that "Con-"gress had appointed the committee to watch the conduct of "the war; and unless this state of things should be soon changed "it would become their duty to make the testimony public "which they had taken, with such comments as the circum-"stances of the case seemed to require." General Meade was not removed, but General Grant was, within a week, given command as general-in-chief, and assumed personal direction of the movements of the Army of the Potomac.

During 1864 and 1865 the committee (besides considering many minor matters) also investigated, with care:

1. The disastrous assault upon Petersburg on July 30, 1864; their report exonerated General Burnside from the responsibility for the repulse, and held that the disaster was attributable to the interference with his plans of General Meade, whose course in the matter was severely censured.

2. The unsuccessful expedition of 1864 up the Red river in Louisiana, which the committee (Mr. Gooch dissenting) emphatically condemned.

3. The first Fort Fisher expedition, the committee, in its report, approving of General Butler's course in withdrawing from the projected assault.

During the inquiry into the Petersburg fiasco, the sub-committee were in session at General Grant's headquarters, and Mr. Chandler was his guest, renewing there an early acquaintance and laying the foundations of their future close friendship. Some incidents of their intercourse were characteristic.

General Sherman had just reached Savannah, and the mystery of the objective point of his great "march to the sea" had thus been solved for the public. This memorable exploit was discussed at length between General Grant and Mr. Chandler. The former said that the suggestion was Sherman's, and so was the entire plan of the campaign. Sherman had urged it for a long time before he (Grant) would consent, but finally the conditions were ripe, and the order was given. General Grant added that Sherman was the only man in the army whom he would have entrusted this campaign to, as he was especially adapted for such a command, and said: "Congress ought to do something "for Sherman. He deserves a great deal more credit and honor "than he has ever received." "What can we do for him?" asked Mr. Chandler. "Increase his rank," was the reply. "We have made you lieutenant general," responded Mr. Chandler, laughingly, "and I suppose we could make him a general, and thus put him over you." "Do it," said Grant, promptly. "If "he carries this campaign through successfully, do it. I would "rather serve under Sherman than any man I know." General Grant also said that when he received a dispatch that Thomas had attacked Hood, he felt that a great victory was already won. He added: "I did not have any anxiety about the "result; when Thomas attacks, a victory is sure. He is a slow "man, but he is the surest man I know. Once in motion, he "is the hardest man to fight in this army. He never precipi-

" tates a battle unless he is all ready, and knows his points, and
" you may rest easy when he attacks, for the next news will
" be the enemy's rout. When Thomas once gets in motion the
" rebels have not force enough to stop him."

Upon the final adjournment of the Thirty-eighth Congress
(on March 4, 1865) it continued the existence of the Committee
on the Conduct of the War for ninety days, in order to afford
it time to finish its work. During this period it closed up some
pending inquiries and prepared its final reports. Its last action
was an examination into General Sherman's unauthorized and
unfortunate negotiations with General Johnston, which the committee disapproved and that officer's superiors promptly repudiated. The final report of the committee bears the date of the
22d of May, 1865, and its closing passages are as follows :

Your committee, at the close of the labors in which the most of them
have been engaged for nearly four years past, take occasion to submit a few
general observations in regard to their investigations. They commenced them
at a time when the government was still engaged in organizing its first great
armies, and before any important victory had given token of its ability to
crush out the rebellion by the strong hand of physical power. They have
continued them until the rebellion has been overthrown, the so-called Confederate government been made a thing of the past, and the chief of that
treasonable organization is a proclaimed felon in the hands of our authorities.
And soon the military and naval forces, whose deeds have been the subjects
of our inquiry, will return to the ways of peace and the pursuits of civil life,
from which they have been called for a time by the danger which threatened
their country. Yet while we welcome those brave veterans on their return
from fields made historical by their gallant achievements, our joy is saddened
as we view their thinned ranks and reflect that tens of thousands, as brave as
they, have fallen victims to that savage and infernal spirit which actuated
those who spared not the prisoners at their mercy, who sought by midnight
arson to destroy hundreds of defenseless women and children, and who hesitated not to resort to means and to commit acts so horrible that the nations
of the earth stand aghast as they are told what has been done. It is a matter
for congratulation that, notwithstanding the greatest provocations to pursue a
different course, our authorities have ever treated their prisoners humanely
and generously, and have in all respects conducted this contest according to
the rules of the most civilized warfare. . . .

Your committee would refer to the record of their labors to show the spirit and purpose by which they have been governed in their investigations. They have not sought to accomplish any purpose other than to elicit the truth ; to that end have all their labors been directed. If they have failed at any time to accomplish that purpose, it has been from causes beyond their control. Their work is before the people, and by it they are willing to be judged.

The volumes which contain the official record of the proceedings of the Committee on the Conduct of the War are and always must be regarded as the most valuable single magazine of historical material relating to the Great Rebellion. They have been liberally used in the preparation of every important account of our civil strife yet published, and the men, who shall in the light of another century estimate the greatness and significance of that "throe of progress," will inevitably look in their pages to the graphic narratives of those who were parts of memorable movements and actors in famous battles as a means of information, and to the conclusions of those who prosecuted inquiries so zealously when the events were yet fresh in the memory as a source of guidance. Infallibility is not a human attribute, and the work of this committee was not free from misapprehension and mistake. Time, which has shown some of its errors and will correct others, has also sustained the essential justice of its most important conclusions, which will stand unreversed on the pages of impartial history.

But the chief value of the labors of this committee is not to be found in its collection of rich materials for the future chronicler. To its unrecorded but potent influence upon the conduct of the war, adequate justice has not yet been done. Its unwearied investigations constantly exposed corruption, incompetence, and insubordination, and placed in the hands of the authorities the means of discovering and punishing the knavish, the weak, and the disloyal. Its activity was a perpetual prompter to energy, and a vigilant detective by the side of inefficiency and disaffection. As the result of its labors, the unsuccessful, the half-hearted, and the traitorous gave way to the able and the patriotic; because of the knowledge of its relentless questioning, indolent men were vigilant, and laxity was transformed into vigor. Its unremitting labors stayed up the hands of the War Secretary in the heaviest hours of his great task, and usefully informed the counsels and shaped the decisions of the White House. If its every session had been permanently secret, and not a line of its proceedings existed as a public record, there would still remain an ineffaceable transcript of the results of its action in the correcting of mistakes of organization and that crushing of sham generalship which alone made final victory possible.

CHAPTER XIV

ONSCRIPTION, taxation, and the reverses of the Union arms in the summer of 1862 in Virginia and elsewhere materially affected the political currents of the ensuing fall, and the tide of re-action against the war feeling reached its highest flood in the closing elections of that year. Horatio Seymour was then chosen Governor of New York; the States of New Jersey, Pennsylvania, Ohio, Indiana and Illinois gave anti-Republican majorities, and ten of the principal Northern States, which in 1860 rolled up over 200,000 Republican majority, gave over 35,000 to the Opposition, while the footings of their Congressional delegations showed a Democratic majority of ten replacing a Republican preponderance of forty-one. In Michigan a successful effort was made to fuse all the "conservative" elements in a so-called "Union movement," which obtained some support from lukewarm Republicans and was thus enabled to manifest unusual strength. Its platform was dissent from "radical" measures in general, and the force of its attacks was centered upon Senator Chandler and his record, as representing the most aggressive type of Republicanism. He accepted this challenge unhesitatingly, and fought the campaign through without a hint at retraction or an apologetic word. He defended the "blood letter" and the "McClellan speech" on every stump; he repeated before the people the bold utterances with which he had stirred the Senate; he declared to every audience that his record he would not qualify by a hair's breadth, and that by it he was prepared to stand or fall; and he denounced with unstinted severity the weakness of some of his critics and the disloyalty of others.* The brunt of the battle in his State fell upon him, and the vigor and courage of his personal canvass attracted widespread attention. He spoke in all the leading cities of Michigan during the campaign, and worked uninterruptedly until the day of election The result was the casting of 68,716 votes for the Republican State ticket to 62,102 for the "Union" candidates, and the choice of five Republicans out of the six members of Congress, and of a Legislature constituted as follows: Senate — 18 Republicans and 14 Fusionists; House — 63 Republicans and 37 Fusionists. This Legislature, on assembling in January, 1863, re-elected Mr. Chandler to the Senate in accordance with the unmistakable wish of his party and the universal expectation. The most strenuous efforts were made to detach Republican support from him, but they failed utterly. In the caucus the vote was taken *viva voce*, and it was unanimous for Mr. Chandler. In the Legislature he received the support of the representatives of his party as well as that of one or two members chosen by the Fusionists. The Opposition selected a candidate of Republican antecedents, and its vote was divided as follows: James F. Joy, 45; Alpheus Felch, 2; Hezekiah G. Wells, 1; Solomon L. Withey, 1. In his address of thanks before the nominating caucus, Mr. Chandler said: "I do "not claim my re-election as a personal tribute. It is, rather, a "tribute to principle. It indicates that the patriotic sons of "Michigan stand firm in support of the government and a vigor- "ous prosecution of the war."

---

* I pity the man who, in this hour of peril, stands back and says, "this is an abolition war, and I won't go." . . . There are but two classes of men now in the United States, and there are no middle men; these two classes are patriots and traitors. Between these two you must choose. A man might as well cast himself into the gulf that separated Dives from Lazarus as to stand out in this hour of trial.—*Speech at Ionia on September 6*.

It has taken time to educate us. If we had won certain victories the war would have been over, but the cause would have remained. The proclamation pronouncing emancipation, for which God bless Abraham Lincoln, is educating the people, and soon we will be ready to go forward. . . . We can never secure a permanent peace until we strike a death-blow at the cause of the war.—*Speech at Jackson on October 7*.

Not only did he thus modestly measure the significance of his re-election, but he bent every energy to make that felt which the people meant. Strafford's motto of "Thorough"— although the spirit was that of Hampden and Pym and not of the apostate Earl—expresses the fixity of purpose and the ardor of zeal with which he strove to make irresistible the blows of the Union against its assailants. Before the people, on the floor of the Senate, within the White House, at the private offices of the War Department, in committee-room, and as part of his daily intercourse with men of all ranks and classes, he urged the use of every resource for the defense of the nation and demanded the sternest punishment of those who had dared

> "to lay their hand upon the ark
> "Of her magnificent and awful cause."

As a Senator his vote was recorded for every important war measure, relating to the revenues, the finances, and the armies of the Union. Upon the great questions of public policy which bore so powerfully on the progress of the struggle he uniformly led his party. At the first Congressional session of the war he urged the employment of confiscation as a legitimate and effective weapon for checking and punishing rebellion; the measure he introduced at that time proved to be too sweeping to receive an immediate enactment, but within a few months Congress did advance on this subject to his ground. When General Butler declared that the slaves who fled to his camp from work upon the rebel intrenchments were "contraband of war," and reported his action to the authorities at Washington and asked for instructions, Mr. Chandler was one of the first to appreciate the adroit wisdom of that epigrammatic construction of military law, and his co-operation with Secretary Cameron in urging the approval of General Butler's action upon the President and General Scott was very valuable and effective. Immediately after the battle of

Bull Run he, with Mr. Sumner and Mr. Hamlin, called upon
Mr. Lincoln with a proposition to organize and arm the colored
people. Mr. Chandler even then favored the full exercise of the
President's constitutional war powers, and urged that they should
be used, first, to set the slaves free; and, second, to make the
slaves themselves aid the work of abolishing slavery and maintaining the Union. He believed that this institution was the
backbone of the South, that the war was brought on to save
it from the civilizing tendencies of the age, and that among
the first steps taken by the Federal government, when thus
assailed by slavery, should be the proclaiming of freedom to all
bondsmen and the guaranteeing of the protection of the government to the free. He argued that such a policy, promptly
declared, would produce chaos in the South, would subject the
Confederate government to the danger of local uprisings of the
negroes, and would thus make victory easy. But the Administration was not prepared to take a step so far in advance of
popular opinion, and for some months the prevailing policy was
one which prohibited the soldiers of the Union from protecting
or harboring fugitive slaves, and in some instances made slave-
hunters of the troops. When General Fremont, on the 31st of
August, issued his proclamation in Missouri, declaring free all
slaves belonging to persons engaged in the rebellion, Mr. Chandler was among those who most heartily approved this step. The
President was alarmed, as he feared the country was not ready
for such an act, and greatly modified the Fremont proclamation,
as he also did a still more sweeping order of General Hunter in
the following May. Mr. Chandler's disappointment at this was
extreme, but within a few months he saw emancipation resorted
to by the Administration as a war measure, and a death-blow
dealt to "the relic of barbarism." That part of the report for
1861 of Simon Cameron as Secretary of War, which urged the
most summary attacks upon the institution of slavery as the

surest means of dealing mortal blows to the rebellion, and which
Mr. Lincoln suppressed, Mr. Chandler heartily endorsed, and
every manifestation by Northern commanders of a disposition to
make their armies defenders of the slave system aroused his
indignation. The act of March 13, 1862, prohibiting by an
article of war the use of the troops for the returning of fugitive
slaves to their masters, he earnestly supported, and the act of
April 16, 1862, abolishing slavery in the District of Columbia,
was a measure in which he especially interested himself, and
whose final passage he celebrated by an entertainment given to
its most devoted friends at his rooms in the National Hotel of
Washington. The abortive colonization schemes which were tried
about this time, at Mr. Lincoln's urgent recommendation, Mr.
Chandler privately opposed as utterly inadequate and as a mere
diversion of force into useless channels, but for public reasons
he made no open resistance to the experiment. For the laws of
June 19, 1862, forever prohibiting slavery in the territories, and
of June 28, 1864, repealing the fugitive slave statutes, it need
not be said that he labored with unflagging industry.

Mr. Chandler was very active in advocating the use of
colored troops as soldiers, being months in advance of the
Administration in this respect; he urged this policy upon the
authorities unsuccessfully for weeks, and then worked earnestly
to secure legislation from Congress authorizing the enrollment
and enlistment of negroes. This movement was so strenuously
resisted at the capitol that in the end a compromise was effected
upon a bill, which was approved on July 16, 1862, authorizing
the receiving of colored men as laborers in the army to dig
trenches and do other work of non-combatants. But after the
Emancipation Proclamation black men were accepted as soldiers
by order of the President, and regularly enrolled and paid. Mr.
Chandler always believed that that proclamation and the enlistment of freedmen in the army were two of the most powerful

blows at the rebellion, and often remarked, when talking upon the subject, that they were worth 300,000 men. While the controversy over this important step was unsettled, General Butler, at New Orleans, found himself in need of reinforcements, and was actually compelled to organize and arm several regiments of colored soldiers, whom he knew to be especially well adapted to the performance of a certain class of duties in that region which could not be done by soldiers from the North, who were not acclimated. This step on his part followed his definite refusal, under instructions from Washington, to permit General Phelps to do the same thing (that officer resigning for this very reason.) While the correspondence on this whole topic was in progress with the authorities, General Butler appealed to Senator Chandler, writing him long letters showing the sanitary necessity of having negro garrisons in some localities, and touching upon the other phases of the question. He also asked the Senator's aid in securing arms and equipments for these colored troops, and obtained from him valuable assistance in pushing on the requisitions at the War Department in defiance of official "red tape." On this general question Mr. Chandler said in the Senate, on June 28, 1864:

I believe that this rebellion is to be crushed, is to be exterminated, and I believe that every man who favors it, whether he be a member of this body or a member of the Southern army, is to be crushed and to be exterminated, unless he repents. That is what I believe. . . . I thank God the nation has risen to the point of using every implement that the Almighty and common sense have put in its hands to crush the rebellion. . . . We do not need another man from north of the Potomac. Let us bring the loyal men of the South in to put down treason in the South, and there are men enough and more than enough to do it. We have heard enough about not using black men to put down this rebellion. I would use every thing that God and nature had put in my hands to put down this rebellion ; but first I would use the black element, bring every negro soldier who can fight into the army. A negro is better than a traitor. I say this advisedly. I consider a loyal negro better than a secession traitor, either in the North or the South. I prefer him anywhere and everywhere that you please to put him. A secession traitor is beneath a loyal negro. I would let a loyal negro vote ; I would let him testify ; I would let him fight ; I would let him do any other good thing, and I would exclude a secession traitor.

The seizure of the rebel emissaries, Mason and Slidell, by Captain Wilkes, on the British steamer Trent, was heartily applauded by Mr. Chandler, and he opposed with much earnestness their surrender at the demand of Great Britain. Mr. Seward's policy in the matter seemed to him to be humiliating, and the possibility of a second war, in case Captain Wilkes was sustained, he did not dread, believing that the nation would treble its military strength in the face of such a danger, that the South would suffer from an alliance with a country so long regarded as the hereditary foe of the American people, and that the end would be the conquest and annexation of the British American provinces. He was greatly incensed by Great Britain's prompt concession of belligerent rights to the South and by its blustering bearing in the Trent case, and at one time suggested a policy of non-intercourse with that power, which he regarded as an inveterate enemy. In later years he advocated the most vigorous pushing of "the Alabama claims," and at the time of the British war with Abyssinia offered in the Senate a resolution recognizing King Theodore as a "belligerent" in the general terms of the Queen's proclamation of May, 1861, in regard to the Confederacy. He never ceased to believe that the United States, in the settlement of its war claims with Great Britain, ought to have refused to accept anything less than the annexation of the Canadas.

Mr. Chandler in the Senate favored imposing severe penalties on the gold gambling in Wall street, which affected so injuriously the national credit. In the preparation of the internal revenue laws of 1862, imposing a large number of taxes and affecting vast interests, he gave exceedingly valuable aid, his own business experience and his familiarity with commercial details making his suggestions practical in form and wise in scope. Every measure to secure the stringent enforcement of the laws for the punishment of treason received his hearty support, and his denunciation of traitors and their open or secret allies continued to be vigorous and unsparing.*͜ His industry time alone seemed to restrain, for his zeal was inexhaustible and his magnificent physical powers bore the tremendous strain unyieldingly. His public record during the four years of the war makes it possible to apply to him, without extravagance, Lord Clarendon's description of Hampden: "He was of a vigilance not to be tired out or "wearied by the most laborious, and of parts not to be imposed "on by the most subtle or sharp, and of a personal courage "equal to his best parts."

The "little, nameless, unremembered acts" of these days were of no slight aggregate importance and thoroughly illustrate the characteristics of the man. There was no reasonable service that he was not quick to render to any volunteer who applied to him for aid. A blue uniform gained for its wearer prompt admittance to his room and a careful hearing for any request. Repeatedly private soldiers saw him leave men of rank and influence to listen to their stories, and lay aside matters of pressing moment to act upon their complaints or relieve their distress.†

---

* Extract from a debate in the Senate on April 12, 1864:

MR. POWELL, of Kentucky: The Senator from Michigan, if I understood him, said that I was now the friend of traitors?

MR. CHANDLER: You did understand me properly. You have been the friend of traitors, and I voted to expel you, as a traitor, from this body.

MR. POWELL: Do I understand you to say that I am now the friend of traitors and of treason?

MR. CHANDLER: You co-operated with traitors, and I have never known you to cast a vote that was not in favor of rebellion.

† It is exceedingly gratifying to witness the marked attention Mr. Chandler bestows on soldiers. One day I happened to be in his room, when a major-general and a senator came in. Shortly after a sprightly young soldier came to the door. When about to enter, the young man hesitated to interrupt their conversation, but Mr. Chandler at once gave his attention to the soldier, who, on being asked to take a seat and tell what he desired, said he was a paroled prisoner and wished a furlough home, and that he had been told that all he had to do was to apply to him and he would be sure to get it. Mr Chandler immediately took his papers and secured the furlough for him.—*Washington letter of 1863.*

He visited the hospitals to seek out Michigan men whom he could help, and to see that they were properly provided for, while their applications for furloughs and for discharges, if entrusted to his care, were so pushed as to obtain prompt action from the authorities in spite of routine and official tardiness. He advanced large sums of money to help destitute and invalid soldiers homeward,* or to aid the friends of fallen or wounded men upon their melancholy errands. Upon all occasions he was especially attentive to the humblest applicants, and the case of the private soldier in distress and need touched his sympathies the most quickly. His was a familiar figure in all the departments, often accompanied with a squad of sick, crippled, even ragged, veterans, in search of delayed furloughs, or of arrears of pay, or of the 'medical examinations preceding invalid discharges, or of some service which "red tape" had delayed. In the words of one who possessed abundant opportunities for obtaining knowledge, "This could be said of Mr. Chandler to a greater extent "than of any other public man I ever saw, that he would spare "no pains in doing even little things for men who were of the "smallest consequence to one in his position. He would take "great trouble in hunting up minor matters for enlisted men, "and this it was that made him so popular among the soldiers." His activity in their behalf was not limited by State lines; he answered any appeals that came to him, although he was especially prompt and vigilant in helping the "Michigan boys." †

---

* Mr. Chandler said that during the late war, while he was in Washington, he loaned our soldiers several thousands of dollars, in small sums of from $2 to $10 each, but that the whole amount was repaid to him with the exception of about $10, and he was satisfied that the poor men who owed him that small amount had given their lives for their country. —*Hon. M. S. Brewer in the House of Representatives, Jan. 23, 1880.*

† This tribute comes from a well-known officer of the Michigan volunteer regiments:

DETROIT, February 3, 1880.

Could all the acts of kindness and aid rendered by Senator Chandler to the soldiers of Michigan, their families and friends, during the war, and especially to those who filled the ranks, be gathered together and written out, the volumes that contained them would be large and numerous. No soldier, however humble, ever applied to him, when in distress

At the War Department Mr. Chandler was as well known as (and was reputed to be scarcely less powerful than) the Secretary himself. Mr. Stanton's brusqueness never daunted him, and few stood upon such terms of privileged ·intercourse with that no less irascible than great man. Repeatedly he elbowed his way through · the crowded ante-chamber of the Secretary's office, pushed past protesting orderlies, strode up to Mr. Stanton's private desk, and obtained by emphatic personal application some order which subordinates could not grant in a case needing prompt action.* Where other men would have encountered rebuff he rarely failed. In connection with this phase of his public activity these letters are of interest:

DETROIT, Mich.,.July 29, 1862.
Hon. E. M. Stanton, Secretary of War.

DEAR SIR : Brigadier-General Richardson, of this State, is reported as being absent from duty without leave. This is not true. He is absent on sick

---

or trouble, that he did not receive a patient hearing and, if possible, speedy aid. No soldier's wife, father, mother, or other kin ever wrote him a letter that was not answered. To these facts there are thousands who can testify to-day, and many thousands more who could do so were they not in their graves.

In those dark days he was always sanguine of the final triumph of our armies, and he always assured the soldiers of his positive convictions that in the end they would be victorious. None except those who had experience can ever know what cheerful assurances and hopeful words from those high in authority did to nerve men for the work of severe campaigns.

The trials and fatigues of army life, and the uncertainty of the final results, were lessened vastly by the assuring words of brave, indomitable men like Zachariah Chandler. All honor to his memory, as also to the memory of his great associates in high places during those memorable days !   R. A. ALGER.

*This anecdote is related by a prominent Michigan officer : I accompanied Senator Chandler once to the War Department to secure the re-instatement of a paymaster who, it had been clearly ascertained, had been unjustly dismissed. The papers were in the possession of the proper bureau, and action had been promised, but was delayed. A great body of eager applicants were gathered about the Secretary's door, which was guarded by two sentries with crossed bayonets. He pushed rapidly through the mass of people to the entrance of the private office, where the sentinel said, "The Secretary is very busy, Mr. Senator." "I know he is," was Mr. Chandler's response, and laying a hand on each bayonet he pushed them up over our heads, opened the door, and we were in Mr. Stanton's presence. Once there, he commenced a vigorous denunciation of the tardiness of the Department. upbraided the Secretary because no action had yet been taken in the case according to promise, and astonished me by the earnestness of his criticisms. Mr. Stanton heard him pleasantly, said when he stopped, ' Are you all through, Chandler ?" and then gave the order we needed.

leave, and is not able to join his command. Will you not, in accordance with the wishes of the whole delegation, assign him to the command of Michigan soldiers now being raised? His presence here, and the assurance that he is to command, will greatly stimulate enlistments. We are proud of him as one of the best fighting generals of the army. Very truly yours,

Z. CHANDLER.

DETROIT, July 31, 1862.

Hon. E. M. Stanton, Secretary of War.

SIR: There is a fine company of ninety-five splendid men guarding *three rebel prisoners* at Mackinac. Would it not be well to put those rascals in some tobacco warehouse or jail and send these troops where they are needed? General Terry would like a command in some other division than the one he is in. Can you not accommodate him? The soldiers at Mackinac are anxious for active service and are well drilled. Very truly yours,

Z. CHANDLER.

DETROIT, Aug. 9, 1862.

Adjutant - General Thomas.

DEAR SIR: Are the boys of the Michigan First (Bull Run prisoners) exchanged yet? I promised them it should be done at once, and now find them enlisting again under the supposition that it has been done. The list is with the Secretary of War. Our quota is full, and our blood is up. They were yesterday paying $10 for a chance to enter some of the regiments. Very truly yours, Z. CHANDLER.

DETROIT, Aug. 28, 1862.

Hon. Wm. A. Howard.

DEAR SIR: Will you say from me to the Secretary of War that I deem it of vital importance that some one be authorized to open and examine rebel correspondence passing through the Detroit postoffice? Mr. Smith (of the post-office) informs me that letters come through directed to rebels at Windsor. Truly yours, Z. CHANDLER.

DETROIT, Nov. 15, 1863.

Hon. E. M. Stanton, Secretary of War.

DEAR SIR: I telegraphed you to-night to send heavy guns and ammunition to the lakes. The reason was this: Upon examination I found that we could improvise a navy in about two hours which could cope with a rebel armament which could be placed upon the lakes, *if we had big guns.* But my investigation furnished one 68-pounder, condemned, and four 32-pounders, without powder, at Erie; and this was our whole armament on the lakes, except one 32-pounder upon the Michigan, and a few 6, 10 and 12-pounders. We must have guns of large calibre at each of the principal ports. If you cannot spare eleven-inch guns immediately send us some eight-inch or some old 68 - pounders, with ammunition. A tug, costing not over $30,000, with one eleven - inch gun on board and a crew of twenty men, could destroy a million dollars' worth of property on the lakes every twenty - four hours, and we would be powerless. She would sink the Michigan with one judiciously-placed shell. We are not alarmed, but we want big guns and we *must have them.* The lake marine is scarcely second to the ocean in tonnage and value, and it must be protected. We had no idea of our defenses until the late scare.

Truly yours, Z. CHANDLER.

Mr. Chandler's influence with public men and in the private councils of the nation's leaders at Washington was throughout the war always invigorating. From the very outset, and while the patriotic instinct of the North was "still, as it were, in the gristle and not yet hardened into the bone," he urged upon the executive authorities summary measures, and the striking of hard and quick blows. He advised them to arrest traitors while their treason was still in the bud. He urged them to make early and incessant attacks on the enemy, and counseled implicit reliance on the devotion and loyalty of the North. The Union cause saw no hour so dark that the eye of his courage could not penetrate its gloom; the rebellion won no victory that shook his absolutely "dauntless resolution." Every suggestion of peace except on the basis of Freedom and the national supremacy he denounced. Every hint of conciliating armed traitors he scouted as, in Hosea Biglow's phrase, mere "tryin' squirt - guns on the infernal Pit." To the real statesmanship of that period he thus gave expression in a public dinner at Washington early in 1863: "We must accept no compromise; a patched - up peace will be followed by continued war and anarchy." He chafed like a caged lion before half - heartedness, imbecility and delay. His sincerity and his earnestness revived the discouraged and aroused hope, and his strong convictions inspired men of weaker moral fibre with something of his own inflexibility. He never hesitated to use plain words in dealing with the nation's enemies, he never lost faith, and he never admitted the possibility of defeat. At the White House his visits were ever welcome, his advice received, and the virility of his understanding and the fervor of his patriotism recognized. ^Mr. Chandler appreciated to the full extent the innate strength of Abraham Lincoln's remarkable character and its rare loftiness, and, different as were their dispositions and widely divergent as often were their opinions, he never lost confidence in the President's aims and never ceased to be one of his trusted counselors. Many features of executive policy he condemned plainly and boldly to the President himself, but frankness and sincerity prevented his criticisms from becoming unpalatable, and Mr. Lincoln often acknowledged his indebtedness to the practical wisdom and the tireless zeal of the Michigan Senator.

Cecil said to Sir Walter Raleigh, "I know that you can toil terribly." This Mr. Chandler did through those eventful years. His labor was without cessation. The great demands upon the energies of the public man were equaled by appeals for private effort which he would not decline, and in every channel of profitable work for the Union cause he made his strong will and his aggressive vitality felt. Industry, so unusual and efficient, multiplied the power of his Roman firmness, and these qualities, guided by his strong understanding, high courage, sincerity of conviction, and the ardor of his patriotism, made him a leader of men in years when leadership without strength was impossible. His·impress is upon the events of that era, and of the war for Emancipation and the Union he could say with Ulysses, "I am part of all that I have met." Through the tempest of civil strife his strong spirit battled its way unflinchingly to the goal, and title was fitly bestowed in the people's knighting of Zachariah Chandler as "The Great War Senator."

CHAPTER XV.

THE Republican reverses of the fall of 1862 were not repeated in 1863. Gettysburg and Vicksburg, the anti-draft riots in New York, and the formal acceptance of Vallandigham as a trusted party leader by the Democracy stimulated and strengthened the Union spirit of the North, and the State elections of that year were emphatic endorsements of the party of freedom and of its policy. The political verdicts of the spring of 1864 were equally gratifying to the friends of liberty and the advocates of a vigorous prosecution of the war, and, with the accession of General Grant to the command of the Union armies and his "advance all along the line," it became evident that nothing but discord among the Republicans could deprive them of a sweeping victory in the presidential election. The masses of that party were unequivocally in favor of Mr. Lincoln's re-nomination; the common people saw one of themselves in the White House and fully met his firm trust in them with an answering confidence. But among men of influence within the Republican ranks there was an exceedingly earnest opposition to his second candidacy. Some of this sprang from rival aspirations; more of it from disappointed office-seeking and from personal pique; but there was outside and above such considerations a strong feeling, entirely disinterested in origin and honorable in character, and held by thousands of sincere men, that the President was unduly conservative in policy and that a man of more aggressive temperament ought to be elected in his stead. There were also not a few experienced politicians who regarded the personal opposition to Mr. Lincoln as sufficiently formidable to jeopard party success, and who were inclined to think that the selection of some candidate who was not identified with the existing Administration, and thus would not be compelled to defend its acts, was demanded on the ground of superior "availability." The anti-Lincoln wing of the party at that time included such men as Mr. Chase and Mr. Greeley, was represented by many of the leading newspapers, including the entire New York press except the *Times*, and counted among its especially active members not a few of the most earnest and devoted of the original Abolitionists.

In this chaotic condition of party sentiment a call appeared (in April, 1864) addressed "To the Radical Men of the Nation," and requesting them to meet by representatives in convention at Cleveland, O., on May 31. Those of its signers who were best known were B. Gratz Brown, Lucius Robinson, John Cochrane, Frederick Douglass, Elizabeth Cady Stanton, George B. Cheever, James Redpath, Wendell Phillips and Emil Pretorious. Its tone will appear from this paragraph:

The imbecile and vacillating policy of the present Administration in the conduct of the war, being just weak enough to waste its men and means to provoke the enemy, but not strong enough to conquer the rebellion — and its treachery to justice, freedom and genuine democratic principles in its plan of reconstruction, whereby the honor and dignity of the nation have been sacrificed to conciliate the still-existing and arrogant slave power, and to further the ends of unscrupulous partisan ambition — call in thunder tones upon the lovers of justice and their country to come to the rescue of the imperiled nationality and the cause of impartial and universal freedom threatened with betrayal and overthrow.

The way to victory and salvation is plain. Justice must be throned in the seats of national legislation, and guide the executive will. The things demanded, and which we ask you to join us to render sure, are the immediate extinction of slavery throughout the whole United States by Congressional action, the absolute equality of all men before the law without regard to race or color, and such a plan of reconstruction as shall conform entirely to the policy of freedom for all, placing the political power alone in the hands of the loyal, and executing with vigor the law for confiscating the property of the rebels.

This document was widely published, and the New York *Tribune* in advance approved the calling of this convention, although it did not in the end support its action. The call was answered by about 350 persons from fifteen States; while very few of them were men of more than limited reputation, yet they made up a body representing wide-spread convictions strongly and sincerely held. Ex-Governor W. F. Johnston of Pennsylvania was the temporary and Gen. John Cochrane of New York the permanent presiding officer of the convention. It nominated John C. Fremont for President, and General Cochrane for Vice-President, and adopted a platform exceedingly radical in terms, including declarations in favor of unconditional emancipation, a one-term presidency, the Monroe doctrine, and the wholesale confiscation of the property of the rebels. Two letters were received by it which at the time produced a strong impression. In one of them, Lucius Robinson, then Comptroller of New York, severely condemned "a weak Executive and Cabinet," and urged the nomination of General Grant, "a man who has displayed the qualities which give all men confidence." In the second, Wendell Phillips attacked a Republican administration with that polished invective which had made him one of the most formidable assailants of the slave power. He wrote:

For three years the Administration has lavished money without stint and drenched the land in blood, and it has not yet thoroughly and heartily struck at the slave system. Confessing that the use of this means is indispensable, the Administration has used it just enough to irritate the rebels and not enough to save the state. In sixty days after the rebellion broke out the Administration suspended *habeas corpus* on the plea of military necessity—justly. For three years it has poured out the treasure and blood of the country like water. Meanwhile slavery was too sacred to be used; that was saved lest the feelings of the rebels should be hurt. The Administration weighed treasure, blood, and civil liberty against slavery, and, up to the present moment, has decided to exhaust them all before it uses freedom heartily as a means of battle. . . . A quick and thorough reorganization of States on a democratic basis — every man and race equal before the law — is the only sure way to save the Union. I urge it, not for the black man's sake

alone, but for ours — for the nation's sake. Against such recognition of the
blacks Mr. Lincoln stands pledged by prejudice and avowal. Men say, if we
elect him he may change his views. Possibly. But three years have been a
long time for a man's education in such hours as these. The nation cannot
afford more. At any rate the constitution gives this summer an opportunity
to make President a man fully educated. I prefer that course.

The Administration, therefore, I regard as a civil and military failure,
and its avowed policy ruinous to the North in every point of view. Mr. Lincoln may wish the end — peace and freedom — but he is wholly unwilling to
use the means which can secure that end. If Mr. Lincoln is re-elected I do
not expect to see the Union reconstructed in my day, unless on terms more
disastrous to liberty than even disunion would be. If I turn to General Fremont, I see a man whose first act would be to use the freedom of the negro
as his weapon; I see one whose thorough loyalty to democratic institutions
without regard to race, whose earnest and decisive character, whose clear-
sighted statesmanship and rare military ability justify my confidence that in
his hands all will be done to save the state that foresight, skill, decision, and
statesmanship can do.

Generals Fremont and Cochrane promptly accepted the nominations thus tendered them. General Fremont resigned his
commission in the army before doing so, and in his letter of
acceptance accused the Administration of " incapacity and self-
ishness," of " managing the war for personal ends," of giving to
the country " the abuses of a military dictation without its unity
of action and vigor of execution," and of " feebleness and want
of principle" in its dealings with other powers. He further
vindicated the Cleveland action by declaring that, "if Mr. Lin-
" coln had remained faithful to the principles he was elected to
" defend, no schism could have been created," and added : " If
" the convention at Baltimore will nominate any man whose past
" life justifies a well-grounded confidence in his fidelity to our
" cardinal principles, there is no reason why there should be any
" division among the really patriotic men of the country." There
was a lack of any popular response to this demonstration, and
it at once appeared — and, in fact, this was the sum of the
original expectations of its shrewder promoters — that this movement was only formidable as a rallying point for any serious
disaffection which might spring up in the future.

The "Union National" convention assembled at Baltimore on June 7, with every State, except those still wholly in possession of the rebels, represented upon its floor. It adopted a platform denouncing any peace by compromise, endorsing the Administration, and demanding the abolition of slavery by constitutional amendment. Abraham Lincoln was re-nominated for the Presidency, receiving every vote save that of the delegation of Missouri radicals who supported General Grant, and Andrew Johnson was on the first ballot nominated for Vice-President as the representative of the Union men of the South. The response of the masses and the leading papers of the Republican organization to this action was prompt and hearty; but, notwithstanding this encouraging fact, the political horizon grew rapidly darker. General Grant was in that summer fighting a series of bloody battles on and about the banks of the James, whose immediate results were indecisive, the attendant steady reduction of Lee's available force not being then apparent at the North. In like manner, Sherman was forcing his way through the mountainous regions between Chattanooga and Atlanta, winning no great victories and losing thousands of men; the mortal effects of his blows at the rebels are evident now, but could not be seen then. General Early, in July, swept down the Shenandoah and over the Potomac, burning Chambersburg and threatening the defenses of Washington, finally making good his retreat. In the face of this military situation, so encouraging to discontent and so calculated to invite criticism, the premium on gold rose rapidly to its highest war point. This disastrous depreciation of the paper money of the government was materially helped by the unexpected resignation, on June 30, of Secretary of the Treasury Salmon P. Chase. Differences of opinion as to some details of department management were assigned as the cause of this step, but its real origin was much deeper, and Mr. Chase's course was universally ascribed, and was undoubtedly due, to lack of sym-

pathy with and confidence in the Administration. The effect of
a change in so important a position at such a critical moment
was profound, and it gave a powerful stimulus to Republican
disaffection. This was followed by the abortive peace negotiations at Niagara Falls with C. C. Clay, J. P. Holcombe and G.
N. Sanders. That this was a crafty scheme to place the Administration in a false position before both the North and the South
cannot now be doubted. It failed to yield all that its projectors
hoped, but it did ensnare Mr. Greeley most disagreeably, and it
had the effect of furnishing the enemy with grounds for charging the President with being "hostile to peace except on
impossible conditions." It also materially augmented the public
restlessness and deepened the vague apprehensions which naturally sprang from such exhibitions of cross-purposes among the
leaders of the national cause. Another event followed which was
of still graver moment:

The problem of the reconstruction of the Southern States
after the defeat of the rebel armies was from the outset surrounded with grave difficulties, and the views held upon this
subject by the ablest Republicans were diverse and conflicting.
Bills and resolutions embodying various theories of reconstruction
were presented in Congress early in the war, but nothing was
done with them, and no definite policy was fixed by enactment
or even determined upon in private consultations. On Dec. 8,
1863, and in connection with the transmission to Congress of his
third annual message, Mr. Lincoln issued a proclamation offering
amnesty to all rebels (with a few conspicuous exceptions) who
should take an oath of loyalty, and declaring that whenever, in
any of the seceded States, persons to the number of not less
than one-tenth of the votes cast in such States at the presidential election of 1860, having first taken and abided by the
prescribed oath, should re-establish a State government, republican in form and recognizing the permanent freedom of the

slaves, it should "be recognized as the true government of the State." This plan Mr. Lincoln explained and defended at length in the message, and under it provisional governments were soon organized in Louisiana and Arkansas, and application was made for the admission of their Senators and Representatives to Congress. The President's action in this respect did not receive congressional sanction and was not endorsed by the majority of his supporters at the capitol. Many held that the subject was one which was wholly within the control of the legislative branch of the government, and that his proclamation was itself an unwarrantable assumption of authority by the Executive. Others objected strenuously to the "one-tenth clause," as oligarchical in tendency and certain to leave the real advantages of position within easy reach of the disloyal majority in any State thus reconstructed. As a rule those who opposed Mr. Lincoln's scheme favored establishing provisional governments in the South until there should spring up a loyal majority, which could be safely trusted with political power. Congress, therefore, referred the message and proclamation to special committees, refused to recognize the Louisiana and Arkansas governments, and passed on the last day of the session a reconstruction act differing radically in terms from the President's plan. Its bill provided that provisional governors should be appointed with the consent of the Senate, that an enrollment of white male citizens should be made when armed resistance ceased in any State, and that when a majority of the citizens so enrolled took the oath of allegiance the loyal people should be entitled to elect delegates to a convention to establish a State government; upon the adoption of an anti-slavery constitution by such a convention it was to be certified to the President, who, with the assent of Congress, was to recognize the government thus established as "the lawful State government." This measure the President defeated by withholding his signature. On July 8, 1864, he issued a second proclamation upon the subject, setting forth that he had not signed this bill because "less than one hour" intervened between its passage and the adjournment of Congress, and because he was not ready by its approval to be inexorably committed to this or any other specific plan of reconstruction which would set aside the *quasi*-governments of Louisiana and Arkansas and thus repel their citizens from further efforts in the same direction. He added that he was not yet prepared to admit the "constitutional competency of Congress to abolish slavery in the States," although he did earnestly desire that it should cease through the adoption of a constitutional amendment. The proclamation closed by declaring that he was satisfied with the terms of the bill, and by pledging the hearty co-operation of the Executive with all who might avail themselves of the method therein laid down to return to their places in the Union. In response to this proclamation, which treated the process of reconstruction as a matter of executive discretion merely, there was published early in August a vigorously worded and cogently argued manifesto, addressed "To the Supporters of the Government," and signed by Senator Benjamin F. Wade and Representative Henry Winter Davis, as chairmen of the committees of their respective houses upon the *status* of the rebel States. This document commenced with the declaration that its authors had "read without surprise, but not without indignation," the President's proclamation, and proceeded as follows:

The President, by preventing this bill from becoming a law, holds the electoral votes of the rebel States at the dictation of his personal ambition. If those votes turn the balance in his favor, is it to be supposed that his competitor, defeated by such means, will acquiesce? If the rebel majority assert their supremacy in those States, and send votes which elect an enemy of the government, will we not repel his claims? And is not that civil war for the presidency inaugurated by the votes of rebel States? Seriously impressed with these dangers, Congress, "the proper constitutional authority," formally declared that there are no State governments in the rebel States, and provided for their erection at a proper time; and both the Senate and House of Representatives rejected the Senators and Representatives chosen under the authority of what the President calls the free constitution and government of Arkansas. The President's proclamation "holds for naught" this judgment, and discards the authority of the Supreme Court and strides headlong toward the anarchy his proclamation of the 8th of December inaugurated. If electors for President be allowed to be chosen in either of those States, a sinister light will be cast on the motives which induced the President to "hold for naught" the will of Congress rather than his governments in Louisiana and Arkansas. That judgment of Congress which the President defies was the exercise of an authority exclusively vested in Congress by the constitution to determine what is the established government in a State, and in its own nature and by the highest of judicial authority binding on all other departments of the government. . . . A more studied outrage on the legislative authority of the people has never been perpetrated. Congress passed a bill ; the President refused to approve it, and then by proclamation puts as much of it in force as he sees fit, and proposes to execute those parts by officers unknown to the laws of the United States and not subject to the confirmation of the Senate ! The bill directed the appointment of provisional governors by and with the advice and consent of the Senate. The President, after defeating such a law, proposes to appoint without law, and without the advice and consent of the Senate, military governors for the rebel States ! He has already exercised this dictatorial usurpation in Louisiana, and he defeated the bill to prevent its limitation. . . .

The President has greatly presumed on the forbearance which the sup-porters of his administration have so long practiced, in view of the arduous conflict in which we are engaged, and the reckless ferocity of our political opponents. But he must understand that our support is of a cause and not of a man ; that the authority of Congress is paramount and must be respected; and that the whole body of the Union men of Congress will not submit to be impeached by him of rash and unconstitutional legislation ; and if he wishes our support, he must confine himself to his executive duties — to obey and execute, not make the laws — to suppress by arms armed rebellion, and leave political reorganization to Congress.

If the supporters of the government fail to insist on this, they become responsible for the usurpations which they fail to rebuke, and are justly liable to the indignation of the people, whose rights and security, committed to their keeping, they sacrifice. Let them consider the remedy for these usurpations, and, having found it, fearlessly execute it !

The damaging force of this attack was undoubted. Mr. Wade was a veteran of the anti-slavery "Old Guard," and was known through the North to be as sturdy, true and honest as he was "radical" in his Republicanism No man sat in the

House who surpassed — but few men then in public life equaled — Henry Winter Davis in mental vigor, in brilliant accomplishments, and in moral fearlessness. Originally sent to Congress by the Maryland "Americans," it was his vote which elected Mr. Pennington to the Speakership in 1859; to the formal censure of that act by his Legislature he replied by telling the men who voted for it to take their message back to their masters, for only to their masters, the people, would he reply. He made a magnificent fight against secession in his State, and waged there a still more gallant battle for emancipation, winning both. In the House he spoke always with force, often with impassioned eloquence, and the Republican ranks contained no champion more ardent in patriotism or more firmly attached to the fundamental principles of Freedom. The formal uniting of these two men, both able, influential and unquestionably sincere, in strictures so severe upon the President, materially invigorated the "radical" opposition to the Baltimore ticket, increased Republican discouragement, and furnished the Opposition with additional ground for accusing the President of the gross use of arbitrary power. The series of events thus recapitulated naturally gave to the action of the Cleveland convention a fresh importance, and by the fall of 1864 it had become a factor of moment in the political calculations of the year.

Greatly encouraged by the evident demoralization of the dominant party, the Democrats held their national convention at Chicago on August 29. Its platform in effect declared the war "a failure," and its ticket consisted of George B. McClellan, representing war without vigor, and George H. Pendleton, representing peace by compromise. The most conspicuous figure on its floor was Clement L. Vallandigham, a banished traitor *posing* as a martyr, and the sedition which was thinly disguised in its deliberations was boldly shouted to cheering mobs about its hall and in front of the great hotels which its delegates thronged.

The character and action of this body made clear the issues of 1864; in Mr. Seward's apt language, the people were called upon to decide whether they would have "McClellan and Disunion or Lincoln and Union." To make the latter the accepted alternative was impossible without complete Republican harmony, and to restore that fully and promptly was plainly a matter of the first importance. This task was undertaken by Mr. Chandler, whose relations with all parties peculiarly fitted him for the work. He was a pronounced "radical," and had steadfastly opposed many features of Mr. Lincoln's policy;* but honest disagreement of opinion had not impaired his full confidence in the man, and that firm grasp upon the practical aspects of all political questions, which was one of his marked characteristics then as always, prevented him from putting in jeopardy essentials by unduly magnifying differences as to details. To the wisdom of renominating Mr. Lincoln he assented, and his election he believed necessary to the preservation of the government. With Mr. Wade he was on terms of the closest intimacy; both Mr. Davis and General Fremont were his personal friends; and his record and public attitude gave him a claim upon the attention of the "radicals" everywhere. His qualifications as a mediator were thus numerous and apparent, and were rounded out by his political experience and sagacity.

Mr. Chandler commenced work by visiting Mr. Wade at his

---

* Mr. Chandler explained the ground of his opposition to the ten per cent. loyal basis plan of reconstruction proposed by Mr. Lincoln for the admission of Louisiana and Arkansas. There were not more than seven or eight members of the Senate with him at the beginning of the session on that question, although there was a large majority before its close. The Democrats did not believe in this ten per cent. doctrine, and they voted with those who did not believe in admitting those States without guarantees. This admission was finally prevented by a night of filibustering. Only six Republicans remained and voted during that night. The result, however, proved that those six men were right, and that Mr. Lincoln and the others were wrong. If Louisiana and Arkansas had been admitted, then we would have been compelled to admit all the other States in the same way, and to-day we would have eleven rebel States in the Union. Those two States, Louisiana and Arkansas, had become the most intensely rebel of all the States that were in rebellion.— *Report of his speech before the Republican caucus at Lansing on Jan. 6, 1869.*

18

home in Ohio, being accompanied thither by his intimate friend and adviser, the Hon. George Jerome of Detroit. The Ohio senator's vigorous common sense was Mr. Chandler's ally in the long interview that followed, and it only required a thorough review of the situation to convince him that, if Lincoln was defeated, the Union cause, and not an individual, would be the sufferer. Mr. Wade, however, urged that Mr. Lincoln himself should make some sacrifices of opinion and preference in the face of the common danger, that the "radical" element of the Republicans was entitled to more considerate treatment at his hands, and that, at least, his Cabinet, which was wholly within his control, should not contain men who were obnoxious to the stanchest members of his own party. Mr. Wade then denounced in the strongest terms the presence in and influence upon the Administration of Montgomery Blair, whom he believed to be at heart a Democrat. Later years have shown how well-grounded were the doubts then felt of Mr. Blair's political trustworthiness, doubts which were, even in 1864, general and strong enough to lead the Baltimore convention to declare in its platform that it regarded "as worthy of public confidence and official trust only those who cordially endorsed" its principles. Mr. Wade readily agreed, as the result of this conference, to pursue any course that should command the approval of his associate in the manifesto, and Mr. Chandler left him to visit Mr. Lincoln at Washington and Henry Winter Davis at Baltimore. He obtained from the President what were practical assurances that Mr. Blair should not be retained in the Cabinet in the face of such strong opposition if harmony would follow his removal. Mr. Davis promptly recognized the logic of the situation, and expressed his willingness to accept Blair's displacement as an olive branch and give his earnest support to the Baltimore ticket.

Mr. Chandler next proceeded to New York, and opened negotiations there with the managers of the Fremont movement.

He had expected Mr. Wade to join him, but was disappointed
in this; he met at the Astor House the Hon. David H. Jerome
of Saginaw and the Hon. Ebenezer O. Grosvenor of Jonesville,
with whom he frequently counseled, and he also obtained the
assistance of George Wilkes of the *Spirit of the Times*. Mr.
Wilkes was well known as the master of a pure and vigorous
English, and no war correspondent equaled him in accurate, lucid
and graphic descriptions of important movements and famous
battles. The public, however, did not know the extent of his
political ability, of his skill in affairs and of his patriotic energy,
and these qualities proved of the highest usefulness to Mr.
Chandler in the completion of his delicate mission. Without the
aid so intelligently and zealously rendered by Mr. Wilkes, Mr.
Chandler doubted whether complete success would have been
possible. The negotiations were protracted for some days, but
ultimately the leaders of the Fremont organization agreed that,
if Mr. Blair (whom General Fremont regarded as a bitter
enemy) left the Cabinet and all other sources of Republican
opposition to the Baltimore nominees were removed, the Cleveland ticket should be formally withdrawn from the field. While
these conferences were in progress Mr. Chandler learned that the
editor of one of the influential evening papers of New York,
who had originally doubted the propriety of Mr. Lincoln's
renomination, had concluded that his election was not possible
and had prepared " a leader " urging his withdrawal, the holding
of a second convention, and Republican union upon either General Fremont or some other candidate who could command the
solid party support. It was not until the day of the intended
publication of the article and after it was in type that Mr.
Chandler learned of its existence, and then by instant and earnest efforts he obtained its withholding until the result of his
labors could be known. Ultimately all obstacles yielded to his
persistence and skill, and he started for the capital to inform

Mr. Lincoln of the close of the negotiations and to ask the fulfillment of the assurances concerning Mr. Blair's removal. On reaching Washington he went instantly to the White House, was admitted to an immediate private interview with the President in preference to a great throng of visitors, and reported in detail the successful result of his labors. On the day of this call upon Mr. Lincoln (Sept. 22, 1864) the newspapers published General Fremont's letter withdrawing his name as a presidential candidate. In it he said:

The presidential contest has in effect been entered upon in such a way that the union of the Republican party has become a paramount necessity. The policy of the Democratic party signifies either separation or re-establishment with slavery. The Chicago platform is simply separation. General McClellan's letter of acceptance is re-establishment with slavery. The Republican candidate is, on the contrary, pledged to the re-establishment of the Union *without* slavery, and, however hesitating his policy may be, the pressure of his party will, we may hope, force him to it. Between these issues I think that no man of the Liberal party can remain in doubt. I believe I am consistent with my antecedents and my principles in withdrawing — not to aid in the triumph of Mr. Lincoln, but to do my part toward preventing the election of the Democratic candidate. In respect to Mr. Lincoln, I continue to hold exactly the sentiments contained in my letter of acceptance. I consider that his administration has been politically, militarily and financially a failure, and that its necessary continuance is a cause of regret to the country.

On the following day this correspondence took place:

EXECUTIVE MANSION, WASHINGTON, Sept. 23, 1864.
Hon. Montgomery Blair.

MY DEAR SIR: You have generously said to me more than once that, whenever your resignation could be a relief to me, it was at my disposal. That time has come. You very well know that this proceeds from no dissatisfaction of mine with you personally or officially. Your uniform kindness has been unsurpassed by that of any friend, and while it is true that the war does not seem greatly to add to the difficulties of your department, as to those of some others, it is not too much to say, which I most truly can, that in the three years and a half during which you have administered the general post-office I remember no single complaint against you in connection therewith. Yours as ever, ABRAHAM LINCOLN.

POSTOFFICE DEPARTMENT, Sept. 23, 1864.

MY DEAR SIR: I have received your note of this date referring to my offer to resign whenever you would deem it advisable for the public interest that I should do so, and stating that in your judgment that time has come. I now, therefore, formally tender my resignation of the office of Postmaster-General.

I cannot take leave of you without renewing the expression of my gratitude for the uniform kindness which has marked your course toward me.

Yours truly,   M. BLAIR.

To the President.

Mr. Blair's resignation was accepted by the majority of Republicans throughout the North as a "cleansing of the Cabinet," * and party lines were at once re-formed. The "radicals" became earnest supporters of the Baltimore ticket, no Republican demand for a new nomination or a second convention appeared, Mr. Davis ceased his trenchant criticisms, and Mr. Wade took the stump and made a series of exceedingly effective speeches in Ohio and Pennsylvania. Military success also came with its powerful help. General Sherman crowned his campaign by the capture of Atlanta, General Grant drew the coils of "the anaconda" daily tighter about the rebel capital, and General Sheridan fairly "swept" Early from the valley of the Shenandoah. The results of the September elections had been dubious in significance, but those of October were decisive Republican victories and preceded an overwhelming triumph in November. Mr. Chandler (who had in 1863 taken an active share in the campaigns in New York and Illinois,† Michigan not holding any general election in that year) returned from his labors of mediation to his own State and spoke to almost daily mass-meetings

---

* Mr. Greeley's comment in the New York "Tribune" was: "Precisely why Mr. Lincoln thought this action called for at this moment, rather than at any other time in the "last four months, we are not told." This chapter shows that Mr. Chandler could have "told" him.

† If the North had been a unit the rebellion would long ago have been crushed. But the rebels found out we were not a unit at any time, so they persevered, so they invaded Pennsylvania, so they hoped to take Washington, and to raise insurrection all over the land. The only hope of the South to-day is in the traitors of the North. . . . They will fail in the contest. Instead of having established a slave empire they will have, by their own acts, destroyed all the securities that slavery ever possessed. They will have swept away all the compromises by which slavery has been tolerated by a forbearing people.— *Senator Chandler at Springfield, Ill., on Sept. 7, 1863.*

in its chief towns throughout the month of October. Michigan gave to the Lincoln electors a majority of 16,917, and sent only Republicans to the Thirty-ninth Congress. Mr. Chandler's contribution to this result was not unimportant, but it was of meagre value compared with his labors upon a broader field in healing grave dissensions and in quietly removing a cause of danger which was deeply founded, and which, although now almost forgotten, was then of no slight actual proportions and of very serious possibilities. It was characteristic of the man that this self-prompted and successful service, one of the greatest he ever rendered to Republicanism, was rarely mentioned by him afterward, and never as if it was more than was due to the cause of his political faith nor as if it gave him any especial claim upon the party gratitude.

CHAPTER XVI.

N the evening of April 14, 1865, Abraham Lincoln was assassinated at Ford's theater in the city of Washington. The universal grief was fitly described by Disraeli, who said, in the British Commons, that the character of the victim and the circumstances of his death took the event "out of all the pomp of history and the ceremonial of diplo-"macy; it touched the heart of nations and appealed to the "domestic sentiment of mankind." Its effect upon the American people was profound, and it deepened vastly the public appreciation of the essential barbarity of the prejudices, passions and ambitions which had plunged the republic into civil war.

The members of the Committee on the Conduct of the War returned on the evening of this crime from Richmond, having made an unsuccessful attempt to visit North Carolina for the purpose of taking testimony in regard to the Fort Fisher expedition. On the following morning they met, and addressed a formal note to Andrew Johnson, who had, while a Senator, served upon that committee, expressing the wish of his "old associates" to call upon him and acquaint him with "many things which they had seen and heard at Richmond." They were promptly admitted to his apartments at the Kirkwood House, and were among the first to talk freely with the man who had been so tragically made President of the newly-restored Union. Mr. Johnson had just been sworn into office by Chief Justice Chase in the presence of some of the Cabinet and a few Congressmen, and naturally the conversation chiefly turned upon the pursuit of the assassins, and the proper punishment of the men who had inspired or countenanced this crime, as well as of its actual committers. As a sequel of this conference, an important meeting was held on the following day (Sunday, April 16, 1865) in the President's rooms. By appointment Senators Chandler and Wade and John Covode (an original member of the Committee on the Conduct of the War, then a contestant for a seat in the House) called upon Mr. Johnson, and proceeded to consider with him what policy should be pursued toward the chiefs of the conquered rebellion. They believed that the public interest required that examples should be made of a few of the more guilty of the Southern traitors, and urged such a course upon the President. They found him — confronted as he was with the danger of assassination, and recollecting his own sufferings as a Southern Unionist — eager for measures of extreme rigor, and were compelled at the outset to seek to moderate a violence of intention on his part, which was certain to defeat the aim they were anxious to secure, namely: that of impressing the public with a sense of the justice as well as the severity of the punishment of deliberate and inexcusable treason. Andrew Johnson's disposition was to give to the contemplated proceedings rather a revengeful than a sternly retributive complexion. The relations of Mr. Chandler, Mr. Wade and Mr. Covode with their former fellow-committeeman were then exceedingly intimate, and they labored to restrain his vehemence and to direct his determination into a channel of action which should be just and not passionate, and should thus yield wholesome influences. It had been suggested that Davis and other fugitive rebels should be allowed to escape to Mexico or Europe, and the question of their punishment thus evaded; this plan was promptly condemned by all the participants in the conference, and there was a general agreement that the leaders of the rebellion should be arrested as rapidly as possible and held to answer for their offenses. The next question that arose related to the best method of procedure after these men had been captured, and then it was decided than Gen. Benjamin F. Butler should be sent for to give his advice as a lawyer. Mr. Covode undertook this errand and soon returned with him. Mr. Chandler then stated to General Butler the subject of the conference, and the President added that he was anxious to make a historical example of the leading traitors, for its moral effect upon the future, and took exceedingly extreme ground on this point, much more so than the other gentlemen were willing to approve. All of those present expressed their opinions in turn, after Mr. Johnson had concluded, and all agreed upon one point, namely: that in the case of the seizure of . Jefferson Davis he should be summarily punished by death. Mr. Chandler remarked, with emphasis:

"You have only to hang a few of these traitors and all will "be peace and quiet in the South. A few men have done the "mischief, and the masses of the people were misled by them. "They have put the country in great peril to gratify their "political ambition and they ought to suffer the penalty of "treason as a warning to all men hereafter."

To this Andrew Johnson replied that Mr. Chandler could not know the full enormity of the crime Davis and his associates had committed, that Northern men could never realize the sufferings the rebellion had brought upon the loyal people of the South, and that no punishment could be too severe. He added that he was determined that a precedent should be established that would be forever a terror to such men as had conspired to overthrow the government.

After some further conversation, the President asked General Butler for his professional opinion, as to whether Davis, Benjamin, Floyd, Wigfall, and the other civil officers of the Confederacy, could be tried by a military commission. General Butler replied that if they could be arrested in the insurrectionary States — in any locality under military control and where no civil authority existed or was recognized — they could be arraigned before such a tribunal, but a court of this character would have no jurisdiction if the criminals should get upon foreign soil, or, before being apprehended, reach any district where the civil law was in force. Mr. Chandler then urged that Davis should, by all means, be secured before he had a chance to leave the seceded States; and inquired as to the situation of the troops in the South and the probability of their defeating an attempt by Davis to fly through Mexico, or by boat on the Gulf. President Johnson replied that no way was open for his escape, but that he would be captured, dead or alive. The supposition that Davis was implicated in the assassination plot was then discussed with some difference of opinion, and finally the President asked General Butler to indicate a plan for the prosecution and punishment of Davis and his associates, for the use of the government. General Butler consented and the conference ended.

With the preparation of the memorandum thus requested, General Butler occupied almost his entire time for several weeks, investigating precedents, and examining authorities with the utmost thoroughness. During this work he was repeatedly in consultation with Mr. Chandler, who saw all of his notes and made many suggestions; before its completion, Davis had been captured and sent to Fortress Monroe. General Butler's plan was submitted to President Johnson in the latter part of May, 1865. It was long and elaborate, was based upon an exhaustive examination of the history of all military tribunals, and set forth in substance these propositions:

1. That Davis could be tried by a military commission, having been captured while in rebellion in a locality where no lawful civil authority existed. This tribunal could sit at Fortress Monroe, where Davis was a prisoner, as that was still within the military lines.

2. That this commission should be composed of the thirteen officers of the highest rank in the army; this provision would have made it consist of Lieut.-Gen. U. S. Grant; Major-Generals H. W. Halleck, W. T. Sherman, George G. Meade, Philip H. Sheridan, George H. Thomas, and Brigadier-Generals Irwin McDowell, Wm. S. Rosecrans, Philip St. George Cooke, John Pope, Joseph Hooker, W. S. Hancock, and John M. Schofield.

3. That in case of conviction, before the sentence should be executed, Davis should be allowed an opportunity to appeal to the Supreme Court of the United States; this would silence criticism, secure Davis all his legal rights, and establish a precedent which might stand for all time.

4. That the only doubt that existed as to the conviction of Davis was to be found in the question of the jurisdiction of the military commission.

5. That the prosecution should hold Davis's assumption of military authority against the United States as the overt act of treason, and that his military orders, his commissions of officers, his official announcements of himself as "commander-in-chief of the military and naval forces of the Confederate States," his official reviews of troops, the official reports made to him by commanders of armies in rebellion, should be proven to establish the case.

6. That the record of the oaths taken by him as an officer in the United States army, as a Senator, and as Secretary of War, should be shown with evidence that he had violated them.

7. That the various acts of cruelty to prisoners of war committed by his orders should be proven; other minor counts could also be introduced in the indictment to secure an accumulation of charges.

General Butler's memorandum further set forth that the prosecution should expect to be met by the defense:

1. With the question of jurisdiction.

2. With an attempt to prove the right of secession.

3. With the claim that the duty of allegiance to a state was superior to the duty of allegiance to the general government.

4. With the claim that the acts of which Davis was accused were performed by him as the head of a *de facto* government, to which office he had been elected under forms of law.

5. With the further point that the recognition of this *de facto* government by the United States in the exchange of prisoners, in the acceptance of terms of surrender, in the observance of flags of truce, and in correspondence of various kinds, amounted to such a recognition of the existence of a government with which it was at war, as must prevent the United States from claiming that participation therein was treason.

These were the chief points which General Butler thought the defense would set up, and in his brief he grouped a powerful array of precedents and decisions upon which the prosecution could rest its case and meet these objections. During the early stages of this work, Mr. Chandler, General Butler and others, who firmly held that stern punishment should be meted out to a few conspicuous rebels — not in a spirit of vengeance, but from a belief that salutary results would follow if it should be established as a historical fact that in the United States treason is a high crime whose penalty is death — were constantly anxious lest the President should by some violent act or word destroy the moral effect of their position. In public he said repeatedly at this time that "the penalties of the law must be in a "stern and inflexible manner executed upon conscious, intelligent "and influential traitors," but his private utterances far outstripped this language, and were often scarcely less than bloodthirsty. Mr. Chandler, on one occasion, came away from the White House greatly disturbed by Mr. Johnson's disposition to treat this subject with mere anger, and characteristically said to

Senator Wade and Mr. Hamlin, "Johnson has the nightmare, and it is important that he should be watched." General Butler's memorandum Mr. Chandler heartily approved as clear in scope, just in spirit, and certain to prove effective in operation, but, by the time it was fully completed, a great change had taken place in the disposition of the President. In April he was in favor of hanging every body; in June he was opposed to hanging any one. He finally ignored entirely the memorandum which General Butler had drawn up at his request, and decided that Davis should be tried by the civil authorities at Richmond, where his crimes had been committed. As a result the arch-rebel was allowed to remain in prison at Fortress Monroe for nearly two years, because of the lack of a civil court competent to take jurisdiction of his case. In 1866 he was indicted and arraigned, and in 1867 was admitted to bail; a year later a *nolle prosequi* was entered, and the case against him dismissed. Before this matter had reached its second stage even, Mr. Chandler had become convinced that Andrew Johnson had determined to desert the party which had elevated him to the vice-presidency, and with that knowledge ceased to act as his adviser and became one of the most active of his political enemies. The leniency of the course finally pursued toward Davis Mr. Chandler then and afterward regarded as a grave public mistake, and believed that the failure to enforce the death penalty where it was so thoroughly deserved was exceedingly unfortunate in its influence upon popular opinion, and did more than any other one cause to encourage the disloyal classes of the South in their plans for ultimately recapturing the political supremacy they had forfeited by rebellion.

Precisely the causes which led Andrew Johnson so quickly back into close fellowship with the men whom he had regarded as his inveterate enemies will never be known. It is probable that originally they were slight, but his temperament rapidly

widened disagreement into irreconcilable hostility. His maudlin
speech on Inauguration - day so incensed many of his supporters
that the Republican senators, at a formal gathering, actually considered a proposition (urged by Mr. Sumner) to request him to
resign the office he had disgraced. The conference decided
against such a step, but Mr. Johnson heard of the movement,
and regarded those who approved it with much bitterness; his
hatred of them undoubtedly fed his growing dislike for the
party of which they were influential leaders. Again, he was a
thorough representative of the "poor whites" of the South. He
felt their jealousy of the planting aristocracy which monopolized
political power in his section, and this made him such a vigorous
opponent of the secession conspiracy which that oligarchy organized and led. But he also shared in the prejudice of his own
class against the negroes, and, when he saw the disposition of
the Republicans to accord to the freedmen equal rights and
privileges before the law, he refused to join in that movement
and set doggedly about defeating such plans. Precisely how
great Mr. Seward's influence over him was at this time is not
clear, but it is certain that the change in his attitude toward
Republicanism was simultaneous with the slow recovery of his
Secretary of State from the blows of Payne's dagger. His
combative obstinacy also made him fiercely resent the vigorous
criticisms which his "policy" of reconstruction invited when first
announced; Congress did not meet for months after his accession
to the presidency, and its leaders were not in position to check
his course, either by organized remonstrance or by legislative
interposition; the rebels who had been denouncing him savagely
were prompt to flatter his vanity and to offer promises of support; and, as a result, when the Thirty - ninth Congress met on
December 4, 1865, the break between the President and the
Republican party had passed beyond mending. Mr. Johnson
entered at once upon that shameful course, which included the

betrayal of those who had trusted him and the disgrace of his high office by lamentable public exhibitions of passion and boorishness, and which led to great and durable public injury by trebling the difficulties surrounding the delicate and important work of reconstructing the " Confederacy." Mr. Chandler's distrust of the President commenced with his change of tone in regard to the punishment of treason and with the first manifestation of his intention to assume full. control of reconstruction and to practically restore the rebels to power in the subdued States. They had one stormy interview at the White House, in which Mr. Chandler, after touching upon the implicit character of his confidence in the President during their senatorial service, denounced his new course as a violation of his sacred pledges and a base surrender to traitors, and left him indignantly and forever. From that time he regarded Andrew Johnson as a public enemy, whose opportunities for evil were to be lessened by every possible lawful restriction. He did not oppose the efforts made by his more hopeful associates in December, 1865, to re-establish harmony between the Capitol and the White House, but he predicted their failure. All the legislation which diminished Johnson's power for harm he ardently supported. The bills to admit Nebraska and Colorado (the Colorado bill failed at this time) he was especially active in pushing, from a belief that it was important to increase the Republican ascendency in the Senate while there was an uncertainty as to how much strength the " Johnson men" proper (Senators Doolittle, Dixon, Norton, and Cowan) might develop. It was largely through Mr. Chandler's untiring exertions, also, that the Fortieth Senate elected Benjamin F. Wade as its President, and thus made him the acting Vice-President of the United States, a position of the very highest responsibility in the then critical state of national affairs.

Mr. Chandler aided in shaping and passing the reconstruction measures of 1866-'67-'68, not for the reason that they precisely

embodied his ideas of the true method to be pursued, but
because they presented a plan upon which the Republicans
could be united, which was practicable, and which promised to
reorganize the Southern States on the basis of the supremacy
of the loyal elements in their population. When Andrew Johnson took the first step in unfolding his "policy" (by his general
amnesty proclamation and by the appointment of a provisional
governor for North Carolina, both acts bearing the date of May
29, 1865) the "Confederacy" had ceased to exist, its chieftain
was a captive, its armies were prisoners of war on parole, its
capacity for resistance had been consumed in the furnace of
battle, but its bitterness still glowed and the prejudices and
ambitions which gave it being were undestroyed. The amnesty
proclamation relieved, with a few exceptions, those who bore
arms against the government and the most virulent supporters of
rebellion who remained at home from all pains and penalties on
the sole condition that they should subscribe to an oath of
future loyalty. The provisional government proclamations permitted all persons thus amnestied, who were voters according to
laws of the States previous to the rebellion, to elect delegates
to conventions to amend the local constitutions and restore the
States to their "constitutional relations with the federal government." By this process the loyal colored men of the South
were denied the right to participate in the work of reconstruction and the entire machinery of reorganization was placed in
the control of men whose hands were yet red with Union blood.
Their discretion was only hampered by three conditions, compliance with which was made essential to the presidential approval
of their work. They were required to annul the secession ordi-
nances, to formally recognize the abolition of slavery, and to
repudiate all debts created to promote rebellion. Beyond this,
the disloyal classes of the South were left in undisputed mastery
of the situation. The control of the insurgent States, and of the

lives and fortunes of the loyalists, white and black, were surrendered absolutely to the men who but a few weeks before had been wrecked in the catastrophe which overwhelmed the rebellion. That they were prompt to improve this unexpected, undeserved and mistaken leniency need not be said. Their use of their new power was both presumptuous and intolerant. In elections, which proscribed Union men as unworthy of trust, conventions were chosen which accepted ungraciously the mere fact of emancipation, and which repudiated the rebel debts only under repeated presidential compulsion. State governments were then organized, which placed men whose disloyalty had been conspicuous in responsible positions, and which sent unamnestied leaders of the rebellion in the field and in council to Washington as claimants of Congressional seats. The State legislation which followed embodied in shameful laws the unquenched diabolism of the slave power. In statutory phraseology these enactments declared, "politically and socially this is a white man's government," and, impudently asserting that Congress was without any power over the matter, the men who had, in form, admitted the death of slavery proceeded to establish peonage in its stead. No body of laws adopted by any civilized nation in this century has equaled in studied injustice and cruelty those by which the "Johnson governments" of 1865 and 1866 sought to prevent the freedmen from rising from the level of admitted and hopeless inferiority, and to convince the blacks that in ceasing to be slaves they had only become serfs. Colored people were denied the right to acquire or dispose of public property. It was made a crime for a negro to enter a plantation without the consent of its owner or agent. Freedmen were declared vagrants, and punished as such for preaching the gospel without a license from some regularly organized church. Colored men failing to pay capitation tax were declared vagrants and the sale of their services was permitted as a penalty. Black persons were prohibited from renting

19

or leasing lands except in incorporated towns or villages. Their owning or bearing arms was declared to be a violation of the peace. For a negro to break a labor contract was made an offense punishable by imprisonment. Colored laborers on farms were prohibited from selling poultry or farm products, and it was made a misdemeanor to purchase from them. This class was also denied the right of forming part of the militia, and it was made an offense for any freedman to enter a religious or other assembly of whites, or go with them into any rail car or public conveyance. White persons "usually associating themselves with freedmen, free negroes, or mulattoes" were also declared to be vagrants in the eye of the law. The colored people were prohibited from practicing any art, trade or business except husbandry, without special license from the courts. And most infamous of all were the statutes for the compulsory apprenticeship of colored children with or without the consent of parents, which practically re-established over the next generation of the freed people slavery with the whipping-post and overseer's lash. One State by joint resolution tendered thanks to Jefferson Davis "for the noble and patriotic manner in which "he conducted the affairs of *our* government while President of "the Confederacy," and other resolutions were adopted declaring that "nothing more is required for the restoration of law and order but the withdrawal of federal bayonets." [The fell spirit and tendency of the reaction which was thus revealed found still more significant expression in the revolting butchery in and around the Mechanic's Institute of New Orleans on the 30th of July, 1866.] Some of these infamous measures were adopted in all the insurrectionary States, others in only some of them, but without exception the new Southern governments which Andrew Johnson's "policy" created were founded upon the traditions of the slave system and the memories of "the lost cause." The objection that the President had, in thus taking the work of reconstruction into his own hands, usurped authority devolved upon Congress by the constitution, was a strong one, but it received but little popular attention. Anger at the results of that "policy" obscured the mere disapproval of its methods. When it was seen that the rebellion had merely changed its theater of action, and that what it lost on the battle-field it proposed to secure by legislation, there was but one opinion among the masses of the people who had heartily supported the war and were sincerely anxious to preserve its fruits. Their emphatic demand was that the illegal and reactionary governments set up by the President should be overturned, and the South reconstructed in the interests of loyalty and liberty. Congress, as part of its stubborn contest with Andrew Johnson, undertook this work. It refused to recognize the pretended State governments or to admit their Congressmen. It divided the territory of the conquered States into five military districts, and placed it under the control of the army until a juster system of reconstruction could be applied. It then provided that in the calling of conventions to frame new constitutions colored men should be permitted to vote; that those revised instruments must confer the elective franchise upon all loyal colored people and all whites not disfranchised for rebellion; that the work of the conventions must be submitted to the colored and white people not disfranchised for approval; that the Thirteenth and Fourteenth Amendments to the national constitution must be ratified; and that the State constitutions so adopted must be submitted to and accepted by Congress. Upon this general plan the South was reconstructed, not without much friction, not wholly to the satisfaction of the men who marked out this course of procedure, but with the faith (or at least the trust) on their part that it would restore that section to the Union with genuinely free institutions, that it would protect the emancipated slave in his rights, and that it would substitute for disloyal communities

States controlled by those whose interests and traditions lay with the national cause. The reconstruction laws were not vengeful in character; the aim of the men who passed them was not retaliation, not even retribution except in so far as the application of mild penalties to treason might increase the security of the future. To prevent a repetition of the terrible struggle which had just closed was the aim; that a political system had been devised, which both recognized human rights, and by its natural operations would exclude from political power the men who had plunged the country into civil war, was the hope. Within ten years the scheme failed utterly, and what it was designed to prevent had been accomplished upon its ruins. No body of laws can maintain itself in the face of organized murder and terrorism which authority refuses to either punish or prevent.

The reconstruction measures, while they commanded Mr. Chandler's general assent, were laxer in details than he would have made them. He felt, as Thaddeus Stevens said, that much that they ought to have contained was "defeated by the united "forces of self-righteous Republicans and unrighteous Copper- "heads," but held that the bills which were passed deserved support as a whole on the ground that it was not wise to "throw away a great good because it is not perfect." Schuyler Colfax closed one of his speeches upon this subject as follows: "Loyalty must govern what loyalty preserved." Mr. Chandler complimented him warmly and said, "You got it all into one sentence," and that doctrine and the belief in equal rights for citizens of every color guided his share of the work upon all measures affecting reconstruction. His chief regret was that the process of this reorganization was not prolonged until the loyal sentiment of the South had become strong enough and intelligent enough to maintain itself. If his wishes had prevailed, the provisional governing of that section would have been continued until the education of the blacks, the death of the rebel leaders, and the extinguishment by time of the prejudices and animosities of the war had accomplished such a wholesome revolution in sentiment throughout that section as would in itself have been a loyal and durable reconstruction. As this was not possible, he spared no effort to make successful the experiment which was attempted; if others had been as resolute and faithful as he, it would not have failed. He did not share in the disposition of so many Republicans to abandon what had been just commenced because of the imperfection of its first fruits. He stood manfully for the maintenance by Northern opinion and by the aid of the United States of the loyal State governments of the South, not claiming they were faultless, but because they were based on justice and were far better than that which would take their place if they fell. When they were assailed by assassination, by massacre, and by systematic terrorizing, he believed that it was the duty of the general government to use all its authority and all its force to protect its citizens in their rights and to prevent the harvesting by unpunished traitors of the fruits of atrocities as brutal and bloody as Saint Bartholomew. The policy of political murder triumphed finally at the South, not through any weakness of such men as he, nor through any failure upon his part to denounce that vast crime. He labored strenuously to kindle Northern opinion into such a flame of just wrath as would have made impossible that victory of organized brutality.

Mr. Chandler was often described by political opponents as "the relentless enemy of the South;" nothing was farther from the fact. That small minority of the Southern people, who ruled that section with oligarchical power before and during the war, who organized and led the rebellion, and who have now regained supremacy by outrage and murder, he always distrusted and attacked. But the great majority of the people of the South — the blacks whom those men rob of their rights and the whites whom they mislead—he profoundly pitied, and their cause he espoused. For them he demanded equal rights before the law, a free ballot box, the common school, and an opportunity to prove their manhood. Those who resisted a policy so just and civilizing he was quick to denounce in unstinted terms, and upon them he did not waste conciliation. They—not "the South"—found him the inappeasable, but still "the avowed, the erect, the manly foe."

In the elections of 1866 the issues were chiefly those connected with reconstruction, and Mr. Chandler as usual spoke in his own and other Western States, exposing the malign results of Mr. Johnson's "policy" and in advocacy of the Congressional plan and the Fourteenth Amendment. The general tenor of his speeches will appear from this extract from an address delivered at Detroit, at the close of the political campaign:

These perjured traitors are permitted to live here, but we say to them they can never again hold office unless Congress by a two-thirds vote shall remove the disability; why, a man who has committed perjury alone, right here in Michigan, you would not allow to testify before a justice of the peace in the most petty case. But we forget the perjury of the rebels which would send them to the State prison, we forget the hanging which follows treason, and say to them simply, that for the future they can never hold office. Personally I am not in favor of the last clause of this section which gives Congress the power to remove this disability by a two-thirds vote. I would have let this race of perjured traitors die out, out of office, and educate the rising generation to loyalty. But it is in the amendment and I advocate its adoption as it is.

Often during the progress of the obstinate struggle between Andrew Johnson and Congress his attempts to evade law and his encroachments upon the powers vested in the legislative branch of the government led to the serious consideration in the House of Representatives of the question of impeachment. Sevearl resolutions ordering the preferring of charges against him at the bar of the Senate were presented without action, but on the 7th of January, 1867, the Hon. J. M. Ashley of Ohio offered a preamble, beginning, "I do impeach Andrew Johnson, Vice-"President and acting President of the United States, of high "crimes and misdemeanors. I charge him with usurpation of "power and violation of law in that he has corruptly used the "appointing power; . . . corruptly used the pardoning "power; . . . corruptly used the veto power; . . . "corruptly disposed of public property; . . . and corruptly "interfered in elections." With this preamble was a resolution referring the charges to the Judiciary Committee to inquire if the President had been guilty of acts which were "calculated to overthrow, subvert or corrupt the government." By a vote of 108 yeas to 39 nays this reference was ordered, but no report was made until November 25, 1867, and then a resolution of impeachment was submitted by Mr. Boutwell in behalf of the majority of the committee. On December 7, this resolution was rejected by a vote of 57 to 108. Encouraged by this result Mr. Johnson, who had suspended Edwin M. Stanton from the Secretaryship of War during the Congressional recess of 1867, and whose action had been disapproved by the Senate under the Tenure of Civil Office act, undertook to force Mr. Stanton out by a second suspension on February 21, 1868, accompanied by an order appointing Gen. Lorenzo Thomas Secretary *ad interim*. Mr. Stanton declined to acknowledge the President's power to take this step, refused to give place to General Thomas, and for many days and nights remained in constant occupation of the department offices. The House of Representatives at once arraigned the President before the Senate for this attempted violation of the Tenure of Office act, and his trial followed. Chief Justice Chase presided; the proceedings lasted from February 25 until May 26, 1868; and in the end Mr. Johnson was acquitted, exactly the number of Republican Senators necessary to defeat conviction voting with the Democratic minority. These proceedings Mr. Chandler watched with the liveliest interest, and the failure of the impeachment was one of the most bitter disappointments of his political career. He sincerely believed that Johnson's course fully merited a verdict of "guilty," and he felt that the great difficulties surrounding the problem of the loyal reconstruction of the South would disappear if the executive department of the government was administered with the Jacksonian vigor and patriotism of Benjamin F. Wade. Mr. Stanton's refusal to permit the President to displace him without the consent of the Senate he endorsed with the utmost heartiness, and, while the Secretary remained in his office to prevent its seizure by Mr. Johnson's *ad interim* appointee, Mr. Chandler spent night after night with him, and did all that was possible to strengthen his resolution and to lighten his voluntary confinement. On one occasion, when there were signs of an intention on the part of the claimant to use force, Mr. Chandler, General Logan, and a few others gathered together about a hundred trusty men, who occupied the basement of the department, and there did garrison duty until the danger was past. During Johnson's trial Mr. Chandler was not forgetful of his position as a judge, and was an attentive listener to the evidence and the arguments before and in the court of impeachment. He was restive under the length of the proceedings, however, and did advise the managers on the part of the House to push the case along as rapidly as possible, urging that the public interest required the ending of the general suspense. He felt then, and said afterward, that the delay was used to effect combinations with, and apply pressure to, individual Senators, which would induce them to favor acquittal. That this was done he never doubted, and he repeatedly denounced in the strongest terms, both in public and private, the action of the seven Republicans (Senators Fessenden, Trumbull, Grimes, Henderson, Fowler, Ross and Van Winkle) who voted "not guilty" with the Democrats and the "Johnson men." He was especially indignant at the course of Mr. Fessenden and Mr. Trumbull, and on several occasions in after years came into sharp personal collision with them during the Senate debates. The final failure of the impeachment movement he felt as a blow. One who knew him well has said: "He believed that republican govern-"ment was at stake and impeachment a necessity. Never was "there a time when he came so near despairing of the republic "as at that event."

The Thirty-ninth and Fortieth Congresses remained in nearly continuous session for over three years "watching the White House." Outside of the exciting political topics which received so large a share of their attention, they were compelled to deal with important financial, commercial and material questions affecting vitally the general interest. The currency and public debt demanded simplification; the tax system was to be changed from a war to a peace footing; the commercial wrecks of many years called for a bankrupt law; bounties were to be equalized, pensions provided, and war claims adjusted on wise bases; neglected internal improvements clamored for renovation and extension; the ocean commerce required national care; and innumerable minor interests, long neglected under the stress of civil war, needed instant attention. Mr. Chandler worked with characteristic energy and practical wisdom in all these branches of legislative activity, and rendered public services of varied and permanent usefulness.

CHAPTER XVII.

N the presidential election of 1868 Mr. Chandler was even more than usually active, both as an organizer and speaker. He delivered nearly forty addresses in his own State, which gave to the Grant and Colfax ticket 31,492 majority, and elected a Republican Congressman in each of its six districts. The Legislature chosen at the same time had 66 Republican majority upon joint ballot, and re-elected Mr. Chandler for his third Senatorial term, the Democratic vote being cast for the Hon. Sanford M. Green of Bay City. In the Republican caucus there was practically no opposition to Mr. Chandler's renomination, and he received on the first and only ballot 78 votes, 13 other ballots being cast for seven gentlemen by way of personal compliment. The inauguration of President Grant, on March 4, 1869, renewed Mr Chandler's influence with the executive branch of the government, and the political and personal friendship between him and the modest, resolute, and illustrious soldier who succeeded Andrew Johnson grew mutually stronger and more appreciative from that day.

Very much of the legislation of President Grant's first term, which received Mr. Chandler's vigilant attention and absorbed no small share of his energy, related to the details of the public business, and furnishes no biographical material of permanent interest. He supported the Fifteenth Amendment in all its stages, and also the Civil Rights bills, which he regarded as incomplete, but still as the taking of steps in the direction of justice.* It was his firm purpose to contribute his share toward making American citizenship mean something, for both black and white, and, if life was spared, to cease not his labors until the humblest freeman in the United States should be in firm possession of every natural and constitutional right, should have free access to an honest ballot-box, should suffer no proscription for his political opinions, and should be amply protected in his liberty to think, say, go, and do as he pleased within the limitations laid down by law for the regulation of the conduct of all. The battle, in which he was so eager and stalwart a leader, will not be finished until that result is forever secured.

Early in General Grant's term the friends of Edwin M. Stanton determined to secure for him such an official appointment as should be congenial to his tastes and guarantee him an adequate support in old age. His iron constitution resisted the enormous labors of the civil war successfully. For many months he worked from fifteen to twenty hours in each day; his assistant secretaries were energetic and trained men of affairs, but their strength successively gave way in attempting to keep up with their chief. When the strain was finally withdrawn, it was perceived that his own powers were greatly exhausted. Rest restored their tone somewhat, and he made one or two legal arguments and public addresses, which showed that his intellectual vigor was undiminished, but these efforts were followed by extreme nervous prostration. Under these circumstances, Mr. Stanton's friends determined to secure for him a judicial appointment. For such a position he was qualified by eminent professional attainments, and this fact and the permanency of

---

* To a letter of confidence and congratulation, written to him at the time of his last Senatorial election, by a committee of the colored citizens of East Saginaw, Mich, Mr. Chandler replied (under date of Feb. 20, 1879): "I hope to be able to assist in the grand "but unfinished work of securing equal political rights for every citizen of this country, 'black as well as white, South as well as North."

tenure made the tender of a place upon the bench grateful to him. Accordingly, when Judge Grier resigned his position as a member of the Supreme Court, Mr. Stanton's appointment to the vacant Associate Justiceship was at once urged upon President Grant. Mr. Chandler was very active in this matter and pressed it with all his energy. The effort was successful, and on Dec. 20, 1869, this nomination was sent to the Senate and promptly confirmed. Four days afterward, and before his commission was made out, Mr. Stanton's overtaxed constitution broke down, and he died after a brief illness, in the fifty-fifth year of his age, as thorough a sacrifice to the nobility of his own patriotic devotion during the war as the bravest soldier who fell on any of its battle-fields. During his fatal illness, Mr. Chandler was a frequent watcher at his bedside, and was one of the last persons with whom the dying statesman conversed. After his death it was found that the man who had controlled the disbursement of hundreds of millions had died poor, and had not left an estate adequate to the support of his children. Congress directed a year's salary of a Justice of the Supreme Court to be paid to his heirs. Mr. Chandler and others of his friends also set on foot a movement to raise a national memorial fund. A meeting of Republicans was called at the residence of Congressman Samuel Hooper of Massachusetts, and a committee was there appointed who collected over $140,000 (Mr. Chandler contributing $10,000 and President Grant $1,000), which was invested in United States bonds and placed in the hands of a few trustees, of whom Surgeon-General Barnes of the army was chairman, for the benefit of the Stanton family.

During General Grant's term the subject of "war claims" commenced to attract national attention. Originally the Republican Congresses dealt liberally with the South in the matter of compensation for damages inflicted upon its loyal citizens during the rebellion. By a series of carefully-guarded laws (and by a few private relief measures passed to meet exceptional cases) a large sum was paid to residents of the rebel States who suffered war losses, and were able to produce satisfactory proof of their fidelity to the Union. In this matter the national government certainly went to the extreme verge of generosity. The experience attending the disbursement of the money thus appropriated established conclusively the fraudulent and outrageous character of a large percentage of these claims. In thousands of cases investigation showed conclusively that arrant rebels were willing to swear that they had been "Union men," and that small losses had, by false affidavits, been magnified into great sums. As reconstruction broke down, and the survivors of the rebellion gained in strength at the Capitol, a new danger arose. No statute of limitations barred the indefinite presentation of claims to Congress, and it soon became evident that, not merely Southern loyalists, but avowed rebels who suffered losses in the war were looking to the general government for compensation for the damages which their own treason had invited. The movement on the Treasury in their interest did not take on the form of an attack in front, but by the flank. It commenced with plausible applications for the "relief" of Southern institutions and corporations, and not of individuals. It further manifested itself in propositions for such a relaxation of the terms of the laws and regulations governing this class of claims as would abolish all distinctions of "loyalty" and put the "Confederate" upon an equal footing with the Union applicant for this kind of "relief." The precise dimensions of this scheme, which has been well characterized as "an attempt to make the United States pay to the South what "it cost it to be conquered in addition to what it cost to con- "quer it," have not yet fully appeared, but the cloven hoof has been sufficiently revealed to justly arouse and alarm the loyal sentiment of the North. Mr. Chandler's record upon this question affords a striking illustration of the soundness of his judg-

ment as to the scope and tendency of any particular line of
public policy. When this subject first demanded attention, he
took the position which his party substantially assumed ten years
later. His clear and practical mind saw what the consequences
would be of any general re-imbursement of war losses, and he
strenuously resisted the taking of any false steps at the outset.
Thus, on March 2, 1865, upon the bill to pay Josiah O. Armes
for the destruction of property within the rebel lines, he said in
the Senate:

> I hope this bill will not pass the Senate. . . . If you pass it, if you
> set this precedent, if you say to every rebel and every loyal man, and every
> man throughout the South, by the passage of this bill, that you intend to pay
> for every dollar of property that has been destroyed by order of our generals,
> you will give a more fatal blow to the credit of the government than by any
> other act that you can perform in this body. I should look upon the passage
> of this bill as a national calamity, and one that we cannot afford at this time
> to bring on our heads. It will do more to shake the faith of our own citizens
> and of the moneyed centers of the world in the credit of your securities than
> any other act you could perform.

In his address before the Republican caucus which renominated him for the Senate in January, 1869, he also said:

> The moment this government begins to allow claims for damages accruing
> to individuals during the war in the South, it is placed in a position of great
> peril. Every rebel in the South who lost a haystack or barn by fire during
> the war will prove his loyalty and secure damages. It requires the greatest
> vigilance to prevent some of these claims from being allowed, as they are
> continually being pressed upon Congress, and probably will be for many
> years. The laws of war do not require nor justify the allowance of this class
> of claims even to loyal men. If they are loyal, then they have served the
> government, and that is compensation enough. If they are disloyal, they have
> no claim.

These quotations indicate his original position on this issue,
taken in the days when it had received but the slightest public
attention. They are exactly in the line of the vigorous utterances upon the same topic which formed one of the important
features of his public addresses in 1879, when the subject had

aroused marked popular interest, and other leaders had stepped up to the platform he had so long occupied.

But Mr. Chandler did more than strenuously oppose the payment of the "war claims" of Southern disloyalists; his far-sightedness placed in their path a serious practical obstacle. In 1873, a Colonel Pickett, who had been confidentially connected with the War Department of the "Confederacy," came to Washington and offered to sell to the authorities a vast quantity of the archives of the rebel government, which he had secreted before the capture of Richmond. Congress was not in session, and the Secretary of War, having no authority in law, refused to buy the documents. Mr. Chandler was in that city at the time, and Pickett was referred to him as a man of means and as one who would be apt to appreciate the importance of such a purchase. After one or two calls, Mr. Chandler determined that the matter deserved investigation at least. He asked for a schedule of the documents and for a statement of their prices. Pickett promptly furnished the former and offered to sell them for $250,000. Mr. Chandler, after a careful examination of the schedule, replied with a proposition that, if the papers corresponded with the list furnished, he would pay $75,000 for them. This offer was at last accepted, and Mr. Chandler deposited that sum in a Washington bank, subject to Pickett's order after a thorough examination of the documents had been made. Confidential clerks were at once set at work upon them, and it was found that they even surpassed their owner's representations as to value. The purchase was therefore completed, and the documents became the private property of Mr. Chandler, who had them locked up in a vault. When Congress met, a bill was passed authorizing the Secretary of War in general terms to purchase the archives of the Confederate government if it was ever possible, and appropriating $75,000 for this purpose. As soon as the bill became a law Mr. Chandler transferred the doc·

uments to the Secretary of War, and they are now in the
possession of that department and constitute one of the most
valuable and useful features of its record of the rebellion. The
amount that has been saved to the government by this purchase,
in furnishing evidence to defeat rebel claims, already exceeds
many - fold the original price. Case after case in the Quartermaster - General's office, before the Southern Claims Commission,
and before the Court of Claims has been defeated by evidence
found among these papers.* One single conspicuous instance

---

* The value of this class of documents will further appear from two quotations from
the official "Digest of the Report of the Southern Claims Commission upon the Disal-
lowed Claims," only two being taken where many might be. "Claim No. 193" was preferred before this Commission by W. R. Alexander of Dickson, Ala., for $13,443, for cotton
and horses furnished to the Union army. Mr. Alexander produced evidence to show, and
swore himself, that he had been a consistent Union man. The Digest (1 vol., p. 55) says:
"Among the papers of the rebel government found at Richmond is a letter, now in the
"War Department, a copy of which Adjutant-General Townsend has furnished to us. It
"reads as follows :

"' DICKSON, Ala., August 1, 1861.

"SIR : I have heard that the War Department was scarce of arms, and I have taken
"it upon myself to look up all the old muskets I can find and I now send them to you,
"and I hope they will kill many a Yankee. I have had one musket fixed to my notion,
"which I send with the others for a model. All here are delighted with our victory, both
"white and black. Yours, respectfully,   WM. R. ALEXANDER.

"P. S. I send these guns, ten in number, to the Ordnance Department, Richmond,
"Virginia.   .   W. R. A.

"The Hon. L. P. Walker.'

"On October 11, 1872, the counsel for the claimant, John J. Key, Esq., appeared
"before the Commissioners and requested that the claim be withdrawn, admitting the dis-
"loyalty of the claimant. The claim is rejected."

"Claim 135" was preferred by J. P. Levy of Wilmington, N. C., for $10,000. After he
had sworn to his own loyalty, he was called upon to face some letters found in the rebel
archives. The Commisssion say (p. 33, 1 vol., Digest) : "The original letters were fur-
"nished the Commission by the War Department from the captured rebel archives, and
"copies of several of them were filed with this report. . . . We have in them the
"claimant at the outbreak of the war calling upon the rebel government to punish the
"superintendent of his brother's plantation for insulting the rebel flag; and, again, asking
"the rebel Congress to pass a law granting him his brother's plantation on account of his
"signal service to the rebel cause ; and, again, offering a ship, to be commanded by him-
"self, for the rebel service; also, tendering for the benefit of the rebel army. patent
"fuse train and soda baking-powders, and boasting and complaining of the large amount
"due him from the rebel government for supplies for the rebel army And now this
"shameless traitor, perjurer and swindler comes before us and swears, with brazen effront-
"ery, that the government of the United States owes him, as a loyal adherent to the
"cause of the Union and the government throughout the war of the rebellion, for sup-
"plies furnished the army, the sum of $10,000. We reject this claim."

in which they saved to the Treasury more than four times their
entire cost attracted much deserved attention at the time. On
Nov. 16, 1877, an effort was made by leading Southern Democrats in the House of Representatives to pass under a suspension
of the rules, and without debate, a joint resolution ordering
the immediate payment of several hundred thousand dollars to
mail contractors in the rebel States who forfeited their contracts
at the commencement of the rebellion. An objection from the
Hon. Omar D. Conger prevented action on that day, but the
resolution came up again on Feb. 15, 1878. Representative John
H. Reagan of Texas, who had been the Postmaster-General of
the rebel Cabinet, then took charge of the measure, and assured
the House that the resolution was a purely formal matter, that
it only provided for the payment of liabilities incurred before
the war commenced, and that the rebel government had never
paid these men for the same services. The Hon. Edwin
Willits of Michigan, by a timely examination of the phraseology
of the resolution, discovered that it provided for the payment of
these contractors, not down to the actual beginning of the rebellion, but until May 31st, 1861, many weeks after the rebel
government had been formed and after the firing upon Fort
Sumter. Calling attention to this fact, he obtained the further
postponement of the consideration of the resolution. When it
came up again (on March 8, 1878) Mr. Willits came to the
House armed with a volume of the rebel statutes and with
important extracts from documents contained in the rebel
archives. With this evidence he demonstrated in ten minutes'
time, beyond question, that the rebel government had assumed
the payment of this class of claims, that it confiscated United
States money and applied it to that purpose, that the men so
paid agreed to refund to the rebel treasury any money subsequently given them on this account by the United States, and
that the joint resolution was but an attempt to pay a second

20

time contracts already paid and also properly declared forfeited through treason. The scene attendant upon this *expose* was a dramatic one, and it resulted in the virtual abandonment then of the measure by those who were responsible for it. This result would not have been possible, had not the rebel archives thus opportunely yielded up their secrets. Their possession by the government is undoubtedly worth millions to the Treasury.

In 1871, the second term of Jacob M. Howard, as Senator from Michigan, expired, and Thomas W. Ferry, then a member of the House of Representatives, was chosen as his successor. With his new colleague Mr. Chandler's relations were always close and cordial, and upon the questions of reconstruction, equal rights, and the national supremacy their accord was complete. Mr. Ferry rapidly attained distinction in the upper branch of Congress, and was for several successive years the President *pro tempore* of the Senate. The death of Vice-President Wilson in 1875 made him Acting Vice-President of the United States, and he held that responsible position throughout the trying weeks of the electoral dispute of 1876–'7, when his good sense, the perfect discretion of his course, and the dignity and impartiality with which he discharged duties of the gravest character amid vast and dangerous excitement, both deserved and received universal praise. Mr. Ferry was re-elected during this critical period, and, as Mr. Chandler's term as Secretary of the Interior was then about to close, it was suggested in some quarters that Michigan should send him back to the Senate in Mr. Ferry's stead. The quality of Mr. Chandler's fidelity as a friend and of his estimate of Mr. Ferry's public usefulness was shown in the fact that, anxious as he avowedly was to become again a Senator, these suggestions obtained from him only peremptory negatives, and his advice and influence contributed to Mr. Ferry's unopposed re-election. Mr. Howard died suddenly at Detroit from apoplexy shortly after the close of his Senatorial service. As

further illustrating the nature of the friendship existing between
him and his colleague from Michigan, and the estimation in
which he was held by the eminent men with whom he came in
contact, this private letter from Mr. Chandler to President
Grant, with an endorsement made thereon by the latter, is here
given :

WASHINGTON, Sept. 21, 1870.

MY DEAR SIR : Secretary Cox has done my colleague an unintentional
but a serious injury.

In 1869 the whole Michigan delegation united in recommending the Rev.
W. H. Brockway, one of the most popular Methodist clergymen in the State,
for Indian Agent.

He was nominated and confirmed, but acquiesced in the transfer of Indian
affairs to the military. Since the adjournment of Congress, my colleague
made a personal request to the Secretary of the Interior, that the Rev. Mr.
Brockway be commissioned as Indian Agent for Michigan. Instead of sending
the commission, he has sent a man from New Jersey to attend to our Indian
affairs. This has given offense to the most numerous and powerful religious
denomination in the State and seriously injured my colleague. I ask for my
colleague that the New Jersey commission may be immediately revoked, and
Mr. Brockway may be at once commissioned. . . .

It is really important that this be done at once. Very respectfully, your
obedient servant, Z. CHANDLER.

To President U. S. Grant.

AUTOGRAPHIC ENDORSEMENT BY PRESIDENT GRANT.

Referred to the Secretary of the Interior.

I think Mr. Brockway might with great propriety be assigned to the
Indian agency in his own State, to which he has once been appointed and
confirmed.

He is a minister, and therefore the new rule adopted will not be violated
by his appointment.

I want, besides, to accommodate Senator Howard, whom I regard as an
able supporter of the Republican party and of the Administration.

Sept. 22, 1870. U. S. GRANT.

Mr. Chandler was a member of one or two of the special
Congressional committees appointed to investigate those atrocious
political murders which made infamous the return of the disloyal
classes to power in the South. This general subject received no
small share of his attention ; the facts which investigation dis-

closed deepened his conviction of the essential barbarity of much
that passes for civilization in that section, and added to the
inflexibility of his opposition to a political system, which was
responsible for the atrocious crimes of the Ku-Klux-Klan, "the
Mississippi plan," the White League, and the "rifle clubs," and
for the horrible massacres of Colfax and Coushatta, of Hamburg
and Ellenton.

Two of his speeches in the Senate in 1871 and 1872
attracted general attention and were widely republished. One of
them was delivered on January 18, 1871, in reply to Mr. Cas-
serly of California, who had challenged a comparison between the
records of the Republican and Democratic parties. In the course
of twenty minutes Mr. Chandler rapidly sketched the services of
the Republican party in defeating the Democratic plot to surrender the territories to slavery, in crushing a Democratic
rebellion, in emancipating four million slaves, in building a
trans-continental railway to the Pacific coast, in inviting the settlement of the Great West by a homestead law, in establishing
the national banking system, in maintaining the public credit
against Democratic attack, and in reconstructing the South on
the basis of freedom and loyalty. He closed as follows:

> These measures were carried, not with the Democratic party, but in spite
> of the Democratic party. Sir, we are not to be arraigned here and put on
> the defensive, certainly not by that old Democratic party.
>
> And now, Mr. President, they ask us to do what? To forgive the past
> and let by-gones be by-gones. You hear on the right hand and on the left,
> from every quarter, "Let by-gones be by-gones; let us forget the past and rub
> it out." Sir, we have no disposition to forget the past. We have a record of
> which we are proud. We have a record that has gone into history. There
> we propose to let it stand. We never propose to blot out that record. There
> are no thousand years in the world's history in which so much has been
> accomplished for human liberty and human progress as has been accomplished
> by this great Republican party in the short space of ten years. Blot out that
> record? Never, sir, never! It is a record that will go down in history
> through all times as the proudest ever made by any political party that ever
> existed on earth. But, sir, do gentlemen of the Democratic party want to

blot out their record? I do not blame them for wanting to, for that record is a record of treason. It, too, has gone into history, and there it must stand through all ages. Sir, the young men of this country are looking at these two records, and they are making up their minds as to which they desire their names to go down to history upon; and I am happy to say that of the young men now coming upon the stage of action, nine out of every ten are joining this great Republican party. They desire that their record shall be associated with those who saved this great nation, and not with those who attempted its overthrow. The day is far distant when that old Democratic party that attempted to overthrow this government will again be entrusted with power by the people of this nation. . . . Mr. President, if this record of the two parties does not please my Democratic friends, I have only to say to them that they made it deliberately and they have got to stand by it.

On June 6, 1872, Mr. Chandler replied in the Senate to that part of Mr. Sumner's elaborate attack upon General Grant in which he declared that Edwin M. Stanton had said, in his last days, "General Grant cannot govern this country." The excessive egotism, which marred Mr. Sumner's character and which inspired that unfortunate speech, was always a cause of impatience with Mr. Chandler, and this display of it aroused his anger. In his reply, he challenged squarely the credibility of Mr. Sumner's statement. He first read from Mr. Stanton's reported speeches, to show that their enthusiastic and repeated commendation of General Grant by name proved that Mr. Sumner's assertion that Mr. Stanton had also said, " In my speeches I " never introduced the name of General Grant; I spoke for the " Republican cause and the Republican party," was exactly contrary to the fact. He then proceeded:

Mr. President, I had occasion with Mr. Wade, formerly Senator from Ohio, as member of the Committee on the Conduct of the War, to see Mr. Stanton, I think once a day on an average, during the whole war, and I was in the habit of visiting him up to the time of his death, and never, under any circumstances, did he express in my presence any but the highest opinion of General Grant, both as to his military capacity and as to his civil capacity.

Mr. President, on the Friday before the death of E. M. Stanton, I had occasion to visit him in company with two friends, members of the other House, one Hon. Judge Beaman, then a member for Michigan, the other Judge Conger, now a member from Michigan. We had that day a long interview of not less than an hour and a half, wherein Mr. Stanton expressed the highest opinion of President Grant, both as to his military and civil capacity. I awaited an interview with these parties before making this statement, and their recollection is the same as my own.   I have likewise held two or three interviews with Senator Wade since then, and his recollection of the expres· sions of the late E. M. Stanton is equally strong as my own to-day.   Mr. Stanton said, in the presence of two witnesses, "The country knows General Grant to be a great warrior ; I know he will prove a great civilian." . . .

Mr. President, the relations between the President of the United States and the late Secretary Stanton were of remarkable kindliness. Never did I hear either express any but the highest esteem and regard for the other. . . . I think the last interview he ever had was the interview with me in the presence of these two living witnesses. . . . Surgeon-General Barnes was his attending physician at the hour of his death. According to his testimony, from the hour I last saw him up to the time of his death, there was no change, so far as can be known.

In another part of this speech the President is arraigned as a great gift-taker. Sir, General Grant was a great taker. Few men have ever. been as eminent as takers. He took Fort Donelson with some twenty or thirty thousand soldiers ; and he took Shiloh, and took Vicksburg, and took the Wilderness, and took Murfreesboro' and Appomattox and all the rebel mate-rial of war. He, with his army, took the shackles from 4,000,000 slaves. And, sir, after he had taken the vitals out of the rebellion, he was urged by his friends to accept a small donation to take himself out of the hands of poverty, a thing that has been done by all nations and by all grateful peoples in all ages of the world. Sir, he is to be arraigned as a great gift-taker because he accepted the voluntary contributions of a grateful people !

Why, sir, there were few men of capacity, few men of fitness to occupy positions under this government who did not subscribe, gratefully, anxiously subscribe, to that fund to relieve U. S. Grant from his poverty. And yet, he is to be arraigned here as a gift-taker, as though that was a crime !

Mr. President, there are two classes of people in this world, and we see specimens of them both. We have great *o-ra-tors* and great men of business. On this floor our *o-ra-tors* have occupied the time of this session to the exclu-sion of business, and while these *o-ra-tors* have been wasting the time of this body to the detriment of the business of the nation, willing to indulge in windy orations at the expense of the government, U. S. Grant, President of the United States, has been managing the affairs of this nation better than they were ever managed before. While your *o-ra-tors* were here delivering windy words, he was paying the national debt faster than these *o-ra-tors* could count it. While they were *o-ra-ting*, he was negotiating treaties and attending to the civil service of the nation. While they were *o-ra-ting* on this floor during the war, he was winning victories in the bloodiest part of the fight. And now, while they are *o-ra-ting* on this floor, he is endearing himself to the hearts of the whole people of this land as no other man ever did. Stanton was prophetic ; he is not only great in war, but he is greater as a civilian.

The act of March 3, 1873, which raised the annual salaries of Congressmen from $5,000 to $7,500, gave also to this increase a retroactive effect and made it apply to the members of Congress who passed the measure and whose official terms ended on that very day. Public opinion did not approve of any aspect of this change, but it condemned vehemently the voting by Congressmen to themselves of $5,000 each for services already rendered and in addition to liberal salaries fixed at the time of their acceptance of office. So emphatic were the manifestations of popular wrath at both this act and its methods, that the next Congress promptly repealed "the salary grab," as it was commonly called. Mr. Chandler's integrity and good sense kept him from any participation in this obnoxious performance. He opposed the increase of compensation earnestly in the Senate, voted against it at all stages of the contest, and refused to accept his "back pay." When the bill had been passed and the increased salary had been placed to his credit on the Senate books, he went to the Treasury with his colleague and they deposited the difference between the old and the new rate to the credit of the government, writing the following letter to the Secretary of the Treasury:

WASHINGTON, March 28, 1873.

SIR : Herewith find drafts on the Treasury, one of $3,906.80 payable to Z. Chandler, the other of $3,920, to T. W. Ferry, being avails of retroactive increase of salary passed during the expiring days of and for the Forty-second Congress, and this day placed in our hands by the Secretary of the Senate.

Not willing to gain what we voted against, we request that the same be applied toward the cancellation of any of the six per cent. interest-bearing obligations of the nation. Lest such return be distorted into possible reflection upon the propriety of dissimilar disposition by others, you will oblige us much by giving no publicity to the matter. Very respectfully, yours,

Z. CHANDLER,
T. W. FERRY.

The amount refunded was the exact difference between the sums allowed under the old and the increased rate. The new law gave an increase of salary for the term, without mileage. The old law allowed $5,000 less salary, but gave mileage in addition. Mr. Chandler and Mr. Ferry took the amount due them under the old system, and returned the additional sum which was allowed them under the new. The spirit of scrupulous honesty which dictated this proceeding is shown in the last sentence of the joint letter, asking that publicity might not be given to their action. They took this step voluntarily and not under any constraint from public opinion.

In the general elections of 1870 and 1872 Mr. Chandler was exceedingly active, making the usual number of public addresses, and also devoting much time to organization and to the general distribution of political literature. The latter branch of party effort had become the special province of the Republican Congressional Committee. For more than twenty years there have been two distinct executive organizations within the Republican party, independent of each other, but always working in harmony, namely: The National Committee, and the Congressional Committee. The latter is composed of a Representative in Congress from each State, chosen by the Republican members of the respective delegations. No man can serve upon this committee unless he holds a seat in Congress, and States which have no Republican Congressmen are unrepresented in its membership. Mr. Chandler and James M. Edmunds were the founders of the Congressional Committee as a practical and influential working body; their plans and efforts first made it a power in American politics, and it remained under their joint control until Mr. Chandler became chairman of the National Committee. The special objects which it aimed to accomplish were the securing of a uniform treatment of political topics by newspapers and speakers throughout the country, and the circulation (under the franking privilege, or otherwise) of instructive and timely documents. During the reconstruction era it also devoted much attention to the work of Republican organization in the South, where special efforts were necessary to form into effective voting masses the emancipated slaves, not yet freed from the blindness of bondage or familiar with the responsibilities of citizenship. But the great aim of the committee — all else that it did was subsidiary to that — was the circulation of political literature. This end it sought to reach by two methods: First, by the publication and mailing to individuals and to local committees in all parts of the country of such Congressional speeches as treated thoroughly and effectively any phase of the current political situation; second, by furnishing the Republican press, through the medium of weekly sheets of carefully prepared matter, with accurate information as to the facts underlying existing issues and with suggestions as to their best treatment before the people. Obviously this work could be done to much better advantage at Washington than elsewhere, for the capital city is the focus of the thousand currents of political opinion and the depository of the official statistics of the nation. Hence it was deemed wise to establish a system of guidance from that point of the public discussions of each' national campaign, so that increased intelligence, cohesion, and efficiency could be given to the general attack on the enemy; this idea — which is, in brief, that the systematizing of the political education of the people is an important element of well-planned party warfare — James M. Edmunds always held tenaciously; aided by Mr. Chandler's friendship, influence, means, and co-operation, he proved its soundness most conclusively.

Early in his Senatorial service Mr. Chandler was made the chairman of this committee, and Mr. Edmunds its secretary. The two men were admirably matched. Mr. Edmunds was a natural planner, keen in his intuitions, shrewd in observation, and a skillful judge of the bearing and tendency of party and public policies. In determining what was the most promising line of attack, where the weakest points of the enemy's lines were to be found, wherein the strength of any position lay, or what strategy would make victory the most certain and complete, he had no superior. When his acute and experienced judgment was re-inforced by Mr. Chandler's vigor in execution, influence with public men, and large wealth great results never failed to follow. These two men quickly made the Congressional Committee one of the most powerful agencies of party warfare known in American politics. In many campaigns its influence was almost literally felt in every Northern township, and its labors were not without some effect, more frequently greater than less, in unifying and invigorating the contest in every Congressional district from Maine to Texas and Florida to Oregon. Its work was done quietly, but most thoroughly; its managers rather shunned than courted publicity; and the people at large, who were informed and inspired by its labors, knew nothing of its methods and activity, hardly the fact of its existence. From 1866 to 1874 Mr. Chandler was very active in connection with this committee, and never failed to provide the agencies and the resources for the adequate carrying on of its work. When its treasury grew empty his private check made good any deficiency, and repeatedly his advances upon its account reached tens of thousands of dollars. His confidence in Secretary Edmunds was implicit, and the latter's mature recommendations never failed because of any lack of means. In 1870 the work of this committee was especially productive; its value became much more clearly apparent then than had ever been the case before, and Mr. Chandler repeatedly said to the President and other Republican leaders, "Judge Edmunds is the Bismark of this campaign." In 1872 Mr. Edmunds first suggested the necessity of meeting the Greeley movement by the thorough searching of the files of the New York *Tribune* and of Mr. Greeley's record, for the ample material therein contained which would make impossible his support by the Democratic masses. Mr. Chandler approved of this plan, and promised that the money needed should be forthcoming. Before all the work was completed, his

JAMES M. EDMUNDS.

advances had reached nearly $30,000. At times, in the course of efforts of this character, Mr. Edmunds guided the pens of upward of three hundred writers gathered under his general supervision, while the results of their labors informed the editorial pages of thousands of Republican newspapers, and thus reached millions of voting readers. For some time, also, a

monthly periodical named *The Republic* was issued, which preserved in durable form the most careful and elaborate articles
prepared under the committee's supervision. This work of the
political enlightenment of the people, clearly the most rational
agency of party warfare, has never been executed on this continent with the thoroughness, intelligence and efficiency which
marked the labors of the Congressional Committee when Mr.
Chandler was at its head and Mr. Edmunds was its executive
officer.

The man whose name is so closely coupled in these pages
with that of Mr. Chandler deserves the grateful and lasting
remembrance of the Republican party. James M. Edmunds was
a natural politician of the best type. Patriotic instincts and sincere convictions were interwoven with his nature. The party
whose tendencies satisfied those instincts, and whose policies most
nearly accorded with those convictions, he served loyally and
with rare capacity; more than this, he served it unselfishly. He
cared nothing for prominence, and never sought after reputation.
He made no speeches, he rarely shared in any public demonstration, he held no conspicuous positions, he manifested no personal
ambition, but for twenty years he was the trusted counselor of
famous men at the capital, his influence was felt in national
legislation and party movements, and important events with
which his name never was and never will be connected received
the impress of his acute observation and sagacious judgment.
Especially in Republican political management was he a wise
and strong "power behind the throne." Mr. Edmunds was a
native of Western New York, but emigrated to Michigan in
1831. He was for many years a prominent business man at
Ypsilanti, Vassar and Detroit, in that State, and was always
politically active. The Whigs sent him repeatedly to the Legislature, and made him their (unsuccessful) candidate for Governor in 1847. He was chairman of the Republican State Central

Committee from 1855 to 1861, and Controller of the city of Detroit for two of those years. At the commencement of Mr. Lincoln's administration he removed to Washington, and was there successively Commissioner of the General Land Office, Postmaster of the Senate, and Postmaster of the city of Washington. Personally he was a tall and spare man, exceedingly plain in his manners and simple in his tastes, utterly without either the liking for or faculty of display, retiring in disposition, firm of purpose, of strict integrity, and exact in his dealings and habits. Mr. Edmunds's remarkable strength as a politician consisted in his experience, in his lack of any personal aspirations, in his skill in controlling men and the accuracy of his judgment as to their motives, and in an almost prophetic ability to reason out the probable direction and effect of any given plan of action. He became a man whom those charged with great responsibilities could profitably and safely consult, and his well-considered and shrewd advice often had decisive weight at the White House, on the floors of Congress, and in the private councils of eminent men. Outside of the Congressional Committee, he did much campaign work in directing organization and suggesting plans. He was one of the founders of the Union League, and directed its operations during the years of its great political usefulness in the South. It may be said without exaggeration that no single member of the Republican party ever rendered it services as great and as slightly requited as were those of James M. Edmunds.

Mr. Chandler's close friendship with Mr. Edmunds covered a period of nearly half a century, and included an implicit confidence in the man himself and in his prudence and the sagacity of his judgment. The comment made upon their intimacy by one who knew them both well was, "Sometimes it seemed to "me that no man could be as wise as Mr. Chandler believed "that Judge Edmunds was." They were in almost constant consultation upon public questions, their co-operation was ever hearty, and this friendship the Senator valued as a priceless possession. "In death they were not divided;" the dispatch, which announced that Mr. Chandler's busy life had ended so suddenly in Chicago, came to Mr. Edmunds while infirm in health; it affected him powerfully, and his spirit did not pass from under the shadow of this blow; within a few weeks his own death followed.

CHAPTER XVIII.

N 1873 the bubble of an irredeemable currency, inflated prices, and wild speculation burst in the United States, and the era of universal shrinkage, commercial collapse, and industrial stagnation began. The financial condition of the government and the people at once became the absorbing topic of public discussion, and for five years the questions connected with the currency and the national credit were those which most completely absorbed popular attention. Mr. Chandler's share in the prolonged controversy over the financial problem was a conspicuous one; he came into it equipped with clear ideas and a consistent record; he contended for the causes of rational finance and public honesty without wavering in the face of the strongest opposition, and without any departure from sound doctrine; and he saw the courage and persistence of those with whom he acted finally rewarded by the enlightenment of the people, the restoration of a convertible currency, and the raising of the credit of the United States to the highest standard. For obvious reasons his record upon all the phases of "the financial question" can be most satisfactorily treated in a single chapter. That record will show that he began at a point to which many other public men were brought only by years of education, and it well illustrates the clearness of his conceptions of the principles underlying questions connected with what may be called the practical departments of statesmanship.

Not the least of the difficulties, which at the outset confronted the administration of Abraham Lincoln, was the fact that

the public treasury was empty and the national credit impaired.
In October, 1860, the government had contracted a five per
cent. loan of $7,000,000 at a small premium; four months later,
a six per cent. loan had been sold with difficulty at about ninety
cents on the dollar. It was true, by way of offset, that the
country was in a generally prosperous condition. The commercial
wrecks of 1857 had disappeared, crops were abundant, and general business had become again remunerative. This was an
element of national strength, but it was not a quickly available
resource. War meant large immediate expenditure, for which
the means must be promptly provided. There was no time to
create and organize upon an extensive scale the machinery of
direct taxation, and some doubts were then felt as to whether
the people would not grow restive under any general imposition
of new burdens. The entire stock of coin in the North was
estimated at but about $121,000,000, while the paper money in
existence was exclusively composed of the notes of state banks
organized under diverse and often insecure systems, and much of
it circulated only at a discount. This condition of the currency
created the fear that the rapid negotiation of large government
loans could not be accomplished without the serious derangement
of the money market; the withdrawal of considerable sums from
circulation, even. temporarily, business men believed would be
impossible without great injury to domestic enterprise and commerce. All these circumstances forced the government (which
found itself facing absolutely without preparation organized
rebellion) to resort at once to the issue of a national paper currency in the form of non-interest-bearing treasury notes of
small denominations. Congress, at its extra session in July,
1861, passed the necessary act for this purpose, and $50,000,000
of these notes ($10,000,000 more were subsequently authorized)
were placed in circulation; originally they were made redeemable in coin on demand at any United States sub-treasury, and

thus violated none of the established principles of sound finance. This expedient facilitated the negotiation of loans, and provided "the sinews of war" for 1861. But, when Congress met in December of that year, it. had become plain that the struggle would be of indefinite duration, and that past expenditures would be greatly exceeded in the months to come. To add to the embarrassments of the situation, at about this time the banks of the North suspended specie payments, and the Treasury Department was compelled as a matter of self-protection to also stop redeeming in coin its own notes then outstanding. It was as a means of escape from this emergency, that the first issue of greenbacks was authorized (by the act of Feb. 25, 1862). These notes were not redeemable on demand, but to secure their free circulation they were made a "legal tender" for all purposes except the payment of duties and of the interest on the public debt. The abandonment of the self-operating method of redemption and the resort to the compulsion of the "legal tender" enactment, as a means of keeping these notes in circulation, constituted a step which the Thirty-seventh Congress took with extreme reluctance. A small minority of its members resisted this measure to the last, but what seemed to be the overshadowing necessities of the situation and the earnest appeals of Secretary Chase finally forced the passage of the law. Mr. Chandler was one of those who, without approving of the principle of this legislation, still voted for it, on the ground that it was essential to the public safety at that moment and justified by the urgency of the situation. But he regarded it as a temporary expedient, a mere plan for an emergency, and not as a permanent policy. The first act authorized the issue of $150,000,000 of "greenbacks" and directed the retiring of the $60,000,000 of treasury notes previously paid out; this $150,000,000 Mr. Chandler believed it was possible to so control and use as to avoid the evils inseparable from inflation. But the proposition to

21

double the amount of "greenbacks," which came in less than half a year from the Treasury officials, he strenuously opposed. On June 17, 1862, he offered this resolution in the Senate:

Be it Resolved by the Senate and House of Representatives, That the amount of "legal tender" treasury notes authorized by law shall never be increased.

On the following day he called up this resolution, and said:

The effect of the recommendation (to issue $300,000,000 of "legal tender" notes) has been most disastrous. The mere recommendation, without any action of Congress on the subject, has created such a panic, and has so convinced the moneyed centers of the world that we are to be flooded with this paper, that gold has risen in price from two and three-quarters to seven per cent. premium. National credit is precisely like individual credit. It is based, first, on the ability to pay; and, second, upon the high and honorable principle which would induce the payment of a liability. When the proposition to issue treasury notes was first made, it was received with great apprehension by Congress and by the nation. . . . There was at that time a vacuum for $50,000,000 that must be filled from some source. . . . I then believed that $100,000,000 was requisite, and that $100,000,000 was enough. I believe so now. When you issue $100,000,000 of currency you must either find a vacuum or you must create one for it. A hundred millions in addition to the existing circulation would at any time create great disturbance in the financial condition of this country. . . . The moment you authorize the issue of $300,000,000 your coin will rise to ten or twelve per cent., and your notes will fall to 90 or 85. The result will be that the government will be paying just so much more for every article it purchases than it would if you kept your circulating notes at or about the value of coin.

Again, the moment you reduce the value of these notes, even to the point at which they now stand, even to seven per cent. discount, you drive out of circulation the coin of the country. The temptation is too strong to be resisted to use something else besides coin for change and for small circulation. Are we to be reduced to a shin-plaster circulation, as is the case to-day all through the South? That will be the result if you force upon the country an amount of circulating notes beyond its requirements. . . . I consider it a duty we owe to the country, a duty we owe to ourselves, to proclaim that under no circumstances shall a currency, irredeemable in coin, beyond the present issue of $150,000,000, be thrust upon the money markets of the country.

But the pressure toward a reckless currency expansion was irresistible, and the pending bill passed. Mr. Chandler's prophecies were promptly verified, for the gold premium rose and the "shin-plaster currency" made its appearance with but little delay.. Moreover, these issues only stimulated the thirst they were intended to quench, and the general inflation of prices soon again produced an apparent scarcity of currency. Early in 1863 a demand came from Mr. Chase for authority to increase the "greenback" circulation to $400,000,000. Congress granted this application, but Mr. Chandler opposed it, saying in the Senate:

When the first proposition was made to issue $150,000,000 of treasury notes, I favored it; but when the proposition was made to increase that to $300,000,000, I opposed it. . . . I prophesied what the result of thus thrusting $300,000,000 of irredeemable paper upon an already overstocked market would be. I said it would carry up coin to an unlimited extent. The result has proved that my predictions were true. Now it is proposed to issue $400,000 000; we propose to thrust them upon an already over-supplied market. . . . It is our duty to protect the people, so far as in our power, from this great depreciation in the specie value of the circulating medium, and this we can only do by decreasing its volume.

The general positions which he stated thus early Mr. Chandler firmly held throughout every stage of the subsequent contest over the "currency question." He believed that irredeemable paper money, although issued by the government itself and made a "legal tender" by supreme authority, was an unmixed evil; that only the most imminent peril could justify an even temporary resort to its use; that it ought never to be employed except within narrow limits; that any excessive issues, if made, should be promptly called in; that it should be made redeemable on demand in coin, "the money of the world," at the earliest possible moment; and that ultimately it should be wholly withdrawn from circulation by the issuing power. Accordingly, he opposed the propositions to still further increase (to $450,000,000) the issue of "greenbacks," supported the principle (while objecting to some of the details) of the act of April 12, 1866, ordering their steady contraction, and was opposed to the act of Feb. 4,

1868, stopping such contraction. The reduction in the volume of the "greenbacks" he believed to be an indispensable preliminary to the resumption of specie payments, saying in the Senate: "The government will never resume so long as it has $400,000,000 of outstanding demand notes." As he opposed during the war excessive issues of the "greenbacks," so after it closed he steadily favored the reduction of their volume with the view to the early restoration of their convertibility and their final redemption and canceling. The hesitating and halting policy, which perpetuated all the unwholesome influences of inflation and added to the severity of the inevitable collapse, was followed against his protest and in the face of predictions, which were inspired by his intimate knowledge of natural commercial laws, and were verified by the event.

In the constant discussions of financial measures during the war, Mr. Chandler did not earnestly oppose the frequent resort to the issue of irredeemable paper without offering as a substitute policies which he believed would yield relief, equally adequate, much less costly, and far less unwholesome in tendency. He proposed to provide the means for meeting the enormous expenditures required of the government by more thorough direct taxation and by larger loans; and he believed that increased imposts, by strengthening the credit of the government, would greatly improve its standing as a borrower in the money markets of the world. Briefly, the policy which he favored, in lieu of the mass of temporary expedients which were adopted, was this: (1.) Declare that the issue of "legal tender" treasury notes should not exceed $150,000,000, and thus stop their depreciation by ending all fear of their inflation. (2.) Tax freely, and by this means convince the world that the United States could and would redeem its treasury notes and pay the interest and principal of its bonds. (3.) Use the credit thus created to borrow on the most advantageous terms, and avoid all measures that might in any way tend to impair the negotiable value of, or the general confidence in, the national securities. He developed these general ideas repeatedly in his speeches and votes, while questions relating to them were before Congress. On May 30, 1862, he said in the Senate:

We voted at an early day in the session that we would raise a tax of $150,000,000 from all sources. . . . What was the result of that vote? On the very day that that solemn pledge was given to the country and the world . . . the six per cent. bonds of the United States stood at 90 cents on the dollar in the city of New York. To-day with an expenditure of more than a million dollars a day, . . . under this simple pledge in advance, of what you would do, your bonds have gone up from 90 cents to above par, and are now sought for, not only at home but abroad. If you violate that solemn pledge given to your country and to the world, what will be the effect on your securities? Let Congress violate that pledge, and you will see your bonds not only not worth 104½ but you will see them below 85. . . . The world abroad does not believe your simple asseveration that you would impose a tax, but the people of this Union do and consequently they themselves have carried your bonds from 90 to 104½. But the world does not take them. Impose your tax ; carry out your solemn pledges, and you will see your bonds eagerly sought for in the moneyed centers of the world. . . . I hope we shall not only carry out this pledge which we have given, but I care not if we exceed it. . . . Under this pledge . . . you are now able to borrow money at six per cent. instead of seven and three-tenths, and you are to day reaping the reward of your pledge of good faith.

All just tax measures Mr. Chandler vigorously supported, as furnishing the solid basis of national credit and public integrity, and time established the ability and the willingness of the people to sustain this war burden. Had the heavy taxation been accompanied by an adherence to sound principles in the management of the currency and a resort to borrowing when needed, it would have reduced the cost of conquering the rebellion by at least $1,000,000,000, probably by nearly one-half.

The maintenance of the public credit at a high standard was exceedingly important during the war, but it was of no less moment after the collapse of the rebellion, and is as great to day as it has ever been. On no public question was Mr.

Chandler more vigilant and outspoken than on this. Any attack on the integrity of the national promise represented by the bonds of the United States he denounced vigorously, whether it it took on the form of the taxation of these securities, or of propositions to pay them in depreciated currency, or of bald repudiation. On May 20, 1862, he said, upon the proposition to tax the bonds:

I believe it to be for the best interest of the government — not for the benefit of moneyed men, not for the benefit of moneyed institutions, but for the benefit of this government — to proclaim in advance that we will never tax these bonds. I believe we shall receive the *quid pro quo* now, to-day, or whenever we negotiate. It is for our interest, not for the interest of moneyed institutions, to offer these bonds. Here is the best security in the world, and we proclaim to the world, if you take these bonds they shall never be taxed. I believe we shall realize more to day, or to-morrow, or this year, or next year, for these bonds by that course, than if we were to impose a tax of one and a-half, or three, or five, or any other per cent. These bonds are negotiable. We are the negotiators. They are not in the hands of third parties. We are to borrow for our daily wants, . . . and I believe it to be for the interest of the government to declare in advance that there shall never be a tax of any sort, kind or description upon these bonds which we are now offering to the world in such enormous quantities.

Mr. Chandler said, in 1868, in a public address at Battle Creek, 'Mich., (on August 24):

The national debt is a sacred obligation upon this government, and it is to be paid, every dollar of it. But it is a Democratic debt, every dollar. If anybody should talk of repudiation it should be the Republican party, who had no instrumentality in creating it. But did you ever hear a Republican talk of repudiating it? It is a large debt. It is the price we pay for government. Is the government worth the cost? If it is, then the debt is not only an honest debt, but it has been worthily contracted. The Democrats propose to pay this debt in greenbacks, and they propose to pay the greenbacks by issuing more greenbacks. What do we gain by that? Issue $2,500,000,000 more greenbacks and they would not be worth the paper they are printed on, because the supply would flood the country and be greater than the demand. . . . It is a measure of fraudulent repudiation. In five or ten years the country might recover financially, but we would never wipe out the national disgrace that would follow that repudiation. It means the absolute annihilation of all values. These extra issues would be utterly worthless.

Mr. Chandler accordingly voted for the act of March 18, 1869, which formally declared that the United States would redeem its "greenbacks" and pay the interest and principal of its long term bonds in coin, and which was simply a new pledge that the government would do what it was already honorably bound to do both by fair construction of its own legislation and by the explicit and repeated promises of its agents. The full maintenance of the public faith, both as a matter of honor and of wise policy, he always upheld, and saw his arguments sustained and his prophecies made good in the steady improvement of the nation's credit and the refunding of its debt at greatly reduced rates of interest.

Of the national banking system Mr. Chandler was an original supporter. He regarded it as certain to become a lasting feature of the fiscal system of the United States, and as destined to ultimately furnish the paper money of the Union. The uniformity of its circulation, the security afforded to bill-holders, and the excellent results attending its method of governmental supervision, he considered as unanswerable arguments in favor of its permanent maintenance. It was his firm opinion that ultimately these banks would furnish all the national currency, and that their notes would supplant the "greenbacks." If national banking should be kept free, and redemption in coin required by law, he believed that the result would be a thoroughly-secured and readily-convertible paper currency, whose volume would be controlled by commercial demand and not by legislative caprice or political agitation, and which would lubricate and not obstruct the machinery of trade.

When the national bank bill first made its appearance in Congress, Mr. Chandler (in February, 1863) favored it as a measure of relief offering a quick market for $300,000,000 of government bonds, and as sure to supply "a better currency than the local banks now furnish." Holding the views he did, he supported the measures which promised to substitute bank notes for "greenbacks," although he opposed those which contemplated any expansion of the aggregate volume of both issues. For instance, in 1870, when the inflation element in Congress introduced a bill to add $52,000,000 to the national bank circulation (banking was not then free, it not being deemed prudent to leave the issue unlimited while all the paper money was irredeemable), he offered on January 31 an amendment to make the sum $100,000,000 and to withdraw "greenbacks" to an amount equal to the bank notes issued under this provision. He said:

> The simple effect of my proposition, if adopted, will be to keep the circulation to a dollar where it is. If no new banks are started, no greenbacks are withdrawn, and if banks are started anywhere, then an amount of greenbacks must be withdrawn equal to the amount of national bank bills put in circulation. Should the whole $100,000,000 be taken we will be just $100,000,000 nearer to specie payments than we are to-day, . . . and in the meantime the amount of national currency will not be changed in the slightest degree.
>
> MR. SUMNER: There is salvation in that.
>
> MR. CHANDLER · Of course there is salvation in it; that is why I offer it.

All proposals made at the time to increase the aggregate paper circulation he resisted, saying:

> That is a step in the wrong direction. . . . If you let it go out that this is to be the policy of Congress, you will see gold go up immediately, . . . because it will show that the Congress of the United States is in favor of expansion instead of a reduction of the currency.

After the panic of 1873, when there was such a universal clamor for further inflation, and scores of propositions were introduced to add many millions to the existing volume of "greenbacks" and of bank notes, Mr. Chandler again insisted at all proper opportunities that resumption was the most essential step toward financial soundness, and that the substitution of bank notes for "greenbacks" would aid greatly both in reaching and in maintaining specie payment. On Feb. 18, 1874, he offered an

amendment to a pending bill, directing "the Secretary of the
"Treasury to retire and destroy one dollar in 'legal tender' notes
"for each and every dollar of additional issue of bank notes,"
and spoke upon this proposition at length. He did not urge it
as a complete remedy for the existing situation (contraction and
resumption would alone furnish that), but he said:

> This is a step in the right direction. In 1865 I advocated upon this floor
> the substitution of bank notes for greenbacks as a step toward the resumption
> of specie payments, and a rapid step toward that resumption. I am now sim-
> ply advocating what I advocated then.

Mr. Chandler's wishes on this subject were not gratified at
that time nor during his life, but before his death he saw the
demand that the Treasury should cease to be a bank of issue
approved by the soundest financial sentiment of the country.
His belief, that the paper money of the Union should be furnished by commercial institutions operating under properly regu-
lated governmental supervision, that is, by the national banking
system perfected and enlarged, has been long held by the
ablest and clearest students of monetary problems in the United
States; it is to-day constantly growing in popular strength, and
the result it aims at will form part of any durable settlement of
"the currency question."

In 1873 the vacillating and halting financial policy of the
nation — which had tried and abandoned contraction, and while
looking toward the resumption of specie payments had, in fact,
retreated from it — bore fruit in speculative collapses, followed
by a panic in business circles and widespread commercial disaster.
Congress met amid the crumbling of unsound enterprise, and
was called upon to meet a terrified demand for a renewed inflation of the already excessive volume of irredeemable paper. To
cure the fever, men demanded more miasma. To repair the ruin,
which all history proved to be the natural result of an over-
supply of currency, it was proposed to still further increase that

supply.   Measures to this end were introduced at once, and pushed with great vehemence.   They were sustained by a misled but powerful public sentiment, which was especially strong in the West and influenced the great mass of that section's representatives at Washington.   Mr. Chandler never served his country better than he did in that hour.   Unmoved by the clamor about him, and refusing to listen to the cries of even his own people when they demanded false leadership, he firmly resisted every measure of inflation and every suggestion that added embarrassments to the business of the future, or increased the difficulties of preserving the public faith.   The pressure in favor of the inflation bill which President Grant vetoed was unusually strong. The Western Congressmen were almost a unit for its passage, but no solicitations, no force of numbers, prevented Mr. Chandler from opposing and denouncing it.   His speech in opposition to this bill (on Jan. 20, 1874) commenced with one of his terse sentences, which went straight to the marrow of the situation, and furnished a motto for the cause he championed.   It was, " We need one thing besides more money, and that is better money."   This phrase furnished the text for many addresses and editorials, and stood upon the title-page of the weekly circular issued by the friends of a sound currency in Boston during the controversy which preceded the passage of the Resumption act of 1875.   In the same speech Mr. Chandler said :

To insure prosperity we ought to have something permanent, something substantial.   Then the business of the country will conform itself to the facts and regulate itself accordingly.   This panic (of 1873) was exceptional, as indeed all panics are.   A panic among men is precisely like a panic among animals.   I once saw 2,000 horses stampede, and they were just as the same number of thousands of men would be in a panic.   It is the feeling of animal fear, and one encourages the other, and so it goes on until it becomes a perfect insane rush for something, nobody knows what.   Prior to this late panic, as is well known, many of our capitalists had over-invested in wild railroad schemes ; they had undertaken to do impossible things ; when the panic struck them it ought not to have had the least effect outside of Wall street and operators in railroad stocks. But the panic swept like a tornado all over the land, affected values everywhere, values of all kinds. Whoever had money in bank sought to draw it out and hide it away. The panic was universal, and yet this nation was never more prosperous than it was the day before the panic struck. And to-day there is as much money in the Union as there was then. Every dollar that was here then is here now. Besides, the enormous borrowers, the men who would pay any price for money — one-half per cent. a day, one per cent. a day, or any other given price — have failed and gone out of the market. And now the money is seeking the legitimate channels of commerce for interest and use. . . . The best time for the resumption of specie payment that has occurred since the suspension was in 1865, at the close of the war, when gold had fallen from over 200 to 122. In a few days values had shrunk, and the people of the nation were comparatively out of debt, and were ready then for a resumption of specie payments, but the government was not. The government owed more than $1,000,000,000, that was maturing daily in the shape of compound interest notes, seven-thirties and other obligations that must be funded or disposed of. Hence the government was not prepared for specie payments at that time, although the people were. . . . From that day to this we have been drifting and floating further and further away every hour from the true path — the resumption of specie payments. I have advocated from the first the earliest possible payment in coin. I believe there is no other standard of value that will stand the test, and I believe the time has arrived, or very nearly arrived, for coming to it. I have not the same timidity in fixing a date that some of my friends on this floor have. I believe that if we were to resolve to-day that we would resume the payment of our greenbacks in coin on the 1st day of January, 1875, and authorize the Secretary of the Treasury to borrow $100,000,000 in coin to be used in the redemption of the greenbacks, and sell no more gold until the 1st of January, 1875, on that day we would have $200,000,000 of coin in the Treasury for the redemption of the greenbacks. I am not particular as to date. I merely suggest the 1st of January, 1875. But I would accept an earlier date than that if it were deemed more advisable, but certainly I would not extend it more than six months thereafter. . .

It is no part of the business of this government to issue an irredeemable currency. We cannot afford to place ourselves beside the worn-out governments of Europe — we cannot afford to place ourselves on a par with Hayti and Mexico We are too rich a people to do it; and it is a disgrace to us as a nation that we have allowed it to continue one single hour beyond the hour when it was in our power to remedy the wrong.

The proposition to increase our paper currency is a step in the wrong direction, and I, for one, am utterly opposed to taking even one step in the wrong direction when I know what the right direction is.

As part of the same general discussion, Mr. Chandler made
a carefully prepared financial speech in the Senate on Feb. 18,
1874, in which he first graphically sketched the history of "wild-
cat banking" in Michigan, and then said:

After the failure of these banks the cry was still, "More money ; and we
must have more money ; the country is suffering for more money." The cry
was responded to, and more money was furnished. The Treasury of the
State of Michigan, already owing $5,000,000, undertook to furnish more
money, and the State issued treasury notes *ad libitum*, and the "more money"
men got more money until the value of the state treasury notes, which have
been paid to the last dollar at par, ran down to thirty-seventy cents on the
dollar ; and almost every city in the State, including the city of Detroit,
responded to the cry of "more money," and issued shin-plasters ; and individuals, realizing that "more money" was needed, issued shin-plasters. So
the State of Michigan was flooded with more money.

Well, sir, you can see at a glance that the State of Michigan needed more
money. We had as a people been speculating almost to a man. It was not
confined to the merchant, the banker, the man of wealth ; but the mechanic,
the farmer, the laborer, every man who could buy a piece of property of any
sort, kind, or description, bought it, ran in debt, laid out a town, sold the
lots, gave a mortgage, and then wanted "more money" to pay that mortgage.

When the collapse came it was absolute ; there was no mistake about it ;
the collapse was perfect. Then the people of Michigan had enough of "more
money ;" and when our constitutional convention met, as it did a few years
later, they put into the constitution a clause prohibiting the Legislature forever from chartering a bank or affording the means of furnishing "more
money ;" and the people acquiesced in it. They had enough of the "more
money" cry ; and for twenty-five years there was no more cry in the State
of Michigan for irredeemable money. . . . The losses to which I have
referred did not fall upon the moneyed men of the State of Michigan, the
men who were in sound condition. They fell upon the laboring man, the
farmer, and the mechanic. They fell upon the men who could least afford to
submit to the loss. So it is now. Why, sir, our values are fixed by a foreign
market, and in coin. There is not a bushel of corn or a bushel of wheat
raised in Indiana, or Illinois, or Michigan, the value of which is not fixed by
the foreign value in coin of that particular article. When you enhance the
cost of production by an inferior currency you put that loss upon the producer, and the loss falls not upon the wealthy man, but upon the laborer and
producer. Money will take care of itself all over the world. If it is not safe in
this country, it will find a country where it is safe, and it will go to that
country, no matter where that may be. Hence, capital requires no protection
whatever from this body ; money will take care of itself ; but the poor man,

the laboring man, the man who submits to all the losses from this depreciated currency, is the man who suffers all the pain and all the injury that are inflicted by this false legislation. . . .

Now, sir, we come to the crash of 1873. On the 15th day of September, 1873, this nation was in a more prosperous condition than perhaps it had been for the last twenty-five years. Every branch of industry was prosperous, every interest of the people was prosperous; but in a day, at the drop of the ball at twelve o'clock on the 16th of September, the panic struck. What produced this tremendous panic and crash in this great and prosperous country? It was over-speculating in railroad securities. It was by men undertaking to do what it was utterly impossible for them to do, to wit. for individuals to float untold millions by their own credit; and when the people became alarmed for fear the crash would come, the crash came, and there was no salvation from it. But, sir, on that very self-same day the nation was more prosperous than it had been for the last twenty years in all its interests — business, banking and every other. The crash ought not to have extended one yard beyond Wall street and the few producers of railroad iron who were manufacturing for these defunct railroads. But, sir, the panic was so great that it spread until it became universal, and values sank until there seemed to be no bottom, and everybody was affected throughout the length and breadth of this broad land.

But, Mr. President, that panic was of short duration. Many failures took place, and particularly among stock and railroad operators; but the main business of the country still went on with a few notable exceptions. Some manufacturers stopped for the want of money; others stopped for the want of credit. The men that had been issuing their paper without intending to pay it, issuing millions of dollars of paper which they knew they could not meet at maturity, trusting in luck to meet their obligations — those men cannot borrow money; their lines are full everywhere; nobody will loan them money; but, sir, upon undoubted security money is to-day cheaper than it has been at any time for the last twenty years. These great borrowers, without the expectation of paying at maturity, are to-day all out of the market. No man will loan money to a person who does not pay at maturity. Every man that desires to borrow money for legitimate business can borrow it to-day cheaper than he could borrow it at any time in the last twenty years. Sir, you may legislate for this class who have over-speculated, you may legislate for the benefit of the men who have built factories, built steamboats, built mills, bought mills, bought mines, bought everything for sale, and given their paper knowing they could not meet it unless they could borrow the money over again; you may legislate them $100,000,000 or $1,000,000,000, and you will not help them in the slightest degree. . . .

Now, Mr. President, I will ask the attention of the Senate while I show the effect upon the purchasing value of money of issuing your greenback circulation from the day it was first issued to the present time. In 1862 we commenced the issue of greenbacks. In January, 1862, the premium on gold was 2.5 per cent.; in February it was 3.5; in March, 1.8; in April, 1.5; in May, 1.3; in June, 6.5; in July, 15.5; in August, 14.5; in September, 18.5; in October, 28.5, in November, 31.1; in December, 32.3. It will be remembered that the then circulating medium (which was at that time state bank notes) amounted to about $200,000,000. This circulation was increased during the year 1862 by the addition of $147,000,000 in greenbacks, and that increase of circulation carried the value of gold from 102.5 on the 1st of January to 132.3 on the 31st day of December following.

In 1863 the necessities of the government compelled us to increase the greenback circulation to a yet larger extent. We issued during that year $203,500,000 additional, carrying up our greenback circulation to $411,200,000, in addition, of course, to our bank circulation, whatever it may have been. During the month of January of that year the premium on gold was 45.1 per cent.; during February, 60 5; March, 54.5; April, 51.5; May, 48.9, June, 44.5; July, 30.6; August, 25.8; September, 34.2; October, 47.7, November, 48; December, 51.1. In other words, the average rate of premium upon gold during that whole year was 45.2 per cent. I hold in my hand a paper showing the cash value of this emission for 1863. The emission of greenbacks at that time was $411,200,000 The average premium on gold was 45 2 per cent. The actual cash purchasing value of that $411,000,000, during the year 1863, was $283,195,000, and that was the whole purchasing value of that money during that year.

Then we come to the next year, 1864. That year, we increased our circulating medium by the addition of $237,900,000, making the whole amount $649,100,000. In 1864 the price of gold was, in January, 155.5; February, 158.6, March, 162.6; April, 172.7; May. 170.3; June, 210.7; July, 258.1, or less than 40 cents on the dollar in coin for your greenbacks after you had carried the amount up to $649,000,000. In August the price was 254.1; in September, 222 5, in October, 207.2; in November, 233.5, in December, 227.5. There is not a man here who does not remember, nor is there a farmer or mechanic throughout the length and breadth of the land who does not remember, that he then paid 60 cents for cotton goods that he had been in the habit of buying for 12½ cents, and that he paid for everything else in the same ratio. The merchant took care that he met with no loss; but the laboring man, the farmer, the man of muscle, was the man who submitted to this great loss, while the merchant and while every man with money took care of himself.

During that year the average price of gold was 203.3 per cent., or your money was a fraction less than 48½ cents on the dollar during the whole year. You had out that year $640,100,000, and the value of gold was 203.3, and the purchasing value of your $649,100,000 was $319,281,000, and that was the whole of it.

In 1865 you again increased the volume of your circulating medium by the amount of $49,800,000; making the whole amount of your circulation

$698,900,000. During the month of January, 1865, the price of gold was 216.2; during February, 205.5; in March, 173.8; in April, 148.5; and after that it stood at 135.6, 140.1, 142.1, 143.5, 143.9, 145.5, 147, 146.2. The average of the year 1865 was 157.3; and what was the purchasing value of your greenbacks that year? Every man here will remark that that year we were disposing of our bonds at the rate of hundreds of millions of dollars a month; money was passing through the Treasury almost without limit. We had $1,000,000,000 that must be negotiated, and negotiated at once — seven - thirties and compound - interest notes and other floating liabilities that must be funded; and during that year the war had closed, and while we were negotiating at this enormous rate, the price of gold fell to 153.3, and during that year the purchasing value of our circulation attained a higher rate than during any other year. That year, although our circulation of greenbacks was $698,900,000, and the premium on gold 57.3, the actual purchasing value of that $698,900,-000 was $444,310,000.

In 1866 we retired $90,000,000, leaving $608,900,000, and the average premium on gold that year was 40.9 per cent. The purchasing value of the $608,900,000, with the premium on gold at 40.9, was $432,150,000.

The next year, 1867, we retired $72,300,000, and premium on gold fell to 38.2. So we went on reducing until we got down to $400,000,000, and then we struck 14.9, 11.7, 12.4 and 14.7 as the premium on gold. There the matter has stood, and I have here from year to year, the purchasing value for each year. . . .

Mr. President, what we want is purchasing value, because the intrinsic value is measured by the purchasing value. There is not a bushel of wheat that goes from your State or from mine the purchasing value of which is not fixed by the gold value on the other side of the Atlantic. We are shipping millions and tens of millions and hundreds of millions of our agricultural products every year, and the value of these products is fixed in gold on the other side of the Atlantic; and yet by this increase of circulation we enhance the value of everything that the producer raises, but when the product comes to the market its value must be fixed by its price in gold across the Atlantic. . . .

Mr President, I know of no way to substitute the Treasury of the United States for the banking experience of the last ten centuries. We have the experience of the past, we have the experience of our own nation, we have the experience of the world. Now, do we propose to throw aside this experience, and to launch our boat upon a wild and uncertain sea, an ocean of expansion and no payments?

Sir, there are very few persons within the range of my acquaintance who desire expansion of an irredeemable currency. Certainly the people of Michigan have had abundance of experience of that kind. But wherever you go you will find two classes of men who are making a great noise about "more money." One is the speculator, the impecunious speculator, who has, perhaps, bought real estate and given a mortgage, and thinks that his only chance is to reduce the value of your currency until it falls so low that the people would rather take his land than hold your money ; and the other is the man who has issued his paper without intending to pay when it matures, and who can borrow no more money upon any terms until he pays what he already owes.

On the 14th of January, 1875, the act for the resumption of specie payments became a law. Mr. Chandler was a member of the Senate when this bill passed. He had but one objection to it; the time fixed for resumption was unnecessarily remote. Neither present exigency nor needed preparation required the delay, and he believed it to be opposed alike to economy, patriotism, and public honor. But it was the best that could be secured ; insistence upon an earlier date would have divided the friends of resumption, prevented the passage of any bill at that time, and postponed the day of specie payments. For these reasons Mr. Chandler favored the measure, and a few weeks later, when he retired from the Senate, it was with the consciousness that he had only voted for an irredeemable and inconvertible currency to meet the imperious exigencies of civil war, that he had opposed its undue expansion, that he had sustained every measure of contraction calculated to lessen the difficulties of the return to a sound basis, and that he finally had crowned his Senatorial career by support of a measure which insured the return of the government to the constitutional standard of values. ·

CHAPTER XIX.

EIGHTEEN Hundred and Seventy-four was a year of unusual political disaster. The prevalent commercial depression both naturally and seriously injured the party in power, and this and other causes combined to produce a general relaxation of Republican vigor, which bore its inevitable fruit in a series of damaging reverses in the fall elections throughout the Union. The contest in Michigan was complicated by an organized movement on the part of the opponents of Prohibition to secure a repeal of that State's stringent law against the liquor traffic, and to more surely reach that end its License League formed an alliance with the Democracy, by which the latter was greatly aided. The result was that the Republican plurality upon the State ticket was reduced to 5,969 in a total vote of 221,006, that three of the nine Congressional districts were carried by the Opposition, and that a Legislature was chosen in which the Republican majority upon joint ballot was but ten. Upon this body, so closely divided, devolved the choice of an United States Senator. To a man of Mr. Chandler's positive qualities and aggressive methods an active public life was impossible without creating strong enmities, and the attention which, had he been more subtle, he would have given to conciliating hostility his direct nature preferred to devote to showing appreciation of friendship. The equality of parties in the Legislature, and the passing disposition among Republicans to look with disfavor upon what has been since termed "stalwart leadership," supplied the local opposition

22

to Mr. Chandler with the looked-for opportunity for successfully resisting his re-election. Michigan Republicanism as a whole gave him its usual hearty support, and, so far as the contest was waged within the recognized lines of partisan warfare, his personal triumph was flattering and signal. In the regular caucus he received fifty-two votes against five ballots cast for three other candidates, and his nomination was made unanimous with but one dissenting voice. A small Republican minority refused to participate in the caucus, and after a prolonged and exciting struggle a combination was formed between six of these men and the solid Democratic and Liberal Opposition, which (on the second ballot in the legislative joint convention) gave precisely the necessary majority of all the votes cast to Isaac P. Christiancy, then one of the Justices of the Supreme Court of Michigan. Mr. Christiancy was an original Republican, but had in some instances in the past so far satisfied the Democrats by his public course that he had been once re-elected to the Supreme Bench without opposition, his name having been placed at the head of the Democratic State ticket after his nomination by his own party. This fact materially facilitated the coalition which secured Mr. Chandler's defeat. Like results in pending Senatorial contests in Wisconsin, Minnesota and Nebraska showed that more than merely local influences had contributed to bring about this event.

Mr. Chandler, with that strong faith in his own position which was so useful a characteristic of the man, did not believe that his defeat was possible until it was accomplished. His disappointment was keen, but he bore it manfully, and, assuring his friends that he should be "a candidate for *that seat* when Judge Christiancy's term ended," he started for Washington to close up his eighteen years of continuous Senatorial service. Many and sincere were the expressions of grief among earnest Republicans everywhere at what seemed to be the abrupt termination of the public career of so influential a man. Mr. Chandler himself was as strongly affected by his fear that Republicanism might have received a severe blow from the method by which his re-election had been prevented as by any sense of mere personal failure. In a letter written in the following March, in response to an invitation from the great majority of the Republican legislators of Michigan to address them on political topics, he said:

> Thanking you cordially for your continued confidence, I assure you most sincerely that when I enlisted in the Republican ranks it was for the whole war. which, I trust, is to be continued until the complete and final triumph of Republican principles, the pacification of the whole people, and the establishment of equal and exact justice for all men in every section of our common country. It will be my pride to prove to my friends, and to my enemies, if there are such, that I can be useful as a private soldier. In all the future contests of the Republican party with its opponents you may order me into the ranks with full confidence that I will respond with all my time, if need be, and with such ability as I can command. . . . We shall not yield in the forum the great principles which have triumphed in the field, nor shall we further waste in internal strife the strength which should be organized against our opponents. I have faith in the future of our country, because of my confidence in the continued success of the Republican party.

Ultimately it became evident that his defeat in 1875 was not a personal calamity, he himself afterward saw that it had opened the way for him to broader fields of public usefulness, and that in what then seemed to be a fall he had in fact only "stumbled up stairs."

After the termination of Mr. Chandler's third Senatorial term (on March 3, 1875), his name was connected, both in current rumor and in the deliberations of influential men, with several prominent positions. It was at one time predicted that he would be nominated for the St. Petersburg embassy, and at another that he would succeed Mr. Bristow as Secretary of the Treasury. Ground was not lacking for both reports, but the appointment which was actually made involved a far more complete test of his faculty of administration than would have attended either of the others. The Interior Department is the most complex division of the executive branch of the government. A great diversity of interests are under its charge, and its duties are dissimilar, widely ramified, and encumbered with a perplexing multiplicity of details. During President Grant's second term this Department, notwithstanding the personal honesty of Secretary Columbus Delano, had fallen into bad repute. It sheltered abuses and frauds which tainted the atmosphere, but were not hunted down and removed by its chiefs. From the scandals which this state of affairs created, Mr. Delano finally sought escape by a resignation, which took effect on Oct. 1, 1875. General Grant, who was determined to appoint to the place a man whose integrity, sagacity and vigor should make it certain that he would not tolerate incompetence and rascality among his subordinates, tendered the position to Mr. Chandler. After some hesitation, and no little urging by his friends, that gentleman accepted, and on Oct. 19, 1875, his commission as Secretary of the Interior was executed and sent to him. (His nomination was, on the meeting of Congress in December, promptly confirmed by the Senate, all of the Republican and three of the Democratic Senators voting affirmatively, with only six Democrats recorded in the negative). Mr. Chandler entered at once upon the discharge of his new and difficult duties. No man could have had less of the professional "reformer" about him — in fact he was not chary of expressing the most contemptuous skepticism concerning much that paraded itself as "reform" — but the exemplification which he gave of practical reform was at once thorough and brilliant. Without ostentation, without the faintest savor of cant, he went at his work in unpretentious, business-like, manful, and clear-sighted fashion. A firm believer himself that "corruption wins not more than honesty," he gave durable lessons on that theme in every bureau of the Interior Department.

The first step of Mr. Chandler's administration was the infusion of new blood. He applied to James M. Edmunds for aid in the selection of a Chief Clerk, and was by him advised to tender that important position to Alonzo Bell, then holding a

THE INTERIOR DEPARTMENT.*

place in the Treasury. What followed illustrates some of Mr. Chandler's methods of transacting business:

Mr. Bell, at his desk in the Winder Building, received a

---

*This massive edifice is popularly known as "The Patent Office," because its main halls are occupied by the magnificent model rooms of the Bureau of Patents.

dispatch on the afternoon of Nov. 8, 1875, which read: "The Secretary of the Interior desires to see you." On the next morning at nine o'clock he was in waiting in the ante-chamber of Secretary Chandler's office, and shortly thereafter that gentleman entered. In a few moments Mr. Bell was summoned into his room, and Mr. Chandler said, "Good morning, Mr. Bell. "I suppose General Cowen (the then Assistant Secretary) has "told you what the business with you is?" Mr. Bell answered, "I have had a very pleasant talk with him, but there has been no business alluded to by us." Mr. Chandler then said, "I have "concluded to appoint you Chief Clerk of the Interior Depart- "ment; will you accept?" "Yes, sir," was the reply. "Very well," said Mr. Chandler, "go ahead." Mr. Bell went at once to the Treasury, filed his resignation, and within an hour returned to the office of the Secretary of the Interior. He found him in conference with two Senators, and this conversation followed: "Mr. Secretary, I have taken the oath and I am ready to go to work." "Very well, do you know where to find the Chief Clerk's room?" "No, sir." "Well, sir, it won't take long to look it up." Mr. Bell started on the search for it, and within a few moments had relieved the gentleman temporarily in charge, taken possession of its desk, and commenced business. Mr. Chandler, also on recommendation of Mr. Edmunds, promoted John Stiles from a minor place to the Appointment Clerkship. The Assistant Secretaryship of the Department he requested the President to tender to Charles T. Gorham of Michigan, who had lately relinquished the embassy of the United States at The Hague. He believed that Mr. Gorham's business training, practical ability and personal attachment to himself would greatly aid in the re-organization of the Department, and only felt doubtful as to whether that gentleman would accept the position. In the end, Mr. Gorham was induced to take it, and the Assistant Attorney-Generalship was given to Augustus S. Gaylord of

Saginaw, well-known to Mr. Chandler as a good lawyer and a vigilant and trustworthy man. These changes in his executive staff the new Secretary of the Interior regarded as an essential part of the work of investigation and purification which was to be accomplished.*

Within less than one month after the commencement of Mr. Chandler's term, all the clerks in one of the important rooms in the Patent Office were summarily removed. Examination had supplied satisfactory proof of dishonesty in the transaction of the business under their care, and the Secretary concluded that all of them were either sharers in the corruption or lacked the vigilance necessary for their positions, and he declared every desk vacant. To the Hon. Jay A. Hubbell, whom he met on the evening of the day upon which he had taken this vigorous step, he said, "I have been 'reforming' to-day. I "have emptied one large room and have left it in charge of a "colored porter, who has the key, who cannot read and write, "and who is instructed to let no one enter it without my orders. "I think the public interests are safe so far as that room is "concerned until I can find some better men to put into it." To the remonstrances which followed this action he was reso-lutely deaf, and to some influential friends of one of the men thus displaced he said significantly, "That man is competent "enough; if he thinks that the cause of his removal should be "made public, he can be accommodated; I don't advise him to "press it." Later in Mr. Chandler's term, and without warning,

---

* Much of Secretary Chandler's confidence arises from the well-known integrity and personal reliability of the several gentlemen sustaining the nearest official relation to him, all of whom were selected by his own free choice, and from his own personal knowledge of these essential characteristics. General Gorham did not seek the office of Assistant Secretary; the office sought him, and Mr. Chandler himself would take no denial. So, also, of Mr. Gaylord, his able and untiring Assistant Attorney-General for the department. And the same is true of Mr. Partridge, his discreet and trusted private secretary. Sur-rounded by such aids he well knows that no material interest can suffer by any temporary contingency, such as the one which now occurs.—*Washington dispatch to the Philadelphia " City Item " of Oct. 20, 1875 (referring to Mr. Chandler's temporary absence).*

the monthly pay - rolls of the Patent Office employes were placed in the custody of a new officer, and the full name and city address of every one who signed them was taken. The result was that for upward of a score of names no owners appeared, and it was thus found that money had been dishonestly drawn in the past by some one through the device of fictitious clerkships. It was also ascertained that in a few cases work requiring expert skill had been given to unqualified persons who had "farmed it out" to others at reduced rates, and were thus receiving pay without rendering service. These disclosures led to further prompt removals of those implicated in the frauds, and to the eradication of the abuses thus exposed. In this bureau some change of methods was also made which simplified the transaction of business, and increased the facilities for procuring patents while lessening their cost to the public.

The Bureau of Indian Affairs Mr. Chandler found to be more utterly unsavory in reputation than any other division of his Department. Besides securing a new Commissioner and Chief Clerk, he instituted a series of quiet inquiries into the methods of doing business there, and soon determined upon removing a number of subordinates, whose records were unsatisfactory and whose surroundings were suspicious. He then sent for the Commissioner and notified him of this decision, but that officer replied that they were the most valuable men he had, and that it would be almost impossible to conduct the business of the bureau without them. The urgency of his protest finally induced Mr. Chandler to delay action for a few days. While matters were in this state of suspense, President Grant, who was watching with keen interest the examination into the Interior Department offices, said to its Secretary, "Mr. Chandler, "have you removed those clerks in the Indian Bureau whom we "were talking about?" Mr. Chandler replied, "No, sir; the Com-"missioner said it would be almost impossible to run the office

" without them." The President answered, " Well, Mr. Secretary, you can shut up the bureau, can't you?" The answer was, " Yes, sir." " Well then," said General Grant, " have those men " dismissed before three o'clock this afternoon, or shut up the " bureau." Mr. Chandler went over to the Department, sent for the Commissioner, told him that the suspected clerks must go that afternoon if the bureau was closed as the result, and gave the necessary orders of removal which were promptly executed. In regard to the dismissal of these men, he said, " I have n't " evidence that would be regarded in a court as sufficient to " convict them of fraud or dishonesty, but to my mind the " proof of their crookedness is strong as Holy Writ." This was only one of many instances in which President Grant actively interested himself in the work of hunting out fraud, and there was no step which Mr. Chandler took in the direction of honest and cheaper administration in which he was not cordially and powerfully sustained at the White House.

The " Indian Attorneys " also came under and felt the weight of the new Secretary's just displeasure. One of the glaring impositions practiced upon the ignorant aborigines was that of inducing them, winter after winter, to send " agents " to Washington to look after their interests, upon representations made to them that the government would otherwise deprive them of some of their rights. Many of these men were paid eight dollars a day and their expenses, while others contracted for certain sums secured on the property of the Indians. In fact, these " attorneys " rendered no needed service and preyed upon the ignorance of their clients. These men Mr. Chandler banished from his Department; he also declined to allow the payment of claims preferred by representatives of the Indians for " expenses incurred in procuring legislation," on the ground that such outlay was illegal and immoral. His decision on these points was embodied in this order (addressed on Dec. 6, 1875, to the Commissioner of Indian Affairs, and still governing the proceedings of that bureau), which saved large sums of money to the Indians:

> Hereafter no payment shall be made and no claim shall be approved for services rendered for or in behalf of any tribe or band of Indians in the procurement of legislation from Congress or from any State Legislature, or for the transaction of any other business for or in behalf of such Indians before this Department or any bureau thereof, or before any other Department of the government, and no contract for the performance of such services will hereafter be recognized or approved by the Indian Office or the Department. Should legal advice or assistance be needed in the prosecution or defense of any suit involving the rights of any Indian or Indians, before any court or other tribunal, it can be procured through the Department of Justice.
>
> This regulation will govern the Indian Office, and application for compensation for such services must not be forwarded to the Department for action hereafter, it being understood that the regularly-appointed Indian Agent, the Commissioner of Indian Affairs and the Secretary of the Interior are competent to protect and defend the rights of Indians in all respects, without the intervention of other parties, and without other compensation than the usual salaries of their respective offices.

Mr. Chandler's experience as Secretary of the Interior made him a firm believer in President Grant's policy of seeking to civilize the American savages by dealing with them through the agency of the Christian churches. Originally he favored turning the management of Indian affairs over to the military arm of the government, but actual contact with this knotty problem convinced him that the so-called "peace policy" was, with all its conceded imperfections, the true one. He held that, if firmly adhered to and improved as experience should dictate, it would ultimately yield the largest and best returns. To make any policy successful he knew that honest and competent service was indispensable, and that he spared no efforts to secure.

In the Pension Bureau there was also some wholesome investigation, and the efficiency of its administration and the vigilance of its scrutiny into fraudulent claims upon the government were materially increased, with the result of saving to the Treasury

President Grant. Hamilton Fish. J. D. Cameron. Alphonso Taft. Z. Chandler. J. N. Tyner.

Lot M. Morrill. G. M. Robeson.

PRESIDENT GRANT'S CABINET—1876-'77.

[From a Sketch by Mrs. C Adele Fassett.]

hundreds of thousands of dollars annually. In the Land Office a series of extensive frauds in what was known as " Chij pewa half-breed scrip" were discovered during the first six months of Mr. Chandler's term. The matter was one that had been brought to the attention of the Department under other Secretaries, but no detection of rascality had followed. Mr. Chandler ordered a thorough investigation, which was pushed vigorously by Mr. Gorham and Mr. Gaylord. The end was the breaking up of a strong and corrupt combination, the prompt removal of all officers connected with its past operations, and the reporting of the facts to the proper Congressional committees for further action. The Secretary also ordered a consolidation of the seven stationery divisions of the Department into one central office, securing thereby a lessened cost of management which was and is worth $20,000 annually to the Treasury.

The result of this exhibition of executive vigor need not be described in detail. Under the impetus of shrewd insight, disciplined business habits, and firm purpose, the *morale* of the various bureaux improved rapidly. Abuses withered up, inefficiency became industry, and fraud took flight.* The Interior Department became a strongly-officered and well-administered branch of the government. Men saw that it had at last a head who meant that his subordinates should be honest and should render efficient service, and who could push his intentions into acts. Mr. Chandler, who had originally doubted as to whether

---

* No appointment was ever more thoroughly justified by the result than Mr. Chandler's. It gave him a new field for his energy and his masterly executive ability, and it is conceded that he made the best Secretary of the Interior that the nation has had in our day. He made no boasts of what he intended to accomplish, but instituted reforms and uprooted abuses. He hated dishonest men, and they feared him.—*Gen. J. R. Hawley, in the "Hartford Courant."*

On no occasion was Mr. Chandler known to use his official position for his own pecuniary gain—directly or indirectly. His death has ended a long career of public service in executive and legislative capacities, and throughout his hands were ever clean of unjust or illegitimate gain—nor did his bitterest political foe (and no man evoked stronger personal criticism) ever charge, or ever suspect him, with making personal profit out of his political station and opportunities.—*T. F. Bayard in the Senate, Jan. 23, 1880.*

he could still command his old mercantile faculty of mastering and managing a host of details, convinced both himself and others that this was still one of his powers. His administration made evident the benefits of the supervision of the public business by a practical man of affairs, and no member of President Grant's Cabinets made a record more enviable for unostentatious and efficient discharge of duty.

The anecdotes of Mr. Chandler's Cabinet service are many and entertaining. He commenced by arming himself for the chronic battle of all heads of departments with the claimants of patronage. One of his first orders prohibited clerks from recommending applicants for position, and another provided him with a statement of the number of employes in the Department from each Congressional district. A memorandum book, containing this information, was constantly by his side, and was used almost daily. A Congressman would apply for the appointment to a clerkship of some constituent whom he was anxious to oblige or assist. The record would be produced, and something like this conversation would follow: " You see your quota is full, but " that don't matter; pick out any man you want me to remove " and I'll put your man in his place at once." "But," the Congressman would reply, "I can't do that. If I ask you to turn out any of these men I shall get myself into hot. water." "You " don't mean to say that you're asking me to get myself into " hot water for you?" the Secretary would answer, and with this weapon, thus used half banteringly but still effectively, he, with perfect good-nature, turned aside the Congressional pressure for positions.

He also carefully kept memoranda of the official records of his subordinates, and charges against any one of them coming from responsible sources were certain to be thoroughly investigated. But no man could be more wrathful at mere backbiting or at efforts for the secret undermining of reputation.

His repugnance to injustice was no less keen than his sense of justice. One afternoon a man of clerical aspect and garb called at his office, and said, after introducing himself, "Mr. Chandler, "I presume it is your intention to have none but correct people "in your Department."

"That is my intention."

"Well, do you know, sir, that you have a woman in one of the bureaux of your Department who is of bad character."

"No, sir, I do not know that I have any such persons in my Department."

"I thought you didn't know it, Mr. Chandler, and so I decided to come and inform you."

The name of the clerk in question was then given and the charges against her made still more explicit. Mr. Chandler listened quietly, and finally picked up a pen and handed it to his caller, saying, "Just put that down in writing, sir, and I will dismiss the woman." The accuser hesitated and said, "Now, "I hope, Mr. Chandler, you will not connect my name with this "matter. I don't want to be known." The Secretary thereupon leaned back in his chair and said, "You know all about this "woman and I know nothing about her, except what you state "to me; but you want me to put a stain on her reputation "upon charges you are unwilling to even substantiate with your "name. Never! Leave the office." Upon the abrupt departure of the visitor so dismissed, Mr. Chandler turned to one of his clerks and said, " He belongs to that class of informers who are "always willing to stand behind and ruin a person, but who "don't want to be known. I don't propose to be a party to any "such transaction."

A contractor, whose rascality had been conclusively exposed and whose contract had been unceremoniously annulled, came to him one day to remonstrate. The conversation ran in this wise.

"Mr. Secretary, I have been badly used —— "

"I'm glad of it," interrupted Mr. Chandler; "you're a scoundrel, and it's time you were getting your deserts."

The man attempted explanation, but Mr. Chandler was too impatient to listen, and finally sent him away with orders to write a letter setting forth his grievances, which should be investigated. "Although," added he, as the contractor retired, "it's my opinion that the worst treatment you could get would "be too good for you."

In the few cases where genuine hardship followed his quick decisions and their enforcement, he was ready to make good the injury he had not intended to inflict. One morning a prominent officer of the army entered Mr. Chandler's office with a small pamphlet in his hand and said, "What kind of a fool is it, Mr. Secretary, that you have at your door distributing tracts?" Upon Mr. Chandler's denying all knowledge of this variety of colportage, he said, "Here is a tract a fellow out there gave me, and told me to read it, and said it might be good for my soul." Mr. Chandler was nettled at this violation of discipline, and made inquiries which showed that one of the clerks was distributing tracts about the Department under circumstances that implied neglect of his official duties, and thereupon he was dismissed. In a short time an earnest letter came to the Secretary from the wife of the displaced man describing the distress that had been brought upon their home, whereupon Mr. Chandler directed his reinstatement, saying, as he issued the order, "I "guess he won't circulate any more tracts. I don't object to "their distribution, but when a man is doing the government "business he should give that his attention." For a clerk discharged because of dishonesty, no amount of personal solicitation, even by close friends of Mr. Chandler, availed anything. At one time when he was most vehemently and persistently urged to restore a suspected and dismissed subordinate, he finally said to the Senator who was pressing the matter, "There is but one

" way by which you can have that man re-appointed, and that
" is to first have me turned out."

In the early part of his term a letter came to Mr. Chandler
from a man in California, who had a case pending before the
Department upon an appeal from the Commissioner of the Land
Office. He wrote that if the Secretary would decide that case
in favor of the appellant, he would remit $300 in gold. Mr.
Chandler read it and said to his clerk, "Call the attention of
" the Attorney-General to that, cite the law that man has
" violated, and ask the Department of Justice to prosecute the
" fellow," and this course was taken. At about the same time,
a dispatch came from the Pacific coast stating that a man was
at San Francisco who claimed to be Mr. Chandler's brother, and
was seeking to borrow money on that statement. To this Mr.
Chandler's answer was this telegram: "I have no brother.
Arrest the scoundrel."

By the clerks, whose official record satisfied him, he was
universally liked. He was easily approached, ready to listen,
quick to perceive, and prompt in decision. He scarcely ever gave
reasons, but his rapid judgment was rarely found to require
reversal or even revision. With those who did business with
the Department on honest principles, and only asked for
promptitude and efficiency in its service, his popularity was great
and deserved. The fact that he was at its head was kept constantly fresh in the minds of all. Soon after the commencement
of his term he exchanged offices with the Commissioner of
Patents, thus obtaining an apartment much more desirable than
the one previously occupied by the Secretaries. One of the
Patent Office *attaches*, in replying to the comment of somebody
who expressed surprise at the fact that this change had not been
sooner made, said, "To tell the truth we have generally regarded
" the Secretary himself as an interloper in the Department. Mr.
" Chandler has started a new order of things."

While the investigating mania was at its height, the House Committee on the Expenditures of the Interior Department determined to look into his books and business system. He

THE SECRETARY OF THE INTERIOR'S OFFICE.

accordingly received from them a formal letter asking what time would be convenient for the investigation. The Chief Clerk submitted this communication to Mr. Chandler, who said, "Tell "them to come down any day, and I want you to put the best

23

"room we have at their disposal, and give them all the facilities
"you can to investigate the affairs of any bureau of the Depart-
"ment that they want to look into. If they can find anything
"wrong that I haven't found, I shall be very much obliged to
"them. They will be pumping a dry well. The work is done."
The committee came, but only held a few brief sessions, and
finally never concluded their labors and never made a report in
relation thereto.

Active as were Mr. Chandler's party sympathies, and little
disposed as he was to consult his political opponents as to his
course, or to admit them to any share in the patronage at his
disposal, he did not manage the Department upon merely partisan principles. He did not make removals of Democratic
subordinates except for cause; he never appointed any Republican whom he did not believe to be thoroughly upright and
competent. That to fill any vacancy he always sought to find
the right kind of Republican was true. His civil service theories
stopped with honesty and efficiency, and did not exclude pronounced political sympathy with the appointing power nor party
activity. Still, he did not on any occasion enforce the payment
of political assessments by his subordinates, and their work for the
Republican cause was left voluntary in character. The nearest
approach to mere partisanship in his use of the appointing power
was the giving of places in the Department to crippled soldiers
who had been discharged from the employment of the House of
Representatives by the Democratic Door-keeper, and even in
that it was far more the indignation of the patriot than of the
Republican that stirred him. At the close of Mr. Chandler's
Secretaryship, the clerks of the Department waited upon him
in a body, and thanked him for the kindness they had received
at his hands. While farewells were being exchanged Mr. Schurz,
the new Secretary, came in and was introduced to his staff of
subordinates. Mr. Chandler then said:

Mr. Secretary, I welcome you to this office. When I came here this Department was greatly tainted with corruption, especially in the Patent Office and the Indian Bureau. With the aid of the gentlemen you see around you, I have been able to cleanse it, and I believe, as far as I am able to ascertain, that no abuses exist in the bureaux I have named. I had to use the knife freely, and I believe this Department stands to - day the peer of any department of the government.

Mr. Chandler further commended the corps of employes as honest, faithful men, and Mr. Schurz replied:

I think I am expressing the general opinion of the country when I say you have succeeded in placing the Interior Department in far better condition than it had been in for years, and that the public is indebted to you for the very energetic and successful work you have performed. I enter upon the arduous duties with which I have been entrusted with an earnest desire to discharge them conscientiously, and I shall be happy when leaving the Department to have achieved as good a reputation for practical efficiency as you have won. I thank you, sir, for this cordial welcome, and I will say to the gentlemen to whom you have introduced me that they shall have my protection; and I ask from them the same faithful assistance they have given you.

The tribute which Secretary Schurz at the outset thus paid to the practical efficiency of his predecessor merely expressed the public verdict which greeted the close of Mr. Chandler's term. Examination did not compel any modifying of this praise, and after Mr. Chandler's death his successor in the Interior Department — a man very exacting in judgment and one with whom his political differences had been numerous — again said: " In " the course of the last two years I have frequently discovered " in the transaction of public business traces of his good judg- " ment and his energetic determination to do what was right." `

CHAPTER XX.

THE Michigan delegation to the Cincinnati Convention of 1876 selected Mr. Chandler as the member of the National Republican Committee for their State, and at the first formal meeting of that body (at Philadelphia, early in July) he was chosen its chairman after a close triangular contest between his friends and those of the Hon. A. B. Cornell and Gen. E. F. Noyes. The committee at once opened rooms at the Fifth Avenue Hotel in New York, with its Secretary, the Hon. R. C. McCormick of Arizona, in immediate charge. Mr. Chandler made frequent visits to the headquarters throughout the campaign, superintending the general plan of operations and meeting with the executive committee; as election-day approached his attendance became more constant.

Originally he felt confident of Republican victory, not believing that in the centennial year the American people would render a political verdict whose result would be the restoration of the disloyal classes of the South to national supremacy. But, in September, evidences of Republican apathy in the important States of Ohio and Indiana — more especially in the former, which was the home of the Presidential candidate — greatly disturbed him, and made it plain that the situation was critical. It had become evident that organized brutality would give all the close Southern States to the Democrats and even make doubtful those which were strongly Republican, and that the merchantable and criminal classes of New York city would be so used as to also cast the electoral vote of that great State for the Opposition. The gravity of the prospect then brought out Mr. Chandler's best qualities of party leadership. Prompt aid was rendered in Ohio, and the National Committee did more than its full share (Mr. Chandler making large personal advances) to carry that State in the important October election. After the serious loss of Indiana, measures were at once instituted to organize the party for decisive work on the Pacific Slope, to see that in those Southern States where there was any hope all lawful measures were taken to defeat the plans of "the rifle clubs" and "the white leagues," and to carry New York if that was possible. Nothing was spared that would arouse the spirit of the party, and Mr. Chandler saw that the means were forthcoming for every effort that promised to make success more certain.

The elections showed that the calculations of the managers of the Republican campaign were accurate, and were also adequate to "snatching victory from the jaws of defeat." The effort to save New York failed, and it and the neighboring States rewarded with their electoral votes the unscrupulous and subtle skill of Governor Tilden's personal canvass. But the Republican victories beyond the Rocky Mountains, and the resolute resistance offered in South Carolina, Louisiana and Florida, to the seizure of those States by political crimes ranging from shameless fraud to wholesale massacre, still left success with the Republicans after a contest without an American parallel in obstinacy, bitterness and excitement. Mr. Chandler showed throughout the prolonged electoral dispute "the courage which mounteth with the occasion," and his firmness, vigor and activity were among the important factors in the work of saving the fruits of the so narrowly-won victory. As soon as the smoke lifted from the battle-field his dispatch appeared, "Hayes has 185 votes and is elected," and he maintained that position to the end without a shade of faltering. Knowing that the Republicans were rightfully entitled to the electoral votes of, at least, Mississippi, Alabama, Florida, Louisiana and South Carolina, he determined that in the three States where the existence of Republican officials afforded some ground for hope nothing should be left undone to deprive fraud and violence of their prey, and he pushed every measure which seemed needed to uphold the Republicans of Florida, Louisiana and South Carolina in their lawful rights. In some of the important closing phases of this exciting contest his counsels were not followed. The Electoral Commission act was not a measure that he approved. Firmly believing in the constitutional power of the President of the Senate to count the electoral votes and announce the result, he held the position that that officer should discharge that duty, and that the candidate thus constitutionally declared elected should be duly inaugurated at all hazards; and revolutionary threats were without effect upon his firm purpose. The negotiations between the opposing party leaders which attended the closing hours of the struggle, and which culminated in the abandonment by the new administration of the Republican State governments of the South, received no sanction from him. He regarded such a policy as essentially perfidious, and as clouding the title of Mr. Hayes to his high office, a title which Mr. Chandler believed to be as clear as that possessed by any President chosen since the formation of the constitution. Much else that attended the surrender of the South to the bitter enemies of the republic he deprecated as exceedingly harmful to the party of his faith, as unwise in tendency, and as unjust in principle. He was not demonstrative in his criticisms upon the new "policy," and his retirement to private life enabled him to maintain a general silence upon the subject. But his disapproval of a "conciliation," which he regarded as cowardly in its treatment of friends and as foolish in its manifestation of undeserved confidence in enemies, was profound.* Within two years the vindication of his opinions was complete.

The indebtedness of the Republicans to Mr. Chandler's attitude and efforts in the presidential election of 1876 and the subsequent electoral dispute can scarcely be exaggerated. Without his firmness, the spirit with which he held his party up to the thorough assertion of its rights, the liberality with which he advanced the large sums required for legitimate expenditures, and the influence of his indomitable resolution, the final victory would have been at least vastly more difficult of attainment, if not actually impossible. In him the enemy never found the slightest traces of failing will or flagging strength. While the excitement was at its height, a Democratic periodical published a cartoon, in which Mr. Chandler was caricatured as standing colossus-like over a yawning chasm, holding up an elephant, labeled "The Republican Vote," by a double-handed grasp upon its tail. The humor of the rough sketch greatly delighted its subject, and he kept it with him for the entertainment of his friends. He first saw it after one of the Cabinet sessions, when it was produced by President Grant and passed through the hands of the other Secretaries, until it reached Mr. Chandler, who, after looking it over, said, gravely pointing out his position in the cartoon: "Mr. President, one of three things is certain: "either the rocks upon which my feet are resting will crumble, or "the elephant's tail will break, or I shall land the animal." Into

---

* In the fall of 1877 Mr. Chandler delivered the annual address before the Branch County Agricultural Society, and while in Coldwater was the guest of the Hon. Henry C. Lewis of that city, who invited a few friends to meet him socially. In the course of the conversation Mr. Chandler said that he was going to his Lansing farm to spend a few days. His reticence in regard to the Hayes administration was then a matter of remark; and the Hon. C. D. Randall said to him : "Well, Mr. Chandler, when you get out in the center of "your great farm and alone, you will have a fine opportunity to express your opinion "about the Hayes 'policy.'" Mr. Chandler's reply was : "No, sir ; that Lansing farm "will never answer my purpose. To do that I shall have to be on the top of a high hill "behind the meeting-house and with the wind blowing the other way !" The audience responded with a hearty laugh.

the methods of his work he never feared examination. No cipher dispatch disclosures have cast infamy upon his name, and eager investigation by his political enemies still left his personal honor untainted.

After the conclusion of Mr. Chandler's term of Cabinet service, he remained in Washington for several weeks, and then accompanied General Grant to Philadelphia, and was one of the party who escorted the Ex-President down the Delaware when, on May 17, 1877, he commenced his tour around the world. The next two years were spent by Mr. Chandler in Michigan. His only prolonged absence from his Detroit home during this period was caused by a two months' trip to the California coast in June and July of 1877. A special car was placed at his service by the Pacific Railroads (he was one of the earliest and most energetic supporters of the trans-continental railway project), and he was accompanied by Charles T. Gorham of Marshall, H. C. Lewis of Coldwater, and S. S. Cobb of Kalamazoo. Denver, Salt Lake City, Los Angeles, San Francisco, and the Yo Semite Valley were visited during the journey, and everywhere Mr. Chandler was welcomed with noteworthy public and private entertainments; his attractive social qualities shone throughout the jaunt. Not a great traveler, yet he saw during his life much of the world. In 1875, in company with Senators Cameron, Anthony and others, he visited the leading cities of the South. During one of the Congressional recesses of his second term, he passed some months in Europe, and while still in active business he spent a winter in the West Indies. His knowledge of the resources and points of interest of the North and Northwest was extensive and thorough.

The marsh farm, which Mr. Chandler bought near the city of Lansing, and the experiments in extensive and systematic drainage which he made thereon, always received a generous share of his attention when he was in Michigan. This enterprise was one in which he unhesitatingly made large investments with the view of settling definitely questions of manifest public importance. In 1857 the State of Michigan gave to its Agricultural College the public lands in the four townships of Bath, De Witt, Meridian, and Lansing, which were designated on the surveyor's maps as "swamp lands;" in the main the sections covered by the grant were marshy, although their rectilinear

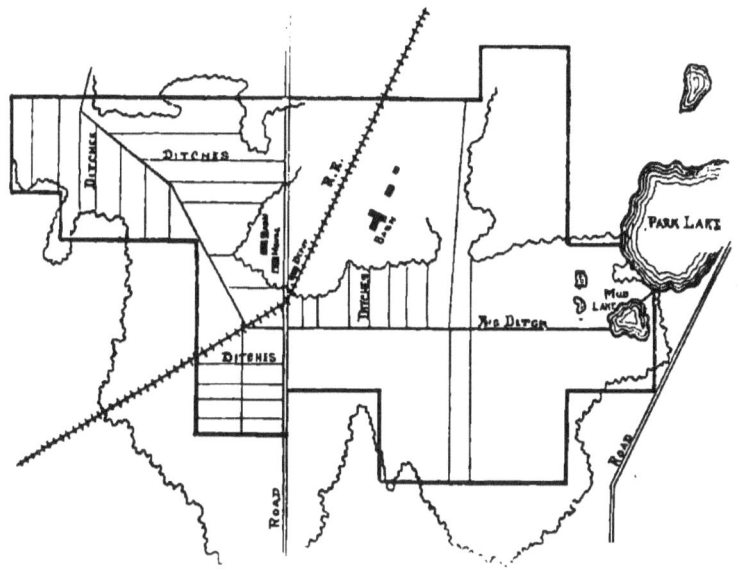

PLAT OF THE MARSH FARM.*

boundaries included some solid ground. Mr. Chandler purchased from the college and other owners a farm of 3,160 acres, located four miles (by railroad) from Lansing, in the towns of Bath and De Witt in Clinton county; it included about 1,900 acres

---

*The heavy black lines in this map are the boundaries of the farm; the waving lines indicate the border of the uplands surrounding the marsh. The drainage is from Mud Lake via "the big ditch" to the Looking-glass river. The lateral ditching (of which there are over fifty miles) is shown on the plat by the fine lines.

of marsh meadow, 500 acres of tamarack swamp, and 800 acres
of oak-opening uplands. The marsh was traversed by a slender
water-course, deviously connecting some small lakes with a stream
known as the Looking-glass river. The upland portion of the
farm was thoroughly fertile, but its development and cultivation
did not specially interest Mr. Chandler, except as furnishing
the needed base for his experiments upon the marsh. He said:
"Michigan contains thousands of acres of precisely this kind of
"land. The drainage of this particular marsh is difficult, as much
"so as is the case with any land in this peninsula which is not
"a hopeless swamp. If this tract can be reclaimed, others can
"be, and I propose to give the experiment of reclamation a
"thorough trial. I have the money, and I believe I have the
"pluck. If I succeed, it will be a good thing for the State, for
"it will show how to add millions of dollars worth of land
"to its farms. If I fail, it will also be a good thing, for it will
"settle an open question, and no man need repeat my attempt."
He pushed this experiment vigorously from the time of its
commencement until his death, and gave to it his frequent personal supervision. His investments in the marsh farm soon
came to be counted by many tens of thousands of dollars.
Originally, practical farmers were inclined to regard his operations as sheer folly, but as they saw the purpose, methods and
thoroughness of his work, a just appreciation of its aim followed. Mr. Chandler never disguised the character of this enterprise. Repeatedly he said to visitors at the farm and to friends,
"I have a theory — that is a remarkably expensive thing to
"have — and I propose to test it here; it will make me poorer,
"but it may make others richer some time." The public value
of his experiment he believed to be great, and that fact he was
quick to make prominent whenever it seemed necessary.

The general plan of drainage operations consisted in connecting by a large ditch Park lake (which has an area of 235 acres)

with the Looking-glass river. This main ditch was constructed by straightening the bed of Prairie creek, and possessed descent enough to ensure a slow current in wet seasons. It is about four miles in length, and averages fourteen feet in width by four in depth. At intervals of forty rods are constructed lateral ditches, as a rule five feet in width at the top by three in depth. This part of the work had not been completed at the time of Mr. Chandler's death, but still the lateral ditching

THE "BIG DITCH" (WINTER SCENE).

had reached about fifty miles in aggregate length, and had well drained about 1,000 acres in the western end of the marsh near the outlet into the Looking-glass. In that portion of the farm the first results of the drainage — the rotting down of the peaty surface of the marsh into a vegetable mold — have already manifested themselves satisfactorily. The extent to which this decomposition will continue is not completely tested, nor does it yet appear what will be the full measure of the arability of soil, which will be created by this process, supplemented by the tile draining which will follow the subsidence of the marsh to a permanent level. This peaty surface varies from two and a half feet to a rod in depth and promises to become an enormously productive soil. The experiments thus far tried upon it have resulted hopefully. Much of the native grass furnished excellent hay, and stock fatted upon it thoroughly with no more than the usual allowance of grain. The tame grass sown was chiefly Fowl Meadow and Timothy. The former Mr. Chandler had seen growing in Holland on reclaimed land, and he determined to give it a trial; he was only able to find the seed in the Boston market, and there paid for it four dollars per bushel of eleven pounds. It is a species of Red Top, and soon yielded from one and a half to two tons of excellent hay per acre. For four seasons this seeding-down with tame grasses was tried with satisfactory results, and then other experiments followed. In the fall of 1878, twelve acres of marsh, then well seeded-down with grass, were thoroughly plowed by Superintendent Hughes, who, in the following season, raised thereon corn, potatoes, rutabagas and oats. The results conclusively showed that the marsh possessed general productiveness, although the experiment itself was marred by the unseasonable frosts of 1879. The corn looked well at the outset, but was severely injured in the end. The potato crop was a good one, and the yield of oats was also large. In the fall of 1879 another tract of twelve acres was plowed, and the same experiment was put in process of repetition. Superintendent Hughes is of the opinion that within another year, the reclaimed marsh will produce 100 bushels of corn to the acre. A short time before his death, Mr. Chandler said that, in view of the success which had attended the experiments already tried, he now felt confident that in time his farm would be pointed out as an ague-bed transformed into one of the most valuable pieces of property in Central Michigan, and would demonstrate the reclaimability of large tracts of swamp land in that State. About 500 acres of the marsh are seeded with Fowl Meadow grass; about 300 acres of this is mowed, and the remainder is used for pasturage. Over 400 tons of excellent hay were cut there in the season of 1879.

THE SUPERINTENDENT'S HOUSE AT THE MARSH FARM.

Outside of the interest attaching to it by reason of the drainage experiments, the Chandler farm would deserve notice as one of the most thoroughly equipped and stocked of the new farms of Michigan. It is traversed by a state road, and by the Jackson, Lansing and Saginaw Railroad (which has established a signal station near the farm-house). Its buildings are located upon the highest ground. They are substantially constructed, and surrounded with all the evidences of thrift. The main house of the farm, which is occupied by the superintendent and his family, is a commodious frame structure, two stories in height, and conveniently partitioned off into spacious and airy apartments. Near it is the house-barn (32 by 54 feet in dimensions) with sheep-sheds adjoining. About a half-mile to the east are two tenant houses, occupied by families employed on the farm. On the east side of the state road, at a distance of half a mile, is a large barn, erected in 1879; its main portion is 41 by 66 feet in dimensions, with a wing 38 by 90 feet; its height is 44 feet to the ridge; attached are sheds 250 feet in length and "L" shaped. This barn is largely used for storage purposes, and will receive 250 tons of hay. The basement of its wing is divided into 60 cattle stalls, 30 on each side, with a broad passage through the center. The stalls are ingeniously arranged in the most improved style, and with a special regard for cleanliness. In the basement of the main barn is a large root cellar (capable of holding 2,000 bushels of potatoes, turnips, etc.), stabling accommodations for eight horses, two large box-stalls for stallions, a feed-room 20 by 25 feet in size, numerous calf-pens, and many other conveniences. Located above are two granaries, each 12 by 26 feet in dimensions. Attached to the barn, but in a separate building, is a 12-horse-power engine, used for cutting feed, and for other farm purposes. A large automatic windmill and pump supply water in abundance.

The farm is well stocked; on it are seventeen horses, including "Mark Antony," an imported Normandy stallion, which is a fine specimen of the Percheron breed. There are also 120 head of handsome graded cattle on the farm, 300 sheep graded from Shropshire Down bucks, and 23 pure-bred Essex swine. In wagons and implements of every kind the equipment is complete, and all are of the best manufacture and most improved quality. The force of laborers on the farm as a rule includes five men in summer and three in winter, large gangs being employed during the two months of the haying season, and also when there is any extensive fencing or ditching enterprise to be pushed.

Mr. Chandler's experiments were closely watched by the farmers of Michigan. Visits were frequent from them singly,

THE MAIN BARN OF THE MARSH FARM.

in small parties, and in club or grange excursions to the marsh, and they always met a hospitable reception. Letters of inquiry also came from many parts of the State, giving evidence of the widespread character of the interest felt. Mr. Chandler himself when in Michigan visited the farm at least once a month, inspecting the work thoroughly, discussing plans with the super-

intendent, making suggestions, and giving orders. His experience
as a farmer in his boyhood furnished ideas which were yet useful and a judgment which was well-informed; still he was ready
to welcome all innovations that promised good results, and he
closed many discussions with his superintendents by remarking,
"If you come at me with facts, that is enough; I never argue
against them." At the farm he also found the most congenial
relaxation. He would come there jaded out with the excitement
and labor of political contest and public life; in stout clothing
and heavy boots he would scour the meadows, examine ditching,
look up the stock, oversee labor, and work himself if there was
an inviting opportunity. A day or two of this life would bring
rest, hearty appetite, and sound sleep, would relieve his nerves
from tension, and restore his vital powers to their natural
activity. He always rated his visits to the marsh farm as a certain and delightful tonic.

In private life Mr. Chandler kept up the habits which
marked his public career. His voluminous correspondence was
never neglected. Napoleon's method of leaving letters unopened
for three weeks, because within that time most of them would
need no replies, he reversed. As a rule, every communication
addressed to Mr. Chandler was promptly answered; to even
mere notes of compliment brief responses were sent. Of course
this practice made a confidential secretary indispensable, and that
position was held for some years by a Mr. Miller; after his
death (in 1870) it was discreetly and faithfully filled by George
W. Partridge. Matters entrusted to Mr. Chandler's care by constituents always received early attention; the same statement is true
of applications from the humblest stranger who preferred a claim
upon his attention, and it includes political enemies as well as
friends. Mr. Chandler regarded meeting these demands as part
of his public duties; no other prominent man of his day gave
to such matters a tithe of the time and energy devoted to them

by him, and this was one source of his hold upon the popular affection. Of course much labor was involved, but this was offset by the fact that in all his duties he was regular, punctual

MR. CHANDLER'S RESIDENCE IN WASHINGTON.

and systematic; his mercantile training helped him greatly in this respect, and it was said of him truly, "He has never been excelled as a 'business Senator' at Washington." While not a student, he was a man who prepared for every important action.
24

In his speeches he aimed at nervous strength and effectiveness.
For oratorical finish he cared nothing, but simple language, terse
sentences, some plain word whose meaning was an argument in
itself — these he sought for unceasingly. He apologized for the
length of one of his brief speeches because he had not had time
to make it shorter. Not rarely he would put into a sentence of
ten Saxon words the power of a philippic, and this rough
missile would crush where mere rhetoric would have only irri-
tated. Mr. Chandler never failed as a speaker to command the
popular attention, and his force and the simplicity of his diction
were greatly aided by the sincerity which illuminated them.
The vigor and truth of conviction, which made him so ardent a
champion of the party of his political faith, marked his speeches,
and made his appeals potent with his hearers. "His words
were simple and his soul sincere." In fact, his sincerity and
honesty were the salient qualities of the man. His was not a
faultless character; but it was above baseness, and it was free
from affectation, from cant, and from hypocrisy. The record of
his public life recalls Emerson's estimate of Bonaparte: "This
"man showed us how much may be accomplished by the mere
"force of such virtues as all men possess in less degree —
"namely, by punctuality, by personal attention, by courage, and
"by thoroughness." But more honorable to his memory is the
fact that concerning the man himself can be justly quoted
Carlyle's eloquent tribute to Burns: "He is an honest man.
". . . In his successes and his failures, in his greatness and
"his littleness, he is ever clear, simple and true, and glitters
"with no lustre but his own. We reckon this to be a great
"virtue — to be, in fact, the root of most other virtues."

Mr. Chandler's social nature was a hearty one. His manners
were easy, he was affable with all, and he was without the
slightest tinge of aristocratic tastes or prejudice. No false dignity
surrounded him; with his friends his laugh was ready; he liked

MR. CHANDLER'S RESIDENCE IN DETROIT.

a game of whist, enjoyed a good story, found pleasure in social gatherings, was entertaining in conversation, and easily gave way to the natural jollity of his spirits. Exact and stern as he often was, his intimates found him a most agreeable companion. Few men have ever bound friends to themselves more firmly.

He surrounded his homes with the comforts that wealth could supply, and yet was not ostentatious. His Washington residence he purchased for about $40,000 in 1867 from Senor Bareda, the Peruvian Minister. It is located on H between Thirteenth and Fourteenth streets, and is a handsome house with spacious parlors and dining room upon the first floor; commodious apartments occupy the upper stories, which are connected by rich staircases of black walnut. Mr. Chandler's office was located in the basement, and has been the scene of many important consultations between famous men on questions of party policy and public concern. His Detroit home was the mansion on the Northwest corner of Fort and Second streets, which he built in 1855 –'56. It is situated in spacious grounds, and is of the plain Roman style of architecture, which aims at the simple in outline and massive in effect. A semi-circular drive and path lead to it through the gate-ways of a heavy and handsome fence and into a large *porte cochere*. Thence wide stone steps rise through solid mahogany doors to a broad hall, whose floor of inlaid woods is partly hidden by rich rugs. On the right is the drawing room, a spacious apartment furnished in blue and gold, and abounding in tasteful ornaments and handsome paintings. In it stands Randolph Rogers's marble bust of Mr. Chandler, executed about 1870. Opposite and connected by folding doors are the library and dining room. The former's shelves are well filled with the best works of standard authors, including many ancient chronicles seldom found in private book collections. Back of the dining room and across a transverse hallway is the apartment that was Mr. Chandler's private office;

its walls are literally covered with shelving containing Congressional annals and reports and many public documents. The appointments of the numerous other rooms are tasteful and complete, and all the surroundings of the house are in keeping with its quiet elegance. In 1858 Mr. Chandler met there with an accident of nearly fatal results. He followed his little daughter upon a search for some escaping gas, and was caught with her in a room in which a large mass of that inflammable vapor was exploded by a lighted candle. To add to the danger of the situation the door was closed upon them by a frightened servant. Mr. Chandler seized his child and sheltered her from serious danger, and groped his way out blinded and scorched. It was then found that his hands and face were badly burned, and the loss of his eyesight was threatened. Careful treatment and his vigorous constitution ultimately brought about a full recovery, and the only traces left of the casualty were some slight affections of the facial muscles and an unusual pallor of countenance.

Mr. Chandler's domestic life was a thoroughly happy one. He married Letitia Grace Douglass of New York, a noble Christian woman, whose social accomplishments blended dignity with grace, and who met to the full her large share of the exacting duties attendant upon public life and high station. Their only child was a daughter, Mary Douglass Chandler, who was married, while her father was a Senator, to the Hon. Eugene Hale of Ellsworth, Maine. She inherited many of her father's traits, and his affection for her was rooted in the inner fibres of his strong nature. Her children, his three little grandsons, often knew him as a rollicking playfellow, and he counseled with her freely and often, and she shared in his confidence as well as his love. Throughout his life he expressed his appreciation of the devoted attachment of his wife and child by many acknowledgments that do not belong to a public chronicle; his will left his great estate to them as his sole heirs, "share and share alike."

CHAPTER XXI.

THE township elections in Michigan in April, 1878,
revealed an astonishing growth in the number of the
advocates of an irredeemable paper currency. "Hard
times," Democratic disgust over the result of the electoral dispute, and Republican disappointment at "the Southern
policy" of the new administration greatly relaxed existing party
ties, and made the way ready for the expounders of the seduc-
tive theory that prosperity depends upon a great volume of the
currency, and that large issues of paper bearing the government
stamp must greatly add to individual wealth. Throughout the
West and South, Republican and Democratic leaders had fostered
these fallacious ideas, and thus prepared the field of public sentiment for this "Greenback" sowing. In Michigan the result
was that the National party (which in 1876 gave only 9,060
votes to Peter Cooper for President) in April, 1878, cast over
70,000 votes for its township candidates, elected a large number
of supervisors in the most populous counties of the State, and
showed greater strength than either of the old parties in four
Congressional districts. This was the gravest situation the Republicans of Michigan had ever been called upon to face. A conference of their representative men was at once held, at the call
of the State Central Committee, and the situation was thoroughly
discussed. Among those participating was Gov. Charles M.
Croswell, who said that he believed that the party should boldly
declare for a sound currency, and resist with all its power the

further spread of financial heresy; for himself, he preferred defeat on that platform to a victory won by any surrender to false theories. The endorsement of his views was substantially unanimous, and an aggressive campaign was determined upon. The State Convention was promptly called, and met in Detroit on June 13. It was the ablest political gathering ever held in Michigan, and its delegates included the foremost men of the party from every county. Mr. Chandler presided; Governor Croswell was renominated at the head of a strong State ticket; a platform, admirable for its soundness of doctrine and clearness of statement * (its author was Frederick Morley, formerly editor of the Detroit *Post*), was adopted; and Mr. Chandler was, amid the . prolonged cheering of the convention, placed at the head of the State Committee. He had at that time about completed his plans for a European journey, and it was suggested to him by friends that his chairmanship of the National Committee afforded a valid excuse for declining this new appointment, which would make him responsible for the result of a doubtful fight, with the certainty that defeat would greatly impair his political prestige. To this advice Mr. Chandler simply replied, "If Michigan Republicanism goes down, I will go with it." He promptly canceled all other engagements, appointed his confidential secretary, G. W. Partridge, secretary of the committee (with the consent of its members), and threw his energy and vigor into that State campaign. The contest that followed under his leadership preserved the spirit of the convention and upheld the doctrines of the platform. The financial question was discussed in every phase "upon the stump" and by the press. Mr. Chandler himself

---

* The Michigan Republicans have done well. Their platform has about it the clear ring of honest conviction, undulled by any half-hearted and halting compromise. So lucid and courageous an enunciation of the financial creed of the Republican party has certainly not been made this year, nor has the irreconcilable hostility of the party to all forms of tampering with public credit and national honor been so resolutely and judiciously stated as by the Detroit Convention.—*New York Times, June 14, 1878.*

spoke in all the leading cities of the State, and was seconded
by many other orators, including James G. Blaine, James A.
Garfield, and Stewart L. Woodford, whose addresses were masterly examples of the candid, luminous and popular treatment
of a topic usually regarded as too abstruse and dry for profitable public discussion. The courage and honesty of this fight
were justly rewarded. The Republicans carried the State by
over 47,000 plurality, and elected every Congressional candidate and a Legislature with a large Republican majority upon
joint ballot. The victory was a signal one. In no Western
State had financial heresy ever been as resolutely grappled with
and as thoroughly beaten, and his prominent share in this battle
must rank among Mr. Chandler's most unselfish and honorable
public services.

An unforeseen but almost poetically just result of this
triumph was his own return to Congress. Senator Christiancy's
failing health compelled him in the winter of 1879 to seek
(under physician's advice) rest and a change of climate. The
President offered him the embassadorship at Berlin, or at Mexico, or at Lima, and he finally decided to accept the latter. His
nomination was sent to the Senate on Jan. 29, 1879, and confirmed without reference to a committee. On February 10, his
resignation as Senator was laid before the Michigan Legislature,
and on the 18th that body filled the vacancy by election. With
the earliest hints of the possibility of Senator Christiancy's retirement, Republican opinion and the popular expectation had
agreed that Mr. Chandler would be chosen for the remaining
years of what the Republicans of Michigan had unsuccessfully
sought to make his fourth term. This was regarded as due
to him, as still more due to the party which had in 1875 been
deprived of its choice, and as securing the restoration to public
activity of a man of national influence and prominence, at an
hour when the sagacity of his political judgment had been vin-

dicated by the alarming attitude of the South, and when the sturdiest qualities of leadership were needed in Washington. The legislative action reflected this strong current of public sentiment. In the Republican caucus (held in the new Capitol of that State), Mr. Chandler was nominated for Senator on the first formal ballot, receiving sixty-nine of the eighty-nine votes cast. In the Legislature he was elected by the vote of every Republican in his seat in either branch.

THE MICHIGAN CAPITOL AT LANSING.

On Feb. 22, 1879, Mr. Chandler's credentials were presented and read in the Senate, and he was escorted by Senator Ferry to the Vice-President's desk, where the official oath was administered to him by William A. Wheeler. He took the seat upon the outer row of the Republican side, which he had occupied in other Congresses. The circumstances of his return to public life attracted national attention, and his re-appearance in the Senate was everywhere accepted as significant of the growth of Republican courage and resolution. But what followed outstripped all expectation and was dramatic in its accessories. Upon February 28, he first addressed the Forty-fifth Senate, speaking briefly upon a bill providing for pension arrears, and in advocacy of an amendment to make more efficient the methods of detecting pension frauds by taking expert examiners from one part of the country and sending them to another. In this connection he referred to his own experience as Secretary of the Interior, saying that he had declared that with $100,000 to so use he could save $1,000,000 to the Treasury yearly. Upon the same day, he also spoke briefly upon the Sundry Civil Appropriation bill, opposing a proposition in it to re-open a settled claim of the war of 1812, based on expenditures made by some of the older States for military purposes. He spoke from recollection of a discussion in 1857, when this matter came up, and showed that the principal of the claims had been already paid, and that this was an attempt to collect compound interest. This measure, which Mr. Chandler repeatedly opposed during his Senatorial career, was again defeated at this time. On March 1, a proposition to pay Georgia over $72,000 compound interest upon advances alleged to have been made in 1835-'38 in the Creek, Seminole and Cherokee wars was strenuously and successfully opposed by him. On the 28th of February, a bill had been passed by the Senate making appropriations for the arrearages of pensions. To this an amendment was offered and adopted extending to those who served in the war with Mexico the provisions of the law passed in 1878, giving pensions to the surviving soldiers of 1812. This amendment was adopted without full consideration, and on the evening of Sunday, March 2, a motion was made and carried for a reconsideration. Then an amendment was offered excluding persons who served in the Confederate army or held any office under the "Confederacy" from the benefits of this bill. This amendment was defeated by the votes of the Democrats and two Southern Republicans. Another amendment was offered by Senator Hoar excluding Jefferson Davis from the benefits of any pension bill. An astonishing debate followed. For some hours the Senate Chamber rang with fervent eulogies upon the arch-rebel of the South. Senator Garland declared that Davis's record would "equal in history all Grecian fame and all Roman glory." Senator Maxey pronounced him "a battle-scarred, knightly gentleman." Senator Lamar characterized the proposition as a "wanton insult," springing from "hate, bitter, malignant sectional feeling, and a sense of personal impunity;" he added, "The only difference between "myself and Jefferson Davis is that his exalted character, his "pre-eminent talents, his well-established reputation as a states- "man, as a patriot, and as a soldier enabled him to take the "lead in a cause to which I consecrated myself;" he further declared that Davis's motives were as "sacred and noble as ever inspired the breast of a Hampden or a Washington." Senator Harris pronounced him "the peer of any Senator on this floor." "I will not," said Senator Coke, "vote to discriminate against Mr. Davis, for I was just as much a rebel as he." Senator Ransom said, "I shall not dwell upon Mr. Davis's public serv- "ices as an American soldier and statesman. He belongs to "history, as does that cause to which he gave all the ability of "his great nature." There was no lack of Republican protest against this apotheosis of unrepentant treason, but it was not wholly free from a certain deprecatory tone. The Senators who spoke in support of Mr. Hoar's proposition rather remonstrated against than denounced the assumption that it was their duty to quietly assent to legislation which would place the unamnestied and still defiant representative of the Great Rebellion on the pension-rolls of the nation. After the debate had lasted for over two hours, Mr. W. E. Chandler of New Hampshire, who was

watching its progress from the reporters' gallery, said to Senator
E. H. Rollins of his State, "Tell Zach. Chandler that he is the
man to call Jeff. Davis a traitor." Mr. Rollins delivered the
message, which was received with a nod of acquiescence in the
direction of the gallery. Senator Morgan of Alabama was
speaking at the time, with Senator Mitchell of Oregon in the
chair. As Mr. Morgan closed, Senator Chandler rose and said:

Mr. President, twenty-two years ago to-morrow, in the old Hall of the
Senate, now occupied by the Supreme Court of the United States, I, in company with Mr. Jefferson Davis, stood up and swore before Almighty God that
I would support the Constitution of the United States. Mr. Jefferson Davis
came from the Cabinet of Franklin Pierce into the Senate of the United States
and took the oath with me to be faithful to this government. During four
years I sat in this body with Mr. Jefferson Davis and saw the preparations
going on from day to day for the overthrow of this government. With treason
in his heart and perjury upon his lips he took the oath to sustain the government that he meant to overthrow.

Sir, there was method in that madness. He, in co-operation with other
men from his section and in the Cabinet of Mr. Buchanan, made careful preparation for the event that was to follow. Your armies were scattered all
over this broad land where they could not be used in an emergency; your
fleets were scattered wherever the winds blew and water was found to float
them, where they could not be used to put down rebellion; your Treasury
was depleted until your bonds bearing six per cent., principal and interest
payable in coin, were sold for 88 cents on the dollar for current expenses, and
no buyers! Preparations were carefully made. Your arms were sold under
an apparently innocent clause in an army bill providing that the Secretary of
War might, at his discretion, sell such arms as he deemed it for the interest
of the government to sell.

Sir, eighteen years ago last month I sat in these halls and listened to
Jefferson Davis delivering his farewell address, informing us what our constitutional duties to this government were, and then he left and entered into the
rebellion to overthrow the government that he had sworn to support! I
remained here, sir, during the whole of that terrible rebellion. I saw our
brave soldiers by thousands and hundreds of thousands, aye, I might say
millions, pass through to the theater of war, and I saw their shattered ranks
return; I saw steamboat after steamboat and railroad train after railroad train
arrive with the maimed and the wounded; I was with my friend from Rhode
Island (Mr. Burnside) when he commanded the Army of the Potomac, and
saw piles of legs and arms that made humanity shudder; I saw the widow
and the orphan in their homes, and heard the weeping and wailing of those

SENATOR CHANDLER DENOUNCING THE EULOGIES UPON "JEFF." DAVIS.

[In the Senate Chamber, at 3 A. M., Monday, March 3, 1879.]

who had lost their dearest and their best. Mr. President, I little thought at that time that I should live to hear in the Senate of the United States eulogies upon Jefferson Davis, living—a living rebel eulogized on the floor of the Senate of the United States! Sir, I am amazed to hear it; and I can tell the gentlemen on the other side that they little know the spirit of the North when they come here at this day, and, with bravado on their lips, utter eulogies upon a man whom every man, woman, and child in the North believes to have been a double-dyed traitor to his government.

This speech was made at about the hour of half-past three in the morning of Monday, March 3, 1879. But few people were in the galleries at that time, and the Senate had lapsed into a listless state. Mr. Chandler's bearing as he arose to speak, and the first sentence that resounded through the Senate Chamber in his strong voice, aroused instant attention. The spectators above listened with new and eager interest, Senators came in from the lobbies and cloakrooms, sleep was shaken off by drowsy *attaches*, and his closing words "a double-dyed traitor to his government" fell in ringing tones upon an intent audience and were answered by an applause from the galleries which the gavel of the presiding officer could not check. His excited hearers listened eagerly for a reply, but none came. After some silent waiting the presiding officer stated the pending question, and was about to put it to vote. Senator Thurman then rose and began the discussion of another branch of the subject, and no answer was attempted to Mr. Chandler's just denunciation of the eulogizing of the man, whose past history and present attitude unite to make him at once the representative of treason's crimes and the embodiment of its unrepentant spirit. When the vote was taken, one majority was given for Mr. Hoar's amendment, and after that result the original amendment itself was defeated.

This speech was a masterpiece in its way—in its brevity, in its skillful use of the speaker's early official association with Jefferson Davis, in its vivid epitome of the history of American treason, and in the rugged power of its simple language. It most profoundly stirred the people. It may be said without exaggeration that years had passed since any Congressional utterance had received such public attention. Democratic and Southern denunciation of Mr. Chandler followed abundantly, but this was wholly overshadowed by the enthusiasm of the response of the patriotic sentiment of the Union to his indignant refusal to let treason raise its head in insolence without branding it as it deserved. The Northern press reprinted the speech with unstinted praise. Public men hastened in person, by telegraph, and through the mails to tender their congratulations. Letters of fervent thanks poured in by the hundreds; from utter strangers, from the rich and the humble, from veteran soldiers, from mothers whose sons were buried on Southern battle-fields, from the colored men, from the Republicans of the South, from every State and Territory came the expressions of gratitude for the utterance given at so opportune a moment and with such force to the loyal feeling of the republic. It was this spontaneous approval of the masses of the people that Mr. Chandler especially prized.

On March 18, 1879, the extra session of the Forty-sixth Congress commenced, and the Democrats made their abortive attempt to force the repeal of the laws relating to the supervision of national elections by withholding appropriations. Their reactionary programme (the striking of the last vestige of the war measures from the statute books was even threatened) and revolutionary menaces aroused the North, and in the end they quailed before the rising popular wrath. Mr. Chandler denounced their schemes vigorously on the floor of the Senate, even charging explicitly that twelve of the Southern Senators "held their seats by fraud and violence." He also earnestly opposed all propositions to compel the unlimited coinage of the silver dollar of 412½ grains, a measure which would have given to the country a superabundance of silver currency of depreciated value to the exclusion of gold. His last Congressional speech was this carefully prepared and forcible "arraignment of the Democratic party," of which tens of thousands of copies were circulated throughout the Union in the following campaign:

We have now spent three months and a half in this Capitol, not without certain results. We have shown to the people of this nation just what the Democratic party means. The people have been informed as to your objects, ends, and aims. By fraud and violence, by shot-guns and tissue ballots, you hold a present majority in both Houses of Congress, and you have taken an early opportunity to show what you intend to do with that majority thus obtained. You are within sight of the promised land, but like Moses of old we propose to send you up into the mountain to die politically.

Mr. President, we are approaching the end of this extra session, and its record will soon become history. The acts of the Democratic party, as manifested in this Congress, justify me in arraigning it before the loyal people of the United States on the political issues which it has presented, as *the enemy of the nation* and as the author and abettor of rebellion.

1. I arraign the Democratic party for having resorted to revolutionary measures to carry out its partisan projects, by attempting to coerce the Executive by withholding supplies, and thus accomplishing by starvation the destruction of the government which they had failed to overthrow by arms.

2. I arraign them for having injured the business interests of the country by forcing the present extra session, after liberal compromises were tendered to them prior to the close of the last session.

3. I arraign them for having attempted to throw away the results of the recent war by again elevating State over National Sovereignty. We expended $5,000,000,000 and sacrificed more than 300,000 precious lives to put down this heresy and to perpetuate the *national life*. They surrendered this heresy at Appomattox, but now they attempt to renew this pretension.

4. I arraign them for having attempted to damage the business interests of the country by forcing silver coin into circulation, of less value than it represents, thus swindling the laboring-man and the producer, by compelling them to accept 85 cents for a dollar, and thus enriching the bullion-owners at the expense of the laborer. Four million dollars a day is paid for labor alone, and by thus attempting to force an 85 cent dollar on the laboring-man you swindle him daily out of $600,000. Twelve hundred million dollars are paid yearly for labor alone, and by thus attempting to force an 85-cent dollar on the laboring-man you swindle him out of $180,000,000 a year. The amount which the producing class would lose is absolutely incalculable.

5. I arraign them for having removed without cause experienced officers and employes of this body, some of whom served and were wounded in the Union army, and for appointing men who had in the rebel army attempted to destroy this government.

6. I arraign them for having instituted a secret and illegitimate tribunal, the edicts of which have been made the supreme governing power of Congress in defiance of the fundamental principles of the constitution. The decrees of this junta are known although its motives are hidden.

7. I arraign them for having held up for public admiration that arch-rebel, Jefferson Davis, declaring that he was inspired by motives as sacred and as noble as animated Washington; and as having rendered services in attempting to destroy the Union which will equal in history Grecian fame and Roman glory. [Laughter on the Democratic side and in portions of the galleries.] You can laugh. The people of the North will make you laugh on the other side of your faces!

8. I arraign them for having undertaken to blot from the statute-book of the nation wise laws, rendered necessary by the war and its results, and insuring "life, liberty and the pursuit of happiness" to the emancipated freedmen, who are now so bulldozed and ku-kluxed that they are seeking peace in exile, although urged to remain by shot-guns.

9. I arraign them for having attempted to repeal the wise legislation which excludes those who served under the rebel flag from holding commissions in the army and navy of the United States.

10. I arraign them for having introduced a large amount of legislation for the exclusive benefit of the States recently in rebellion, which, if enacted, would bankrupt the national Treasury.

11. I arraign them for having conspired to destroy all that the Republican party has accomplished. Many of them breaking their oaths of allegiance to the United States and pledging their lives, their fortunes, and their sacred honors to overthrow this government, they failed, and thus lost all they pledged.

Call a halt. The days of vaporing are over. The loyal North is aroused and their doom is sealed.

I accept the issue on these arraignments distinctly and specifically before the citizens of this great republic. As a Senator of the United States and as a citizen of the United States, I appeal to the people. It is for those citizens to say who is right and who is wrong. I go before that tribunal confident that the Republican party is right and that the Democratic party is wrong.

They have made these issues; not we; and by them they must stand or fall. This is the platform which they have constructed, not only for 1879 but for 1880. They cannot change it, for we will hold them to it. They have made their bed, and we will see to it that they lie thereon.

25

CHAPTER XXII.

THE closing hours of the Forty-fifth Congress and the extra session of the Forty-sixth may be said to have revealed Mr. Chandler to the country. While he had been well known he had not been truly known. He then became a central figure in the public attention. His utterances were universally discussed, and with discussion came a juster appreciation of the man. The people at last saw him as he was, the possessor of strong common-sense, a cool and indefatigable worker, a sagacious and fearless leader, a man who had never sacrificed principle to policy, who had never compromised with crimes against liberty or the nation's honor, whose most malignant enemies had not accused him of being influenced by corrupt motives, and one gifted with the rare capacity of saying the right thing at the right time in terse, impromptu sentences, in epigrams which became political mottoes.

The campaign of 1879 followed closely upon the midsummer adjournment of Congress, and invitations to address the people came to Mr. Chandler from a score of States. No public speaker was in more urgent demand, or aroused a keener interest. The popular gatherings, which, during the summer and fall, greeted his every appearance from the shores of the Great Lakes to the Atlantic seaboard, amounted to a genuine ovation. His first address was delivered before the Republican State Convention of Wisconsin, at Madison, on July 23. In August he made six speeches in Maine to immense mass meetings. In September he visited Ohio, and spoke at Sandusky, Toledo, Warren, Cleveland, and other important points. His audiences in that State were uniformly large, and his Warren speech was delivered in the afternoon to an enormous crowd, one of the greatest ever called together upon such an occasion in the Western Reserve. He was greatly pleased by an invitation, which came to him at about this time, from Senator G. F. Hoar, to visit Massachusetts in October. It was unexpected, and he had believed that the Republican leaders in the Bay State were inclined to look upon him with distrust. He accepted it promptly, and spoke to enthusiastic audiences in Boston, Worcester, Lynn and Lowell. Some brief remarks made at a dinner of the Middlesex Club, in which he urged the national importance of the pending contest, were especially useful in stimulating Republican activity and directing it into proper channels. He next addressed meetings in New York at Flushing, Albany, Troy, Potsdam, Lowville and Buffalo, amid increasing public interest. On returning home from that State in the last days of October, he revisited Wisconsin, and spoke to great crowds at Milwaukee, Oshkosh and Janesville, returning to Chicago, where, on the evening of October 31st, he made the last address of his life.

The striking evidences of his hold upon the popular confidence, which manifested themselves during the summer and fall of 1879, led to the frequent mention of Mr. Chandler as a possible presidential candidate in 1880. His friends in his own State were eager to formally present his name to the National Convention, and the Republican press of Michigan united in earnestly advocating such a course. This movement also manifested strength in other States, and steadily increased in importance up to the hour of his death. Although Mr. Chandler was not insensible to this growing sentiment, little or nothing was done by him to promote it; he favored the renomination of General Grant, and the presidential ambition he rated as the

most fatal malady to which public men are subject.* To one
friend, who spoke of the popular feeling and his own desire in
this matter, Mr. Chandler replied: "You may vaccinate me with
the presidency and scratch it deep, but it won't take." To
another he said: "No! no! Men recover from the small-pox,
"cholera and yellow fever, but never from the presidential fever.
"I hope I will never get it." The movement in that direction,
which his death so abruptly checked, was spontaneous and sincere,
and that it was growing in strength was undoubted. What limit
that growth might have reached and with what result can only
be conjectured.

Repeatedly, during the arduous labors of the year, did Mr.
Chandler's physical powers manifest signs of rebellion against
excessive effort. In one of his Ohio speeches his voice suddenly
failed, compelling him to cease speaking. He suffered several
times from what seemed to be violent attacks of indigestion,
and was on one or two occasions dangerously distressed by
them. At Janesville he caught a severe cold, but when he

---

* This letter, written to a prominent Republican of the Pacific coast, did not reach the
gentleman to whom it was addressed until after Mr. Chandler's death, and was then given
to the public :

REPUBLICAN STATE CENTRAL COMMITTEE, }
DETROIT, Mich., Sept. 23, 1879.   }

MY DEAR SIR : Your favor of 11th inst. is at hand, and contents noted.

The prospects for the success of the Republican party in the national election next
year look much more favorable now than they did the year preceding the election in 1876.
Republicans are united, and earnestly preparing for success as the only hope of saving the
country from the shot-gun rule of the Confederate Democracy. The Tammany bolt
promises to give us New York both this year and next.

Ohio is sure to go Republican, and there is hardly a doubt that every Northern State
having a general election this fall will score a victory in favor of a free ballot and an honest count.

Each Territory is entitled to two delegates in the National Republican Convention,
under the rules heretofore adopted. I am under the impression now that Grant's chances
for the nomination are better than those of any other person ; but unless he is nominated
without a contest he will be out of the field, and there will be a trial of strength between
the friends and supporters of a few stalwart radicals.

No unknown man of lukewarm sentiments or obscure antecedents will be nominated.

It is very possible that Michigan will present a name in the convention as well as
Maine, New York, Ohio, and perhaps other States ; but I know nothing special in regard
to the matter, only that, if General Grant is a candidate, no one else will be. Very truly,
yours,   Z. CHANDLER.

THE GRAND PACIFIC HOTEL, AT CHICAGO.

[Where Mr. Chandler died on the night of October 31, 1879.]

reached Chicago, on the last day of his life, he seemed to be in his usual robust health, and showed but slight signs of fatigue. Those who called upon him on that day at the Grand Pacific Hotel noted his fine spirits. His address in that city was delivered before the Young Men's Auxiliary Republican Club in McCormick Hall, and he never spoke with more animation, nor more effectively. The audience applauded almost every sentence, and under that stimulus he rose to even more than his usual fervor of speech. His ringing sentence, "The mission of the "Republican party will not end until you and I, Mr. Chairman, "can start from the Canada border, travel to the Gulf of Mex- "ico, make Black Republican speeches wherever we please, vote "the Black Republican ticket wherever we gain a residence, and "do it with exactly the same safety that a rebel can travel "throughout the North, stop wherever he has a mind to, and "run for judge in any city he chooses," was followed by cheer after cheer, until the entire audience was standing and shouting. After closing his speech, Mr. Chandler returned to the Grand Pacific Hotel; a few friends chatted with him in his rooms for a short time, and at about midnight Representative Edwin Willits of Michigan, who had been one of his hearers, made a short call, and congratulated him upon the power of his closing appeal. After that, no man saw Mr. Chandler alive. At seven o'clock on the following morning, in accordance with orders, one of the employes of the hotel knocked at his door. There was no answer, and a look over the transom showed a figure lying in an unnatural attitude on the edge of the bed with the feet almost touching the floor. In alarm the room was entered with a pass-key, and Mr. Chandler was found in a half reclining posture, with his coat about his shoulders, unconsciousness having apparently seized him while he was attempting to rise and summon help. Medical aid was promptly at hand, but life was extinct. "A Power had passed from earth." Zachariah Chandler was dead!

BUST PROFILE OF ZACHARIAH CHANDLER.

[A sketch from Leonard W. Volk's plaster cast.]

The news spread at once throughout the great city in which he had so suddenly fallen; friends were soon by his bedside, while a large crowd gathered about the hotel. A coroner's jury was at once impaneled, listened to the testimony of the physicians, and returned a verdict that death had resulted from cerebral hemorrhage. Impressions of the features were taken by Leonard W. Volk, the eminent sculptor, and the lifeless body was then arranged by kind, if strange, hands for the funeral casket. Before its removal to Detroit, thousands who cherished the memory of the man looked mournfully upon the dead face.

The telegraph bore the intelligence of this sudden death promptly throughout the country, and the announcement was answered by unusual demonstrations of national grief. Throughout the cities and towns of Michigan, at Washington, and in many other places where his name was well known, the insignia of mourning were at once displayed. Public men sent prompt dispatches of sympathy to his family, upon whom the blow had fallen with prostrating force. Especially significant were the newspaper tributes to the memory of the bold, resolute, and successful leader of men, whose star had not set, but had gone out at the zenith. The President of the United States issued this official order:

EXECUTIVE MANSION, WASHINGTON, Nov. 1, 1879.

The sad intelligence of the death of Zachariah Chandler, late Secretary of the Interior, and during so many years Senator from the State of Michigan, has been communicated to the government and to the country, and, in proper respect to his memory, I hereby order that the several executive departments be closed to public business, and their flags, and those of their dependencies throughout the country, be displayed at half-mast on the day of his funeral.

R. B. HAYES.

From the Executive Mansion also came this dispatch of personal condolence:

WASHINGTON, D. C., Nov. 1, 1879.

Mrs. Z. Chandler.

Mrs. Hayes joins me in the expression of the most heartfelt sympathy with you in your great bereavement.   R. B. HAYES.

A nation, as well as the
State of Michigan mourns
the loss of one of her most
brave, patriotic & truest
Citizens. Senator Chandler
was beloved by his associates
and respected by those who
disagreed with his political
views. The more closely I
become connected with him
the more I appreciated
his great merits

U. S. Grant

Galena Ill
Nov, 9th 1879.

GEN. U. S. GRANT'S TRIBUTE.

[His endorsement on W. A. Gavett's official notification, as a member of the
Detroit Commandery K T to attend Mr. Chandler's funeral.]

The following proclamation was published by the Governor
of Michigan:

EXECUTIVE OFFICE, LANSING, Nov. 1, 1879.

To the People of Michigan:

An eminent citizen has suddenly been taken from us. Zachariah Chandler was found dead in his room at the Grand Pacific Hotel in Chicago early
this morning. For nineteen years he has represented this State in the National
Senate. He held this exalted position at the most perilous period in the
history of the nation, and unfalteringly supported every measure for the maintenance of the Union. A member of the Cabinet under the recent administration of President Grant, he proved himself a public officer of keen sagacity,
of incorruptible integrity and of admirable ability. A resident of Michigan
during the whole period of his manhood, he has been active in advancing the
interests of the State and promoting its growth. By his energy he secured a
competence, and by his integrity the confidence of all. A statesman and a
leader among men, he combined in an unusual degree qualities which commanded respect and admiration. Taken from us so unexpectedly, we cannot
but deeply feel and deplore his loss. I, therefore, as a tribute to his memory
and to his public services, hereby direct the several State offices to be closed
to public business, the flags to be displayed at half-mast, and the other demonstrations of public grief usual to be made, on the day of his funeral.

CHARLES M. CROSWELL.

An unofficial tribute, highly prized by Mr. Chandler's friends,
was that of Gen. Ulysses S. Grant, who wrote upon the reverse
of a funeral order issued by the Detroit Commandery of Knights
Templar (shown him by W. A. Gavett) these lines:

A nation, as well as the state of Michigan, mourns the loss of one of
her most brave, patriotic and truest citizens. Senator Chandler was beloved
by his associates and respected by those who disagreed with his political
views. The more closely I became connected with him the more I appreciated his great merits.   U. S. GRANT.

GALENA, Ill., Nov. 9, 1879.

On the morning of Sunday, November 2, an escort of the
militia and of the people of Chicago accompanied the body of
the dead Senator from the Grand Pacific Hotel to the depot, and
delivered it to a committee of prominent citizens of Michigan,
who had arrived to receive it. The burial-case was wrapped
in the national flag, and, when it had been placed in the car, its

lid was opened and the face exposed. The train stopped at Niles, Kalamazoo, Marshall, Jackson, and Ann Arbor, and at each place crowds came on board to look at the remains. When Detroit was reached, thousands of grief-stricken people were at the depot, and in solemn procession they joined the military escort in the march to the Chandler mansion. There a few loving friends received and looked upon the silent and lifeless form. To gratify the earnest desire of the many who wished to behold again the strong, earnest face of Zachariah Chandler before it was forever covered from mortal sight, the body was removed on the morning of November 5 to the City Hall, where it lay until one o'clock; a guard of honor kept watch at the head and foot of the casket, and on either hand, for five hours, a double file of men and women passed in steady march. Thousands of mournful glances were given at the placid face of the dead, and many affecting incidents made touching this parting tribute of the people. Then, from the City Hall, the body was borne to the Fort street residence for the last time. The day was cold and blustering; a blinding snow-storm set in. Yet the streets were thronged by the sad multitude, while every train brought from Michigan and from other States hundreds to increase the sorrowing concourse; among them were men of great reputations founded on useful and honorable public careers. After impressive funeral services at the house, the remains of Michigan's great Senator, escorted by the militia of Detroit and of the neighboring cities, by the United States troops, by civic societies, by Governors, Senators, Congressmen, Legislators of Michigan and of other States, and by hundreds of friends, passed slowly through the streets draped in mourning, and lined with dense crowds of people who braved the storm to pay this last honor to Zachariah Chandler. At the gates of Elmwood Cemetery the militia and civic societies halted, presenting arms as the hearse rolled slowly on under its trees.

Upon a high knoll, fronting on Prospect Avenue, it halted; the coffin was drawn slowly out, poised a moment over an open grave, lowered to its resting-place, and "I am the resurrection and the life" rose up in solemn tones above the sobbings of family and friends. Living green branches and flowers fell softly down upon the casket, and a new mound grew up beside where Senator Chandler's brother already lay.

Thus was Zachariah Chandler buried. Living, he was honored. Dead, he was mourned. Though dead, his labors and his example remain, and they form his fittest monument.

APPENDIX.

THE LAST SPEECH

OF

ZACHARIAH CHANDLER,

DELIVERED IN McCORMICK HALL, IN THE CITY OF CHICAGO, ON THE
NIGHT OF HIS DEATH, OCTOBER 31, 1879.

[Republished by permission of Ritchie & Williston, Stenographers, Room 23, Howland Block, Chicago.]

MR. CHAIRMAN AND FELLOW-CITIZENS: It has become the custom of late to restrict the lines of citizenship. In the Senate of the United States and in the halls of Congress you will hear citizenship described as confined to States, and it is denied that there is such a thing as national citizenship. I to-night address you, my fellow-citizens of Chicago, in a broad sense as fellow-citizens of the United States of America. [Applause.] A great crime has been committed, my fellow-citizens — a crime against this nation, a crime against republican institutions throughout the world ; a crime against civil liberty, and the criminal is yet unpunished — that is to say, he is not punished according to his deserts. [Applause.] And I shall to-night devote myself chiefly to the history of a crime, and shall endeavor to hold up the criminal to your execration. [Renewed applause.]

But, first, it is proper for me to allude to certain matters of national importance, which are at this present moment living issues. Twelve years ago an idea was started in the neighboring State of Ohio, called the "Ohio idea," which spread and bore fruit in different States. That idea was to pay something with nothing. [Laughter] From this Ohio idea sprang up a brood of other ideas. For example, the greenback idea, an unlimited issue of irredeemable currency, and a party was inaugurated in different States called the greenback party. It took root in Michigan last year, had a vigorous growth, put forth limbs, blossomed liberally, bore no fruit, and died. [Laughter and cheers.] Therefore, I shall pay no attention to the greenback party. It is not a living issue. [Laughter.] But the Ohio idea is still a living issue, and even during the last session of Congress a demand was made, and persistently made, to repeal the Resumption act that had been in existence for years. The resumption of specie payment was virtually accomplished when, in 1874-5, that Resumption act became a law, for at that time we made that act so strong that there was no power on earth that could defeat the resumption of specie payments after it had once been inaugurated. [Applause.] We authorized the Secretary of the Treasury to use any bonds ever issued by the government, and in any amount that was necessary, to carry forward to success specie payments, as soon as the time arrived for the resumption. We carefully guarded that law. True, we are under an obligation to the man who executed the law, but the resumption of specie payments was as much a fixed fact when that law was signed as it is to-day, and all the powers on earth combined could not break that resumption when it had once been inaugurated.

But this Ohio idea, as I said, was to pay off your bonds with greenbacks. Well, my fellow-citizens, we have paid off $160,000,000 of your bonds in greenbacks within the last sixty or ninety days, and what more do you want? Ah! But the Ohio idea was something different from that. It was, as I said before, to pay something with nothing, and up to the final adjournment of the last regular session of Congress the attempt was still made to issue irredeemable paper and force it upon the creditors of the nation. Now, if this paper which they propose to issue in paying off the bonds of your government was properly and truthfully described, it would read thus: "The government of the United States for value received"—for it was for value received; no greenback was ever issued except for value received; no bond of the government was ever issued except for value received—"for value "received, the government of the United States promises to pay nothing to "nobody, never." [Applause and laughter.] That was the paper with which it was proposed by these men, entertaining then, and now entertaining the "Ohio idea," to redeem the bonds of your government.

Now, you have heard, I presume, here in Chicago, the denunciation of the holders of your government bonds. The "bloated bondholder" was a term of reproach, both on the floor of Congress and in the streets of Chicago and all over these United States. But who were the bloated bondholders? Why, my friends, every single man who has a dollar in the savings-bank is a bloated bondholder, for there is not a savings-bank in the land, which ought to be entrusted with a dollar, whose funds are not invested in the bonds of your government. [Applause.] There is not a widow or orphan who has a fund to support the widow in her widowhood and the orphan in its orphanage, in a trust company, who is not a bloated bondholder; for there is not a trust company in the land that ought to be trusted which has not a large proportion of its funds in the bonds of your government. Every man who has his life insured, or his house insured, or his barn, or his lumber, or who has any insurance, is a bloated bondholder; for there is not an insurance company, life, fire, marine, or of any other class of insurance, that ought to be trusted, which has not its funds invested in bonds of your government. You may go to the books of the Treasury to-morrow and inquire and you will find ninety-nine men who own $100 and less of the bonds of your government, directly or indirectly, where you will find one man who owns $10,000 or more. And these men, entertaining the Ohio idea, would ruin the ninety-nine poor men for the possible chance of injuring the one-hundredth rich man. And yet you may destroy the bonds of the rich man and you do him no harm, for he has but a small amount of his vast wealth in the bonds of your government, while the poor man, owning $100 or under as his little all, is utterly ruined. [Applause.]

You would not find a man, woman, or child in America who would touch the kind of paper I have described, if proffered to them. You say you would stop the interest on your bonded debt. Very well! The holder of your bonds would say: "You do not propose to pay any interest. I hold a bond "for value received, with a given amount of interest payable on a given day. "Now I will hold your bonds until you men entertaining the Ohio idea are "buried in your political graves, and then I will appeal to an honest people, "to an honest government, to pay an honest debt." [Applause.] "But," say these men, "pay off your foreign bonds." I see men before me who remember the days of General Jackson, and they likewise remember that in the time of General Jackson the government of France owed to the citizens of the United States $5,000,000, which France did not refuse to pay, but neglected to pay. It ran along from decade to decade, unpaid. General Jackson sent for the French minister and said: "Unless that $5,000,000 due to the citizens of the United States is paid, I will declare war against France." [Applause.] General Jackson was remonstrated with. It would disturb the commercial relations, not only of this country, but the world. Said he, "Unless France pays that $5,000,000, by the Eternal, I will declare war against France." [Applause.] Every man, woman and child and the King of France knew that he would do it, and the $5,000,000 was paid to the United States. It is not $5,000,000 that your government owes to the citizens of the world, but it is more than fifty times five million, and it is scattered in every nation with which we have commercial relations, or where money is found to invest in your bonds. You say you will stop the interest on those bonds. How long do you think it would be before a British fleet would come sailing to your coast, followed by a French fleet, and a German fleet, and a Russian, and an Austrian, and a Spanish and an Italian fleet, and the British Admiral would step ashore and say: "I have $50,000,000 of the bonds of this government belonging to the citizens of Great Britain, which I am ordered to collect!" The answer is: "Your account is correct, sir. The government of the United "States owes just $50,000,000 to the citizens of Great Britain, and here is "your money, sir."

[Mr. Chandler, suiting the action to the word, held out a sheet of paper with $50,000,000 written upon it, and the audience burst out into loud and long-continued laughter.]

26

The British Admiral looks at it and says: "What's that?"

"Why, money. Don't you see? Why, it is a first mortgage on all the "property of all the citizens of all the United States." [Laughter.] "Don't "you see the stamp of the government?" [Laughter.]

Says the Admiral: "Where is it payable?"

"Nowhere." [Laughter and applause.]

"To whom is it payable?"

"Nobody." [Laughter.]

"When is it made payable?"

"Never." [Renewed laughter and cheers.]

"Why," says the Admiral, "I don't know any such money. My orders "are to collect this $50,000,000 in the coin of the world, and unless it is so "paid my orders are to blockade every port of these United States, and here "are all the navies of the earth to assist me, and to burn down every city "that my guns will reach."

Honesty is the best policy with nations as well as with individuals. [Cheers.] "Well," they say, "perhaps you are right about this bond busi- "ness. It is an open question, and we will abandon that, but the national "banks — down with the national banks! [Laughter and applause.] Abolish "national banks and save interest." What do you want to abolish the national banks for? That is a living issue to-day — a present proposition of the Democratic party that I propose to hold up to your abhorrence before I get through to-night What do you want to "down with the national banks" for? I was in the Senate of the United States when that national banking law was passed. I was a member of that body and voted upon every proposi- tion made in it. I had had a little experience in state banks myself. [Laughter and applause.] Michigan had a very large state bank circulation at one time [loud applause], and we called that "money" in those days wild-cat money [laughter], and it was very wild. [Renewed laughter and applause.] Chicago also had a little experience in those days as well as Michigan. In those days it was necessary for any man liable to receive a five-dollar note to carry a counterfeit detector with him for three purposes First, to ascertain whether there ever was such a bank in existence. [Laugh- ter and applause.] Second, to ascertain whether the bill was counterfeit, and, third, to ascertain whether the bank had failed [laughter] — and as a rule it had failed. [Laughter and applause.] Now, we had two objects in view in getting up that national banking law. First, we wanted to furnish an abso- lutely safe circulating medium, so that no loss could ensue to the bill-holder. Second, we wanted to furnish a market for our bonds which had become somewhat of a drug. We might just as well have put in state bonds as security for those bank notes. It would have been just as legal, just as right, but we didn't know which one or how many of those rebel States would repudiate their bonds, and therefore we didn't put in any. [Laughter and applause.] We might just as well have put in railroad bonds, but we didn't know how many railroads would default in their interest. We might just as well have put in real estate, but we didn't know whether the neighbors of the banker would appraise the real estate at its actual cash-selling value. [Applause and laughter.] And therefore we put in the bonds of your government at 90 cents on the dollar ; so that to-day for every single 90 cents of national bank notes afloat there is 100 cents —(worth 102½ cents)—of the bonds of your government deposited with the Treasurer of the United States for the redemption of the 90 cents. [Applause.] And you don't know and you don't care whether the bank is located in Oregon, in Texas, in South Carolina, Mississippi, New York or Illinois, because you know there is 102½ cents to-day of the bonds of your government deposited with the Treasurer of the United States for the redemption of every 90 cents of national bank notes you hold. You don't know and you don't care whether the bank whose note you have in your pocket failed yesterday, last week, or last year, or whether it ever failed. And you never find that out, for if trouble comes the bonds are sold and your bank notes are redeemed the day after, or the week after, or the year after your bank has failed, precisely the same as though it had never failed. [Applause.]

Now you say, "Call in your bonds ; abolish the national bank notes." Very well ! You pass a law to-morrow repealing the charters of all your national banks. Call in the national bank notes ! Every national bank in America takes the exact amount of the circulation which it has, either in silver or gold or greenbacks, to the Treasury, leaves it there to redeem its notes, takes the bonds and distributes them among the stockholders of that bank, and the day after you have called in every national bank note that you have out, you pay the self-same amount of interest on your bonds that you paid the day before, not one farthing more nor less. You don't gain one cent, but you lose $16,500,000 of taxes paid this year and last year and every year upon the stock of the national banks to national, state and municipal governments. [Applause.] You gain nothing, and you lose $16,500,000. You distress the whole community of these United States by compelling your banks to call in $850,000,000, now loaned and now being used in commerce, manufactures and all the industries of the nation. You distress the people by forcing a recall of that amount. No, my friends, in my judgment you had better devote yourselves to something you understand, and let the national banks alone. [Applause and laughter.]

But they say, "There is one thing that we know we are right on, and that is the free coinage of silver." Every man who holds 85 cents worth of silver shall go to the Treasury or the mints of the United States and take a certificate of deposit for 100 cents, which shall pass as money. This was the Warner bill. This the Democratic party as a party was committed to, and is committed to, and on the very last day of the extra session by a majority vote of one, and only one, in the Senate of the United States we substantially laid that bill upon the table, every Republican voting aye, and every Democrat, except four of five, voting no. [Applause.] Now, to-day, the laboring man can take gold or silver or paper, as he chooses, for his day's labor I am in favor of the dual standard. I am in favor of a silver dollar with 100 cents in it. I am in favor of an honest dollar anywhere you can find it [cheers], and I stand by an honest dollar. To-day the laboring man can take gold or silver or paper, and they are all of equal value, because they are all interchangeable into each other. The paper dollar costs nothing; a silver dollar costs the government 85 cents — a fraction more now; it has been a fraction less. But all three are of equal value. Now the very moment you commence issuing those certificates of deposit freely to every man having bullion you banish gold from your circulating medium and make it an article of traffic and nothing else; and you have but a single standard, and that is a depreciated standard. Now there is paid out in these United States every day for labor alone $4,000,000. By compelling the substitution of the silver dollar alone, you swindle the laboring man out of $600,000 a day. The laboring man who receives a dollar gets but 85 cents. The man who receives $10 a week gets $8.50, and no more. The farmer who sells a horse, or the man who sells a load of lumber, or a load of wheat, or anything else amounting to $100, receives but $85, and no more. You have but one single standard, and that the silver standard, which, having banished gold, is worth precisely the metal that is in it. Who is benefited by this substitution? Why, my friends, not a living mortal is benefited, except the bullion-owner and the bullion-speculator. I do not charge these men with being bribed to pass that law, because I have no proof of it; but I do say that the bullion-owners and the bullion-speculators can afford to pay $10,000,000 in bullion for the privilege of swindling the laboring men of the country out of 15 per cent. of all their earnings. [Applause.] They say, "That may all be true; we don't know how it is; we have not been bribed" — and I never knew a man that would own up that he was bribed in my life. [Laughter.] I don't say that they are, but I do say that they are engaged in a mighty mean business. [Laughter and applause.]

But there is another question which is of vital interest to every man, woman and child in America, and that is this question of the enormous rebel claims against your government. I hold in my hand a list of the claims now before the two houses of Congress, and being pressed — cotton claims, claims for the destruction of property, for quartermaster's stores, for every conceivable thing that war could produce. I have a list of claims right here [holding up several sheets of paper containing names and amounts] aggregating many hundreds of millions. And the only thing to-day — the Senate and the House both being under the control of those Southern rebels — the only protection, the only barrier between the Treasury of the United States and those rebel claims is a presidential veto [cheers], and thank God for the veto! [Long-continued applause.] But these claims are not all. There are claims innumerable which they dare not yet present. You may go through every State in the South, and somewhere, hidden away, you will find a claim for every slave that ever was liberated. In the files of the Senate and the House you will find demands for untold millions of dollars to improve streams that do not exist — where you will have to pump the water to get up a stream at all. [Laughter and applause.] Demands; for untold millions to build the levees of the Mississippi river ! We have already given the Southern people 32,000,000 of acres of land which would be reclaimed by those levees, and now they propose to bankrupt your Treasury by telling you, people of the North, to build the levees to make the lands which you gave them valuable.

To show you that I am not over-stating this idea of Southern claims, I will read you a petition which is now being circulated throughout the South :

"We, the people of the United States, most respectfully petition your "honorable bodies to enact a law by which all citizens of every section of the "United States may be paid for all their property destroyed by the govern-"ments and armies on both sides, during the late war between the States, in "bonds, bearing 3 per cent. interest per annum, maturing within the next one "hundred years."

Every soldier who served in the Northern army has been paid. Every dollar's worth of property furnished to the Northern army has been paid for. Every widow or orphan of a wounded soldier entitled to a pension has been pensioned, so that there is no claim from the North ; but this means that you shall do for the South precisely what you have done for your own soldiers.

But I have not yet reached the milk in this cocoa-nut. [Laughter.]

"And we also petition that all soldiers, or their legal representatives, of "both armies and every section, be paid in bonds or public lands for their "lost time [laughter], limbs, and lives while engaged in the late unfortunate "civil conflict." [Laughter and applause.]

That all soldiers be paid for their lost time while fighting to overthrow your government ! That they shall be paid for their lost limbs and their lost lives while fighting to overthrow your government !

Ah, my fellow-citizens, they are in sober, serious, downright earnest. They have captured both houses of Congress, and the only obstacle to the ·payment of these infamous claims is the presidential veto, and there is not a man before me who has not a personal, direct interest in seeing to it that the rebels do not capture the balance of Washington. [Applause.] These rebel States are solid — solid for repudiating your debt, solid for paying these rebel claims ; they have repudiated their individual debts through the bankrupt law ; they have repudiated their State debts by scaling, and then refusing to pay the interest on what has been scaled ; they have repudiated their municipal debts by repealing the charters of their cities, towns, and villages. And do you think they are more anxious to pay the debt contracted for their subjugation than they are to pay their own honest debts ? I tell you, No. They mean repudiation, and do not mean that your debt shall be of any more value than their own. When you trust them you are making a mistake, and

I do not believe you will ever do it again. [Laughter and applause, and voices : " We won't ! "]

But we have a matter under consideration to-night of vastly more importance than all the financial questions that can be presented to you, and that is, Is this or is it not a Nation ! We had supposed for generations that this was a Nation. Our fathers met in convention to frame a constitution, and they found some difficulty in agreeing upon the details of that constitution, and for a time it was a matter of extreme doubt whether any agreement could be reached. Acrimonious debate took place in that convention, but finally a spirit of compromise prevailed, and the constitution was adopted by the convention and submitted to the people of these United States. Not to the States, but to the people of the United States, and the people of the United States adopted the constitution that was framed by the fathers, and for many long years the whole people of the United States believed that we had a Government. The whisky rebellion broke out in Pennsylvania, and was put down by the strong arm of the Government, and we still believed that we had a Government. We continued in that belief until the days of General Jackson, when South Carolina raised the flag of rebellion against the Government. Armed men trod the soil of South Carolina and threatened that unless the tariff was modified to suit their views they would overthrow the Government. This was under the leadership of John C. Calhoun, in carrying out his doctrine. Old General Jackson took his pipe out of his mouth when he was told that Calhoun was in rebellion against the Government, and said : " Let South Carolina commit the first act of treason against this Government, and, by the Eternal, I will hang John C. Calhoun ! " and every man, woman, and child in America, including Calhoun, knew that he would do it, and the first act of treason was not committed against the Government, for even the State of South Carolina, under the leadership of John C. Calhoun, had bowed to its power.

We remained under that impression until I first took my seat in the Senate on the 4th day of March, 1857. Then, again, treason was threatened on the floor of the Senate and on the floor of the House. They said then : " Do " this or we will destroy your Government. Fail to do that, and we will " destroy your Government." One of them in talking to brave old Ben. Wade one day repeated this threat, and the old man straightened himself up and said : " Don't delay it on my account." [Laughter.] Careful preparations were made to carry out these treasons. Jefferson Davis stepped out of the Cabinet of Franklin Pierce, as Secretary of War, into the Senate of the United States, and became chairman of the Committee on Military Affairs. There was an innocent-looking clause in the general appropriation bill which read that the Secretary of War might sell such arms as he deemed it for the interest of the government to dispose of. Under that apparently innocent clause, your arsenals were opened ; your arms and implements of war went together with your ammunition ; your accoutrements followed your arms ; your

navy was scattered wherever the winds blew and sufficient water was found
to float your ships, where they could not be used to defend your government.
The credit of the government, whose 6 per cent. bonds in 1857 sold for 122
cents on the dollar, was so utterly prostrated and debased that in February,
1861 — four years afterward — bonds payable, principal and interest in gold,
bearing 6 per cent., were sold for 88 cents on the dollar, with no buyers for
the whole amount. Careful preparations were made for the overthrow of
your government, and when Abraham Lincoln [cheers] took the oath of
office as President of the United States [cheers], you had no army, no navy,
no money, no credit, no arms, no ammunition, nothing to protect the national
life. Yet with all these discouragements staring us in the face, the Republican
party undertook to save your government. [Applause.] We raised your
credit, created navies, raised armies, fought battles, carried on the war to a
successful issue, and, finally, when the rebellion surrendered at Appomattox,
they surrendered to a Government. [Applause.] They admitted that they had
submitted their heresy to the arbitrament of arms and had been defeated,
and they surrendered to the government of the United States of America.
[Applause.] They made no claims against this government, for they had
none. In the very ordinance of secession which they had signed they had
pledged their lives, their fortunes, and their sacred honor to the overthrow of
this government, and when they failed to do it, they lost all they had pledged.
[Cries of "Good."] They made no claims against the government because
they had none. They asked, and asked as a boon from the government of
the United States, that their miserable lives might be spared to them.
[Applause.] We gave them their lives. They had forfeited all their property
— we gave it back to them. We found them naked and we clothed them.
They were without the rights of citizenship, having forfeited those rights, and
we restored them. We took them to our bosoms as brethren, believing that
they had repented of their sins. We killed for them the fatted calf, and
invited them to the feast, and they gravely informed us that they had always
owned that animal, and were not thankful for the invitation. [Great laughter
and cheers.] By the laws of war, and by the laws of nations, they were
bound to pay every dollar of the expense incurred in putting down that
rebellion. Germany compelled France to pay $1,000,000,000 in gold coin for a
brief campaign. The seceding States were bound by the laws of war and by
the laws of nations to pay every dollar of the debt contracted for their subjugation, but we forgave them that debt, and, to-day, you are being taxed
heavily to pay the interest on the debt that they ought to have paid.
[Applause.] Such magnanimity as was exhibited by this nation to these
rebels has never been witnessed on earth [applause], and, in my humble
judgment, will never be witnessed again. [Cheers.] Mistakes we undoubtedly
made, errors we committed, and I will take my full share of responsibility
for the errors, for I was there, and voted upon every proposition ; but, in my
humble judgment, the greatest mistake we made, and the gravest error we

committed was in not hanging enough of these rebels to make treason forever odious. [Prolonged cheers.] Somebody committed a crime. Either those men who rose in rebellion committed the greatest crime known to human law, or our own brave soldiers, who went out to fight to save this government, were murderers. Is there a man on the face of the earth who dares to get up and say that our brave soldiers, who bared their breasts to the bullets of the rebels, were anything but patriots? [Cheers.]

And now, after twenty years—after an absence of four years from the Senate—I go back and take my seat, and what do I find? The self-same pretensions are rung in my ears from day to day. I might close my eyes and leave my ears open to the discussions that are going on daily in Congress, and believe that I had taken a Rip Van Winkle sleep of twenty years. [Applause.] Twenty years ago they said . . "Do this or we will shoot "your government to death! Fail to do that or we will shoot your govern "ment to death!" To day I go back and find these paroled rebels, who have never been relieved from their parole of honor to obey the laws, saying: "Do "this! obey our will, or we will starve your government to death! Fail to "obey our will, and we will starve your government to death!" Now, if I am to die, I would rather be shot dead with musketry than be starved to death. [Laughter and applause.]

These rebels—for they are just as rebellious now as they were twenty years ago—there is not a particle of difference—these rebels to-day have thirty-six members on the floor of the House of Representatives, without one single constituent, and in violation of law those thirty-six members represent 4,000,000 people, lately slaves, who are as absolutely disfranchised as if they lived in another sphere, through shot-guns, and whips, and tissue ballots; for the law expressly says, wherever a race or class is disfranchised they shall not be represented upon the floor of the House. [Applause.] And these thirty-six members thus elected constitute three times the whole of their majority upon the floor of the House. Now, my fellow-citizens, this is not only a violation of law, but it is an outrage upon all the loyal men of these United States. [Applause.] It ought not to be. It must not be. [Applause.] And it shall not be. [Tremendous cheers.]

Twelve members of the Senate—and that is more than their whole majority—twelve members of the Senate occupy their seats upon that floor by fraud and violence, and I am saying no more to you in Chicago than I said to those rebel generals to their faces on the floor of the Senate of the United States. [Enthusiastic applause.] Twelve members of that Senate were thus elected, and with majorities thus obtained by fraud and violence in both houses, they dare to dictate terms to the loyal men of these United States. [Applause.] With majorities thus obtained they dare to arraign the loyal men of this country, and say they want honest elections. [Laughter and applause.] They are mortally afraid of bayonets at the 'polls. We offered them a law forbidding any man to come within two miles of a polling place with arms of any description, and they promptly voted it down [laughter and applause], for they wanted their Ku-Klux there. They were afraid, not of Ku-Klux at the polls, but of soldiers at the polls. Now, in all the States north of Mason and Dixon's line and east of the Rocky Mountains there is less than one soldier to a county. [Laughter.] There is about two-thirds of a soldier to a county. [Laughter and applause.] And, of course, about two-thirds of a musket to a county. [Laughter.] Now, would not this great county of Cook tremble if you saw two-thirds of a soldier parading himself up and down in front of the city of Chicago. [Loud and long-continued applause and laughter.] But they are afraid to have inspectors. What are they afraid to have inspectors for? The law creating those inspectors is imperative that one must be a Democrat and the other a Republican. They have no power whatever except to certify that the election is honest and fair. And yet they are afraid of those inspectors, and then they are afraid of marshals at the polls. Now, while the inspectors cannot arrest, the marshals under the order of the court can arrest criminals; therefore, they said: "We will have no marshals." What they want is not free elections, but free frauds at elections. They have got a solid South by fraud and violence. Give them permission to perpetrate the same kind of fraud and violence in New York city and in Cincinnati and those two cities with a solid South will give them the presidency of the United States; and once obtained by fraud and violence, by fraud and violence they would hold it for a generation. To-day eight millions of people in those rebel States as absolutely control all the legislation of this government as they controlled their slaves while slavery was in existence. Through caucus dictation now I find precisely what I found twenty years ago when I first took my seat in Congress. In a Democratic Congress, composed of twenty-eight Southern Democrats and sixteen Northern Democrats, they decreed that Stephen A. Douglas of Illinois should be degraded and disgraced from the Committee on Territories, and there were but just two Northern Democratic senators who dared even to enter a protest against the outrage. To-day there are thirty-two Southern Democratic senators to twelve Northern, and out of the whole twelve there is not a man who dares protest against anything. [Applause.] I say, that through this caucus dictation, these eight millions of Southern rebels as absolutely control the legislation of this nation as they controlled their slaves when slavery existed.

Now, if every man within the sound of my voice should stand up in this audience and hold up his right hand and swear that a rebel soldier was better than a Union soldier, I would not believe it. [Laughter and applause.] I would hold up both of my hands and swear that I did not believe it. [Cheers.] And yet, to-day, in South Carolina, in Alabama, in Louisiana, in Mississippi and in several other States the vote of a rebel soldier counts more than two of the votes of the brave soldiers of Illinois; for they vote for the negro as well as for themselves, and their vote weighs just double the weight of that of the brave soldier in Illinois. It is an outrage upon freedom, an outrage upon the gallant soldiers of Illinois and Michigan. [Applause.]

Now, my fellow-citizens, I have undertaken to show you the condition in which the country was placed when the Republican party assumed the reins of power. When the Republican party took the reins of power, the country had no money, no credit, no arms, no ammunition, no navy, no material of war. When the Republican party took the reins of power in its hands, there was no nation poor enough to do you reverence. You were the derision of the nations of the earth. You had but one ally and friend on earth, and that was little Switzerland. [Applause.] Russia sent her fleet to winter here for her own protection, but there was not a nation on God's earth, that did not hope and pray that your republican government might be overthrown, and there was no nation on earth poor enough to do you reverence. We fought that battle through; we raised the nation's dignity, and the nation's honor, the national power and the national strength, until now, to-day, after eighteen years of Republican rule, there is no nation on earth strong enough not to do you reverence. [Loud and continued applause.] We took your national credit when it was so low that your bonds were selling at 88 cents on the dollar, bearing six per cent. interest and no takers, and we elevated your credit up, up, up, up, up until to-day your four per cent. bonds are selling at a premium in every market of the earth. [Applause.] So your credit stands higher than the credit of any other nation. [Applause.] We saved the national life and we saved the national honor, and yet, notwithstanding all this, there are those who say that the mission of the Republican party is ended and that it ought to die. If there ever was a political organization that existed on the face of this globe, which, so far as a future state of rewards and punishments is concerned, is prepared to die, it is that old Republican party. [Cheers.] But we are not going to do it. [Laughter and applause.] We have made other arrangements. [Renewed laughter and cheers.]

The Republican party is the only party that ever existed, so far as I have been able to ascertain — so far as any record can be found, either in sacred or profane history — it is the only party that ever existed on earth which had not one single, solitary, unfulfilled pledge left [cheers] — not one [renewed cheers]; and I defy the worst enemy the Republican party ever had to name one single pledge it gave to the people who created it which is not to-day a fulfilled and an established fact. [Cheers.] The Republican party was created with one idea, and that was to preserve our vast territories from the blighting curse of slavery. We gave that pledge at our birth, that we would save those territories from the withering grasp of slavery, and we saved them. [Voices. "Yes, we did."] It is our own work. We did it. [Cheers.] But we did more than that; we not only saved your vast territories from the blighting curse of slavery, but we wiped the accursed thing from the continent of North America. [Tremendous cheering.] We pledged ourselves to save your national life, and we saved your national life. We pledged ourselves to save your national honor, and we saved your national honor. [Applause.] We pledged ourselves to give you a homestead law, and we gave you a homestead law. [Applause.] We pledged ourselves to improve your rivers and your harbors, and we improved your rivers and your harbors. [Applause.] We pledged ourselves to build a Pacific railroad, and we built a Pacific railroad. [Applause.] We pledged ourselves to give you a college land bill, and we gave it to you; and, not to weary you, the last pledge ever given and the last to be fulfilled was that the very moment we were able we would redeem the obligations of this great government in the coin of the realm, and on the first day of January, 1879, we fulfilled the last pledge ever given by the Republican party. [Cheers and long-continued applause.]

Notwithstanding all this, you say: "Your mission is ended and you ought to die." [Laughter and applause.] Well, my fellow-citizens, if we should die to-day, or to-morrow, our children's children to the twentieth generation would boast that their ancestors belonged to that glorious old Republican party [applause] that wiped that accursed thing, slavery, from the escutcheon of this great government. [Cheers.] And they would have a right to boast throughout all generations.

Senator Ben. Hill of Georgia said, in my presence, that he was an "ambassador" from the sovereign State of Georgia [laughter] to the Senate of the United States. Suppose Ben. Hill should be caught in Africa or India, or some of those Eastern nations, and should get into a little difficulty, do you think he would raise the great flag of Georgia over his head [laughter] and say: "That will protect me.". [Renewed laughter and applause.] My fellow-citizens, you may take the biggest ship that sails the ocean, put on board of her the flags of all the States that were lately in the rebellion against this government, raise to her peak the stars and bars of the rebellion, start her with all her bunting floating to the breeze, sail her around the world, and you would not get a salute of one pop-gun from any fort on earth. [Loud and continued laughter and applause.] Take the smallest ship that sails the ocean, mark her "U. S. A."—United States of America—raise to her peak the Stars and Stripes, and sail her around the world, and there is not a fort or a ship-of-war of any nation on God's footstool that would not receive her with a national salute. [Cheers.] And yet the Republican party has done all this. We took your government when it was despised among the nations, and we have raised it to this high point of honor; and yet you tell us we ought to die. [Laughter and applause.]

Suppose there was a manufacturing concern here that failed about the year 1857, and the citizens of Chicago thought it very important that it be reorganized and resume business. You would buy the property for fifty cents on the dollar and reorganize it under your general laws, elect officers, and look about for a competent man to manage it. Finally you find what you believe to be the very man for that business and put him in possession. He finds that the machinery is not up to the progress of the age, and goes and buys new. He brings order out of confusion, he manages the business so that the stock of the concern rises to par; dividends are paid semi-annually and they grow larger and larger. The stock rises to two hundred, and none for sale. After eighteen years of successful management the manager comes in with his account-current and his check for the half-yearly dividend, and lays it before the president and the directors. The president has had a little conversation with his directors, and says:

"This statement is very satisfactory, but we have concluded that after the first day of July next we shall not require your services any longer."

"Why," says the manager, "what have I done?"

"Nothing that is not praiseworthy. We will give you a certificate that "we think you have managed this establishment with great ability and great "success. We will certify that we think you have no equal in the city of "Chicago or State of Illinois. Everything you have done is praiseworthy, and "we give you full credit for it; but eighteen years ago one of our employes "was caught stealing and sent to the penitentiary. He has now served his "time out, and we propose to put him in your place." [Prolonged laughter and cheers.] Wouldn't you say that the president and all of the directors should be put into a lunatic asylum on suspicion at once? [Applause and laughter.]

Now, I tell you, Mr. Chairman, the mission of the Republican party is not ended. [Cheers.] I tell you, furthermore, Mr. Chairman, that it has just begun. [Cheers.] I tell you, furthermore, that it will never end until you and I can start from the Canada border, travel to the Gulf of Mexico, make black Republican speeches wherever we please [applause], vote the black Republican ticket wherever we gain a residence [cheers], and do it with exactly the same safety that a rebel can travel throughout the North, stop wherever he has a mind to, and run for judge in any city he chooses.

[This hit at the Democratic candidate for judge of the Cook County Superior Court, who was a rebel soldier during the war, set the audience wild, and they cheered and swung their hats and handkerchiefs frantically.]

I hope after you have elected him judge he won't bring you in a bill for loss of time. [Laughter.]

You are going to hold an election next Tuesday which is of importance far beyond the borders of Chicago. The eyes of the whole nation are upon you. By your verdict next Tuesday you are to send forth greeting to the people of the United States, saying, that either you are in favor of honest men, honest money, patriotism, and a National Government [cheers], or that you are in favor of soft money, repudiation, and rebel rule. [Cheers.] It is a good symptom, Mr. Chairman, to see 600 young men like you in line, prepared to carry the flag of the Republican party forward to victory. [Cheers.] It is a good symptom to see 600 young men like my friend, the chairman here, in the front ranks, ready to fight the battles of their country now, and vote as they shot during the war. [Cheers.]

Now, I want every single man in this vast audience to consider himself a committee of one to work from now until the polls close on Tuesday next.

[Cheers.] Find a man who might stay away, who has gone away and might not return ; secure one man besides yourself to go to the polls and vote the Republican ticket ; and if you cannot find such a man, try to convert a sinner from the error of his way. [Applause.] You have got too much at stake to risk it at this election. The times are too good. Iron brings too much. Lumber is too high. Your business is too prosperous. Your manufactories are making too much money for you to afford to turn this great government over to the hands of repudiating rebels. You cannot do it. Shut up your stores. Shut up your manufactories. Go to work for your country, and spend two days. and on the night of election, Mr. Chairman, send me a dispatch, if you please, that Chicago has gone overwhelmingly Republican. [Loud cheers.]

The Doric Pillar of Michigan.

A MEMORIAL ADDRESS,

DELIVERED IN THE FORT STREET PRESBYTERIAN CHURCH, DETROIT, MICH., THURSDAY MORNING, NOV. 27, 1879,

BY

THE REV. ARTHUR T. PIERSON, D. D.

"There were giants in the earth in those days," is the simple record of the age before the flood.

There has been no age without its giants; not, perhaps, in the narrow sense of great physical stature, but in the broader sense of mental might, capacity to command and control. Such men are but few, in the most favored times, and it takes but few to give shape to human history and destiny. Their words shake the world; their deeds move and mold humanity; and, as Carlyle has suggested, history is but their lengthened shadows, the indefinite prolonging of their influence even after they are dead.

One of these giants has recently fallen, at the commanding signal of One who is far greater than any of the sons of men, and at whose touch kings drop their sceptre, and, like the meanest of their slaves, crumble to dust.

This giant fell among us. We had seen him as he grew to his great stature and rose to his throne of power. He moved in our streets; he spoke in our halls; in our city of the living was his earthly home, and in our city of the dead is his place of rest. He went from us to the nation's capital, to represent our State in the Senate of the republic; he belonged to Michigan, and Michigan gave him to the Union; but he never forgot the home of his manhood. Here his dearest interests clustered, and his deepest affections gathered; and here his most loving memorial will be reared. As he belonged peculiarly to this congregation, surely it is our privilege to weave the first wreath to garland his memory.

The annual Day of Thanksgiving is peculiarly a national day, since it is the only one in the year when the whole nation is called upon by its chief magistrate to give thanks as a united people. By common consent, it is admitted proper that, on that day, special mention be made of matters that affect our civil and political well-being. There is therefore an eminent fitness in a formal commemoration upon this day of the life and labors of our departed Senator and statesman.

With diffidence I attempt the task that falls to me. The time is too short to admit even a brief sketch of a life so long in deeds, so eventful in all that makes material for biography ; a life full, not only of incidents, but of crises ; moreover, I am neither a senator nor a statesman, and feel incompetent to review a career which only the keen eye of one versed in affairs of state can apprehend or appreciate in its full significance ; but, if you will indulge me, I will, without conscious partiality or partisanship, calmly give utterance to the unspoken verdict of the common people as to our departed fellow-citizen ; and try to hint at least a few of the lessons of a life that suggests some of the secrets of success.

History is the most profitable of all studies, and biography is the key of history. In the lives of men, philosophy teaches us by examples. In the analysis of character, we detect the essential elements of success and discern the causes of failure. Virtue and vice impress us most in concrete forms ; and hence even the best of all books enshrines as its priceless jewel the story of the only perfect life.

To draw even the profile of Mr. Chandler's public career the proper limits of this address do not allow. There is material, in the twenty years of his senatorial life, which could be spread through volumes. His advocacy of the great Northwest. whose champion he was ; his master-influence, first as a member, and then as the chairman of the Committee of Commerce ; his bold, keen dissection of the Harper's Ferry panic ; his sagacious organization of the presidential contests ; his plain declarations of loyalty to the Union as something which must be maintained at cost both of treasure and of blood ; his large practical faculty for administration, made so conspicuous during stormy times ; his efficiency as a member of the standing Committee on the Conduct of the War ; his exposure of those who were responsible for its failures, and his defense of those who promoted its successes , his marked influence in changing not only the channel of public sentiment, but the current of events . his watchful guardianship of popular interests, political and financial ; his intelligence and activity in senatorial debates ; his attentive and persistent study of the problem of reconstruction ; and his fearless resistance to all Southern aggression and intimidation, are among the salient points of that long and eventful public service, whose scope is too wide to allow at this hour even a hasty survey.

But, happily, it is quite needless that in such a presence I should trace in detail the events of his life ; to us he was no stranger ; and the mark he has made upon our memory and our history is too deep not to last. His foot-prints are not left upon treacherous and shifting quicksands; and no wave of oblivion is likely soon to wash them away.

Zachariah Chandler had nearly completed his sixty-sixth year; forty-six years he had been a resident of the City of the Straits. New Hampshire was the State of his nativity: Michigan was, in an emphatic sense, the State of his adoption. In our city his first success was won in mercantile pursuits, where also was the first field for the exhibition of his energy, ability and integrity. Here, as this century passed its meridian hour, he passed the great turning-point in his career; and his large capacities and energies were diverted into a political channel. First, Mayor of the city, then nominated for Governor; when, more than twenty years ago, a successor was sought for Lewis Cass in the Senate, this already marked man became the first repre-sentative of the Republican party of this State in that august body at Washington. There, for a period of eighteen years, he sat among the mightiest men of the nation, steadily moving toward the acknowledged leader-ship of his party, and the inevitable command of public affairs. After three terms in the Senate, his seat was occupied for a short time by another; but, upon the resignation of Mr. Christiancy, he was, with no little enthusiasm, re-elected, and was in the midst of a fourth term, when suddenly he was no more numbered among the living. It may be doubted whether, at this time, any one man, from Maine to Mexico, swayed the popular mind and will with a more potent sceptre than did he; and many confidently believe and affirm that, had death spared him, he would have been lifted by the omnipotent voice and vote of the people to the Presidency of the Republic.

Mr. Chandler took his seat in the Senate in those days of strife when the storm was gathering, which, on the memorable 12th of April, 1861, burst upon our heads, in the first gun fired at Fort Sumter. He entered the Senate chamber, to take the oath of office, in company with some whose names are now either famous or infamous for all time. On the one hand, there was Jefferson Davis; on the other Hannibal Hamlin, Charles Sumner, Benjamin F. Wade and Simon Cameron.

Those were days when history is made fast. Every day throbbed with big issues. Kansas was a battle-ground of freedom; and the awful struggle between State Sovereignty and National Unity was gathering, like a volcano, for its terrible outbreak. The Republican Senator from Michigan took in, at a glance, the situation of affairs. Devoted as he was to the State, whose able advocate and zealous friend he was; earnest and persistent as he was, in pro-moting the commercial and industrial interests of the lake region; he was yet too much a patriot to forget the whole country; and as the great conflict, which Mr. Seward named "irrepressible," moved steadily on toward its crisis, he armed himself for the encounter and planted his feet upon the rock of·unalterable allegiance to the Union; and from that position he never swerved.

Mr. Chandler was a zealous party-man; in the eyes of some he was a partisan, in the strenuous advocacy of some measures; but I believe that when history frames her ultimate, impartial verdict, she will accord to him a candid, conscientious adherence to what he believed to be a fundamental principle, absolutely essential to our national life. He saw the South breathing hot hate toward the North, planning and threatening to rend the Union asunder. To him it was not a question simply of liberty and slavery, of sectional prejudice, of political animosity; but a matter of life or of death. He saw the scimitar of secession raised in the gigantic hand of war—but what was it that it was proposed to cleave in twain at one blow? A living, vital form! the body of a nation, with its one grand framework, its common brain and heart, its network of arteries and veins and nerves. It was not dissection as of a corpse—it was vivisection as of a corpus—that sharp blade, if it fell, would cut through a living form, and leave two quivering, bleeding parts, instead. Divide the nation? Why, the same mountain ranges run down our eastern and western shores; the same great rivers, which are the arteries of our commerce, flow through both sections. Our republic is a unit by the decree of nature, that marked our nation's area and arena by the lines of territorial unity, a unit by the decree of history that records one series of common experiences; and, aside from the decree of nature and of history, it is one by the decree of necessity, for we could not survive the separation. Those were the decisive days, and they showed whose heart was yearning toward the child; and God said, as he saw a unanimous North pleading with Him to arrest the falling sword and spare the living body of a nation's life— "Give her the child, for she is the mother thereof!"

Mr. Chandler has been charged with violent and even vindictive feeling toward what he deemed disloyalty and treason.

You have heard the story of the Russians, chased by a hungry pack of wolves, driving at the height of speed over the crisp snow, finding the beasts of prey gaining fast upon them, and throwing out one living child after another to appease the maw of wolfish hunger, while the rest of the family hurried on toward safety.

There are sagacious statesmen that have declared, for a quarter of a century, that State Rights represents the pack of wolves and the Sovereignty of the Union the imperilled household. For scores of years, the encroachments of the South became more and more imperious and alarming.

Concession after concession was made, offering after offering flung to the sacrifice, but only to be followed by a hungrier clamor and demand for more; and, at last, even men of peace said, "We must stop right here and fight these wolves;" and, when it becomes a question of life and death, men become desperate.

I have never supposed myself to be a strong partisan. As a man, a citizen, and a Christian, I have sought to find the true political faith, and, finding it, to hold it, firmly and fearlessly. The question of the unity of our nation

27

and the sovereignty of the national government has ever seemed to me to be of supreme moment, transcending all mere political or party issues ; and, as a patriot, I cannot be indifferent to it.

When the long struggle between State Rights and National Sovereignty grew hot and broke out into civil war, it was a matter of tremendous consequence that the Union be preserved. History stood pointing, with solemn finger, to the fate of the republics of Greece and Switzerland, reminding us that confederation alone will not suffice to keep a nation alive. Mexico, at our borders, was a warning against dismemberment or the loss of the supremacy of a republican unity. And men of all parties forgot party issues in patriotic devotion. It may be a question whether State Sovereignty, however fatal to national life, deserved the hideous name of treason, before the war. But, after the matter had been referred to the arbitrament of the sword, and had been settled at such cost of blood and treasure, it can never henceforth be anything but treason, again to raise that issue. Hence, even men that were temperate in their opposition to Southern aggressions before the war, now are impatient. They set their teeth with the resolution of despair, and say, "We make no further effort to escape this issue, and we throw out no "more offerings of concession. We shall fight these wolves ; and either State "Rights or National Sovereignty shall die."

This was Mr. Chandler's position : if it was a mistaken one, it is the unspoken verdict of millions of the best men of all parties in the whole country ; and every new concession to this great national heresy is only making new converts to the necessity of a firm and fearless resistance.

Some one has suggested that the old division of the church into militant and triumphant is no longer sufficient ; we must add another, namely, the church termagant In our country both sections were militant, and one was triumphant ; the other has been very termagant ever since. General Grant, at his reception in Chicago, declared that the war for the Union had put the republic on a new footing abroad. A quarter of a century ago, by political leaders across the sea, "it was believed we had no nation. It was merely "a confederation of States, tied together by a rope of sand, and would give "way upon the slightest friction. They have found it was a grand mistake. "They know we have now a nation, that we are a nation of strong and "intelligent and brave people, capable of judging and knowing our rights, "and determined on all occasions to maintain them against either domestic or "foreign foes ; and that is the reception you, as a nation, have received "through me while I was abroad."

On the same day we have a significant voice from the South. General Toombs, in response to a suggestion that Governors of various States and prominent Southern men should unite in congratulations to the ex - President on his return, telegraphs in these words : "I decline to answer except to "say, I present my personal congratulations to General Grant on his safe "return to his country. He fought for his country honorably and won. I

"fought for mine and lost. I am ready to try it over! Death to the
"Union!"

Here we have simply two representative utterances; one is the voice of a
solid North; the other is, we fear, the voice of a South that is much more
"solid" than we could wish. It is no marvel if, after a war of so many
years, that cost so many lives and so much money, and left us to drag
through ten years of a financial slough, loyal men are impatient and even
angry, when they discover that the question is still an unsettled one, and that
we have not even conquered a peace! Even the interpretation now attached
to this seditious utterance by General Toombs himself, that "the result of
"war was death to the Union, and that the present government is a consoli-
"dated one, not a confederacy," does not essentially relieve the matter.

Mr. Chandler could not brook what he regarded as sentiments rendered
doubly treasonable by the fact that a long, bitter but successful war had
burned upon them with a hot iron the brand of treason. He fought those
sentiments, and it was as under a black flag that announced "no quarter."
But this does not prove malicious or vindictive feeling toward misguided men
who hold such views. There is a difference between fighting a principle
and fighting a person. In fact the only way to prevent fighting men is often
a vigorous and timely opposition to their measures. And if we wish to
avoid another war, and that a war of extermination, the ballot must obviate
the necessity for the bullet: we must stand together, and by our voice and
vote, by tongue and pen, by our laws and our acts, in the use of every
keen weapon, exterminate the heresy of State Rights. We need not do this
in hate toward the South: a true love even for the South demands it, for
to them as to us it is a deadly foe to all true prosperity and national
existence. How can a man who candidly looks upon the present attitude
of the South as both suicidal and nationally destructive be calm and cool?
The philippics of Demosthenes were bitter, but they were the mighty beat-
ings of a heart that pulsed with the patriotism that could not see liberty
throttled without sounding a loud and indignant alarm. The North owes a
big debt to every man who at this crisis will not suffer an imperilled
republic to sleep.

Mr. Chandler was not a college graduate. His early training was got in
the New England common school and academy. Yet he was in a true sense
an educated man: for education is "not a dead mass of accumulations," but
self-development, "power to work with the brain," to use the hand in cun-
ning and curious industries, to use the tongue in attractive and effective
speech, to use the pen in wise, witty or weighty paragraphs. Somehow he
had learned to hold, with a master hand, the reins of his own mind, and
make his imagination and reason and memory and powers of speech obey his
behests. That is no common acquirement: it is something beyond all mere
acquirement; it is the infallible sign and seal of culture. His addresses, even
on critical occasions, were unwritten, and, in some cases, could not have been

elaborated, even in the mind; yet in vigor of thought, logical continuity and consistency, accuracy of diction, and even rhetorical grace, few public speakers equal them.

The power to command the popular ear is a rare power, whether it be a gift of nature or a grace of culture. With Mr. Chandler it was held and wielded as a native sceptre. He had the secret of rhetorical adaptation; he could at once go down to the level of the people and yet lift them to his level. They understood what he said and knew what he meant. He threw himself into their modes of thought and habits of speech; he culled his illustrations mainly from common life. If he sacrificed anything, it was rhetorical elegance, never force; his one aim was to compel conviction.

The simplicity of his diction was a prime element and secret of his power. He did not speak as one who had to say something, but as one who had something to say, and whose whole aim was to say it well: with clearness, plainness, force and effect. If he could not have both weight and lustre, he would have weight.

Walter Scott has exposed the absurdity of "writing down" to children, and shown that it is really writing up, to make oneself so simple as to be plain even to the child-mind. Simplicity is the highest art. To have thought faintly gloom and glimmer through obscure language, like stars through a haze or mist, may serve to impress the ignorant with a supposed profundity in the speaker; but it is no more a sign of such profundity than muddy water signifies depth in a stream; it may suggest depth because you can see no bottom, but it means shallowness! It is a lesson that all of us may learn through the life of our departed Senator, that the first element of good speaking is thought; and the second a form of words fitting the thought, which, like true dress, shall not call attention to itself but to the idea or conception which it clothes. Any man who is long to hold the ear of the people must give them facts and thoughts worth knowing and thinking of, in words which it will not take a walking dictionary or living encyclopædia to interpret, or a philosopher to untangle from the skein of their confusion.

Mr. Chandler was such a man, a man for the people. Free from all stately airs and stilted dignities, he took hold of every political and national question with ungloved hands. He understood and used the language of home life, which is the "universal dialect" of power. His speeches were packed with vigorous Saxon. He thought more of the short sword, with its sharp edge and keen point and close thrust, than of the scholar's labored latinity, with its longer blade, even though it might also have a diamond-decked hilt; and in this, as in not a few other conspicuous traits, he was master of the best secrets that gave the great Irish agitator, O'Connell, his strange power of moving the multitude. His last speech, even when read, and without the magnetism of his personal presence, may well stand as the last of his utterances.

The simplicity of Mr. Chandler's style of oratory amounted to ruggedness, in the sense in which we apply that word to the naked naturalness of a landscape, whose features have not been too much modified by art. There is in oratory an excessive polish, which suggests coldness and deadness. Some speakers sharpen the blade until there is no blade left ; the mistaken careful-ness of their culture brings everything to one dead level of faultlessness ; there is nothing to offend, and nothing to rouse and move. Demosthenes said that kinésis — not "action," but motion, or rather that which moves — is the first, second, third requisite of true oratory. He is no true speaker who simply pleases you : he must stir you to new thought, new choice, new action.

We must beware of the polish that is a loss of power, and, like a lapi-dary, not grind off points, but grind into points. Demosthenes was more rugged than Cicero ; but he pricked men more with the point of his oratori-cal goad. Men heard the silver - tongued Roman and said, "How pleasantly he speaks !" They heard the bold Athenian and shouted, "Let us go and fight Philip !"

Carlyle says, "He is God's anointed king whose simple word can melt a million wills into his !" That melting wills into his own is the test of eloquence in the orator ; and a rugged simplicity has held men in the very fire of the orator's ardor and fervor, till they were at white heat, and could be shaped at will ; while the most scholarly display of culture often leaves them unmoved, to gape and stare with wonder, as before the splendors of the Aurora Borealis, and feel as little real warmth. Emerson is right : "There is no true eloquence unless there is a man behind the speech," and men care not what the speech is if the man be not behind it, or, on the other hand, what the speech is, if the man be behind it ! And so it is that Richard Cobden compelled even Robert Peel, who loved truth and candor, to become a convert to his free - trade opinions ; and so it was that John Bright, another model of a simple utterance with a sincere man behind it, swayed such a mighty sceptre over the people of Britain. The mere declaimer or demagogue may win a temporary hearing ; but the man who leaves a lasting impress on the mind of the people must have in himself some real worth.

To Mr. Chandler's executive ability reference has been made. It was never better illustrated than in his vigorous and faithful administration as Secretary of the Interior. It was Hercules in the Augean stables again — purging the department of incompetency and dishonesty. He sent a flood through the Patent Office, that swept all the clerks out of one room ; and another through the Indian Bureau, that cleaned out its abuses and exposed its frauds. It is said that the reconstruction of that department saved millions annually to the treasury of the nation. Mr. Schurz, in becom-ing his successor, paid a very handsome tribute to the retiring Secretary, acknowledging the great debt of the country to Mr. Chandler's energy and fidelity, and modestly declaring that he could hope for no higher success than to keep and leave the department where he found it.

If there be any one thing for which the Senator from Michigan stood above most men it was in this practical business ability. He had, in rare union, "talent" and "tact." His good sense, clear views, ready and retentive memory, prompt decision, patience and perseverance, quick discernment and instinctive perception of the fitness of ways to ends, qualified him for energetic and successful administration anywhere. Webster said, "There is always room at the top." Even the pyramid waits for the capstone, which must be, itself, a little pyramid. And he who has inborn or inbred fitness for the top place will find his way there ; no other will long stay there, even if some accident lifts him to the nominal occupancy of such a position.

He had rare tact, that indefinable quality of which Ross says, that "it is the most exquisite thing in man." Literally it means "touch," and is suggested by the delicacy often found in that mysterious sense. It describes, though it cannot define, the nice, skillful, innate discernment and discrimination which tells one what to say and do, even on critical occasions ; how to reach and "touch" men, when a blunder would be fatal. This wisdom of instinct may be cultivated but cannot be acquired ; and it seems to be close of kin with that common sense which, though by no means exceedingly "common," represents a sound intuitive sense in common matters, such as would be the common sense or verdict of wise and sagacious minds.

The Senator impressed men as one whose powers were varied and versatile. Thomas F. Marshall, the "Kentucky orator," maintained that fine speaking, writing and conversation depend on a different order of gifts. "A "speech cannot be reported, nor an essay spoken. Fox wrote speeches ; "nobody reads them. Sir James Mackintosh spoke essays ; nobody listened. "Yet England crowded to hear Fox, and reads Mackintosh. Lord Bolingbroke "excelled in all, the ablest orator, finest writer, most elegant drawing-room "gentleman in England."

Whether or not this philosophy be sound and this estimate correct, we shall all agree that few men combine power of speech with force in composition and grace in conversation. Our departed Senator certainly had more than the common share of versatility. That last speech at Chicago thrilled a vast audience when spoken, and kindled a flaming enthusiasm ; yet it reads like the compact and complete sentences of the essayist.

Versatility, however, is not to be coveted where it implies a lack of concentration. An anonymous writer has left us a very discriminating comparison of two great British statesmen. He likens Canning's mind to a convex speculum which scattered its rays of light upon all objects ; while he likens Brougham's to a concave speculum which concentrated the rays upon one central, burning, focal point. There are some men who possess, to a considerable degree, both the power to scatter and the power to gather the rays. At times they exhibit varied and versatile ability, they touch delicately and skillfully many different themes or departments of thought and action ; but when crises arise which demand the whole man, they become in the best sense men of one idea, for one thought fills and fires the soul ; every power is concentrated in one burning purpose.

The Senator, whose deserved garland we are weaving, was one of these men. There were times when he seemed to turn his hand with equal ease to a score of employments; now giving wise counsel in gravest matters, now playfully entertaining guests at his table; now studying the deep philosophy of political economy, now holding a Senate in rapt attention; now reorganizing a department of state; now pushing a new measure through Congress; now closeted with the President over the issues of a colossal campaign, and again conducting a pleasure excursion; to-day leading on the hosts of a great party, and to-morrow managing the affairs of an extensive farm. But, when the destiny of the nation hung in the balance, or history waited with uplifted pen to record on her eternal scroll the final decision of some great question, he gathered and condensed into absolute unity all the powers of mind and heart and will, and flung the combined weight of his whole manhood into the trembling scale. When he felt that a thing must be, a mountain was no obstacle to surmount, a host of foes no occasion for dismay. With intensity of conviction, with contagious courage and enthusiasm, with indomitable resolution, with tireless energy of action, he went ahead, and weaker men had to follow; his conviction persuaded the hesitating, his courage emboldened the timid, his determination inspired the irresolute. He was the unit that, in the leading place, makes even the cyphers swell the sum of power.

It is no slight praise of Mr. Chandler to say that he was a man of industry; the results he reached were won by work. There is a great deal of blind talk about genius. That there is such a thing, apart from the practical faculty of application, even great men have doubted or boldly denied; but certain it is that there is such a thing as the genius of industry, and that rules the world! Alexander Hamilton disclaimed any other genius than the profound study of a subject. He kept before him a theme which he meant to master, till he explored it in all its bearings and his mind was filled with it. Then, to quote his words, "the effort which I make the people are pleased to call the fruit of genius. It is the fruit of labor and thought."

And so for us all there is no royal road to a true success. We must simply plod on, along the plain, hard, plebeian path of honest toil, and climb up the hills, if we would get on and up at all. Spinoza grandly says that that there is no foe or barrier to progress like "self-conceit and the laziness which self-conceit begets." We venture to add that no conceit is surer to beget laziness than the conceit of "conscious genius." Our peril is to learn to do our work easily; that means poor work, if indeed any work at all, shallow acquirements, superficial attainments, and no real scholarly or heroic achievements.

Our regretted Senator did not despise honest work, and never claimed to be a genius. He had a hearty contempt for all that aristocracy of intellect that frowns on mental toil.

He spoke without manuscript, and without memorizing; or, as we say, "extempore." That is another much-abused word. Extemporaneous speech is not the utterance of words that shake the world, or any considerable part of it, unless such speech be the fruit not of that time, but, as Dr. Shedd says, "of all time previous." But when the orator first becomes master of his theme and then of the occasion, and is thus fitted to deal with the real vital issues before the people, he may, without having put pen to paper, o, having framed a single sentence beforehand, often find himself master also of his audience. The careful study of his subject, the habit of thinking in words, and of weighing words when he reads and talks, scoops out a channel in the mind ; and when he rises to speak he finds his thought flowing naturally and easily in this channel.

No man can carefully read Mr. Chandler's public utterances without detecting a brevity and terseness, a simplicity and plainness, an accuracy and vigor, and often a rhetorical beauty, which shew care in preparation. These qualities are not the offspring of indolence. Years of drill lie back of the exact and daring touches with which the artist makes the canvas speak and the marble breathe ; and the extempore speech of the eloquent orator tells of long, hard discipline that has taught him how to think and how to talk ; it may have taken him fifty years to learn how to hold and sway an audience at will for fifty minutes. The ease and grace of true oratory are the signs of previous exertion ; of that systematic exercise of the intellect that has suggested for our training schools the name, gymnasia. The laws of brain and of brawn do not differ much in this respect. Men are not born athletes, either in mind or muscle ; and to all who have a true desire to succeed, in any sphere of life, the one voice that, with the growing emphasis of the successive centuries, speaks to us, is, "Whatsoever thy hand findeth to do, do it with thy might." Your sword may be short ; "add a step to it!" it may be dull ; add force to the blow or the thrust. There is no encouragement from history, more universally to be appropriated by us, than the testimony she furnishes to the power and value of honest endeavor. To will and to work is to win. The highest endowments assure no achievements ; all success is the crown of patient toil !

While thus speaking a word in favor of hard work, one word of caution and of qualification may not be out of place. I think God means that the sudden decease of public men when in life's prime, shall not be without warning. No thoughtful man fails to feel the force of this fact that somehow the average duration of human life, especially on these shores and among men of mark, is shortening ; and that apoplexy, paralysis, angina pectoris, cerebral hemorrhage, and softening of the brain are amazingly common among brain-workers. The fatality among journalists is especially startling.

We are a fast-living and a fast-dying people. Our habits are bad. We work hard half the time and worry the other half. We eat and sleep irregularly ; we tax our powers unduly, keeping the bow bent until the string snaps simply from constant tension, lack of relaxation. We turn night into day, without restoring the balance by turning day into night. We live in an atmosphere of excitement, and push on to the verge of death before we know our peril or realize our risk. We are tempted to put stimulus in the place of strength, that we may do, under unnatural pressure, what we cannot do by nature's healthy powers. Instead of repairing the engine, we crowd fuel into the boiler and get up more steam ; and, by and by, something breaks, or bursts, and the machinery is a wreck.

I believe it is not hard work that kills us, so much as work under wrong conditions. To do, with the aid of even mild stimulants, like tea and coffee, not to say tobacco, opium, quinine, etc., what we cannot do by the natural strength, is the worst kind of overwork ; and yet our public men are subject to such strain, that they are almost driven to such resorts. Where they ought to stop, and sleep and rest, they "key up" with a kind of artificial strength, and get the habit of unnatural wakefulness ; and then wonder why they are victims of insomnia.

Professor Tyndall, one of the most tireless men of brain in our day, says to the students of University College, London : "Take care of your health ! "Imagine Hercules, as oarsman in a rotten boat ; what can he do there but, "by the very force of his stroke, expedite the ruin of his craft ! Take care "of the timbers of your boat !" And Dr. Beard adds : "To work hard with- "out overworking, to work without worrying, to do just enough without "doing too much — these are the great problems of our future. Our earlier "Franklin taught us to combine industry with economy ; our 'later Frank- "lin' taught us to combine industry with temperance ; our future Franklin "— if one should arise — must teach us how to combine industry with the art "of taking it easy."

The qualities that fitted Mr. Chandler for the conduct of affairs were, however, not purely intellectual ; they belonged in part to another and a higher order, viz.: the emotions and affections.

He had great intensity of nature. Even his political opponents could not doubt the positiveness of his conviction and the profoundness of his sincerity ; and here, as Carlyle justly says, must be found the base blocks in the struct- ure of all heroic character. It is no small thing to be able to command even from an antagonist the concession and confession of one's sincerity. Candor atones for a host of faults. Men will, at the last, forgive anything else in a man who tries to be true to his own convictions and to their interests. The utterances of impulse and even of passion, stinging sarcasm and biting ridicule, unjust charges and assaults, all are easy to pardon in one whose sincerity and intensity of conviction betray him into too great heat ; men would rather be scorched or singed a little in the burning flame of a passionate earnestness than freeze in the atmosphere of a human iceberg — beneath whose rhetorical brilliance they feel the chill of a cold, calculating insincerity and hypocrisy that upsets their faith in human honesty.

He was also peculiarly independent and intrepid. The determination to be loyal, both to his convictions and to his country, inspired him to a bold, brave utterance and invested him with a courage and confidence that were almost contagious. We cannot but admire the political fidelity expressed by Burke, in his famous defense before the electors of Bristol, when he said : "I "obeyed the instructions of nature and reason and conscience ; I maintained "your interests, as against your convictions." Few men have ever dared to say and do what Mr. Chandler has, in the face of such political risks and even such personal peril. One brief address delivered by him in the Senate, soon after he resumed his seat, will stand among the classics of our language, and, if I may so say, among the "heroics" of our history.

He was also a man of great political integrity. In the long career of a public life spanning more than a quarter of a century, no suspicion of dishonesty or disloyalty has ever stained his character or reputation. Michigan may safely challenge any Senatorial record of twenty years to surpass his, either in the quantity or quality of public service.

Those who knew him best affirm that he was, politically and personally, an incorruptible man. The position of a legislator is one of proverbial peril. From the days of Pericles and Augustus till now, the men who make laws and guide national affairs are peculiarly in danger of defiling their consciences by "fear or favor." Bribery sits in the vestibule of every law-making assembly. Greed holds out golden opportunity for getting enormous profits from unlawful or questionable schemes and investments. Ambition lifts her shining crown, and offers a throne of commanding influence if you will bow down and worship, or even make some slight concession in favor of, the devil. Only a little elasticity of conscience, a little blunting of the moral sense ; a little falsehood, or perjury, or treachery, under polite names ; a lending of one's name to doubtful schemes ; and there is a rich reward in gains to the purse and gratifications to the pride, which more than pay for the trifling loss of self-respect. And so not a few who go to Congress with unsullied reputation, come back smutched with their participation in "Credit Mobilier" and "Pacific Railroad" schemes, or any one of the thousand forms of fraud.

So far as I know, Mr. Chandler has never been charged with complicity as to dishonest and disgraceful measures such as have sometimes made the very atmosphere of the Capitol a stench in the nostrils of the pure and good. His name does not stand on the pay-roll of Satan, but with the honored few whose eyes have never been blinded by a bribe and whose record has never been blotted with political dishonor.

To have simply done one's duty is no mean victory. To stand—like the anvil beneath the blows of the hammer—and firmly resist the force of a repeated temptation is grand and heroic. To be venal is no venial fault ; no price which can be weighed in gold can pay a man for the sale of one ounce of his manliness. Conscience is a Samson, whose locks are easily shorn, but they never grow again ; whose eyes, once put out or seared with a hot iron, no prayer will restore. And men, as great and wise as Bacon, have like him been compelled to confess to their own meanness and the mercenary character of their virtue.

One of the worst signs of the times is this corruptibility of popular leaders. One of the greatest of European journals moves like a weather-vane, just as the day's wind blows. Much of the best talent of Europe is for sale for or against despotism. Some of the most gifted men in the House of Lords are of plebeian birth, bought by the bribe of a title, as Harry Brougham himself was, when his great influence became a terror to the aristocracy; and the Duke of Newcastle is said to have bought one-third of the House of Commons. There is scarce a measure, however infamous, that may not be pushed through our common councils and legislative bodies if the lobbyists are only "influential and numerous," and the money is only plenty enough. Let us give God thanks for every man in the community who is not on the auction block to be knocked down to the highest bidder. In these days of abounding fraud and falsehood, men are beginning to feel the value of simple honesty. We have, in our admiration of the genius of intellect, forgotten the genius of goodness, which has power to inspire men with hero-ism. Better to strengthen a few timid hearts in loyalty to principle than to have deserved the encomium of Augustus, who "found Rome brick, and left it marble." The Earl of Chatham refused to keep a million pounds of gov-ernment funds in the bank and pocket the proceeds; as Edmund Burke, on becoming paymaster-general, first of all introduced a bill for the reorganiza-tion of that department of public service, refusing to enrich himself, through the emoluments of that lucrative office, at public expense.

No wonder George the Second should have said of such "honesty" that it is an "honor to human nature!" Such words were worthy of a king, but it is only a crowned head bowing to royal natures that need no crown to tell that they are kingly. The distinguished Hungarian exile will never be for-given for saying that he would praise anything and anybody to aid Hungary. There is an instinct in the great heart of humanity which not even wicked-ness kills, that no quality is so fundamental to character as absolute loyalty to truth; it is the base-block of the whole structure; and great has been many a "fall," where there is no better foundation than the treacherous and shifting quicksands of what is called "policy," and which is to many the only standard of honesty.

Mr. Chandler was known in politics as an enthusiastic and radical advo-cate of his party and its measures. It was not in him to do anything by halves, and it is difficult to see why one may not as naturally be zealous in politics as in religion; in fact, none are more likely to charge upon him parti-sanship than those who in their attachment to the opposite party shew their own lack of moderation.

It has been well said that religion demands "a faith, a polity and a party." The faith and the polity belong to it as necessary features; the party is that on which it depends for organization and onward movement. There is a philosophy, a political creed and economy, which are to the state what religion is to the church; and no man can be a patriot without a political faith and polity and party; though he may stand alone, he represents all three. He may be in the largest sense a patriot, and adopt the sublime motto of Demosthenes, "Not father, nor mother, but dear native land!" yet his patriotism may compel him, as he looks at the matter of his country's interest, to take a position on the side of a political party, and to hold it in the face of ridicule and reproach and even of a pelting hail of hate. Others may not be wrong in their espousal of a different political creed, but he is not wrong, but right, in his honest adherence to his. It is so in religion; an honest, intelligent man is loyal to his own denomination, yet is he none the less, because of that, a Christian in the breadth of his charity.

In fact, religion is not the only sphere where self-sacrifice, for duty and for conscience, may be pressed even to martyrdom. St. Ignatius, facing the wild beasts in the arena, calmly said, "I am grain of God; I must be ground between teeth of lions to make bread for God's people." That was the grand confession of a Christian martyr. Tell me, how much lower down in the scale of the heroic does he belong who, for the sake of the best good of a constituency blinded by passion or prejudice, like the great English statesman, consents to be hurled from his shrine as the idol of the people, and calmly says, "I am under no obligation to be popular, but I am under bonds to myself to be true!" When Regulus refused to buy his own liberty and life, at the cost of Rome's disgrace, and persuaded the Senate to reject the very overtures which he was commissioned to convey, himself returning as his pledge required him if the negotiations were unsuccessful, and surrendering himself to the will of his enemies that Carthage might put him to death by slow torture, it seems to me something like the martyr-spirit burned in that bosom. And, if there be nothing akin to moral martyrdom in bravely standing in one's place and boldly holding one's ground, advocating what one believes to be the only true creed in politics, and the only true policy for the country, in face of sneer and threat, daring the blade and the bullet, the open affront and the secret assault, for the sake of being true to one's self and to one's native land — if there be nothing sublime and heroic in all this, the verdict of reason is unsound.

This lamented statesman had also a genial temper, which won for him a host of friends. Public men are prone to one of two extremes; either the hypocritical suavity of the demagogue, or the arbitrary bluntness and curtness of the despot. Some swing away from the fawning airs of the puppy, but it is toward the repulsive manners of the bear. The man who, as you tip your hat with a polite good morning, sweeps by, saying, "I have n't time," is too often the typical man of affairs, who thinks the quick dismission of applicants and intruders is the price of all energetic public service. It is said of the great French statesman, Richelieu, that he could say "No," so gracefully and winningly, that a man once became applicant for a position, upon which he had not the least claim, just to hear the great Cardinal refuse. If common testimony may be trusted, Michigan's esteemed Senator seldom lost the

hearty cordiality and courtesy of his manners, even under the fretting friction
of public cares.

I am tempted to add that, though a representative Republican, Mr.
Chandler was, in the best sense, a democrat. He weighed a man according
to the worth of his manhood. He could recognize true manliness beneath a
black skin as well as a white one, and behind the rough dress of a poor man,
as behind broadcloth ; and, because he was the friend of humanity and of
human rights, you will find some of his warmest friends among the common
people and in the lower ranks.

I think both justice and generosity demand that among the tributes we
weave for him, there should be distinct and emphatic mention of this simplicity
of character. He was a man among men. From the first, he had none of those
assumptions of conscious superiority that mark the aristocrat. If anything,
he was rather careless than careful of his dignity, and would sooner shock
than mock the fastidious airs and tastes of those who prate about culture, or
pride themselves on their "nobility." Fox quaintly said, of the elder Pitt,
that he "fell up stairs" when he was elevated to the peerage. Many a man
cannot stand going up higher. He becomes haughty, proud ; he affects dignity, he lords it over God's heritage, he becomes too big with conscious
superiority. Like Jeshurun, he waxes fat and kicks. He falls up stairs, if not
down.

The warm, soft, genial side of Mr. Chandler's nature was unveiled in
social life and most of all in the domestic circle. The play of his smile, the
roar of his laughter, the delicacy and tenderness of his sympathy, his stalwart
defense of those whom he loved, the childlike traits that drew him to
children and drew children to him, none appreciate as do those who knew
him best as friend, husband and father. The man of public affairs, he could
lay one hand firmly on the helm of state, while with the other he fondly
pressed his grandchildren to his bosom, or playfully roused them to childish
glee.

This aspect of his many-sided character makes his death an irreparable
loss to his own household. Even the great grief of a nation cannot represent
by its "extensity," the intensity of the more private sorrow that secludes
itself from the public eye. He was, to those whom he specially loved, both
a tower for strength, and a lover and friend for comfort and sympathy.
Those who were "at home" with him, and especially those who were the
peculiar treasures of his heart, knew him as no others could. Happy is the
minister who forgets not his parish at home—the church that is in his own
house—and happy is the public man, whose private life is not simply the
revelation of the hard, coarse and unattractive side of his character.

That is I am sure no ordinary occurrence, which has made forever memorable the Calends of this November. Death, however frequent and familiar
by frequency, can never, to the thoughtful, be an event of common magnitude ; the exchange of worlds cannot be other than a most august experience.

But this death has about it colossal proportions; it stands out and apart like a mountain in a landscape. It is recognized as a calamity not only to a household, but to the city, the State, the Nation; and it may be doubted whether, since the assassination of Abraham Lincoln, any single announcement has so startled the public mind and moved the popular heart as when on the 1st day of November it was announced that Zachariah Chandler was found sleeping his last sleep.

Ulysses S. Grant is a man of few words—and like his shot and shell they weigh a good deal and are well aimed. Let us hear his verdict on Mr. Chandler:

"A nation, as well as the State of Michigan, mourns the loss of one of "her most brave, patriotic and truest citizens. Senator Chandler was beloved "by his associates and respected by those who disagreed with his political "views. The more closely I became connected with him the more I appre "ciated his great merits.   U. S. GRANT.
    "GALENA, Ill., Nov. 9, 1879."

It is evident that it is no ordinary man who has departed from among us. It is not "a self-evident truth that all men are created equal," if we mean equality of gifts and graces, capacity, opportunity or even responsibility; and the people of these United States do not need to be told that Mr. Chandler was no common man. It was by no accident that he held in succession, and filled with success, posts of such importance and trusts of such magnitude. He did not drift into prominence; he rose by sheer force of character and by the fitness of things. Born to be a leader, endowed with those qualities that mark a man destined to leadership, having rare business faculty, and sagacity, tact and talent, large capacity for organization and administration, his hand was naturally at the helm.

Mr. Chandler's leadership reached beyond and beneath the visible conduct of affairs. As Moses was the inspiration, of which Aaron was the expression, he was often the power behind the throne. He who has now left us, forever, belonged to the illustrious few who were the special counselors of Mr. Lincoln and the instigators of many of his wisest and best measures. There is an inner history of the war which has never been written and never will be. The lips that alone could disclose those secrets are fast closing in eternal silence, and the scroll will find no man worthy to loose its seals.

Mr. Chandler could not have been wholly ignorant of the risk he ran in his laborious and prolonged campaign-work; but when his country seemed in peril his tongue could not keep silence. Just before starting on his last journey westward, he said to me: "In my judgment the crisis now upon us is "more important than any since Lee surrendered, and as grave as any since "Sumter was fired on." Those who knew him best will not be surprised that, with such an impression of the magnitude of the issues now before the American people, he could not spare himself, but gave himself without reserve to his country, sacrificing his life itself on the altar of his own patriotism.

And so our stalwart statesman has fallen, and we have a· new lesson on human mortality. Anaxagoras, when told that the Athenians had condemned him to die, calmly added, "And nature, them!" All our riches, honors, dignities cannot stay the steps of the great destroyer. The manliest and mightiest leaders, and the humblest and meanest followers bow alike to the awful mandate of death. And as Massilon said at the funeral of the Grand Monarch, "God only is great!"

Of how little consequence after all are all the things that perish. Temporal things derive all their true value from their connection with the invisible and eternal. How small will all appear as they recede into the dim distance at the dying hour and the world to come confronts us with its awful decisions of destiny! What grandeur and glory are imparted to our humblest sphere of service, here, when touched and transformed by the power of an endless life!

We have reason to be glad that the popular recognition of Mr. Chandler's abilities and services has been so prompt and hearty as to afford him not a little satisfaction. Posthumous tributes are sometimes melancholy memorials, reminding us of the monumental sepulchres of martyr-prophets.

Robert Burns's mother said about his monument, as she bitterly remembered how the poet of Ayr had been left to starve, "Ah, Robbie, ye asked them for bread and they hae ge'en ye a stane!" It can never be said that our departed Senator had to wait for another generation to pronounce a just or generous verdict upon his career; the trophies of victory and of popular esteem were strewn along the whole line of his march; and his last tour of the Northwest was a perpetual ovation.

There is to my mind no little inspiration of comfort in the fact that not even human malice can falsify history. Men sometimes get more than their share of praise or of blame while they live; but sooner or later the cloud of incense or the mist of prejudice clears away and the real character is more plainly seen. We can afford to leave the final verdict to another generation if need be, grateful as it is to be appreciated by the generation which we seek to serve.

But it is still more inspiring to know that God rules this world, and reigns over the affairs of men. If He marks the flight and the fall of the sparrow, we may be sure that no man rises to the seat of power or sinks to the grave without His permission.

God is not dead, and cannot die. Generations pass away while He remains the same. His hand is on the helm, whatever human hand seems to have hold, and is still there when the most trusted helmsman relaxes his dying grasp. If God's hand is not in our history, all its records are misleading, and all its course a mystery. Admit the divine factor, and, from the strange unveiling of this hidden Western world until this day, our national life appears like one colossal crystal; it has unity, transparency and symmetry. We can understand Plymouth Rock, the revolution, the French and Indian wars, the war of 1812, the great rebellion, the Kansas problem and the California problem, the Indian question and the Chinese question, Romanism and Communism, Eastern conservatism and Western radicalism, the freedmen and the emigrant, state rights and national sovereignty — all are the subordinate factors whose harmonizing, reconciling, assimilating factor is the divine purpose and plan in our history. My friends, the republic has a divine destiny to fulfill. The Great Pilot is steering the ship of state for her true haven. Scylla threatens on one side, Charybdis on the other; but He knows the channel. The stormy Euroclydon may strike her, tear her sails to tatters and snap her ropes like burnt tow, and splinter her masts to fragments; but He holds the winds in his fists. Let us not fear. We have only to love, trust and obey the God of our Fathers and He will guide us safely and surely through all darkness and danger. The sins that reproach our people are the only foes we have to fear; the righteousness that exalts a nation the only ally we need to covet. If the people of Michigan would rear a grand monument to the heroic men who have adorned our history, let us be true to the principles which they have defended, and to the God who gave them to us as His instruments.

The DORIC PILLAR OF MICHIGAN has fallen; but the State stands, and God can set another pillar in its place. There is stone in the quarry — columns are taking shape to-day in our homes and schools and churches; and in God's time they shall be raised to their place. Let us only be sure that in the shrine of our nation God finds a throne, and not the idols of this world, and not even the earthquake shock shall shatter the symmetric structure of the Republic.